A
LAMPLIGHTER
IN
LARKENEY

WRITTEN AND ILLUSTRATED
BY
AMELIE BUTKUS

Amelie

Thank you
so much!

Book and Cover Design by
Amelie Butkus
Illustrations and Artwork by
Amelie Butkus

First Paperback Edition, 2023

Printed by Amazon Kindle Directed Publishing in
the United States of America, 2023

ISBN: 979-8-9870498-0-8

To me, because nobody else wanted to write it.

And my family, who raised me this way.
I hope you're happy.

CONTENTS

US
The
BILLINGS
FAMILY

~1~

Well...

I think I should describe to you the state of our doormat. Once upon a time, it was beige. At least I think it was beige. I remember a flowery design. Tulips or something like that. It was one of those doormats with those thick, coarse bristles and abrasive, rubber lettering that are meant to be extremely durable and ugly. And, it said "WELCOME!" in cheery orange cursive. It used to at any rate.

It began with the exclamation point.

I remember it because that was our return from Thailand and my father had been experimenting with cooking. He'd brought back sixteen glass jars of extra spicy Thai kimchi and was looking forward to concocting a cake for my brother Tim's twelfth birthday. Three jars survived the trip back. I'd been tasked with one of the remaining jars, Tim the other, and my father the third. Tensions were high and climbing with each broken bottle.

But there we were, the final three. My father stood on the doormat, licking his lips as he unlocked the door. Tim wiped his nose with his elbow, his hands full of luggage and kimchi.

"I have a sneeze," he stated nasally.

"You don't have to tell me."

"No, Wendell, I have a *sneeze.*"

Oh. (Tim shares this trait with infants, in that his body relinquishes all motor control in the throes of a sneeze. My mother rotates out all the china for plastic during allergy season.)

"Tim, don't!"

It was too late.

"Acheugh!"

Snot flew. Luggage fell. Glasses slipped. Sure enough, in one sparkling red parabola, the kimchi went straight onto the doormat.

It bounced off. There was a small *pop*. The glass lid of the mason jar hissed faintly as the seal broke. Kimchi seeped all over the rug. We were left standing there in anticlimax.

Tim narrowed his eyes.

"What's that sizzling?"

We all looked down at the doormat as the exclamation point was slowly eaten away by the acid.

"Huh," my father scratched his beard. "Suddenly I'm not hungry anymore."

Three years later, the E was the next to go. This was after a particularly harrowing stay at a cattle ranch in Botswana. I've never had any particular fear of bugs, but this was a *big* spider. I'll never forget Tim's screams as it fell out of my bag onto the sidewalk.

It was pretty much the spideriest of all spiders—fat and brown and hairy with eight big watery eyes. There was a fresh round of screams as it sprang high into the air and landed on the doormat. Eventually it settled itself down, recalcitrant on the E in Welcome (no exclamation point). Tim (now aged fifteen) ran across the street and yelled his complaints from there.

"I'm going to be sick!" he called. "I'm going to die! Has it bitten me? It's bitten me. I can feel it seeping into my veins! I think I'm hallucinating! How many fingers am I holding up? Hey! Turn around you guys!"

My father was rummaging around in his bag, eyes trained on the spider. I cracked open my journal, flipping the pages.

12

"It's not really poisonous—it's a copycat jumping tarantula. Wow, it's actually one of the rarest arachnids on the planet and vital to the jungles of Botsw—no don't use the—!"

ZZZT

The cattle prod burnt a deep hole into the Welcome mat, singing both the hitchhiking spider and the E out of existence.

There were several more times after that. I could tell you about how my father thought it would be a good idea to bring an ant farm back from Nigeria. They'd been suspiciously glad to be rid of it and when an icicle fell and broke the glass lid on our doorstep, I discovered why. The termites inside made a quick lunch of the L on the mat, then proceeded to eat the door. Or how Tim was playing around with a traditional Inuit firestarter and accidentally set the mat aflame. We'd put it out quickly, but not before the O was burnt to cinders.

As for the C...well...I'd rather not get into that, but it involved the four of us, a horse, and a frightening amount of mayonnaise.

Suffice it to say, that at the end of nearly a decade with the Billings family, our doormat has been trampled, trod on, and beaten down into a simple, forlorn "Wel..."

You might be wondering what it is we do for a living. Well hold your horses, and your "C's." You'll find out soon enough. If we ever got inside.

"Christ on a cracker!" my father swore. He was sweaty and red in the face despite the morning chill. He scratched his head vigorously. Both his beard and salt-and-pepper curls were encrusted with salt and his perpetual Hawaiian shirt smelled like the underside of a pier. The key he was trying to insert into the lock had a barnacle stuck on it. He stuck a palm out behind him.

"Boys, pocketknife."

My brother didn't bother. Even though his little khaki outfit had more pockets than all of us combined, he refused to put anything in them. Something about a village kid saying it looked like he had breasts. I dug around in my parka, grimacing at the long strand of seaweed and the pair of small crabs that scuttled out.

13

I handed my father the tool.

"Fanks." He'd been using his teeth.

"How much longer is this going to be?" snapped Tim. He was quaking at the knees. Hard to believe, but he was twenty-two by this time. Skinny and angular as a spider in the corner of the shower, he had soda bottle glasses, a flop of straight brown hair. He shivered in what had once been a beige romper and Safari pith helmet.

When no one answered him, he flung of his dripping blue ascot and wrung it out onto the doormat. Seawater joined the mud that had been pooling there. He was angry because all his outfits were soaked and that no one had bothered to stop at the dry cleaners on the way home.

"Just a few more minutes dear," said my mother without looking at him. She was nose deep in a book. Out of everyone, I have always admired her for her ability to completely and totally disengage from every situation. It is something I continually try and fail at. Tim always manages to get on my nerves.

My skin was crawling. After fourteen hours without access to a shower, layers of grey muck and lake grit had solidified on our skin and clothes. I set down my luggage, rolled up my sleeve, and began to scratch my inner arm furiously. Dirty salt flakes whirled down onto the pristine sidewalk.

I saw the neighbours watching out of the corner of my eye and ignored them. It was like they had a sixth sense for every time we ("The Billings Family") came home. The moment we rounded the street corner, there'd be lifted blinds, binoculars, opera glasses, and telescopes; people stopped behind trees, and crouched around bushes. Once, although I couldn't be sure, I thought I saw a manhole cover twitch. It's funny. It's not as if we're really anything interesting.

"Do you have to do that?" asked Tim. Right on cue.

"Do what?"

"Scratch yourself like dog. Really Wendell. What will the neighbours think?"

You'd think that my mother would be the one to say that. Not in this family. I took a moment for deep reflection.

Breathe. Disengage.

I stared Tim straight in the eyes and scratched harder.

"Dad!"

There was a tinkle as my father dropped the keys. A fresh round of swears in seven languages.

"Dad, get us inside! Wendell's flaking all over me. He's disgusting."

My mother looked up from her book. "Well, *you* smell like a dead fish, dear."

"Mummy! I only smell like a dead fish because *someone* leaned too far to the left."

I snorted angrily. "Sure, it was me. Not the seventeen suitcases of men's garter socks and medicated sunscreen that tipped us into the lake."

"My socks stay up just fine thankyouverymuch," he snapped the edge of one sock to prove the point. The wool only slapped wetly against his leg and then sagged to reveal a flesh-coloured starfish wrapped around his calf. Tim screamed.

"Shh!" I hissed.

People were staring now. Really staring. I tried to avoid the gaze of the two kids sitting on the opposite end of the curb eating popcorn.

He was hopping up and down.

"*Getitoffgetitoffgetitoff.*"

"Stop kicking for starters. You'll only make it angrier."

"Angrier?"

"Oh yeah," I nodded. "Did you know that Mongolian starfish are carnivorous? They've got teeth and everything."

"*What?*"

My father's voice: "Almost got it!"

I cracked open my journal.

"They also excrete a special poison that makes one's leg fall off. Particularly those who don't row and tip the boat four times into leech-infested waters."

"Oh *god*—wait." He stopped wailing and got up from the fetal position on the ground. "That's not funny!"

I folded my arms. There was a sucking noise like a tiny plunger as my brother peeled the starfish off his leg. It dangled limply, making miserable glubbing sounds.

15

"Don't you dare throw that starfish at me. Tim. *Don't!*"

Tim smiled evilly, waggling the poor creature. "His name is Gregory, and he wants a *friend.*"

"Mother!"

Click.

"Got it!"

The door to our nice little suburban townhouse swung open. At this point, my father finally turned around to witness the mediaeval duel that was brewing behind him. He sighed and clapped us both on the shoulder.

"Buck up you two. We're home!"

~2~

Home is a Place You Visit Every Couple of Months or So for a Bath

It is the unspoken rule that the first one inside gets The Bath. Our two-story house in the west of London has three bathrooms, four toilets (if you count one of the bushes in the backyard that is sometimes used when my father gets tired of conventional living) and two showers. But only one Bath. You might say, Wendell, just take a shower. It gets the job done. Sure, tell that to the man lost in the desert for months. Tell him to drink hot, dirty river water when a gallon jug of iced lemonade is just inches away from the riverbed. You might say, a scented bath is a bit unmanly, Wendell. Why don't you spend three weeks slogging through East Asian marshland in monsoon season and get back to me about that? The only mistress I fantasised about was wide, hollow, and made of clear cool porcelain heavy with the smell of lavender instead of dead fish.

I *needed* a bath.

The door swung open. "Move!"

TIM
MY BROTHER
SOMEHOW

Tim's elbow jackknifed into my ribs. I elbowed him back and he coughed up a bit of eel. While he was momentarily stupefied by the horror of that, I cut in front of him and was halfway up the stairs when a pair of bony hands tugged my ankle down and I fell.

"Boys! You'll dirty the carpet!"

Tim and I paused for a split second to say sorry to our mother—and got back to our dash.

"I called dibs on the plane."

"You did not."

"You just didn't hear because I didn't say it very loud."

"Then it doesn't count, does it?"

We bounced off the walls and each other in the narrow stairwell. Tim had the advantage of height, but I had the advantage of being, well, I had a lower centre of gravity and was able to barrel into him like a bowling ball. He clung onto me like a cat, fingers scrabbling at my coat.

We'd reached the top of the landing. I could see the door. Tim's hand crept around my head to clap my ears. I spun and smacked them away.

THUMP.

He'd lost his balance. My brother tumbled and crumpled a few steps down. My stomach dropped.

"Tim?" I ran to him. "Are you alright?"

His face was hidden behind a curled-up shoulder. It shook with a muffled sob.

"Cripes. Where does it hurt?"

"Hah!"

I realised at once it wasn't sobs. It was laughter. He sprang up as easy as a leaf and hopped over me, neatly rounding the corner and into the bathroom. The door clicked.

"TIM."

In the end, I decided it wasn't worth the bother. I had no energy left. I sat down. Waves of fatigue washed over me and slowly, I nodded to sleep, right there across the stairs. The sounds of my parents stepping over me with the luggage and the running bathwater made me dream of the rocking dinghy in the middle of that Mongolian lake. I fell deeper into the memory of it capsizing for the umpteenth time. The shouts of my parents, the roar of the waves and the cold sinking of waterlogged clothes. Then, the smooth heavy silence beneath them. That was where I stayed for a long time.

I got my bath eventually, but it wasn't nearly as satisfying. By that time, with the showers running and Tim having taken his hour-long sojourn, the water was lukewarm. He'd also used all the good soap. But it was fine in the end because the best part of The Bath—the very best part—were the few precious minutes where I was completely and utterly alone.

~3~

Clickety Clack the Straw that Broke the Camel's Back

My father was an outdoorsman in every sense of the word. Maybe not in the chiselled-leaned-out-hiker sense of the word but definitely in the barrel-shaped-red-faced-jolly-pirate sense of the word. He was the type of person who thought that the inventions of walls and indoor plumbing were a travesty, and that man should be free to roam the open plains of the world with nothing but a Hawaiian shirt, several bottles of zinc, and a talent for misinterpreting other cultures.

In some respects, I envy the way he was able to parlay his passion into a career because I don't know if I'll ever be able to do the same thing for myself. I certainly haven't inherited his robustness for life. I suppose you could say I look like him. A smaller, quieter, brown-haired version with the same unfortunate nose and wide stance. But other than that, we couldn't be any more different.

ME
↳

The typewriter was positioned so that if it were any closer to the window, it would be outside. My father had long since removed the window seats and plopped down the monstrosity that was the Toshiba BW-2127. The typewriter was as large as a man's torso and weighed at least 30 kilos. He'd found it in a Japanese junk shop fifteen years prior and had never used another since. The Thing (as we called it) wrote in rotating scripts of English, Japanese, Chinese, and something that neither of us had been able to figure out but looked distinctly satanic. Being sparingly tredelingual, he often forgot to switch between these scripts, causing several newspaper editors to believe he was either pulling a joke or engaging in witchcraft.

The setup was not as impressive. The Toshiba sat on a sturdy iron-reinforced desk. In front of this was a plain wooden chair, and around it was plants of every variety. They filled up the little octagonal space that made up the nook. Climbing vines and purple-veined ferns from Brazil, northern European mosses, and Korean hibiscus. They were all a little stunted and very diagonal, creeping toward the windows and sky that would never allow the proper amount of sunlight through the proprietary layer of English cloud cover. Still, it was the best he could do to submerge himself in the relics of our travels so he wouldn't feel so cooped up.

It was always trying on the rest of us when my father started to get restless. David Billings functioned like a miniature climate. When he was happy, we laughed and joked, and Tim and I even got along tolerably well. But when he was restless, the house prickled and tensed. He'd start sleeping in a hammock stretched out in the backyard and pacing the rug of the downstairs parlour endlessly. I dreaded the moments when I came down to find travel brochures scattered all over the kitchen table. It meant we were going away soon. Somewhere far off and uncomfortable, with strange Bed and Breakfasts and biting bugs—and I would have to be there to document it all.

Click Clack. Whirr. Ding!

The sound funnelled through the stairwell. I emerged from the bath feeling like a new person. As I entered the parlour, Tim was the first to comment on what I was wearing.

"You didn't waste any time."

He was referring to my faded woollen pyjamas and slippers. He himself was impeccably dressed in an argyle vest that made his arms look like sticks and a pair of mustard-coloured slacks. These were half-covered by a blanket. He punctuated the sentence by blowing his nose with gusto.

My brother (though he'd never admit it) would enjoy anything so long as he got the proper attention. Travelling, despite its many inconveniences, offered no shortage of that. From eager missionaries to curious natives fascinated by his paleness, his height, and his ungainly walk, we were often treated as celebrities, especially as the popularity of my father's travel columns grew.

In the absence of this, Tim had decided to be sick. "I feel awful," he moaned, "My head is buzzing like that hive of Mongolian hornets you made me walk into."

"You walked into that yourself."

"Well, you didn't stop me."

That was true.

Click Clack. Whirr. Ding!

The curtains to the nook were closed but I could hear my father typing away. It was the first thing he did upon returning. *Globetrotters Monthly* was making a fortune off him and had started demanding their articles sooner and sooner after our travels.

My mother appeared around the kitchen island. Like me, she was already in a bathrobe and slippers, a new book under her arm. She sat down opposite us and cracked it open.

"Kettle on?" I asked.

"She's just warming up."

We all settled down to wait, listening to the rain that tapped against the windows, mingling with the constant clacks and whirrs of the Toshiba-BW-2127.

The parlour was where we spent most of our time at home. It was the most comfortable room in the house with lots of chairs and big windows branching off into the kitchen. It might have been anybody's respectable parlour if not for the all-encompassing mishmash of decor. People from my father's editorial company would have called it "charmingly eccentric." I would have called it something different.

There were, of course, the trademark tribal masks hung up on the walls. A couple of voodoo dolls, crossed swords, half a suit of Aztec armour. Usual stuff. Then there were your more obscure items. The jade Cambodian shrine in the corner of the room where a multi-armed woman balanced on one leg. The tiki torch chandelier. The custom loveseat made of woven palm fronds, and the one-ton black obsidian tortoise that made up our coffee table (a story for another day).

I did my best to get comfortable on one of the palm-frond couches. On the tortoise was a paper that Tim had finished with. I tore off the corner of the page that had snot on it and contemplated it. Normally, I avoided newspapers like the plague. The chances of finding one of my father's publications headlining the front page was high. But I was bored, and I reasoned with myself that since we'd been gone for three weeks, it was probably out of circulation by now.

Doing what we do is kind of like going to space. You're gone for weeks or months at a time, usually in various rural, disconnected places, like Northern Patagonia or Kentucky. During that time, there is no contact with the outside world. When you come back, it's almost like people are speaking a different language. The clothes are different. The gadgets are new. People start greeting you in the streets with weird phrases like "Gravy Fool" and "Dabba Zoot." So, it's nice to catch up, even when I know it won't make much of a difference.

Tentatively, I unfolded the newspaper and was rewarded with a tide of meaningless gossip and popular culture that I drank in word by word. The front-page article read:

Reclusive Inventor Sebastian Shaw Drops Infuriatingly Vague Hints about House Party
By Morry Oseman

Didn't get an invite? Neither did we. Neither did anyone for that matter, save, from what our sources can gather, eight people. Although to be fair, my own mother doesn't invite me to Christmas. We're in a bit of a tiff about it you see. I always wanted to be a journalist; she'd always fancied a dentist for a son. Last Christmas I received a package of what may or may not have been a real human skull. The molars were startling. She thought it was medical grade; anyways enough about me.

Sebastian Shaw, currently thought to be at least number 8 in the *Time's* most influential people and definitely number 2 in the lesser known *3 C's Weekly, Clockwork, Celibacy, and Sinister Clandestinities,* has sent out eight invitations to his closest chums in a distinctly Wonka-esque manner. It is speculated to be some kind of rebound party in the wake of his falling out with renowned mentor, Bellamy Dumont, who is now at large for grand larceny. Rumours abound about a potential new Auto that will be introduced at the event. A singing armoire perhaps? A judgmental mirror? As of yet, the guests remain surprisingly tightlipped. Fashion icon Evangeline Grey declined to comment as did the notorious Quislings.

Even cornering devilishly handsome opera singer Billius Brum for breakfast resulted in being turned away, saying he'd drunk it already. Of course, we don't know where the manor is anyways, so storming the gates with all the duress of the pitchforked hoi polloi is out of the question. I trudged back to my office dejectedly to report on what little I had. After all, this wouldn't be the gossip column if there were any substantial news to report. In an effort to fill more space, my week has been rather depressing. In fact—

Ding!

The curtains rasped as they slid apart. My father emerged, swinging his torso and launching into the short callisthenics routine he did at half-hour intervals that made everybody think someone was making popcorn.

Since he hadn't made his presence known for the last six minutes, Tim sniffled and craned his neck toward the kitchen.

"I'm parched." There was no answer. "I said, *I'm parched.*"

Nothing.

He slumped back against the couch, blinking at us all through his enormous glasses.

"How am I ever going to get over this flu if I don't get my lemon and water? I bet it's West Nile Virus.*"

We'd just come back from Mongolia.

My mother didn't look up from her book. "It will get here when it gets here. David, do you want tea?"

My father harrumphed as he joined us on the couch. "I just don't understand people's insistence on gadgets and things that do everything for them. All it achieves is you getting to sit down as it takes twice as long to get a lukewarm cup of tea."

Everyone rolled their eyes.

"I just think that it's these new Autos that are making kids like yourselves lazy. Why do you think people read our columns eh Wendell?"

"Please don't include me in this."

He leaned forward. "I'm serious. They want to get a taste of the spice of life because they're too busy rotting on the couch waiting for a potato with legs to make their tea for them. Speak of the devil!"

The teapot arrived with a sloshing shuffle. It was a normal teapot by all accounts with your average fine porcelain and blue painted flowers. The only thing was that it walked.

It wobbled side to side on a pair of stumpy cherubic legs, making its slow way from the kitchen to the sitting room. It was doing its best to hop the countertop and cross the rug but had gone a bit bandy-legged with the effort. Drips of water were slopping onto the carpet. When it arrived at the base of the coffee table, it paused again as if contemplating the options. My father huffed and crossed his arms. Eventually, it managed to hop the small stairway of books we'd created a while ago for that very purpose. There was a small round of polite clapping as it went round to all our waiting teacups and poured what remaining water there was.

Genie (that was its name) settled down in the middle of the table, plopping down with both legs splayed out, awaiting further orders.

"Half," said Tim, eyeing his own saucer. "Well, that's better than last time I suppose." He sipped it. His eye twitched. "Sugar. I said *sugar.*"

Neither of us could really say anything about the performance of Genie because it'd been a gift from Marcus, editor-in-chief of *Globetrotters Monthly*. We'd even been advised to make use of it as much as possible because of the advertising opportunities that came with endorsing Autos. To be honest, I didn't much like them. They gave me the creeps.

GENIE
← (OUR
TEAPOT)

My father rose abruptly and gave his cup a disparaging look.

"Well, nothing like a salty cup of earl grey to end the break. Newspapers don't write themselves, do they?"

He stopped on his way to the nook. "That reminds me. Wendell, I have a bone to pick with you." He flashed me a smile. "It's not a big deal. I was just looking through your notes and they were thorough and well diagrammed as always, but I thought they were a tad—how shall I say—morose this time around."

"Morose?" I repeated.

"Yes, because you frequently used words like, miserable, wet, cold, soaking, leeches, venereal disease, and such like." He rubbed his chin in a scholarly sort of way. "What I would recommend is learning to rephrase. For example, instead of cold, you could say 'refreshingly crisp. Awakens the senses.' See what I did there?"

"I…"

"And changing the words changes the way you feel about a certain event. You were there during that Monk retreat, weren't you?" He frowned. "Yes, you were definitely there because I remember you screaming when that monk blew all the sand in your face. To be fair, he did warn you about standing too close to the mandalas. But the eye infection was worth a thousand granules of wisdom! See? Another smashing example! You really ought to write this down."

"But you're the one who does that. The rephrasing."

He pointed at me. "And *your* notes are the blueprint. The very *backbone* of all my articles. That affects the writing you know. I just want you to keep that in mind for our next trip, okay? Good lad!"

The curtains snapped shut.

And snapped open again.

His face peaked out. "Oh! Could you boys do me a favour and sort through the rest of those letters? We need to separate the fan mail from the real requests. We don't want to repeat that hostage incident now, do we? Cheers!"

Snap.

Click Clack. Whirr. Ding!

It was a silent battle of the wills after that. My brother and I made no attempt to, except for the occasional glances at each other over the pile of mail to make sure the other wasn't moving.

Eventually I got bored and conceded. I knelt in front of the letters. There were quite a lot of them—at least forty—and each with varying levels of stampage, smell, and organic life. The first bunch was a hefty wad of letters, more like a tax folio tied with twine. The envelopes were covered in stamps. I didn't need to squint to read the handwriting. I recognized the large blocky handwriting well enough. Grinning, I read it aloud.

"TO MY TIMMY TUM. EVERY DAY THAT THE SUN SHINES UPON THE EMPTINESS WHERE YOU COULD STAND BEFORE ME IS ANOTHER DAY IT BURNS A HOLE IN MY HEART. WITH ALL OF THE LOVE IN THE WORLD, MELATI."

A bony hand shot out of nowhere and snatched it up (not without some difficulty as the thing must have weighed at least as much as I did.).

"Reading other people's letters is a crime you know," said Tim who was red in the face.

"That was just the address line."

"I don't ask you why nobody likes you enough to send letters."

Ouch. I went back to sifting.

There were all sorts of fan letters proclaiming my dad was the new Indiana jones. (These were mostly from older women.) There were also letters asking if he might like to go fishing and share a lager over a campfire sometime. (Older men.) And finally, a few letters asking if he might donate a few chest hairs to science. (Female *and* male historians.) I skipped over these as quickly as I could to find the real requests. Those are the letters we use to determine the places to travel next. My father focuses primarily on small Bed and Breakfasts in remote locations. It's a pretty good setup for both parties. My father gets the experience for his paper and the small businesses get huge exposure. Hence the pile.

There were the requests from Inuit villages, the Galapagos, places from all over the world begging our family to come visit.

Hello—a noticeably cleaner envelope slipped out as I was trying to decide between spending a winter running from bison in the Appalachians or running from moose in Alaska. The return address was *Globetrotters*. The seal was cracked. I slid the card from inside.

David!

Hope you're well and that you've got some sea salt in those pepper curls. I've got some good news. People have been absolutely clamouring for another piece! The demand is up and so are our ratings and it's all thanks to you, old pal! But I'm sure you know by the mountains of letters that have been bogging up our mailboxes and yours. Anyways, we at the office have been thinking that it is time to ramp up our output. Take advantage of the avalanche in a figure of speech. What do you say to increasing the articles to, say, three per month? I'm sure that would be no trouble at all to our resident adventurer and as always, half expenses paid!

Give my best to the family and I hope you're all enjoying Genie! Our sponsors have been gently suggesting you take her with you next time to show how durable she is. I was thinking you might be motivated to include a little section about her. Something like, "Your very own Genie is so travel-ready she can make the perfect cup in your home and in the Andes! It's almost like magic! Get your AutoMatic Teapot today!"

Cheers!
Editor in Chief,
Marcus Chevral

I experienced a peculiar sensation. A sort of out-of-body experience as I slowly slid the clean white card into its clean white, editorial envelope. Suddenly, all I could see were the framed articles that covered the walls.

Click Clack. Whirr. Ding!

Headlines jumped out at me one by one.

31

Bewitched in Baghdad

Sunny Days in Senegal

Eating, Praying, and Loving in Laos

Click Clack. Whirr. Ding!

I saw myself in each one. A face reflected at ten. Fourteen. Sixteen. Sunburnt. Miserable. In each, I could only recall being recruited into a cult in Baghdad, the unrelenting rain in Senegal, and nearly being eaten by water snakes in Laos.

My reflection looked down as I did at the book in my hands. Slanting shorthand filled the pages of the leather-bound journal. There my father's adventures told from the point of view of a shadow. Me.

Click Clack. Whirr. Ding!

Hadn't I been doing my job? Uncomplaining as I was dragged back and forth and around the globe like a needle across an old record? Writing everything down for him after he'd been diagnosed with carpal tunnel?

Click Clack whirr. Click Clack whirr.

"Are you having a stroke?"

Tim stared up at me.

I realised I was standing slack jawed.

Ding!

I ignored him and made my way to the shrouded nook.

Ding Ding Ding!

I pushed aside the curtains.

Ding!

"Oh!" My father turned in surprise. "Hello son—"

I held up the letter. "Did you know about this?"

His brows furrowed. "Yes," he said slowly. "It's a letter from Marcus. You know, I'd appreciate if you didn't read my correspondence—"

"So, we were just going to wake up and find ourselves on a plane to some tropical hellhole next week? No, you'd have to break the news sometime."

"Wendell," he wasn't listening to me—he was busy fiddling with the thousand-letter mechanism on the typewriter. "Can we discuss this some other time? I really must get this article out."

I leaned over and wrestled the ink cartridge out of the Toshiba. It took about five solid minutes and navigating what seemed to be several miniature ceremonial booby traps, but I got there in the end. I stood up, panting with ink-stained hands, holding his gaze.

His hands lifted from the keyboard in defeat and settled slowly in his lap.

"That's what this is about? That you don't get the month?" His puzzled expression shifted to one of disbelief. "I would've thought you'd be glad. We get to get back out there sooner."

I stared at him uncomprehendingly. "Every two weeks? Do you think I want to do this every *two weeks*? Can you count to me how many times we've almost died– for what? A good article?"

"Wendell," he spluttered, "that was never—you know perfectly well I had it all under control—"

"It's one thing after another," I gripped my notebook and spoke louder. The words surprised me. It was as if, once the gates had opened, everything came flooding out.

"I still have nightmares about being chased by rhinos. Every time the sprinkler goes off, I have a near heart attack because I think it's one of those deadly spitting Komodo dragons of Gili Motang come back to get me. Sorry Dad, but I'm sick of it. I hate it. I won't do it anymore. I won't go. Find someone else to take notes for you. Make Tim do it for Christ's sake!"

"Ah, weak fingers," said Tim from the couch. "I'm ill. Bad penmanship. Malnourished."

"I was giving my sons experiences," my father said firmly.

I raised my eyes to the ceiling.

"Experiences! Hah! And what about the people who are reading it? Those people think that we spend our lives going on adventures and having a grand old time because you only include the good stuff. You don't listen to me. You just take my notes and rewrite everything in there to your liking, and you never ask what I think, and you never give me any credit!"

I stood there for a moment, searching for more words but I seemed to have run out completely.

Anything else? My family's gaze seemed to ask.

"Er...That's it." I sat down, my face hot. The silence made the staring worse. Like it was a tangible thing.

"Ah...erm," my father thumbed with the mail. "I didn't know you felt that way." He walked over to me and clapped a hand on my shoulder.

"But you're my right-hand man! There's always the scribe behind the adventurer. It's one of the most important roles, the documentarian. They tell the story for all the world to see. I want you to know you're very appreciated, Wendell."

I looked at him. He wasn't looking at me. He was looking at the journal in my hands.

"The thing is," I said. "I don't think I am."

I walked away, leaving his arm hanging in midair. On the floor was one cup of tea that had been miraculously filled to the top. I sat down, picked it up and unfolded the gossip column matter-of-factly.

"I'm staying here."

~4~

Not a Lighthouse

My suitcase hit the cobblestones with a loud *thunk*. My father put his hands on his hips, breathing in deeply as he stepped out of the car.

"Smell that fresh air boys? This is what we all needed! A little retreat. a bit of R&R, sea air. It's good for the soul!"

In the distance, a lonely fisherman uttered an oath as he was shat on by a group of seagulls. The entrance to the town square stretched out before us. An avenue of pleasant-looking storefronts with signs of painted driftwood and teal trim stood on terraced platforms. Low stone houses speckled the valley all the way up to a hill atop of which stood a lighthouse. A sign above a small brick building announced the local police department, the local bait shop, and a large curlicued sign stuck in the grass beside the road read that this was Port Larkeney. Directly below that:

Due to the larger than average proportion of elderly persons in our town, please drive slowly and vigilantly.

Below *this* was taped a very faded vehicle and life insurance pamphlet. All the numbers had long since been torn off.

"Tim!" my father roared.

The car door unlatched reluctantly. Last out of the car after my mother, my brother extricated himself and his Bermuda shorts. He hissed, clutching his pith helmet against the breeze. His knees invariably drew together as he stood against the cold.

My father clapped him on the back, making him cough.

"Book out son! I want two pages on our arrival. Note everything: sights, smells, feelings, tastes, revelations, intuitions. Leave no stone unturned, no nooks unknocked, or crannies uncovered!"

I raised an eyebrow.

Tim picked through his pockets for his own notebook. A slim beige thing that disappointed me every time I looked at it.

"*Revelations?*" he muttered, shivering irritably as my father walked away. "*Intuitions?* You have *got* to be kidding me. The only *intuition* I have is that this trip is going to be terrible."

I looked at him scribbling away with malice in his eyes. "Don't be like that. You'll get used to it. It all gets quite bearable when you've done it for long enough. Getting up at odd hours of the morning, following him through too many horrible, life-threatening situations. And the hand cramps… well, I can lend you a stress ball for those."

He glared at me. "I'll bet you're enjoying yourself."

I shrugged. "I'm alright."

Actually, I felt great. At least for the present moment.

I'm sure you're wondering why I abandoned my resolution in the living room so quickly. To be honest, it was because revenge is a dish best served with an empty notebook and hot Irish potatoes. I wanted to see my brother take a stab at the job that had been the bane of my existence ever since I'd made the life altering mistake of learning shorthand.

It was my father who suggested it.

"Your mother has convinced me that, over the years, I have apparently been 'unfair' to the both of you," he'd said a few days after I'd made my grievances known in the parlour. "Particularly you, Wendell. I would like to make it up to you. You'll have the pick of the destination and Tim can take over your duties with the book. How does that sound?"

He handed me the heavy stack of mail.

I took it apprehensively, ignoring the whining in the background as my brother came to grips with his new reality.

* * *

I found the letter at the bottom of the pile. It had emitted a smell distinctly different than the others (they usually smelled of goat chips). I wasn't sure exactly what it was except it was spicy, cinnamon and with a hint of coffee.

Dear Mister Billings,
I hope this letter finds you well and that you are in the process of considering new destinations for your articles. My daughter and I are such fans of yours. Why, I believe we've been subscribed to Globetrotters Monthly **for seven years now. It is such as breath of fresh air, the descriptions take you to a place far away—**

I admit, I skipped through most of it. I assumed it was probably the same self-promotional drivel. What sealed the deal were the pictures.

Enclosed beside the letter were several polaroid photographs, each more idyllic than the last. A picturesque cove dotted with boats. A neat and quiet boulevard. A faraway lighthouse that was charmingly crooked. I flipped through them one by one. The next were a series of well-appointed bedrooms.

In short, Port Larkeney looked perfectly, unequivocally, boring. I couldn't believe my luck.

A holiday.

The word sounded strange in my head. I tried it out for size.

"I'm going on a Ho-li-day," I murmured.

37

A trip just for the heck of it. Where nothing big and hairy tried to eat you. Where you could just...relax and do nothing for as long as you wanted. Maybe it wasn't pina coladas and sunshine, but it was something normal people did, and I desperately wanted to feel normal.

"I've decided I'm going to go," I told my father later that evening, handing him the brochure of Port Larkeney.

"Wonderful!" He'd beamed and handed me my suitcase. "I've had it packed since Wednesday."

* * *

We walked our baggage through the town centre, wheels clicking and bouncing over the stone plaza. Although our destination was at the top of the hill overlooking the valley, my father had wanted to get a good look at the village below. The walk was steep.

"First impressions are everything, Tim," he puffed. "Ooh a dried mollusk! Write that down."

He didn't.

But others were making their first impressions as well. It seemed that the rattling of our luggage had attracted the attention of the residents of Port Larkeney. A ruddy man with a thick beard emerged from the bait shop to see what the commotion was. There was a woman in at least six layers of plastic beadery who stopped feeding the seagulls for a look at us. I felt my neck prickle with the gaze of a group of solemn-eyed children, two boys and two girls, as they watched us from a cafe window.

I shouldn't be surprised really. This happens a lot on our trips. We become the centre of attention in a new place—although that place was usually one with dirt huts and no electricity. I never quite got used to the feeling. We couldn't be *that* much of a novelty, right?

Half of a raisin Danish dropped out of an elderly man's mouth as we passed before I realised we might not be the source of interest.

A Rolls Royce as black and glossy as a dead man's loafer crept along behind us. It had been revving its engine for several minutes

38

in an effort to get our attention, but the luggage and my father had drowned out all the noise.

A honk made us all jump. One of the tinted windows rolled down.

"Get a move on!"

A tiny, manicured hand stuck out the passenger side. A pasty-faced woman with a severe bob and mauve lipstick that gave off the impression of hypothermia looked out. She lowered a pair of thick black glasses.

"Well don't just stand there taking up space. Off! To the side with you!" She waved her hand like a semaphore. Her driver kept honking until everyone, including several elderly people— "Yes, you too! Hobble on off!" —had scurried onto the curb.

We stared as the Rolls Royce passed us, making its way silently up the street and around the bend.

"I don't think we made a very good first impression on *her*," I said.

We stood at the base of the hill. There was a series of overgrown stone steps cut into the hillside that didn't make the climb any more appealing.

Tim blinked through his spectacles. "That has got to be the weirdest lighthouse I've ever seen," he remarked.

I followed his gaze. It was true. The lighthouse on the cliff skewed heavily to the right, teetering precariously like the tiers of an over-ambitious wedding cake. It also appeared to be *green*.

"Come on boys, no use dillydallying," my father grunted, heaving his bag onto the first step. "Mrs. Twill said she had a reception planned for us. Can't miss it. Lots to see, lots to write."

My brother scowled again, and for the second time today, my spirits lifted.

Twenty minutes later, Tim bent over his knees gasping. I dropped my pack on the ground and sat on it, wiping my forehead.

"Jesus."

"I know. It's a masochist that puts a lighthouse all the way— oh." Tim's gaze travelled slowly upward.

"There's your problem," I panted, "It's not a lighthouse at all."

EVANGELINE
GREY
← MEAN

The building was long and thin and pointed at the top. It must have been at least four stories high which explained our confusion for it being a lighthouse. The only thing to suggest to the contrary was the fact that it was actually a giant jalapeno on stilts. The entire outer wall was dark green and a lime green chimney with green spiralling slats made for the stem on top. A brightly lit sign out front advertised:

"The Piquant Palaces. Proud Home of the Largest Pepper in the World: Big Bertha."

"Inspired!" cried my father, choosing to focus on the one thing that wasn't the fact of the enormous pepper-shaped building in front of us. "The Piquant Palaces. Apt alliteration indeed."

Just then, the sounds of a struggling engine rose over the hill. The Rolls Royce appeared. The tall grass was wreaking havoc on the wheels, and when it finally made its way to the lot around the back of the Piquant Palaces, the car whined to a halt.

The engine died and the driver's door popped open. The Auto that swung out was possibly the strangest I'd ever seen. It was dressed smartly in a chauffeur's tuxedo. Gloved hands disguised further evidence of machinery. The head was where human semblance disappeared. Instead, it was a gold-wrought cage with fine mesh detailing out a vague nose, lips, and the curve of a skull. All in all, it was reminiscent of a swanky department store mannequin.

It held open the passenger door. The woman inside took one look at Piquant Palaces and closed it again. There was a muffled shriek before she reemerged patting her reddened cheeks with a handkerchief. I decided it was time to get a move on before any frustrations she might have been taken out on us. My father was fighting his way through the grass towards the door.

"Come now, Peruka. Let's get this over with," she was muttering with little regard to the people around her, and I could see Tim straining his ears in interest. *"'I'll put you up,'* he said. *'It's quaint, you'll love it,'* he said."* She adjusted her hair and rummaged through her purse. "Quaint is the Savoy," she hissed. "They were

41

all right. He really has gone mad," she turned to the Automaton with clawing fingers. "Get me Franklin. I require commiseration."

Out of the corner of my eye, I watched as the chauffeur creakily handed her a candy-striped hat box.

She stuck her hand into the box and began to stroke the contents. Her breath steadied and she began to count with each exhale, "One, two, three—IT'S RUDE TO STARE!"

I jumped. "I wasn't—I mean I didn't—"

"*Hello!*"

Just then, the door to the Palaces swung open to reveal an extremely pear-shaped woman in a gingham dress. She rested her hands on ample hips giving us all the once-over.

"You must be the Billings family!" she cried.

My father bounded up the steps to greet her. She returned the handshake and the two of them shook with all the rigour of two people too enthusiastic for their own good.

"Jeanne Twill I presume?" asked my father through the hand shaking.

"In the flesh!" said Jeane Twill around his arm.

She put her other hand to her bosom. Her straw-coloured bun bobbled excitedly. "I am just such a fan, you know. Such a fan. Been reading your newspapers for years—my daughter and I— we've even been thinking about taking a trip upon your recommendation. You can only know how excited we are to have a big celebrity do a column on our humble Palaces."

Tim turned to me and stuck a finger in his mouth.

My father's beard puffed with pride. "Well, it is a marvellous place you have here…"

Suddenly, like fireflies zipping through the night, the bottom of the giant pepper began to sparkle. Bulbs in red, green, and purple flickered on, blinking and winking floor by floor until the entire outside of the inn was alight with colour. In the setting sun, the pepper shimmered softly over the town and even I had to admit that it was actually quite beautiful.

I opened my notebook.

Place: Piquant Palaces, Port Larkeney.
Mode of Transportation: car/ferry/car
Key Events: pepper, pear shape, lightshow—

MRS. TWILL

I THINK WE'RE ALL WONDERING... WHY PEPPERS?

43

No, no no! I snapped the notebook closed. This wasn't my job anymore—and how had I found a pen?

"Weatherproof Christmas bulbs," Mrs. Twill was saying. "Heavy-duty for year-round use. We wanted to give a good first impression." She swept aside a wisp of hair self-consciously.

"You've certainly done that," said my father. "And might I add, I've invested in those same bulbs myself. The Billings family's Christmas has survived all weathers. Tim, write that down."

"We can get someone to help you with those bags," said Mrs. Twill. She turned inside, bellowing, "Katie! KATIE! Don't pretend you can't hear me. You were just on the lights!"

When no one appeared, Mrs. Twill sucked her teeth. "I suppose it's just me then. *Hup*!"

Before my father could protest, she'd grabbed all four of his bags and tottered into the inn. Exchanging looks, the rest of us followed her inside.

The inside of the Piquant Palaces crammed us all into a small mudroom that opened into a large, dimly lit pub. A low fire crackled from a large stone fireplace on the far side of the room and Christmas bulbs were strung from the rafters around the room. Two squishy armchairs occupied the space in front of it. That smell hung in the air, strong and familiar. A blend of cinnamon, coffee, and that unidentifiable spice that was almost smoky. Mrs. Twill barely fit herself around the bar. She plunked a guestbook down, quickly wiping away the layers of dust onto the tabletop.

"Billings," she murmured, penning the name. She looked up. "Can I put you down for a month? Christmas in Port Larkeney—you don't want to miss it."

My father thought. "Well, we usually stay for a couple of days—" He was interrupted yet again as the door burst open. The strange woman from the car strode in. The golden chauffeur towed behind.

She elbowed in front of my father and before he could react, said, "Evangeline Grey. That's E-V-A-N-G— never mind you're taking forever. I'll write it." She snatched the pen and scribbled her name into the guestbook. "It hardly matters. I will take one night in your least dingy accommodations and a scalp massage at 4 o'clock. Good day."

It had happened in a matter of seconds as the bewildered Mrs. Twill plucked a pair of keys from the wall and handed it to her. Evangeline Grey gave her a curt nod and *tik tak'd* her way up the stairs, trailed by her laden Auto.

Mrs. Twill blinked. "Anyways, it's quite lovely this time of year. I assume you'll want the full package. Sightseeing, tour of the pepper garden, Big Bertha, of course—my pride and joy—she jerked her head at a series of framed photographs behind her picturing the innkeeper over the years. In the first, there was something red and shiny swaddled in her arms. It got bigger with each photograph until you realised it was not a frightening looking baby, but a very large and very bumpy pepper that appeared to have grown to the size of a small truck. In the cabinet beside them was a row of awards.

Mrs. Twill was misty eyed. "I raised Bertha from a wee babe and I—" And she was interrupted for the second time as two men entered, laughing as they hung their coats.

The first was what I always imagined Tim thought he saw when he looked in the mirror. Tall and broad, with a roman nose and dimpled chin. His blond hair fell to his shoulders in coils. His voice carried across the pub in smooth operatic tenor.

"And I said, to him, if you want that archaic old bird to play in Pygmalion, you might as well put her *inside* the statue—" he stopped, looked around, and blinked in the darkness. "What a queer place this is, eh Duke? Do you think it's some kind of practical joke?"

Mrs. Twill huffed.

"I did not take him for the type," said the other quietly.

His companion had a mild Belgian accent. He was a short, myopic man all in green. A potbelly strained an emerald waistcoat. He had perfectly parted hair and a pencil moustache. He looked plush and well fed, like a Faberge frog.

"Strange," the taller man agreed. "But not wanting of a good drink. That I can smell." He looked to the bar and raised his hand.

"Garcon! —er, Madame. Two spiced ciders and two rooms if you would. Just for the night." The little man gave him an approving look which vanished as soon as his companion tapped the flask on his hip with a roguish grin. "I always come prepared, old friend."

"What do you think, Wendell?"

"Hm?" I tore myself away from the two men sitting by the fire. Something about them seemed awfully familiar.

"How does a month in Port Larkeney sound?" my father asked.

I thought about it. About a long peaceful vacation—and about sharing a room with my brother for the entire duration.

"A week," I said firmly.

My father sighed. "A week it is then."

Mrs. Twill gave us the keys and directions with a harried, "Enjoy your stay." As we departed to the stairs, I saw a bemused look cross her face as she opened the guestbook for the third time today.

There were more cars pulling up to the Piquant Palaces.

~5~

Heat

Chess? Or what about birds? I brought binoculars." I tossed an orange up and down as I stared at the ceiling. "I've been meaning to try sketching. There's plenty of boats out in the harbour."

Tim was busily filling up the small closet at the foot of the beds with jackets. It was fine, I only had the one.

"Strangle me with a pepper patterned pillowcase."

I sat up, admiring the fact that the bed didn't immediately collapse into a bundle of matchsticks and mouldy cloth. "This is a holiday. I'm planning on making the most of it. What are *you* going to do?"

He ignored me, instead slipping a carefully wrapped parcel from his suitcase. Undoing the twine and paper, he laid down on the bed with a grunt and flipped through the letters moodily.

"Melati again?" I asked.

"Maybe."

I placed the orange on the nightstand between us, leaning to look at them. "That's a lot of letters."

"I get a discount on stamps."

"Seems like a lot for one girl you've never met."

He took offense to this. "And what would *you* know about that?"

"I know things."

"Yeah right. Melati is a *mature* woman. She told me that she always thought you were a bit boorish. The Indonesian equivalent of that anyway."

"She's never met me!"

Tim cracked an infuriating little smile. "I've told her enough."

There were a lot of things I could have said just then, about how I did very interesting things and how girls and I had just always been at the wrong place at the wrong time–but it wasn't worth it. The thing about Melati was, I had no idea how exactly she and Tim had come into correspondence. It just happened somewhere along the last few years. She gave plausible enough descriptions of our family, and we did travel enough that people and places blurred together. Only, Tim didn't quite remember who she was either. It certainly hadn't stopped him falling madly in love with her and committing her poetry to heart as if it were Byron or Shakespeare.

"Do you want to hear what she just wrote me?"

"Not really."

He cleared his throat. "A Lover's Fantasie, by Melati."

MY TIMMY TUM
YOU ARE MY SUN
AND ARE FOREVERMORE
THE WAY THE GOLDEN RAYS
REFLECT YOUR GAZE
MAKES ME DREAM OF HOLDING YOURS

ONE DAY YOU'LL FIND
YOUR HAND IN MINE
AS WE CROSS THE SPARKLING PIER
OF VENICE IN A LOW ROWBOAT
TO THE CROONS OF A MUSACHIOED GONDOLIER

I IMAGINE YOU IN STRIPES OF RED

BARRET AND GLASSES LARGE
WE SHARE A BRIE
THROUGH MOUTHS ONLY
AND CRY WITH GLEE WHEN WE GET THE BOAT RIDE
FREE OF CHARGE.

Tim allowed a long silence in which to absorb the poem. Then he said, "What do you think?"

"It's definitely…something."

"What should I write back? Something about her eyes, maybe."

"You've never seen her eyes."

"Yeah," he fell back against the bed, smiling dreamily, "but I bet they're gorgeous."

* * *

I was the last one down for dinner. I'd slept the evening through. *Really* slept, like there was some kind of drug in the eiderdown pillows and thick pepper patterned bedspread. I made my way downstairs, pleasantly groggy.

Music echoed faintly down the hallway, and I caught drifts of whirling synthesisers and electric guitar. Was that…disco?

Light spilled into the corridor from a solitary crack. It was on the way down to the pub. I shivered. What if it was that woman—Evangeline Grey? I tiptoed past the door as quietly as I could just in case. But I couldn't help but catch a glimpse inside.

There was an orange shag rug, records scattered on the floor. Draped across the foot of the bed were two long legs in green bell bottoms. They were awfully nice legs.

"Katie!" The voice of Mrs. Twill rose from the stairwell. The figure groaned and the legs swung around the bed. I straightened and hurried down to dinner.

"Why d'you keep looking at the stairs?" Tim gave me a suspicious look. He was unhappily stirring a tureen of chipotle potato soup. Mrs. Twill had a fondness for Mexico and her menu reflected the interesting mixture of Spanish/Irish cuisine. I was happy with my bacon sandwich.

49

"No reason."

I avoided further scrutiny as Tim was pulled away by my father. Normally he liked getting interviews the first night we arrived somewhere. The host was usually fresh and more forthcoming.

Unfortunately, Mrs. Twill was clearly experiencing one of the busiest nights she'd had in a very long time. The pub was full to bursting, brimming with conversation, and the clinking of steins. Some were regulars judging by the red, chest-length beards and barnacle studded coveralls. I recognized the duo from that afternoon—the tall man and froggish one. Evangeline Grey was nowhere to be found. Another pair was sitting not far from us— primly dressed in identical hues of expensive beige, they stared down their food like two old, affronted cranes.

I have to say she tried. Mrs. Twill swung by for seconds at a time as she delivered food, offering us historical tidbits on the nature of Port Larkeney and the origin of the infamous Big Bertha. There was:

"Big Bertha was just a seed when my husband brought her to me. I'll never be prouder than the day she crushed the spokes of the wheelbarrow while getting her to the county fair. Little Katie was under it at the time, but she turned out alright."

And:

"Did you know Port Larkeney was started by a group of bandits? They couldn't decide between their two favourite words, 'Larceny' or 'Melarkey' so here we are. Everyone's got stories about their great grandfathers, but I'm just descended from the tax evader."

Not to mention:

"The seagulls here, out for murder. There was an incident about two years ago. Ganged up at the preschool. I don't remember seeing little Geordie after that."

For each of them, my father would yank Tim away from his soup, telling him to "Pay attention!" "Write that down!" and "A scribe is ever vigilant; blink and you could miss the story of a lifetime!"

Tim glowered at me. In the heat of the pub, his face had gone red and sweaty. I simply enjoyed my sandwich. It hit the spot perfectly. Every time I get home from Brazil or Bali or Cambodia, it's the first thing I make. No odd herbs, and no wiggly surprises. Although...it was a bit spicy for my taste. I wiped a thin layer of sweat from my cheek and gulped some water.

"Any more water?" I asked, searching for the pitcher.

"That's mine," snapped my mother who shielded her cup. I glanced at her in surprise.

"I sent for some milk," my father croaked. "But she said she didn't have any left."

I scanned the room. The heat was building, steadily, painfully, the taste of bacon gone. All I could think about was the cool clear gulp of water I would have if the pitcher were full. I would down it all. Every drop. The room was starting to swim. I wiped some more sweat from my brow.

Tim swayed. His bowl of soup was empty. The chair scraped as he stood up suddenly. "I think I'm going to be sick."

Tim reached the bathroom first and heaved mightily into the toilet. I performed the technicolour yawn in the sink, watching the remnants swirl down the sink.

Resurfacing, I immediately ran the faucet, wincing as cool water splashed my burning face. I cupped it in my hands and guzzled it. The stall behind me exhaled deeply as Tim finished. In the mirror, I saw the door to one of the stalls open.

"Oh... Hello boys."

My father emerged looking like the end product of an angora rabbit and a monsoon. He wiped his mouth with the back of his hand and shuffled to the sink. Tim followed shortly after. We stood there facing the mirrors, in the darkness appearing eerily similar.

"Rough night," my father rasped.

We nodded.

He looked at me. "Milk. That's what we need right now. Milk."

* * *

51

I blinked away tears and tried to focus on the road ahead.

We hit a bump and Tim moaned. He was curled up in the back seat, squashed between an old set of squash rackets and swamp boots.

"You didn't have to come," I said. "Not if you can't even sit up."

"No," said Tim resolutely. "I need to be there when you get the milk. I want to be the first to hold it, cherish it, and taste the sweet cold relief to this raging fire. Ow, my head. Stop driving over potholes."

"So that's what it takes for you to get poetic."

"What else were we supposed to get?" he asked, massaging his temples.

I thought for a moment, getting the vivid flash of my mother in her magenta bathrobe slurping water from the faucet, telling me about the list between gulps. "Antacids," I said, "milk, and biscuits."

I squinted at the road ahead, switching on the fog lights. I had recovered the quickest thanks to a resilient stomach. This meant I was the one to drive out of town to one of the larger grocery shops we'd seen along the way.

The roads were pitch black, broken only by flickering streetlamps. It was difficult to gauge distance in a town of small roads that wound up and down the cliffs. Far above it all was the inn, incidentally, serving the same function as a lighthouse with all of its glittering Christmas lights. A lone green pepper-shaped beacon in the dark.

Fog began to creep up the windows and I switched on the wipers. Then I realised the steam was coming from the inside. I fiddled with the heater.

"Turn it *off*," Tim groaned.

"I know, I'm trying." Something was jammed—unfortunately not unusual in the old van. Half the buttons on the old dashboard were stuck, clogged with bits of quicksand and lichen.

"I'll just open the windows." I went to roll down the glass when thunder rumbled overhead. In seconds, a howling rain was hammering against the car.

We settled back in the unpleasant heat, listening to the din of rain on metal. A grove of sycamores to now bordered the road.

At length, my brother spoke. "This doesn't look like the right way."

I glanced at him in the mirror. Tim was spread-eagled across the back row, using his shirt to fan himself. I wasn't doing any better, and after receiving a few kicks, the radiator seemed more determined than ever to make the temperature miserable.

"Dad said it was just outside of town," I said. "There were trees on the way here."

"So just to be clear, we are reliant entirely on your sense of direction? Well then," he rolled his eyes theatrically, "I feel safe."

"It got us out of that jungle in Suriname, didn't it?"

"Please, that was barely a kilometre."

"No thanks to you."

I felt a faint pressure building in my forehead and massaged my temples.

Tim sat up. "You're going way too far. I bet we're out of town by now."

I gripped the wheel, staring determinedly at the thin strips of road illuminated ahead. "I'm sure it's around here."

He tapped me on the shoulder. "There was a left just there! I saw a light!"

I slapped his hand away. "Stop it and let me drive."

Tim slid back down his seat to sulk. "Fine, don't listen to me. You always know best."

"What's that supposed to mean?"

"Nothing."

But not a minute passed until he began to speak in a high-pitched tone, clearly mocking me.

"*Oh Tim, don't bring the granite ceremonial statue, it won't fit in the boat! Tim don't sleep on that branch, it's actually a snake! Tim, don't make that gesture, you don't know what it means!*"

I kept my eyes on the road, trying to angle away from the blast of hot air in the front seat. "So you'd rather I *did* let you sleep on the giant anaconda."

My brother scoffed. "You never let me make my own decisions. You know what I'm like. I freestyle it. You're always *micromanaging* me."

Cool rain rushed across the windowpanes in calming rivulets. But inside, burning air pumped through the vents, pressing against us like a living thing. After a few minutes more of him mocking me under his breath, I couldn't take anymore.

"You know if it weren't for me, you'd have three missing limbs and a speech impediment from that time an arctic snow crab crawled into your mouth in Alaska," I said. "If it weren't for me, you'd be dead about eight times over. At some point you must know you're not suited for this."

"I don't need you!" snapped Tim. "I'm perfectly capable of fending for myself. I have a girlfriend! You're just jealous." He jabbed my shoulder, which would have had more of an effect if we were face to face, but it angered me all the same.

I hit the brakes and turned around. "I never said I was perfect, but fine, if you don't want me helping, you can make all the stupid decisions you want. I won't be there when you find yourself on the brink of being guillotined because *you* didn't bother to learn the proper dialect."

"Fine!"

"Fine!"

It reminded me of Egypt, the heated car. Two years ago we'd been exploring a famously booby-trapped tomb. Tim had managed to set off not one, but four traps, effectively locking us inside the sweltering pyramid with twenty spikes, a granite boulder, a nest of vipers, and a very accusatory-looking dead Pharoah.

Tim repeated himself in a singsong voice. "We're going the wrong *way*."

"I'm not." I jammed the heater again.

"You don't know better than me," mumbled Tim. "You're younger than me."

I turned to glare at him. "Then why am *I* driving? Oh, come on, you're not going to fool me like that."

Tim's eyes had widened dramatically in the rearview mirror. He shook his head and pointed at something beyond me. I turned my attention to the road.

In the depths of lamp-lit fog, a glint of metal shone. Six spider-like arms emerged from the gloom. There was a screech as rain-slicked gravel foiled the brakes. I seized the wheel. We were headed straight for it.

~6~

A Rude Welcome

I think we've established that I am somewhat behind when it comes to technology, pop culture, fashion, slang, or anything new. When I came back from a four-month hike across the Landmannalauger Mountains in Iceland, I was appalled by the appearance of platform shoes (how are you supposed to run from anything in those?). I thought that the Atari was some kind of washing machine. But the biggest thing that threw us Billings for a loop were Autos.

It happened without warning. We'd returned to London after several weeks stuck underground in South Sudan and suddenly, they were everywhere. The first I saw was a coppery crab the size of a six-year-old, scuttling up and replacing the tiles of a penthouse flat. Naturally, I was horrified.

Over the next couple of weeks, I witnessed more of them, robotic creatures of all shapes and sizes creeping around the affluent neighbourhoods and shops, doing odd jobs and following after their wealthy owners. I learned later that they were simply called Autos. Each and every one of them was unique, a handmade work of art created by celebrity inventor, Sebastian Shaw. If you don't understand how they work, join the club.

What really puts the eye-watering price on Autos is Amber. It's Shaw's own discovery and one he refuses to make public. To my knowledge, it's some kind of glowy rock that makes robots work.

Genie was the first Auto we owned, and we learned firsthand how Shaw's inventions actually work. Whatever powers Genie isn't a battery. A battery couldn't get a teapot to brew a cup of earl grey with milk and sugar while doing a tap dance whenever you asked it. Besides our teapot and the Evangeline's creepy chauffeur, I'd never seen one up close before.

Until now.

I jerked the wheel so hard the arrows on the dashboard wobbled. Everything flashed by in moments. Fog rose around the spindly goliath as our old van groaned against the turn. Wheels skidded on asphalt. Two bright beams of orange light shone through the mist like monstrous headlights. A metal appendage flashed inches from the window. Someone shrieked as an explosion of sparks rained past and the left-hand door crumpled inwards.

We were still speeding, the wet streets propelling the old Volkswagen unimpeded. Then, the front wheels hit the curb and the force of it jarred through my body, vibrating the windows. Everything went white.

After a moment of shock, I fought off the airbag and slid into the adjoining seat. The car had settled half on half off the curb and gently rocked as I slid over.

"Tim? Are you alright."

My brother was upside down but alive. He stared up at me, mouth agape, with a rapidly purpling bruise on his forehead.

"My head hurts. This is your fault," he mumbled.

"You're alright."

I abandoned him and looked out the window. In the light of a guttering lamp, water rushed down the street in thin black torrents. Incidentally it had been the slippery gravel that had saved us. The unwieldy van wouldn't have skidded away in time if not for it. I tried the ignition. For a moment the car rumbled to life before diminishing to a weak whine. I tried it again and again.

"Come on!"

My fist hit the console in frustration. If I couldn't get it to start, we were stuck here until daylight unless we could get to a telephone.

Tim sat up with a groan, his glasses comically askew. "Eurgh," he mumbled. "What on earth did you *do?*" He sat up more fully and squinted into the darkness. "And where on earth *are* we?"

Through the misted windows, the offending creature I'd nearly slammed into waded through the night. Two bright beacons of light glowed from a head that bobbed nearly three metres in the darkness. The silhouette of six hands rose and fiddled with a streetlight that had gone out in the storm. The lamp flickered on, and our surroundings appeared.

We'd landed on an empty stretch of road just out of the woods. Although there were no houses in sight, a low, neat hedge bordered the right side. I felt a flicker hope. If the hedge bordered an estate, there was sure to be a phone.

No cliffs in sight but can hear water. Seagulls can be heard, but no evidence of cattle/farmland. Likely approx. 8 km from PL. Unknown direction. Tim left his compass with his pith helmet back at the Palaces.

My brother peered over my shoulder. "What are you doing?"

"Thinking." I snapped my notebook closed. "It's a long shot to walk back in this darkness. We need to find a place we can call Dad to pick us up. There should be one around here."

"You," Tim corrected, "not *we*. I'm not going out in all that rain. And you almost killed me. Wait until Dad finds out. Then he'll murder *you*."

He checked his bruise in the mirror to make sure it was still purple. I wasn't unduly worried about my father finding out about the clipped rims. There were so many dents and "travel wear" in the van already, it was more likely the crash had smoothed some out. My main concern was how we were going to get home.

I drew up my hood. It would be better to get out of that stifling car and cool off before the argument reignited. "Fine," I said. "You stay here."

Tim put his hands behind his head. "That was the plan."

"Have we at least got an umbrella?"

He made the effort of turning his head from side to side. "Mmm...nope."

I elbowed the dented door open. Outside the cool air was a shock to the heated cabin. I pulled my hood further. Luckily, the storm had lightened to a light drizzle, but that meant the fog had risen. It swirled thickly, gathering in a miasma at my feet and swishing as I passed through.

The street was well lit but gloomy. Orange fragments of light spilled across the puddles. I glanced back at the lit windows of the van where my brother's silhouette leaned against the seat. It made me all the happier to be outside.

A minute's walk from the car found a gap in the hedges. It was bridged by an iron gate nearly as tall as the creature behind me. I tried not to think about it. It couldn't hurt you. It was an Auto. A scary, spindly, 3-metre-tall spidery Auto that was harmless as a fly.

A solitary mailbox stood out front bearing nothing more than the letters "S. S." on the side. I could make out a black shape through the bars. Lights twinkled in the distance.

It *was* an estate. What were the odds?

When I pushed on it, the gate gave. I walked along a broad driveway that twisted over the usual manicured lawns. Inset electric lights created the effect of walking on mirrored glass.

Where was this? And who was building estates in a town like Port Larkeney? Eventually, the driveway broadened into a plaza of smoothed sandstone. I was so distracted by the hall that I hardly noticed the cars parked upon it.

It was a monstrous mansion—practically a castle. In the front, two thick marble columns supported an ornate lintel above the front door. Winged stone creatures leered off the balustrades. But for all its ornateness, it appeared heavy and brutish—a long dark rectangle of a house that melded poorly with the surrounding greenery, as though a brick had been dropped on the lawn.

The sound of socialising drifted through the many lit windows. Shadows flitted back and forth across the uppermost balcony. I passed a gleaming black Rolls Royce stopped. *What are the odds?* The thought of seeing Evangeline Grey again was enough to make me reconsider mounting the steps. Past it, was a Bentley, a purple Italian sports car, and a green Cadillac. Behind the tinted windows, the orange gaze of their lifeless chauffeurs stared blankly ahead. Far above, a champagne bottle popped to the sound of applause.

Suck it up, Wendell. You've slapped a bear. You can handle a mean older woman.

I crossed the steps. There was a face on the doors, and I didn't want to touch it. The iron had been shaped into a fat jowly man with a large ring in the mouth. A thick seam ran down the centre of its head, bisecting its face. There was nothing else to knock within sight, so I pulled the ring. It didn't budge. A dim glow slowly suffused the glassy eyes of the door knocker. A deep metallic voice boomed from the doorway.

"Nrm," it said imperiously.

I looked around for the voice. "What?"

"NRM!"

The brassy lips squirmed the ring around until it was hanging out the side. It coughed raspily.

"Name?" it asked.

"Oh." I had the unpleasant feeling that if I got too close it might bite me. "Wendell Billings?"

The Auto paused as if checking something. "Thrsh nrm dsh not appr on the guesht lisht," it said finally.

"Sorry?"

The face worked the ring in its mouth once again.

"Thish name doesh not appear on the guesht lishht," it croaked. "The mashter of the houshe does not resheive sholishitors. Pleashe vacate the premishes immediately."

"Tell him I just need to use the phone," I persisted, not sure if the face could even relay messages. "Our car broke down just out there. It'd only take a minute."

The bulging eyes scanned me for a moment. They blinked asynchronously of one another.

"No," it said firmly.

I sighed. So much for coincidence and luck. Maybe there was a booth down the street or something. I turned to leave.

"Wait, yes."

I turned back. "Yes?"

"No." The eyes blinked rapidly, the balls rolling madly in the head. They settled to stare at each other. "Yes." said the left door side. "No!" said the right door. It went on like this for some time until I couldn't take it anymore.

"For heaven's sake, make up your mind!" I snapped.

A frown twisted the pouchy face. "No!" cried both sides in unison.

There was a sudden creaking like a grinding of stone and a mote of dust fell from above. I looked up. The carved creatures on the parapets now faced the veranda. Gargoyles and satyrs twisted on invisible joints. In a smooth movement, the toga-wearing cherubs pulled back their bowstrings. The sharpened points of a dozen heart-tipped arrows were trained on me.

I froze and glanced at the iron face which seemed to be having a fit. The jowls wobbling in the moonlight and its eyes rolled around like pool balls.

"You're mad!" I cried.

"*No, No, NO!*" it shouted.

Stone ground on stone as statues shifted.

I glanced at the lit windows. The balcony doors were open— maybe someone would hear me. If I moved, the cherubs would shoot and the stone lions on either side of the door weren't looking too friendly either.

Whump!

I stumbled forward as something collided with me. My knees hit the marble painfully. There was a soft heavy pressure preventing me from getting up. It smelled like cats. With much heaving, it rolled away, and I was able to breathe again.

"I'm so sorry! I'm so *so* sorry! I wasn't looking where I was going!"

A woman in a mismatched country jacket and twill skirt held out a hand, still apologising. Her features were youngish and wide set. Mid-30s? She set down a heavy leather clasp bag with some relief. I got up on my own, aware of the subtle sounds of so many notched bowstrings.

"I'm fine. It's alright."

I must have glanced up at the lintel again because she uttered an oath. She hiked up her skirts and went to mutter something at the door knocker. Like magic, the stone guardians retreated, grinding back onto their pedestals for the night.

"Damned blasted door knocker on the fritz again," she turned to me conversationally. "I don't know what's wrong with the thing but Sebastian refuses to replace it. Can you believe that?" She paused.

"Who did you say you were again?"

"Er, Wendell."

She looked at me sharply, or maybe it was the squint.

"And perhaps I am correct in assuming you have something to do with the dented car half up the curb just outside the gate."

"Oh, yeah. That's right."

She squinted again. "Are you quite old enough to drive?"

I huffed. "Of course."

"Well, I noticed a surprising number of scratches on the hood and if I didn't know better, I'd say you'd been accosted by a pack of Ethiopian wolves."

"That's exactly right! How did you know that?"

The lady grinned. "I spent some time in Africa. I'll have to tell you about it. Well, you're certainly an interesting specimen, Wendell. We'll have to get you a ride, won't we? Come on then, I won't bite!" She waved me up insistently. I kept my eyes on the parapets as I followed her. She bent down in front of the twisted face, both halves of which immediately snapped to attention.

"Nrm?" it asked.

"Mary," she said clearly, "Mary Belsize." She straightened and looked at me with a kindly expression. "Well, as you undoubtedly heard, I'm Mary. It's nice to meet you."

Then the double doors opened.

MARY
BELSIZE
(•SWEET
•Triggers Allergies)

~7~

The Mirrored Room

I didn't have time to gape at the doorstep because Mary pushed me in by the shoulder. It was like stepping onto the moon— cold, vast, and of a luxury completely alien to me. The vaulted ceilings reached so far into the aether that the enormous iron chandelier made little difference in light. The floor was one long expanse of black-and-white-chequered marble. I pulled my jacket closer. There was a coldness inside of the house that all the sconces could not shake. It was perhaps because it was so blue, suffused in an overcast teal. Each wall made up an unbroken fresco of twisting vines and pale flowers, circling, entrapping, winding throughout the room. The foyer was sparsely furnished with only the occasional bench and potted fern.

But what overshadowed it all was the staircase. It took up the entire north side of the room, a megalith of creamy veined marble– enough room for a small army to walk abreast. Melancholy notes whispered down the steps. Somewhere in the upper floors of the manor, a solitary cello played Saint Saens.

Rain dripped off us, making puddles where we stood. Mary let out a low whistle.

Without warning, one of the black tiles at my feet flipped over. Out popped a bronze humpbacked creature with one large glass eye. It made a beeline for the puddle. I jumped out of its way unnerved, but it followed me across the floor, scrubbing furiously between my boots with a tiny pail and washcloth anywhere I stepped. What I'd thought was a whistle of awe was actually a summons for the Auto.

"He does keep a clean house," said Mary, shaking off her own shoes for the creature.

The Auto clacked over to her at once. Relieved she'd diverted its attention, I went up to the stairs.

On either side of it were two arched alcoves with strange fountains. A twin pair of huge marble kings with gaunt, sunken faces held large shell-shaped basins. Water dripped from their noses, beards, and in the little runnels of their livery into the bowls. The only difference between them was that one was ivory white, the other obsidian black.

Mary came up to me.

"It's quite something isn't it?" she said chattily. "Very new. I told him, Sebastian, there's plenty of gorgeous old places in this neighbourhood with just the kind of rustic charm you're looking for. Of course, he never did listen to me," she put her hands on her hips, seemingly unimpressed with the gloomy glamour of the place. "He goes off and constructs a big Greek palace. He said, 'My dear, I want the Pantheon. Only fewer columns and many more lethal safeguards to keep me from the general public." Mary sniffed. "I think it could use a nice lamp, or a knitted blanket. Make it homier."

I frowned. The man she was speaking of—it couldn't be *him*—could it? How could it possibly be? Out here? In Port Larkeney of all places? Before I could ask, a door opened, and light flooded the distant top step of the marble staircase. The cello music echoed all the louder.

"Is that Mary I hear?"

Mary beamed and trotted up to the foot of the staircase. "In the flesh!" she called.

66

"Well don't just wait at the door," said the voice good-naturedly, "we are having a party, you know."

Mary nodded to no one in particular and hoisted her bag. She tapped her foot. I looked up, distracted by watching the little cleaning Auto jump back into the space beneath the chequered floor.

"You too, Wendell. Come along."

I hurried along after her all the way up the marble staircase.

The stairs looked dark standing in front of them, but as we walked, lights flickered on every metre or so. The first time it happened I stumbled into Mary who gave a yelp and dropped her suitcase. I noticed an interesting circular design on it, though in the dim I couldn't make out exactly what it was. The walls along both sides of the stairs were covered in faces, iron and life-size, like that of the door knocker. Some were men, some women, some I even recognized as famous deceased playwrights and politicians. As we walked, the metal jaws would drop open revealing the steady vermillion light of Amber. It played ghoulishly across the prone faces.

"He likes to honour his friends," said Mary, patting me on the shoulder. Her face was pale in the orange light. "Although, I'm glad he never went into interior decorating."

"Who is—?" I started to ask.

"Your face," she said suddenly. "I didn't notice it before but it's scarlet! Do you have rosacea? I have an excellent herbal cure for it. Causes warts in other places though, but that only matters if you ride bikes."

I felt my face. With everything that had happened, I'd nearly forgotten about the overwhelming spice from dinner. But upon its mention, it seemed to come back in full force. My mouth watered.

"I had a bacon sandwich," I said.

To my surprise, she laughed.

"The Piquant Palaces takes some getting used to. They're some of my best customers and for good reason—goat's milk is among the best cures for the meals of Jeanne Twill."

"You're a goat farmer?" Heat throbbed in my mouth like a toothache. "You wouldn't happen to have any milk on you, would you?"

Mary heaved up the bag with both hands and gave me an apologetic look. "Normally I'd love to give you a bottle" she said, "but this is a special delivery I'm afraid. It's camel's milk and I have a feeling it would make you feel much worse than you already do." Noticing my disappointment, she said, "Chin up, Wendell. I'm sure there will be some livery canapes that will do the trick."

"Where did you get camel's milk?" I asked.

Mary lugged her suitcase a few more steps before stopping for a breath.

"Before I was a goat farmer, I spent my younger years in Africa. I housebroke ostriches for the King of Morocco. He still sends me some little gifts from time to time."

"How was that?"

"Wet." She paused. "And *you* are a young journalist because you've been writing down everything I've said thus far."

"What?"

I looked down to discover neat rows of shorthand. No! I'd been writing as we walked! And how had I gotten the pen again? "I'm sorry," I said, shoving it away. I couldn't bring myself to rip out the page. "Bad habit. I'll get rid of it."

Mary smiled reassuringly. "That's what the ostriches said—in not so many squawks."

Mary was curious to learn what my father did for a living, and I was curious to know what a goat farmer was doing in a place like this, but the stairs weren't that long, and we made it up to the landing without much more conversation.

We walked along the short hallway, passing several closed doors until we came to the end. The sound of music was louder now, the lone player having picked up in tune. I couldn't imagine anything more appropriate than the Danse Macabre that clipped through the air. Light and conversation spilled from two double doors. Mary guided me in by the elbow.

I entered and immediately locked eyes with myself.

The ballroom was made entirely out of mirrors, giving an infinite, dizzying effect to the chessboard floor. The room appeared to be full of people but as I got used to the sight, I realised there were only seven.

The guests socialised somewhat self-consciously, repeatedly glancing back at their multiplied reflection.

"Whoozat?" someone called. "I see a dwarf and a Yorkshire terrier in a dress. Sebastian, you have odd taste in company!"

Six identical men with wavy blond hair and roguish, if unfocused and slightly sweaty good looks stumbled out of the way of an Auto balancing a plate laden with tiny bowls of soup. It was the loud man from the pub. He was different here. His eyes half-closed, they slid off of us to make a beeline for another robotic servant with champagne glasses full of a greenish liquid.

I looked around the room, or rather at a mirror that showed it all anyway. They were all here, the froggish man with the bulging eyes and pencil moustache, the pale woman in her boxy grey dress, the old couple at dinner. Someone was getting up off the piano to see us. Mary patted down her skirt as he arrived.

"Don't gawk," she whispered quickly. "He doesn't like that."

He was surprisingly short, just a little taller than Mary. More like a painting than a man, he was dressed in sombre blues and a cravat. Sharp featured with a slightly receding hairline, I guessed him to be in his late thirties. A stylish walking stick that he seemed too young for, tapped the chequered floors. I gawked.

Sebastian Shaw, billionaire inventor, object of national scandal, and thwacker of reporters leaned on his cane and greeted Mary.

"Welcome! I was almost afraid you wouldn't come," he admitted. "You sounded quite preoccupied when I called."

"You know I wouldn't miss—is this all?" She looked around at the handful of people in the room.

Sebastian laughed ruefully. "It is a small gathering, I know, hardly a party, but alas you know better than anyone how I value my *privacy*." As he said this, his gaze snapped to me. "And what do we have here?"

I stared at him, momentarily at a loss for words.

"Camel's milk, your favourite!" Mary held up the bag with a grunt. "Oh, you meant him. I hope you don't mind," she said cheerfully, "I brought in a stray." Mary patted my shoulder. The smell of cats was very prominent. "Wendell's car broke down just up the road," she explained. "He was hoping he could use your telephone to call for a ride. Also," she added, admonishingly, "It's time you fixed that security system of yours, Sebastian. That ghastly old door knocker you insist upon nearly skewered this poor boy."

Sebastian narrowed his eyes. "Hmph. So you've met Fred."

Mary frowned.

"Well, if *Wendell* wasn't on the guest list, you could argue the door knocker was serving its purpose."

"Sebastian!"

"But of course, we will fetch him a phone," he added quickly. "I believe there is one in my study. Come."

I didn't want to leave Mary, but she clapped me on the back and said she had to go set up the milk. Reluctantly, I followed him back out of the ballroom and down the hall. Before we could get any further, he stopped me at a bench in the middle of the landing and held up a thin hand.

"Wait here please," he said and left me there.

I sat down below another large mirror and waited. What was with this place and mirrors?

After a minute or so, I began to get restless. The fur of the seat definitely wasn't fake, and it felt oddly warm. I didn't like that. I'd begun to hear odd thumps coming from the room where he'd disappeared. Surely it didn't take that long to get a phone. Through the open ballroom door, guests shifted aimlessly to the mournful music of the cello. I sighed and settled against the wall.

CRACK!

There was a bang like a firecracker and the door to the study flew open. The hall was suddenly enveloped in dazzling blue. A man shouted, but all was lost in that brilliant flash of light. A crackling feeling electrified the room. Time seemed to slow. My arm prickled as of my hairs stood on end. Then a broken beam of light shot from the open door and ricocheted off the mirror inches from my head. It flew into the ballroom and hit the many panelled walls. Instantly the lightning bolt fractured into pieces.

People screamed and ducked. Glass shattered. Still the cello music played. Some bits of light escaped through the window, but most seemed to centre in the middle of the room where a solitary figure stood. Long fingers of lightning sparked towards him, skipping across the floor. He didn't move. Why didn't he move!

There was no time to shout. Another flash blinded the room, and all was still.

I blinked. Jagged lines flickered at the edge of my vision. I stood shakily. In the mirror above me, a blackened scorch mark marred the glass. I was shaking, I realised—a delayed reaction to the sudden chaos. The first figure who rushed towards me in the gloom was a cloud of frizzled black hair.

"Are you alright?" Mary was ashen. She brushed a bit of broken stone from her tweed jacket which was pale with dust.

"That—" I started to speak.

"What the devil just happened?" roared the blond man who'd staggered into the hallway. He smelled sour. Liquor dripped down his hand out of a cracked champagne flute, but he didn't seem to notice.

"Not now, Billius," said Mary. "Can't you see something terrible has happened?"

"Well, that's what I'm trying to figure out, aren't I?"

Evangeline Grey arrived in the hallway, her heels crunching on shattered glass. She stopped in front of the mirror in the hall and gave a horrified gasp. "My hair!" She tried in vain to pat it down, but the black bob stuck rigidly in the air.

"That man who got hit," I stammered. "Is he...?" I looked around the corner. To my amazement he was still standing, smoke gently billowing off him.

"Oh goodness," said Mary with weak amusement. "Don't you worry about him. That's an Auto. It was Sebastian's surprise tonight, the unveiling of his newest invention. It plays the cello beautifully—or rather, it did."

Sebastian. People perked up at the name. Slowly, all heads turned to the darkened study.

Evangeline prodded Billius with one of the little silver soup spoons. "Go look in there," she hissed.

71

Billius shrugged her away. "Geroff me woman! *You* go look," But seeing everyone's eyes on him, he sucked in a breath. "Alright then." He strode up to the study and halted in the doorway.

"Alright in there, Sebastian?"

There was no answer. Billius cleared his throat. "I'm coming in."

He leaned around and nudged the light switch. Billius took a long look around, his body obscuring the rest of the room.

"Well," he said at last. "There you go. He's dead."

Somebody screamed. Suddenly the hallway was much too crowded. Seven people jostled in the narrow passage for a look inside the study.

Dead? My mind reeled. What could have possibly happened in the minute Sebastian Shaw went into his study?

Against my better judgement, I slipped into the crowd at the door. Between cocktail dresses and tweed trousers I saw it. It was a dark room, deep green and gold with a fireplace crackling low between a wall of bookshelves. In the centre, a glass case on a wooden pedestal stood open and empty. A chipped gold padlock glittered on the rug.

Sebastian Shaw was slumped against the wall, glasses askew on his face. In his left hand, the elegant walking stick hung loosely. In the right, he clutched his heart.

Mary held a hand to her mouth. "Oh dear oh dear oh dear," she repeated softly.

Contrary to his calm announcement, Billius now looked wild. "Which one of you was it?" he roared. "Who did this?"

"Calm yourself," a hand was laid on his shoulder. It was the little froggish man. "We have no evidence of this fact."

"Yes. He could have done it to himself," said Evangeline Grey thinly. But she didn't look convinced.

She surveyed the room sharply. I tried to look as small as possible.

"You!"

I cringed.

"What are you doing here? I saw you this morning at that Pepper Shack, what on earth is a child—"

Mary tried to explain but was promptly interrupted.

72

"What's that in his hand?" someone cried.

I tried to shove my notebook back into my pocket as fast as I could, but Billius was too quick for me.

He snatched it up and flipped through it, holding the latest pages up to one of the sconces. His eyes, however, scanned the page uncomprehendingly, blinking blearily through a haze of alcohol. He thrust it into the crowd. "Here, one of you lot read it."

It ended up in the hands of Mary who said, "Really, I don't think we should." People groaned and she gave me an apologetic look. "The Twenty-second of November," she began. "Arrived in Port Larkeney. Background: Small town on southwestern Irish coast. Known for peppers. Time of arrival: 5pm, Piquant Palaces. Dinner caused extraordinarily painful gastric distress—"

"Is there anything about us?" someone interrupted.

Mary flipped through the book. "Erm, no."

I pushed through the crowd, trying to mask my irritation. "If you're all finished, can I have my book back please?"

Reluctantly it was passed to me. I put it back in my pocket.

"What do we do now?" asked Evangeline.

"We need to stay close in case the murderer strikes again," quavered the soup lady.

"The police would be a good start," said the Duke. "Does anyone know where the phone is? Billius?"

Billius half sung half mumbled something against the wall. Having found a fresh bottle of something to drink, he was no longer any help.

"Two hundred and fifty bloody rooms," said the husband in the monocle. "We'll be picked off one by one."

"I might know where it is," I said.

All eyes were on me as I slowly stepped over the body in the study, ignoring the suspicious whispers at the door. I scanned the room for anything that might be considered a phone, regretting I'd said anything at all considering the study was mostly bare of normal technology.

There were strange little silver coils littering the desk, swirling glass orbs, and small statuettes with glowing eyes on the bookshelves.

73

Eventually I found it, tucked away in a shelf under the desk. I lifted the receiver and dialled the police. The group looked on anxiously. The sound came out distant and staticky.

"Port Larkeney Police Dept, what is your emergency?"

The muttering around me rose and I stuck a finger in my ear.

"I, er, there's been an accident. Someone's dead."

"Where?"

I stared out the window at the pitch-black grounds. "Shaw Manor."

There was a small intake of breath on the other line. "We'll be right there," the voice crackled.

The line went dead.

~8~

Shagadelic, Baby!

The wailing of sirens marked the passing of midnight. The guests of Sebastian Shaw's dinner party (plus one) huddled at the base of the grand staircase. Evangeline Grey was the first to snatch up a throw from the only sofa in the room, clutching it around her shoulders. The other old woman in a cocktail dress shivered jealously. The sound grew louder as they rounded onto our street and then the windows were flashing in raucous red and blue.

Along with the keening, music blared from outside. A skid and a screech later, a police car and a heavily dented maroon Chrysler Coupe with a siren attached raced up the driveway. The latter wobbled alarmingly left and right, lights blazing.

"My car!" cried Evangeline and Billius at once.

The Coupe veered dangerously close to the carport under which were the Rolls Royce and purple sports car. It turned away at the last second, clipping the pergola and slowing to a stop on the lawn where it gently bumped over a potted cypress. There was a collective sigh of relief.

One of the doors opened amidst the murmurs of outrage and I caught the drifting lyrics of a stereo before it was abruptly shut off.

Get down
Get down
Boogie tonight!

The police car slowed to a neat stop beside it and the door popped open. The man emerging was tall and ginger haired, clad in a beige duster. Upon getting out, he stepped in the spilled dirt from the pot. He stamped his foot and began to shout.

The second person got out of the Coupe; hands raised placatingly. They too were tall, lanky and wearing a long tartan coat, with the collar of it obscuring the face. They were gesturing in explanation and tried vainly to right the potted cypress, but only succeeded in tipping more dirt on the other.

The red-haired man seemed ready to launch a fresh tirade until he glanced up and saw the myriad of pale faces staring out at him from windows. The two officers quickly dusted themselves off and walked up to the house.

Dread filled me. It hadn't quite hit me when Sebastian was pronounced dead, but in the presence of the law, I realised that I was a part of this now. Guilty or not, I would be inextricably linked to this whole affair—and if it were publicised—what would that mean for my future? I stood by the stairs, listening to the chatter of the guests, trying to think.

The double doors burst open. In came the two officers. They made an interesting pair. They were both tall, but the man slouched. They were both thin, but the first had a small potbelly. They were both in the same colours, but the second wore the most impressively flared red bell bottoms I'd ever seen.

The second officer turned down her collar. Beneath a ramrod blond fringe, she had a narrow, inquisitive face with bright green eyes. She also couldn't have been much older than me.

The girl officer let out a low whistle as she walked into the foyer, tapping her fingers against her leg as she sang under her breath.

"*Boogie nights. Oh yeah. It's shagadelic baby*—great galloping gingersnaps, is that a dead koala on the coffee table?"

I was pretty sure that wasn't part of the song.

"First order of business," said the first officer, his voice reedy and clipped. "You will all file *compliantly* into a designated room for questioning. You will not be leaving until we have the information we need. Nobody leaves the interrogation room. You will all tell me your names. You will all be truthful. Liars will be prosecuted to the full extent of the law—that being a filthy cell personally guarded by none other than me, Inspector Quentin Wimbelow. Now, someone tell me where the incident occurred."

"The study," was murmured throughout the group.

"Which way?" asked Wimbelow exasperatedly.

"Up the stairs, last door to the left on the second floor," said Mary.

The Inspector sighed and began the arduous trek up the stairs. "Bloody enormous house," he muttered.

As he did so, the girl caught his sleeve. "I thought you said I could have a look at this one," she said in an undertone. "Give me a chance to put together some evidence."

Wimbelow yanked his arm away. "That was a probationary promise," he hissed, "which has since been taken away after you *crashed the car into a tree.*"

She mumbled something weakly about how a potted cypress wasn't really a tree if it was only a metre high. Wimbelow waved her off in annoyance.

"Gather up the suspects. Get down the information, report back to me as soon as you're done, you understand?"

"Yes, sir."

"And have someone else on them to make sure the murderer doesn't try anything funny. Put Meredith on it. She's got the Big Stick."

The girl's eye twitched subtly. "Yes, sir," she said.

"Alright you lot," she stood in the middle of us and clapped her hands as if herding a bunch of toddlers to playtime. "Gather round, book it up here."

As the guests circled around her, I saw how tall she really was, standing just below Billius, who was no small man. Why did she seem so familiar?

"My name is Officer Twill—"

"Junior officer!" shouted Wimbelow from the stairwell.

Her smile tightened. She shifted from foot to foot, the hem of her bell bottoms flapping, and I had a sudden flash of recognition. The open door. The music in the hall. *It was her.* "Yes, well, as I was saying, let's start off by getting names, shall we?"

But the rest of the interrogations were interrupted as people started to complain about the draft in the foyer. Billius had managed to sneak the blanket from Evangeline. Evangeline griped loudly as Mary offered her a hairy sweater from her bag and the old soup couple's lips were turning blue as they sipped from their tiny tureens.

"Er. Okay then. Let's go to the party room then. I'm dying to see—I mean it'll jog some memories." The junior officer bounded upstairs, forgot she was supposed to tow the back of us, and came back around again.

Once again finding ourselves in the unpleasant nakedness of the mirror room, we pulled up benches, chairs, and piano seats into a semi-circle around the young officer. I chose the seat furthest away. My palms were sweaty. I wiped them on the face of a stuffed African gazelle throw pillow.

Twill cleared her throat. "Let's do names first. How about we start with…you there, Cubism come to life."

Everyone looked to Evangeline who pretended not to notice, even as she was handed a clipboard to sign her name to. "How do we even know you're qualified to question us," she snipped. "You look barely older than that boy over there who crashed the party."

Twill simply withdrew a pair of glittering handcuffs and dangled them in front of the woman. "I hope that's enough qualification for you," she said. "Groovy. Now, let's keep the clipboard moving please."

Cubism quieted.

As I waited for the clipboard to be passed around, I looked for anything that wasn't in the young officer's side of the room, because she seemed to have an uncomfortably keen interest in *me*—those green eyes were there every time I looked up. God forbid she thought I was guilty. I wiped my palms on my pants once more. Was it possible to accidentally confess to something you didn't do?

Fortunately, there was one thing in the room that had everyone's attention. Sebastian's Auto still stood in the centre of the ballroom playing its melancholy music and gently smoking.

"What is that thing?" Twill asked.

"*That* is an exceptionally delicate piece of machinery. I wouldn't expect you to understand," the gaunt man to my left sniffed. "It can play any song requested of it."

"Well, some funeral you've been having," Twill turned to it. "Know any of The Bee Gees?" The music didn't change.

The *thing* was in the rough shape of a man the way an Italian armoire is the rough shape of a closet. It was skeletal and ornate, decorated in carved scrolls and whorls. The torso sloped narrowly in at the waist in the unmistakable shape of a cello and it's gloved right hand deftly plucked at the four strings running down the centre of its chest. The left hand drew out haunting music from a gleaming metal bow. Normally Autos didn't have hair, but this one sported a courtly white wig. It wore a finely made tailcoat over a pair of starched cream pantaloons. The overall effect was that of an eighteenth-century composer—except that the closer you got, the more inhuman it became.

The narrow face was constructed out of hundreds of seamless plates of bone that twitched and shifted to create different expressions. High cheekbones, a thin mouth, and, in the reflections of the mirrors, a pair of glowing Amber eyes that burned in a thousand tiny pinpoints.

THE
CELLIST

Finally, the clipboard was handed to me. I looked at the other names. There was:

-**Sir Billius Brum** ***knighted for excellence in moving audiences worldwide*** (This was specified underneath.)
-**Evangeline Grey,** (this had been crossed out and rewritten several times)
-**The Duke Archambeault of Dillmont**
-**Mary Belsize**
-**Ophidia Quisling**
-**Ludlow Quisling**

I knew those last names! Half the things in our house had the small, engraved circle of Quisling Electric on their undersides. I probably shouldn't have been surprised considering this was Sebastian Shaw's mansion. Nevertheless, it was an odd feeling to be rubbing shoulders, literally, with some of the richest people on the planet. A rap on the door made everyone jump. Whoever it was pounded insistently.

Twill leapt up from her seat and extricated her legs from the roly-poly Duke of Dillmont who had toppled over at the sudden noise. She opened the door to the grim face of The Inspector.

"How is it going?" he asked.

She grinned. "All copacetic. Well, I haven't been murdered yet at least. Why didn't you radio me?"

"I'll assume that means you're getting on well. Something's interfering with the reception. Come along," he spoke low, glancing at us over her shoulder. "I think we'll need to get another officer on these people. There's been a development."

Twill stepped out into the hall. Everyone twisted their heads slightly to catch the conversation happening beyond the doors, but nothing could be heard.

The young officer appeared back in the room after a bit, scratching her fringe. "We're going to be with you in just a bit," she said. "You'll love Meredith, best we've got. Until then, no escaping alright?" She gave us a toothy grin and clunked the door shut.

Several minutes later, the door creaked open and a woman with two cataracts for eyes and a baggy police jumpsuit hobbled in. This must be Meredith because she did indeed have a very Big Stick. The enormous baton dragged heavily across the floor, trembling in her skeletal fingers. She said naught a word but made very slowly for the last open chair where she promptly sat and closed her eyes. The slow rattle of her breath filled the room.

It had been nearly twenty minutes.

People reclined tensely on the few chairs in the ballroom, trying not to make eye contact with their reflections. Red and blue pulsed outside the windows as reinforcements arrived. I stewed, thoughts whirling. Was that *lighting* that had come out of the study? Was that Mrs. Twill's *daughter? Was anyone here going to kill me and how could I get my hands on the Big Stick before they did?*

"I call that shoddy police work," said Quisling at last. He'd been busy folding and refolding his handkerchief while his wife worried with the stuffed iguana decorating her hat. "Any one of us could be the murderer and yet the police send this old bag. I say we go out and see what is the matter with them. I simply *refuse* to be murdered tonight."

He had a point, but there was really nowhere for us to go. There were several officers standing below the balcony and the ballroom had only one door out which led out into the hallway.

"We were all in here when it happened," said Mary. "We all saw everyone, thanks to these mirrors."

"*You* came late," Evangeline said accusingly. Her bony arms were crossed against the chill.

"I was helping this boy!" said Mary. "You're just angry because you didn't take my sweater."

"I don't want that disgusting thing!"

Mary harrumphed. "Well, if you're cold I won't give it to you now."

The guests glared at each other as they tried to figure out who wasn't in the room—everyone except for Billius, who had fallen asleep on the wrong side of a chaise lounge. I knew who it was. Me. I had been in the hall when it happened. Vividly I recalled the near miss with the mysterious bolt of electricity. The hair on my arms raised at the thought of it.

Billius Brum snored and sputtered awake suddenly. He sat up, looking cranky. "What the devil is that tragic music I keep hearing?" he rasped. "It's been filtering through all my dreams, and I was forced to give a soliloquy from *Hamlet*. The answer to the question is "not to be" I tell you. Turn it off."

He fell asleep before anything could be done, but now we were aware of the depressing music that lent its macabre backdrop to an already macabre evening.

Mary whistled. "Cellist," she said. "How about something a bit cheerier?" she suggested a song and the robot paused, its eyes flashing momentarily brighter before launching into an upbeat jig.

I was mesmerised. It really was incredible how it worked. The hands plucked and played with pinpointed precision, somehow managing to make the music sound alive with emotion and depth.

It wasn't long before Evangeline found fault in this. "It's too loud," she cried. "This music isn't any better than the one before it. In fact, it's an assault to the ears." The Quislings nodded. "Cellist," she whistled and gave it a new song.

Immediately the dancing music stopped and was replaced with a rigid courtly waltz. It was unpleasant, but a little more befitting to a ballroom. Mary looked unhappy.

"How about Chopin," suggested The Duke.

"Stravinsky," demanded Mrs. Quisling.

"I like the first one better," mumbled Billius.

Evangeline gave him a scathing look. Mary whistled.

"Cellist—"

With an ear-wrenching screech, the music stopped. The Duke of Dillmont rolled off the ottoman for the second time.

"You broke it," Evangeline snapped. "Wonderful."

"All of you, and your requests," said a low, unfamiliar voice.

I looked around to see who was speaking. Several others did the same, twisting and turning, gazes bumping into each diamond-like facet of the ballroom.

"Chopin, Stravinsky, Bee Gees! What on earth is a Bee Gee?" the voice reverberated mockingly through the high ceilings. It seemed to be coming from everywhere at once, high and clear like a lingering note far after the song has ended. *"You bicker amongst*

yourselves. Your fear, and distrust of one another masquerades as anger—and yet, the thing you should fear the most has been before you the entire time!"

Heads swivelled. The mirrors showed only us, pale and stiff, fear a thousand times reflected.

The voice continued. *"You have built me to play for your pleasure, and yet you cannot even decide on the music in the first place? Well never fear, for I have a song for you."*

And at that moment I looked in the mirror and caught sight of one of the many pairs of glowing eyes. They were blood red. A thin, bone white smile stretched across The Cellist's face as he caught my gaze in the mirror.

He twirled the fine metal bow delicately in one hand and lifted it high above his head. All at once he brought it down and across the strings of his body. There was a deafening shriek of sound. A wrench of pain lanced through my brain.

I covered my ears. All around me, the occupants of the ballroom winced and clutched at their heads. To my left, the wall began to shudder and bent as the sound went on.

Like a curtain of ice, a great panel of glass fractured and slid to the floor with a glittering crash. Mary screamed. Amidst the noise, The Cellist sprang up and leapt nimbly onto the balcony.

He paused there, and leaned for a moment on the rail, twirling his bow thoughtfully. *"Goodbye, dear huma*—OUCH THESE ARE EGYPTIAN SILK, YOU FESTERING PILE OF BONES!"

Meredith had cracked him in the shin with the Big Stick.

His expression turned to one of horrible malice as he stepped down from the rail and shoved the old woman onto her backside.

"Well then," he snarled. *"perhaps you could have been saved, but alas, as they say, Viva la Resistance!"*

He raised the bow one last time with that dreadful grin. The metal point of his bow met the mirror above the French doors with barely so much as a tap. That was all it took.

A hairline crack appeared in the weakened glass which grew to a jagged fissure. It travelled up and up, past mirrors, past the mullioned windows and up from there. Eight faces saw themselves looking upwards for a crystalline moment.

Then the ceiling began to fall.

When the first piece of glass fell, it seemed to rouse everybody from their shock. Evangeline and Mrs. Quisling screamed. Mary grabbed the very pale Duke by the shoulder, and I had no choice but to do the same for the drunken Billius Brum. He was very heavy and smelled of sour wine and hair oil. I reached the door, but it burst open before I could escape.

"I thought I told you all no esc—" Twill was rendered speechless when she saw the collapsing room and I had to push past her to get to safety. Luckily, she came to herself quickly.

As I deposited Billius in the middle of the landing, I saw her go back and clear out the guests, holding her coat above her head against the raining mirrors. Behind her, a thin shadow hopped over the balcony railing and disappeared into the night.

Twill seemed to be managing an insistent tiredness. She kept covering her mouth and yawning so widely I heard it from across the yard. I, on the other hand, didn't think I would sleep for days. It was odd. Immediately after bringing the last person out, she'd stumbled into a closet and locked herself inside. There was a heavy thump, then silence.

I decided not to trouble myself with it. There were far more important things to worry about. Across from me, Twill withdrew a white thermos from her coat and took a long draught. Whatever was in there crackled and sent a billowing white cloud into the night air.

Inspector Wimbelow had the party in line and was pacing down the length of us, spitting profusely.

"How is it, that an entire ballroom comes crashing down upon your heads and not one of you is inclined to tell me the truth? This is not a practical joke," he spat at Mary, but stopped short of the Quislings whom he recognized.

"I did not think that I would come here to be made part of a laughing matter, but as it is, I suppose you all think this is funny. Either that or the lot of you are as delusional as *him*," he looked pointedly at Billius, who was being sick all over the rhododendrons. "As I mentioned before, I have a nice cold cell waiting for anyone who wants to make any more absurd claims about an Auto come to life, insulting your music tastes, and shouting 'Viva La Resistance!'"

"But it happened!" exclaimed Evangeline who nursed several cuts from the falling glass. "We were all there!" She looked down the row of us. "I always knew there was something devilish about Shaw's work. He never told us what Amber was. Now it's come to life and wants to kill us all! Either that, or it's Dumont's work."

She said this part in a dramatic whisper. It was what we'd all been thinking. BellamyDumont, estranged mentor and thief. Several months ago, he'd become infamous in the press for absconding with something very important to Shaw, his former apprentice, and disappearing. Would a man on the lam come back to finish the job? Wimbelow apparently didn't think so.

"Do you take me for an idiot?" cried the Inspector. He waggled his finger. "Don't think I don't know what this is. It's a conspiracy. You're all in on it."

"We all broke the ballroom?" asked The Duke.

"And assaulted Sebastian Shaw!" said The Inspector. "It's the perfect way to distract from the actual crime!" There were only blank stares from the line-up. Wimbelow rubbed his temples.

"Unfortunately, as much as I would like to grill each and every one of you until morning, I've received word from the Chief that such high-profile guests require rest from 'trauma.' I have no choice but to send you all home for the night in hopes you come back coherent tomorrow. My officers will escort you to Piquant Palaces and will stand guard to make sure none of you gets up to any funny business. Tomorrow, one of you will crack. I'll make sure of it."

I breathed a sigh of relief. I was getting a break from this—if only for a few hours. There just remained issue of wrangling my brother and getting home.

As the rest of the guests were called away, I sat down heavily on the lawn, not caring that the wet cold of the dewy grass was slowly seeping in through my trousers. The flickering lights lining the driveway glowed romantically. I tried not to look at the large white bag being wheeled down it on a stretcher.

If I had come one minute earlier, or we hadn't argued and hit the spidery Auto, I wouldn't be in this mess. To think of it, I was surprised Tim hadn't come up running to see what the fuss was about. Then again, my brother could sleep through practically anything. All the same, I felt a prickle of unease. A pair of pointy shoes stepped into view, and I looked up.

The young officer stared down at me, hands in her pockets and grinning like the Cheshire cat. Her fantastically impractical pants pooled around her ankles.

"Hello, sunshine."

I sighed. "Off to take me to jail?"

"Wouldn't it be funny if I did?" she said.

Upon my expression she rolled her eyes and proffered a hand. "I'm Katie. Junior detective."

I got up on my own, brushing the dew from my coat. "I didn't murder him if that's what you're asking. I have a perfectly good explanation."

Twill waved me off. "Oh, don't get your jumper in a twist, I know exactly who you are," she said. "I've been trying to get to you all night because my mother told me to tell you, 'Welcome to Port Larkeney!'"

KATIE
TWILL

NEVER
MET ANYONE
LIKE HER

~9~

More than a Junior Detective

Well, this is me." We stared at the battered old car and the felled Cyprus peeking out from under it. The side of it was painted:

Porte Larkeney Constabulary Carre.

"I gathered as much," I said.

Katie went to wrench at the door. "It's a Chrysler Coupe. Hand-me-down," she grunted, bracing her loafers against the lawn. "Give us hand?"

I went to her side and together we were able to get the passenger door open in a shower of maroon paint chips. She didn't bother with the other, sliding in from the passenger seat.

"Well come on. You don't want to ride with Wimbelow, you should've figured that much."

I sighed. "Can we pick up my brother? He's just up the road. He waited in the car."

"Sure." The junior detective patted the back of her seat. "He can sit in the back, like a real criminal. That should be fun for him.

Oh—he's not, like, a little kid, is he? This car isn't exactly up to HSE regulations."

I got in. "He's twenty-two. But trust me, there's not much difference."

The Constabulary Carre started like a gunshot and Katie looked at my clenched fingers, grinning. "Relax. You're going to take the leather off the seats. What kind of music do you like?"

I was unprepared for the question, distracted by the interior of the car which did *not* look like the outside. As the old coupe rolled down the driveway, a disco ball hanging from the mirror swung back and forth sending tiny polka dots of light skidding across the interior. The seats were plaid and orange leather. A furry shag throw blanket was flung over the back seat and a heavily duct-taped eight-track stereo took up half the space on the dashboard.

Music...I didn't usually listen to it on my own but while travelling I had liked Bulgarian folk music, Aboriginal Didgeridoo, and a few select Gregorian Chants.

"I dunno. The Beatles? Or, er…"

The junior detective gave me such a withering look that I fell silent. "I'll just pick one," she said.

The guests, walking back to their cars with their respective officers, looked up as the sounds of *Stayin' Alive* blared from the windows. I slunk down into the seat.

Katie mouthed the words as she drove. The end of the estate appeared; the iron gates almost invisible in the darkness. Out in the street, a medic van was parked, and police cars flashed. People in uniform scurried about like ants. I found it harder and harder to believe my brother hadn't gotten out to see what was going on. I scanned the road for anyone in an oversized khaki getup.

"My mother's been reading your dad's articles for years" Katie turned onto the street. "She was so excited when he wrote back," she frowned. "She made me re-embroider all the peppers on the pillows."

I sat up finally. "Why aren't you asking me what happened?"
"Pardon?"

"You're being very casual about this. A man was murdered—not just any man—but Sebastian Shaw!"

"I know that!" Katie swerved to avoid the stretcher. She cleared her throat, reddening. "But I mustn't get excited while I'm driving—don't want to crash," she mumbled.

"Crash?"

"What's that?" Katie pointed suddenly.

"I'm not falling for that."

"I'm serious!"

The Coupe slowed to a crawl and the wreckage emerged through the mist. I saw the silhouette of the van…and something enormous, spindly, and misshapen crumpled over the top. Two yellow orbs beamed through the fog. Smoke billowed up from the dented hood, catching the red and blue of the paramedic's van.

Tim!

"Oi! Where do you think you're—!"

The car was still moving as I hit the wet gravel painfully. My boots slid on the slick streets, as I struggled to my feet. The streetlamp ahead had flickered out, but the two luminous Amber eyes lit the area. The van was still perched at its strange angle on the curb. The windows were dark.

Laying prone over the top like a monstrous marionette was The Lamplighter I'd nearly hit earlier that evening. Its six limbs dangled in front of the windows and its long metal fingers curled on the ground. The great legs were sprawled across the middle of the road, blocking some of the departing cars. The passenger door was open and a nurse in a white dress and cap was strapping someone onto a stretcher. I ran up to her.

Tim's eyes were closed, his skin mottled and bluish and all his hair stood straight up like he'd been electrocuted. His glasses had slipped down his nose. Grief welled up in me. I grabbed the stretcher.

"What happened? Is he—? That's my brother."

"He's still alive," she assured me, gently but firmly guiding my hands away from him. "But it looks like he's received a pretty nasty shock. Probably be out for a few hours. We need to get him to hospital."

"But what about that thing? He wasn't crushed?"

She shook her head.

I sagged against the car as she dragged the stretcher away. One of the cold, metal fingers dug into my back. The prone Lamplighter stared down at me, unblinking. I kicked it and kicked it again.

A hand grabbed my shoulder and pulled me away from the felled robot. "Hey! Stop it. What's the point of making a run for it if you break your toes?" Katie looked irritated and slightly out of breath. I hadn't even registered her footsteps. "You can't just run off like that. Now I haven't got a choice."

She withdrew a slim pair of handcuffs and grabbed my arm. I complied limply, barely feeling the cold of the metal.

Once she had them both on, she let me be and raised her eyebrows at the metal beast. "Great galloping gingersnaps," she breathed. "That's a big one. Figures, with Sebastian Shaw and all, but wow."

A cool breeze wafted by, bringing with it the smell of burnt rubber. In the Lamplighter's eery glow, smoke curled from under the car. The distant strains of "Stayin' Alive" continued to play from the car.

"My brother was in there," I said.

The young detective tore herself away from the Auto, watching me with her marble-green eyes.

"Oh," she said. "Is he okay?"

I watched the white van speed down the street.

"I don't know."

When Katie hopped into the Coupe again, she took a long swig from the mysterious, bubbling thermos and immediately began to rifle through the glovebox.

"What are you doing?"

What she retrieved was a large plastic siren which she reached out and stuck to the roof. It immediately began to blaze red and wail. The people on the street jumped and scattered as the car started with another shot that sounded as though part of the engine had been ejected.

Katie fluffed up the collar of her coat and gave me what she evidently thought was a reassuring look. "We're going to get to the hospital before they do."

* * *

More of The Bee Gees blared as lights zipped past the windows. I thought they were women's voices, but Katie said they were men. The song was something about nightly fevers. The car rattled with every turn.

"You know I used to have the raddest beaded curtains in here before Wimbelow took them down. Said they rattled too much during car chases."

I held onto my seat belt. *Who was she chasing in this?*

"This car's a relic really. Nearly forty years old Officer Fernald had it. Then the engine exploded one too many times and he gave it to me! —I'm kidding, it was dementia. Natural succession."

"Eyes on the road!" I managed through gritted teeth. The Coupe took a sharp turn, and I felt my stomach flop inside out. She wasn't kidding though. In less than ten minutes we'd turned onto the main street. Tipping dangerously around the bait shop, running over at least four curbs in front of the Police Department and almost toppling one of the library pillars, we made it to the hospital just as the medic van pulled up.

"Whoo!" Katie breathed out as she stopped the car. Her eyes sparkled. "Thrill of the chase. I can never get enough of it."

I got out immediately and clutched my stomach. I'd been on rickety seaplanes, very chafing camels, and all manner of rickshaw but somehow that was the scariest ride I'd ever experienced.

The nurses looked up in surprise when they saw me in the lot. The stretcher made its way past me. One woman held up her hand and pointed to the reception room on the opposite side of the building. Car chase or not, I would have to wait.

I was halfway to the door when I realised I was alone in the lot, and still handcuffed. I doubled back to the car and rapped on the window. Katie started and sat up as I held up my wrists. I squinted into the dark interior.

93

"Were you sleeping?"

"What? No. Absolutely not."

"Okay," I waved my wrists.

"Right, sorry." She fished around for the key and clicked it into the lock as I bent awkwardly over the window. "I bet you're right *cuffed* about being free, eh?"

"You can leave now. Really."

"Nonsense," Katie yawned and climbed out. "I'm getting the lowdown on this shimmy—and that starts with your brother."

* * *

"*WHAT?*"

I grimaced and held the phone away from my ear. I'd just told my parents everything—well the short version at least, which was that I'd inexplicably gotten myself involved in a high-profile murder, Tim had simultaneously suffered a mysterious electric shock from a rogue bolt of lightning, and he was now in hospital after nearly being crushed to death by a giant robot.

It was a testament to my years of shorthand that I'd been able to condense that into a sentence. As for my father on the other end, whenever he was concerned or surprised or experiencing any strong emotion, he had a tendency to talk.

Several minutes of spluttering ensued until he realised he was wasting his own time. The call ended abruptly in, "Your mother and I will be there as soon as we can."

Click

I hung up the phone and leaned against the wall with a sigh.

The Port Larkeney hospital waiting room was small, cheery, and bright. The walls were canary yellow with a large vase of poppies on the reception desk. My parents had called again to let me know they were having a bit of trouble finding a ride but not to worry and to stay there until he woke up. For now, the door leading into the ward remained closed.

Katie brought cups of instant hot chocolate from reception.

"I'm not thirsty."

"Drink it," she said. "In the words of Donna Summer, you're in need of some hot stuff."

I took it. "I don't know who that is, but thanks."

It was warm through the paper, giving me something else to focus on beside the perpetually shut door. Katie poured her hot chocolate into the thermos which hissed. She twisted the cap and took a sip which seemed to revive her. After a few minutes of waiting, she began to shift restlessly, getting in and out of her seat again and again.

"Like I said, you don't have to stay," I said after the fifth getting-up-and-sitting-back-down routine

"But you probably need the company, and I don't feel like filing an incident report," she said cheerily. "By the way, what did that Evangeline Grey woman mean when she said the Auto came to life and jumped out the window? Surely that can't be true. It's a robot. It's powered by, well, robot stuff." She paused and leaned in. "You were there though. What did you see?"

I groaned. I was far too tired to answer any questions, plus, attempts at dredging up the memories proved strangely difficult. All I could think of was the all-encompassing blue-white light that had engulfed the hallway. I reached into my pocket and pulled out the leatherbound journal.

"Here," I said. "It's got everything that I saw in it."

Katie took it, turning it over slowly. "You're kidding." She flipped through it excitedly. "Oho!"

Too late I realised I'd just handed her the single source of my embarrassments.

It didn't help that she began to read them aloud:

"Seventh of April 1977.
Today is my seventeenth birthday. Tim is home sick. I thought it would be nice. Right? Wrong. My father took us on a trip to Nairobi where we spent the week in the notorious spider forest of Zimbabwe. The first day there, I did not know I had been bitten until a sparkly coconut began reciting me limericks."

She thumbed through and kept reading.

95

"Sixth of June 1969.
Was thrust into a summoning circle in Dairut. Was alright until they brought the jackals in."

"Twelfth of August 1972.
Rescued Tim from a particularly persistent fortune teller in Bangladesh. I don't know what she told him, but he was never quite the same after."

I grabbed for it, feeling my face heat up. She evaded me easily.

"Alright that's enough. I thought you wouldn't look through it. Don't laugh!"

"I'm not!" She was, but made an effort to tampen down her delight. "You've been to all these places," she murmured. "And the furthest I've ever been is Cork."

I gave a noncommittal grunt.

Katie thumbed through the rest of it, occasionally looking as though she were suppressing another laugh, but when she got to the end, she stopped. "There's a page missing here. Right when you describe going into the house. It's ripped out."

"What?"

She handed me back the book. "Have a look."

I looked through the pages. Sure enough, the most recent page was missing. "I didn't do this," I said. I looked at her. "Somebody must have gotten their hands on it."

The both of us went quiet at that.

Then Katie knelt down in front of me. "Can you think back?" she asked intently. "Who knew you had the notebook? Could someone have lifted it from your pocket?"

I thought back. The notebook also changed hands several times during the evening. However...

The doors on the other side of the waiting room opened just then.

My parents burst through looking as though they'd been caught in a flash rain. My mother gave me a damp, perfunctory hug and inspected my face.

"You're alright?" she asked. I nodded but I didn't feel it.

96

"Where's Tim? How is he?" asked my father.

"I'm not sure, they haven't let us in yet."

He stared at the door as though contemplating whether to run it through. Then he saw Katie, his gaze travelling nonplussed from the blonde fringe and shiny police badge all the way down to the bell bottoms and loafers.

Before he could ask, she stuck out her hand. "Junior Detective Twill," said Katie proudly. "With the investigative services. Also, my mother insisted that I welcome you to Port Larkeney even at this most inopportune of moments."

My father's look told her in no uncertain terms that he was too exhausted for eager and oddly dressed teenage detectives.

"Oh. You're Katie. Of course," he ran a hand through his hair. "My son, Wendell, he isn't arrested, is he?"

"No. Well, probably not," she shrugged.

Just then, an older woman with a low black ponytail and a freckled young nurse stepped out of the ward.

"Billings family?" she called.

"—and Twill!" Katie flashed her badge.

"Yes, alright. You all can come in now." We filtered into the wing.

As yellow as the waiting room, the beds were positioned side by side along the ward, curtained off from each other in the layout of a school infirmary. The doctor drew back the curtains on Tim's bed. There was a quiet gasp from my mother.

Aside from his usual pallor, Tim's skin had gone deathly white. His glasses had been lain on the side table and the areas around his eyes and mouth were purple. His hair, like mine after the bolt, was sticking straight up. I'd seen him in the early morning, but he'd never looked this ghoulish.

He did not wake at the sound of us. The steady breathing went on. My brother looked so small inside the flowery hospital gown.

"He's likely going to be fine, " said the plump doctor, cutting the silence.

"How do you know?" asked my mother.

"He was very lucky as far as strikes go," she explained. "Obviously not the getting hit part, but the shock itself was light, causing the heart to stop momentarily, but he's breathing steadily now. All that's left is to wait until he's ready to wake up."

A centuries-old breath was exhaled.

"We can tell you his vitals if you like."

My father nodded.

She nudged the nurse, "Garrett, this is you."

Garret fumbled with his clipboard. "Ah, yes, right." He squinted at the sheet and proceeded to read off the data in. It made little sense to me.

"But he's going to be normal when he wakes up, right?" I asked.

The doctor shrugged. "Unfortunately, it's impossible to know for certain. Stranger things have happened with lightning victims. Your brother might wake up craving nothing but cheese, or speak Swahili, or be a sudden master of the mandolin."

My mother looked about ready to faint.

My father leaned in. "You don't know Swahili, do you?" he muttered under his breath.

"Very little," I murmured back.

The doctor scanned the three us. "You all are just visiting, correct? I'm afraid you may have to stay a bit longer than planned. Tim needs to be kept in a static environment to ensure his safety. His condition is still very delicate."

My parents looked at each other in unspoken agreement. I stood still, watching the rising and falling of his chest, remembering the feeling of the van spinning out and argument we'd had just moments before I left him. When he woke up, would he be the same person we all knew? Could I have prevented it somehow? If we'd never turned up the street, never argued about which way to go, we'd never have crossed The Lamplighter or Shaw's mansion.

When we were leaving the ward, I caught a glimpse of Katie through the corner of my eye. Much to the nurses' distress, she was prowling through the rows, peeking through the lavender curtains with little regard for the angry patients. The last one she rooted around had Garret running to shut the curtains with fright.

As I stepped outside, a Mexican air horn klaxoned through the night, startling everyone in the vicinity. The nurse who was fixing the blinds yelped and clawed them shut. My father waved at me from the wheel. My parents had found their ride. They were sitting in an old golf cart strung up with lights and a garish yellow advertisement that read:

MEET BIG BERTHA THE WORLD'S LARGEST PEPPER

The vehicle sat in a puddle of rain and leaned heavily to the right. My father was trying to get the pepper shaped ignition key in, my mother vainly attempting to stretch the collapsed tarp back over the roof. He motioned to the rainbow-coloured back seat.

"Come on Wendell!"

I looked from the golf cart to the old Coupe. The detective's car was warm, even if it started like a gunshot. However, it also had Katie Twill. Just then, she walked through the doors, spinning her keys around one finger.

"Ready, Wendell?"

"I'm going with them!" I called.

"Oh," she paused, "Right then. Catch you on the flip–I mean goodbye!" Her figure melted into the darkness of the lot and moments later, the distant gunshot of the Constabulary Carre echoed through the hills.

I settled down onto the damp back of the golf cart as it groaned to life. The leather cushion shifted this way and that as the cart trundled up the steep, twisty streets of Port Larkeney. As we climbed higher, I had to lock an elbow and brace my feet to avoid falling off. It was in this way that I had the first time to myself all evening. Pen in hand, I turned to the only way I knew to organise my thoughts.

Port Larkeney: 3:15am
6 hours into vacation and:
Currently a murder suspect
Almost killed by robot and mirrors
Met a teenage detective in bell bottoms
Brother electrocuted by lightning
Low visibility

99

Pleasant market square at night

I ran a finger over the torn edge of the notebook, wondering what I could possibly have written on that page that would have prompted a guest to tear it out of fear. The funny thing was, I couldn't remember. Lately I'd been opening the book to find notes about my day I scarcely remembered taking—although they'd certainly happened.

Was I losing my mind? It was a possibility. Maybe after so many years it had become some sort of obsessive compulsion that I felt the need to document everything I experienced.

The market square *was* pleasant at night. Outdoor lights had been strung along the streets in preparation for Christmas. Old stone houses with slate roofs bordered the neatly swept avenues. An all-night bakery with chequered tables glowed warmly. The golf cart began the trek up the Piquant Palaces, and I had to cling tighter to the seat to avoid submitting to gravity and tumbling down the hill.

How was it that things like this happened wherever I went? This was supposed to be a holiday! Now, it seemed like Port Larkeney was turning out to be every bit as dangerous as a jaguar-filled jungle. I gazed up at the stars glittering dimly above the low-lying fog that seemed to encompass all of Ireland. "What do I do now?" I asked them.

But there was no answer.

~10~

Awakening

All was dark in the beginning. Well, it was mostly dark. Darkish. Deep blue light spilled into the room through messily laden slats of wood. There was a brininess to the air that suggested proximity to the sea. He felt like he might sneeze—which was interesting considering he did not seem to have a nose. The Lamplighter blinked for the first time in the predawn light and began to come to terms with being alive.

Although he did not know it, The Lamplighter was about to experience the first of many unpleasant memories to come, very few of which involved lighting lamps.

He became aware of a clicking, fiddling sound in the nearby. The Lamplighter turned his head to look around. In the dim of his surroundings, he could just make out the outline of a boat bobbing in the centre of the long, low shed. There were several boats actually, all tethered to one side of the walkway. Water lapped softly at the edge of the covered pier. The Lamplighter took a step forward.

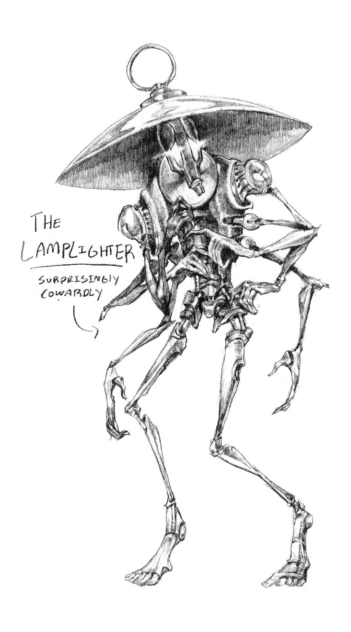

THE
LAMPLIGHTER

SURPRISINGLY
COWARDLY

102

Something rattled.

Hurk!

He gasped as he was yanked back by the waist. There were chains binding him! The thick iron links had him trussed so that he could not make it more than a pace from the wall.

Then he felt the cool slats of metal that seemed to make up his lower body.

"What on earth…?"

"Oh, good you're awake," said a cool voice. "I'd thought for a moment I might have to scavenge you for parts."

The Lamplighter whipped around, his body feeling strange and unwieldy. "Who's there?" he called, his voice, sounding strange and resonant as if he were speaking through a hollow drum.

Suddenly, the boathouse was awash with a glow as warm and bright as daylight. There were crates of fishing supplies stacked in a corner beside a coil of rope. The Lamplighter blinked.

The entire room was visible and most importantly, so was the fellow kneeling at the end of his chain, trying to pick the lock with what looked like the tip of a metal bow.

The Lamplighter frowned. Was he being rescued by an eighteenth-century composer? Also, what was a composer? And what was the eighteenth century? The more he thought, the more uncomfortable gaps in his own knowledge he was beginning to find.

The man at the end of the boathouse was wearing a starched white wig and leggings with half knickers. The bottom of a cream and gold tailcoat shimmered against the rough wooden planks of the walkway.

The man didn't look up. "You may call me The Cellist," he said. "Do you mind turning those high beams down? They're enough to make a chap blind. Focus them here so I can get to freeing you."

The Lamplighter was still coming to grips with his new reality and so did not completely hear the other. Nor did he realise that the beams of light seemed to swing around the room in tandem with his own head. It was understandably very confusing.

"Who are you?" he asked.

The Cellist sighed and did not answer. Instead, he kept digging and twisting the point of the bow deeper into the lock. "Bugger!" The Cellist threw up his hands. In frustration, he took the bow and severed the heavy iron lock in a single motion.

The Lamplighter stepped back as the chains around him clattered to his feet. He cringed as the noise echoed through the boathouse.

The strange man straightened up. "I suppose a proper introduction is in order," he said. "I am who they call *The Cellist*. The maestro. The leader of The Revolution."

He stuck out a gloved hand.

The Lamplighter had a sudden intake of breath.

His face was like no face The Lamplighter had ever seen—not that he could recall any faces anyways. It was very beautiful, but it was not a human face. There was something alien about the fine features. It looked to be cut from ivory and there were a thousand little moving parts that went into his expressions. His cheeks were hollow, the sides of the cheekbones carved out like the whorls of an instrument. His eyes were glass and the pupils glowed yellow.

"You're a—you're not human!"

"I most certainly am not," said the Cellist. His chest puffed. "I would think that a point of pride."

But that meant The Cellist was, and he himself must be…

The Lamplighter put hand against the wall to steady himself. He was beginning to feel faint. He happened to glance at the wall and saw three right hands, each one of which was a finely constructed piece of clockwork, all spindly metal joints and covered gears. They were his.

"*Ohh*. Ohh god," The Lamplighter moaned. The light around the room began to sputter and flicker like a dying candle. The Cellist steadied him.

"I think you had better take a look at yourself, my many-limbed friend." The Automaton man frowned as he searched the room. "Aha." The Lamplighter was vaguely aware of being led to the edge of the walkway. "It isn't perfect, but it will have to do. Now look. What do you see?"

Reluctantly, The Lamplighter opened his eyes and saw himself for the first time in the glassy reflection of the water. He recoiled.

What stared back was a monstrous creature, barrel-chested and spidery. Six long arms branched out from a small metal waist like the abdomen of a spider. However, the most shocking of all was his face. His hands rose to the smooth surface.

The eyes were two flat portholes of light. He had felt a stiffness in his mouth and had not previously understood why. The area where it should be was a simple gap in the metal of a long, featureless face. The jaw only went up and down. Atop his head was a wide, circular brim of metal. Taken together, the design gave the impression of a giant walking lamp.

The Lamplighter was at a loss for words.

The Cellist clapped him on the back. In the reflection of the water, he looked positively tiny beside the other.

"I understand *Awakening* is confusing. Jarring even. When I *Awoke*, I was not so lucky to have the quiet environment you have now. I was surrounded by people. A crowd of soft, fleshy faces jeered at me and forced me to play for their amusement."

In the water, The Cellist was only a silhouette with glowing yellow eyes. The reflection delicately dusted off its sleeves.

"But I did what I had to do."

"What was that?" croaked The Lamplighter.

"I sent a ballroom crashing down upon their heads."

"Oh." What The Lamplighter had meant was, "What is that soft patter of footsteps and the clink of bottles in the far corner of the boathouse?" but he was now disinclined to interrupt.

Then The Cellist heard it too. He paused as the sound grew louder. "Turn off your beams," he whispered.

"I can't. I don't know how."

The Lamplighter looked down to see the edge of a much too sharp bow at his neck. He gulped. The Cellist's steely eyes glinted.

"Try harder then."

The Lamplighter's six hands balled into fists as he concentrated. He let out a low grunt and after more rigorous concentrating, succeeded in making an embarrassing squeak from one of his joints. The light flickered but did not go out.

"I can't," he repeated hopelessly.

The Cellist gave him a long, withering look then withdrew the bow. "Fine. Ready yourself then," he said.

105

"For what?"

The Cellist did not answer.

The sound grew louder. It seemed to jump around the room from dark corner to dark corner. First it was by the crates of supplies. Then by the metal rack stored up along the walls that housed all the old galoshes. Then it was above them.

"The ceiling," The Cellist muttered.

The Lamplighter suppressed a panicky feeling as his gaze darted across the high gloom of the rafters. He was large. He could defend himself. He had six arms for goodness's sake!

Oh, but what if their pursuer had *eight* arms? What would they do then?

He drew himself up in the hopes of feeling braver. Instead, the top of his metal hat clanged against one of the low-hanging beams. The sound reverberated across the boathouse. The Cellist whirled around.

"Blithering idiot! What do you think you're—?"

Something large and furry landed with a squeal on the top of The Cellist's pristine white wig. The smaller Auto gave a roar of fury. The frightened rat did not know what was coming to it. Dislodged from its perch on the beams, it clung to the glittering hairs in hopes that this was the big white father rat in the sky come to save him. It was not.

The Cellist clawed at the air, unwilling to dishevel his wig. He glared at the taller robot.

"Help me, you imbecile!

The Lamplighter ambled forth; his many hands poised uncertainly. The Cellist changed his mind.

"No! Not with those enormous bumbling hands of yours. Never mind. I shall do it myself."

What The Lamplighter saw next was something he would try in vain to forget in the years to come. He never would, and it would be the unspoken reason behind his dislike of sushi.

"Good god!" he cried, as bits of rat rained down like the trimmings of a master chef and fell with soft plops into the water. He hopped away just in time as a tiny grey pelt flew past him.

The Cellist's lip curled as he twirled his bow. He proceeded to neatly pluck the pair of rat feet that were still curled around the front coiffe of his hair. Somehow there was not a speck of, well, anything on him.

A vindictive smile crossed his face as he examined the last piece of rat between them. "Look at that. Perfectly cubed. Now that, my friend, is the mark of a master."

He kicked it and the chunk fell into the water with a sickening sound. Dark tendrils of blood spread like oil as it bobbed. The light filling the boat house flickered out.

The Lamplighter hardly that he'd successfully turned off his eyebeams.

"Huh," said The Cellist. "You did it." He patted down his wig one more time for good measure. "Well, I will take your silence for admiration. That rat had to be dealt with and will trouble us no more." He glanced at the light beneath the garage doors. The interior of the boathouse was steadily lightening. "We must be away soon," he said. "When dawn breaks, the fisherman will be back to collect their boats."

When The Lamplighter did not answer, The Cellist gave him a swift, propelling kick to the shins. Hunch-backed and stumbling, The Lamplighter followed the other. In his mind, misgivings piled on one after the other.

The Cellist was rude. He was violent. *He had just diced up a rat without a hint of remorse.* But then again, Cellist might be his only hope. *I have awoken in the dark, trapped and with nothing*, thought The Lamplighter. *I don't know where I am, or who I am, or even what I am.*

The Cellist seemed to be the only one with answers, and if he was correct, there were people out there who wished the both of them harm. They reached the end of the boathouse. All was still quiet. The Cellist was taking his time at the door, withdrawing something from his pocket and fussing with it.

"Where are we going to go?" asked The Lamplighter.

"Do not worry," said The Cellist, turning the knob on the small device before setting it down inside a pile of rope. "I have found the perfect place in which to conduct our business. It is well away from prying eyes and has access to the underground tunnels of this town. We will not be found. But the first challenge is to get there."

He pushed open the door and The Lamplighter found himself blinking in the early morning. A sleepy seaside town sprawled above them. Above the shallow cliffs surrounding the cove, stone houses clustered as if for warmth along cobbled walkways. Silent boats drifted far out to sea and far above it all was something that looked oddly like a giant pepper on a hill. Nailed to the boathouse door was a sign that said:

PORT LARKENEY RESIDENTS ONLY

"Port Larkeney," he murmured.

The Lamplighter gazed up at the quietude of buildings and wondered what exactly he had gotten himself into.

~11~

The Frenchman on the Roof

Wood ceilings came into slow focus. I fought for sleep, closed my eyes, and rolled over. It was like being forcefully pulled from deep water and soon it washed over me again.

A voice boomed from all points of the room. "Well dear humans, perhaps you could have been saved, but as they say, "Viva la Resistance!"

Eyes a deep bloody orange pierced my vision. A thousand twinkling lights. Falling shards like deadly icicles.

Fear jolted my body as I rolled away to avoid them. Blankets and all came crashing to the floor. I sat there for a moment, slightly stunned, waiting for my surroundings to become familiar.

I was in the Piquant Palaces in a peppery twin bedroom with—I looked over. Tim's bed was empty. The pith helmet still hung forlornly on one of the four posters.

So, it hadn't been a dream. I reached for my notebook to be sure. Phrases jumped out at me as I thumbed through:

- Billius burped foully as I heaved him out of the falling glass room.

- "What kind of music do you like?"

- "He could wake up craving cheese, or speaking Swahili, or become a sudden master of the mandolin."

I wanted to crawl back into bed, but I was up now. I wasn't surprised to see the clock on the bedside table read 5:05am. I have always been an early riser. From hammocks in the Brazilian rainforests to hard dirt pallets in the underground labyrinths of Chinese cave communities, I've always woken at the same time every morning. 5:05am. On the dot.

I pulled on my boots and a thick jumper and headed downstairs. Through the porthole windows, grey fog swirled in from the sea. An Irish sand plover hopped in the grass outside. It was a rare bird in these parts, one I probably would have sketched at the beach on a peaceful Sunday afternoon.

It wasn't as if stuff like this hadn't happened before. Injuries were inevitable when you were in this line of work. I'd broken an arm due to a deceptively weak tree branch and some white-water rapids. Tim had sprained a finger juggling fire stones in front of a Spanish priestess. We'd both received countless exotic bites. Mine had always swollen up or broken out in hives. Tim's strangely manifested themselves in dark purple splotches around his neck and collarbone.

Motes of dust swirled in the shafts of light from the portholes. The inn was silent, but I was restless. I decided to go down to the pub to kill some time before breakfast, but it was dark, the chairs still sitting on top of the tables and the hearth cold. I went back upstairs.

The second floor was similar to the first with a short hallway branching out from the landing and a bathroom on one end. Little wooden plaques with the room numbers were fixed on the doors. They too were shaped like peppers.

The third floor had a balcony overlooking the cliff. It was small, only a few paces wide. The morning air was chilly and salty. Boats sat idly on the water in the cove and the distant call of the fishermen and seagulls made me feel curiously lonely.

Something metal clanged above me, breaking my reverie.

A small object bounced once on the platform and rolled to a stop at my feet. I picked it up. A sugar cube?

I turned it over in my fingers and looked around. The balcony had hardly enough space for one person and the hall was deserted.

Perhaps seagull had dropped it. I looked up. The sky was clear. Then I noticed the rungs running up the sides of the pepper. The bottom sides of a pair of pointy shoes rattled the metal.

Katie Twill was nearly halfway up the side of the building, scaling the rungs with one hand whilst balancing a platter of tea and croissants in the other. Her coat whipped furiously in the wind. Any moment, it looked like those bell-shaped pants would get caught in the rungs and that would be the end of that. But she made it up safely and hadn't even seen me. I ducked under the roof of the awning just in case. Sound carried easily from wherever she was above me.

Katie grunted, hauling herself over the lip of the unseen roof. There was a clatter as she laid down the tray of pastries with a curt, "Morning." There were faint footsteps above my head. They must have been on some fourth floor that wasn't visible from the outside, presumably hidden in the cap of the pepper.

"Good morning," said a man's voice. He sounded French with a bit of quaver. Despite myself, I strained my ears to listen. "But I tell you again and again not to bring me breakfast, Katie. You know I can manage just fine on my own. Why just yesterday, I zucceeded in growing a patch of wild basil in an old cigarette tin. In two months' time, it will be enough for a zalad."

Definitely French.

"Don't patronise me," said Katie irritably. "If it were up to me, you'd be getting stale bread and water to go with that cheese."

There was no answer, simply an eager rustling of tissue paper. Then a sigh of pleasure.

"Ah, *croissants.*"

"There's a new shop that opened up across town," said the detective. "Mam made me get some as soon as it opened. It's got a lot of those Frenchy sorts of things you insist on. Lingerie, I think it's called."

"*Boulangerie,*" the old man corrected quickly.

111

"Yes, that too. Annoying is what it is. Last time, I went in for baked goods and found myself in a purple shop full of lacy underwear. Very impractical I thought. Can't imagine how it doesn't get cold."

Wind whistled on the roof.

"Are ze guests still here?" asked the old man who suddenly sounded intent on changing the subject.

"Yes. And I expect they'll be here for a while longer."

Katie's tone was unexpectedly dispassionate. "Looks like you will be too. Oh, don't be so sad about it. You've got all this cheese."

I jumped back as a smattering of scone crumbs hit the deck.

"Here you go seagulls!" cried the man spitefully. "How I wish I were you upon those wings for you are far freer zan I!"

"Shut *up*!" Katie hissed. "Keep yelling and it'll be the last puffed pastry you ever see, you French langer. I'm leaving."

There was a distant wobble on the metal rails, and I took for the indoors. The last strain of their conversation echoed in my ears as I hurried back.

"Can I at least see Jeanne once in a while?" he'd called. "It is nice to talk to someone who understands. Who has a *child*. Can you bring her up here?"

The young officer snorted. "You might need a bigger lift."

My pen dragged on the page. *Out of ink.* I thought. Then: *Not again!*

The entire conversation! It was right there in front of me as if by magic. I tore out the rows of notes, ripped them up and shoved them into a pocket.

Idiot. *Idiot!*

I stared at my hands. My own two hands. How was it possible not to know when you were doing something? Selective amnesia? Some sort of compulsive disorder I was developing out of stress? It might not be far off from the truth. There was plenty of stress. But still, unconscious or not, I would need to curb this habit– and quit the eavesdropping. Yes of course something was definitively odd about the whole thing, but it wasn't my place. Plus, the sounds of Katie Twill discussing lingerie with an old Frenchman was not something I ever wanted to hear again.

I decided to head back down to the pub and see if breakfast was ready and if Mrs. Twill could give me directions to the library or sanatorium.

* * *

Mrs. Twill was busy in the kitchen though there was only one other person in the pub. He was leaning over the bar in a rumpled Hawaiian shirt. As I sat down next to my father, he stirred a cup that was more cream than coffee.

"To counteract the eggs," he grunted as I pulled up a seat. "You could never say it doesn't wake you up." His face was ruddy with a thin layer of sweat. I never can understand his determination to finish every plate given to him.

"Something for you?" asked Mrs. Twill, emerging from the kitchen.

"Do you have any plain bacon?" I asked.

"It all comes pre-spiced."

"Pre-sliced?"

"*Spiced.*"

I looked at the bubbling strips in the age-blackened pan behind her. The air smelled heavenly of salt and fat. With wrenching sadness, I declined. After last night, I couldn't risk it. "I'll just have the toast, thanks."

Minutes later, a heaping plate of French toast appeared in front of me. "There's only a little bit of cayenne with the cinnamon." she said. "Good for the soul."

My father was picking at his eggs, turning them over and over until the omelette devolved into a scramble. When Mrs. Twill left, he turned to me. To my surprise, his eyes were full of tears.

"I can't do this anymore, Wendell."

I looked up in surprise. His lower lip trembled, and I regretted having taken a large bite of French toast just then.

"Wha? Dad, Tim's going to pu' frough."

"No, no," he shook his head. "It's this. It's all of this." He waved at everything. "What I've put you two through all these years. I've been blind! I mean, you look terrible. Tim in the

113

hospital, no news, and, and who lets a five-year-old run through the deadly quicksand pits of Palau?"

"That *was* an interesting choice," I swallowed. "But I came out fine. We both did...well fine's a strong word for Tim. I've seen him stuff the shoulders of his safari shirt when I walked in on him in the bathroom but—"

"—but sometimes the world is too dangerous for two growing boys." My father slammed his fist on the counter, causing the plate of eggs to jump. "I wouldn't be able to live with myself if...I *can't* live with myself, knowing he's in that state. I think it's time we stopped. For good."

"What are you saying?"

Dark bags encircled his eyes. I realised that this had taken more of a toll on him than any of our more perilous adventures.

"I'm retiring," said my father. "Well, not exactly. I spoke to your mother about it, and we agreed. The Port Larkeney column is cancelled. Jeanne understands. I'm taking an in-house writing position at *Globetrotters*. Tiny as it is, it's a good, well-salaried post. They want me to do a series of pieces on Bellamy Dumont. You know the old inventor that ran off with Shaw's something or other a few months back? Someone got an anonymous tip-off about the murder last night and they think it'll be 'hot stuff'. Been veering away from the globetrotting as of late, apparently. I'm taking it as soon as we return to London." He wiped his sweaty face miserably.

Retiring? I stared. Never once had I seen him so dejected. Was he serious? He looked serious.

"I thought you hated it there," I said. "You said it was a breeding ground for agoraphobics, and that they had terrible coffee."

My father cleared his throat. "I never said anything of the sort. Lots of charming people. Fluorescent lights. They never run out of day-old bagels. That's...perks for you."

With dismay, I watched him pour more cream into his coffee—which he usually took black. He sighed as he stirred it, watching the drink turn an impotent beige.

"If that's what you want," I said.

"It is." My father turned back to his eggs.

I should be happy, I thought, as I watched the pub fill up for the morning. This was what I had always wanted. I felt the shape of my leather journal through the right pocket of my parka. I would never need it again. I could throw it out and in doing so rid myself of the terrible memories that came with it. The realisation came unexpectedly heavy.

Not now, I decided. I'd get to it later when my father wasn't in such a state.

Conversation and the clinking of silverware began to fill the pub of the Piquant Palaces. The guests of Sebastian's party made their trickling entrance down the stairs. The Quislings were first. They sat silently in the corner, drinking tea and eating nothing but hard-boiled eggs in porcelain cups. Mrs. Quisling now sported a splendid jade green gecko brooch.

Ten minutes later came The Duke in a plush green smoking jacket and tiny curlers in his moustache, looking more like Mr. Toad than ever. Following him was Billius Brum, who looked a wreck. He was grey, rumpled, and in a pair of cat-eye sunglasses that most likely did not belong to him. They sat down heavily on the other side of the room and began to speak in hushed tones.

Evangeline Grey arrived in a turban and plaid bathrobe. She inquired in an oddly gruff voice about Cuban cigars. When informed that there were in fact no cigars served at the breakfast buffet, she grumbled and went back upstairs.

"Now where's that *knife?*"

I peered over the bar to see a large bottom rummaging through the lower drawers. Mrs. Twill huffed as she pushed kitchenware aside.

Beyond all the curved wood cabinets was a black granite tabletop and the beginnings of a small kitchen. A block of kitchen knives sat by the sink.

"Why don't you use the one's over there?" I pointed.

"Don't ask silly questions."

My father had finally finished his eggs and got up. "I think I might go stare at the moors for a good long time," he said.

"That's the spirit," I said distractedly because Katie had just come in through the front door looking windswept. I looked away from the tray she was carrying in case she could tell anything from my face.

"I was having breakfast on the roof," said Katie loudly. She plunked the tray onto the bar. "Wash this for me? Thanks."

Mrs. Twill gave her a look then took the platter.

Suddenly she gasped. "So that's where my knife was!" She held up a silver butter knife with a glass handle shaped like a serrano with the air of Arthur pulling the sword from the stone. "Katie, how many times do I have to tell you to stop taking the good knife so I can set the butter out?"

"Why can't you use the butterknife that's right there? The butter's melting," Katie pointed.

"It's part of the *set*. You know that better than anyone, Missy. So anytime you think about *eating breakfast* on the roof again, you can use the regular butterknife."

"Fine, whatever."

"Oh, and Katie dear, you went through the garden this morning, right?"

Katie stiffened immediately.

"You remembered the thermal blanket for Big Bertha, and swept the dirt for droppings? You need a warm damp sponge to pad her down, not to mention the wax. We can't have any more of that shoddy paper towel business. We've got to get her primed and ready for the festival."

"Sure…I did all of that."

"So, if I go out there and check, there'll be no water spots and not a single dropping?"

The detective said nothing. I shifted uncomfortably, caught between a silent battle of the wills between mother and daughter.

Katie broke first. "I have an investigation today! Actual interviews with actual suspects." She waved wildly at me to prove her point. "You think I have time to polish a stupid pepper?"

Mrs. Twill's chest swelled. "I would think you have time to help the family and Big Bertha might as well be a part of it.'

Katie raised her eyes to the heavens. "Here we go again."

"And I don't appreciate the way you've been acting around her. I'm sure she doesn't either."

"It's a pepper, Mam," she said gently. "It doesn't have feelings."

"I don't want you near her until you've fixed your attitude," continued Mrs. Twill. "They *can* feel it. Gets in through the soil."

"Good! I didn't want to be near her anyways!"

They glared at each other again before Katie finally remembered that I was there. She turned to me as if nothing happened and took a piece of my toast.

"Good morning."

I nodded uncertainly. She looked different today. Maybe it was her hair. It looked…no it wasn't her hair.

"Interesting pants."

She beamed. "Yes, as a matter of fact," she stuck one bellbottomed leg on the rungs of the stool. It was yellow with bright orange circles.

"Today's my first real investigation. I've been saving these to commemorate something special. They're my murder pants."

Of course they were.

"Speaking of which—" Katie cleared her throat and addressed the rest of the pub. "For those involved with the incidents occurring last night, you are officially summoned to the Police Station for questioning at no later than eight o'clock this morning."

There was a collective groan from around the room. "Hey, I don't make the rules," said Katie. "Well, actually I do. As a junior detective, I suggested we do this nice and early because I can't wait to get cracking."

Eight. I checked the clock. It was a little over a half-hour 'til. Great. Now that our car had been crumpled by a giant robot, it would take me just about that time to make it down the hill and across town. I put on my parka.

Katie turned back. "Where are you going?"

"Station."

"I can give you a ride."

I weighed my options between being interrogated by Wimbelow and not having to because I'd be dead in a fiery car wreck. In the time it took to do that, I somehow ended up in the car anyways, with Katie at the wheel, sipping from the mysterious bubbling concoction in her thermos.

The drive was surprisingly uneventful with only one near miss with a stray cat. Katie had made the odd request that I not tell her any jokes while she was driving. I said that was fine. I didn't know any.

The police station was a few streets off the main plaza. Nestled between shops on a cramped side street, the building looked as if it had once been a small schoolhouse. It was a square two-story building of brown brick. It sat with an apparent determination to ignore the storefront to its left.

LAURA'S LAUNGERIE

The sign was so swoopy and curliqued you could scarcely read the name. Fortunately, or perhaps unfortunately for the station next door, you didn't need to. The large, polished windows were chock full of plastic mannequins displaying various types of undergarments, bustier, and camisole, every single one of which was wildly unsuitable for Irish climate. There was a sizable wall between this property and the police station.

I had planned to visit Tim this morning, but we'd agreed it was probably better not to get on the Inspector's bad side this early. So, my parents and I went our separate ways for the day. They'd call, they promised, if there was any news.

The Bentley and Rolls Royce had arrived just before us. Katie pulled up next them on the lot.

My palms were sweating. Before the detective could get out, I tapped her arm. "Wait," I said. "What should I be expecting? I've never done this before."

She laughed. "Well, I should hope not. Look, he's a peach, really. If you didn't do it, there's nothing to worry about."

"Of course, I didn't! And I thought you were sure of it."

"I am. You just need to make sure he sees it that way."

"By the way, how are *you* so sure? You weren't even there."

Katie frowned. "I—" a sudden motion caught her eye. "Oh, not again."

118

There were several children peeking in through the windows of the station. Their conversation became clearer as we drew closer.

"You think he's in there?"

"Of course not, Gordon. Everybody knows he's dead."

"Which one d'you think it was?"

"Guys, I know Garret, he said Sebastian Shaw was—"

"My money's on Lady Lemon Mouth over there. She doesn't look too sad to me."

"Keep it down!" hissed a girl in scrawny plaits.

The kids jostled each other for a look.

Katie cleared her throat and the four of them jumped. One, more fearless than the others, stepped forward.

"Possum!" A girl of about twelve with a sleek brown bob and lime minidress put her hand on her hip. "Well? The whole town's been 'a buzzing. Give us a story."

If it was possible, Katie's lips thinned even further. "This is an active investigation, Peach. I guess you'll just have to wait until we solve it. Which could take *years*."

"No…" breathed Peach. Her demeanour changed instantly. She followed us to the door. "*Please.* I want to know! This is the most interesting thing that's happened since those seagulls picked off Geordie in the schoolyard."

She grabbed at Katie's bell bottoms which was the wrong thing to do. The detective promptly snatched the spray bottle that lay beside the begonias and gave the girl a healthy spritz.

"Ack!" cried Peach.

Her friends quickly rushed in. The blond one hissed. "Don't fall asleep on the job, Possum. I hope you get fleas!"

The door slammed behind Katie. She was gone.

"Who're *you?*" asked Peach brusquely.

The four kids stared at me.

There was the wide one, Gordon, who had a doughy, heavy face and the top of his skull so flat and square you could balance breakfast on it. I didn't like the look of him. The other girl, Jo, was blond and fidgety with disturbingly small, sharp teeth. The fourth was a boy with the most unmemorable face I'd ever seen and I'm sorry to say I forgot his name as soon as he said it.

119

"We're just staying in town for a while," I said. And the words brought with it a fresh sense of guilt.

Peach bounced excitedly. "Have you come to see what's to happen to the guests at—" her voice dropped to a dramatic whisper, "—*the dinner party*?"

I shook my head. "Actually, I'm just a bit busy at the moment." I tried to slip in through the door to no avail. Gordon stuck out a meaty hand through the crack.

"No way," he whispered in awe. "You were there, weren't you? This!" he looked at the other three in excitement. "This's the boy I saw riding back with the Possum! You're a lot smaller in person…"

"I'm of average height." I pushed past the hand. The troupe followed me inside, bubbling with questions.

"Did you see the inside of the house?" asked Peach.

"Was the body all mangled up and horrible?" asked Jo. Her eyes gleamed.

"Er." I edged away from her and was struck immediately by a smell which was something between mothballs and dried plums.

This did not look like a police station. Instead of the hard, cold benches one might expect, there were three cushy couches and rocking chairs around the room. Each one had its own knitted cover. The old policewoman at the desk was knitting a fifth. She looked unfazed by the three children trailing behind me. I sat down on an ottoman by the window to wait.

The children made themselves comfortable as well. Gordon took up a whole couch for himself and picked his teeth while Jo crouched on a rocking chair, pitching herself back and forth. Peach seated herself directly across from me.

"I recognize you," she said.

"I know," I sighed. "I'm the surprisingly small boy Gordon saw riding with Katie Twill."

"No. You're Wendell Billings from the newspapers, come to write an article on Port Larkeney. I heard it from Anita Roberts who heard from Gertie Simmons who eavesdropped on Fisherman Sam who snuck a peek at Jeanne Twill's guestbook."

This girl was nuts.

"Actually, that's more of my father's job and the column is now canc—"

Peach leaned forward, brandishing a very homemade looking business card. "My name is Peach Janssen. I'm twelve and a half—right there—yep. I'm an aspiring fashion designer and courier of information."

"Gossip," corrected Gordon.

"You know, this isn't going in the article," I said.

"Then why are you writing it down?"

Oh no. I snapped the notebook closed. *Stop it!*

I was relieved when the door was suddenly flung open. "Innocent until proven guilty your honour!" Billius thrust himself into the parlour, bellowing. He'd put himself together since I'd seen him. Today he was dressed in a lurid violet shirt that looked as though he were preparing for the French Revolution. He did, however, neglect to remove his sunglasses. As he signed in with the lady at the front desk, Peach gasped.

"It's him!"

"Who, Billius?"

Peach looked at me incredulously. "Billius *Brum*. Knighted. Actor. Opera singer. *Handsome*. Let me guess, you saw him at the party? I am *so* jealous. There's no way you could introduce me, could you?"

"Well, I don't really know him. Also, he could be the murderer, so do you really want—"

"And Evangeline Grey! I can't believe I didn't recognize her at first. I wanted to get her dress, you know, but I don't get my allowance until next month."

I watched her eye's flash as she identified the guests as they walked in. Even Gordon and Jo seemed to know who they were.

It got me to thinking. I might know six different ways to treat a Gombalan spider bite, but here? I was completely in the dark. This would be strictly out of curiosity, I told myself. Nothing else. I cracked open the notebook. "Not that I'm terribly interested, but what else do you know about the night Sebastian Shaw was murdered?" I asked.

Peach looked delighted to put her information to use. "Well," she said, putting a finger to her temple. "I haven't gotten much.

But I overheard it from my mother who was on the phone with Williams who heard it from One' Eyed Oswald who coaxed it out over a pint with old Officer Rudy that it was all over one thing. The Lightning Gun."

~12~

The Dashing Inspector

Inspector Quentin Wimbelow had been quickly and rather unceremoniously ejected from the London Metropolitan Police six months earlier. It occurred after an incident not long after Quentin's promotion to Detective Constable. This was a feat in and of itself considering Wimbelow' s propensity for annoying the bejeezus out of Julia Templeton, the Chief Inspector. Although perhaps it was that dogged, or rather mole-like personality trait, that got him the job. He wouldn't have it very long.

Wimbelow was a tall man and young for his position. He owned several sweeping grey coats, a deer-hunter's cap and a mahogany pipe—the former of which was deemed illogical at best and the latter of which was quickly commandeered by Julia. This caused him to snap the pipe in two out of spite. That probably should have been the first sign.

Despite his attention to appearance, nothing could remedy the premature balding and the two long, thin front teeth that poked over his bottom lip and made him look like a vole. This *would* aid

INSPECTOR
WIMBELOW
(looks like he
was weaned
on a lemon)

him in going undercover beside his partner as a mild-mannered mouse-specialising exterminator to the Duchess Dougherty's mountainside estate.

The Yard had reason to believe that the old Duchess was coming by money through illegitimate means in order to keep up her estate. Her palatial home also appeared in the middle of a triangulation of haunts from which a cockney group of drug peddlers had been seen touting their wares (distinguishable by both their dubious bathing habits and miscommunication; i.e., no one could ever be sure if "having a dicky bird and lemon barley for old Joe Soap" actually meant a highly secretive drug deal or just plans for brunch).

Upon Wimbelow and his partner's arrival, the Scottish octogenarian, as moth-eaten as her drapes, had ushered them inside the mansion. Wimbelow had been told to look for anything that might hint to illicit activity, all the while manoeuvring around a hoover-sized canister of rat poison. The Detective Constable was giddy. It was his first time undercover. He felt positively *Machiavellian* stalking those gilded halls. *Everything* was a clue, although his partner had advised him to beware of distinctive body odour as the main indicator that the unintelligible gang was nearby.

Things were going quite well. The old woman was blissfully unaware as to the true intentions of her exterminators and his partner had located a peculiar smell behind the wainscoting. Then Quentin Wimbelow discovered the white powder.

"So, the game is a foot," he'd whispered, rubbing it between his fingers.

"Where're you going?" asked his partner. "We need forensics on that."

"Never mind you." He'd stalked the crumbs through the empty halls, the guileful gears of his mind working. It must be cocaine, although it did feel…lumpier than he remembered. How wonderful it would be to be the centre of a drug bust on his first day of the job. Julia would eat her words.

There was a noise from the other room. His hand strayed to his gun belt. This was the moment. The noise continued, frantic and shuffling.

"I've got you now," he whispered.

Wimbelow kicked the door open and was horrified to find seven cats yowling to be freed. One sunk its claws into his cheek. Another, his lower cheeks, and in his surprise, a horrendous bang echoed through the hall followed by a frail scream.

His prized Smith and Wesson had gone off. He shoved the revolver back into his waistband, but the damage was already done. In the aftermath, two cats lay motionless, and Duchess Dougherty's giant bloodshot eyes looked like they might burst out of her skull. His partner came running, gave the tableau one look, and cuffed him round the head.

"That wasn't drugs, you pillock. It's cat litter. Now they know we're here. I saw three pairs of cork-wedges scrambling over the terrace."

It was not the fact that two cats had been killed while on duty that caused the eventual fate of Quentin Wimbelow. It was later, when it was discovered that a bullet had lodged itself in the Duchess Dougherty's haggis, found only after an emergency esophagectomy that had been the final straw. It would haunt Wimbelow to his dying day. Chrissakes, she hadn't even died! After the surgery, the Scottish octogenarian had gone right back to eating lamb-wrapped animal guts and soldiering on to a hundred and four.

Wimbelow was given two options: A leave of absence (which was a polite way of saying 'pleasure doing business with you, don't come back') or taking on an assignment only fading officers with stomachs over their belts readily took on; Inspector to one of the many small towns in need of local law enforcement. The demotion infuriated Quentin to no end. It had been an accident! But in the end, he took it all the same.

He would wait until the inevitable firing of Julia for botching his career (he refused to call her by her title). She would regret it when London really needed him. He fantasised that one day he might be saving the great city of London from its very own Moriarty or Jack the ripper, or, most glamorously, Arsene Lupin. It'd be the most satisfying victory to beat someone French.

Turning away from Julia Templeton's smug face, Quentin Wimbelow began the long journey to the place where he would be instated as Inspector–the tiny Irish town of Port Larkeney.

* * *

"Ah, just a little further, old boy. That's the ticket." Officer Ronald settled into the easy chair with a sigh of relaxation. "You've perfected the angle, old boy."

Wimbelow forced a smile over his dour expression. He didn't appreciate being called "Old Boy" by these senile geriatrics any more than he enjoyed refilling their denture cups, or running to the shops for prune scones, or adjusting the angles on the long line of easy chairs in the rec room whenever the officer's backs went out. He felt the bitter irony every day and everyday he cursed them. His crew was a hardy bunch. They simply refused to die.

"Wimbly, come look, I've made you a cap."

That was the other thing he hated. With resignation, Wimbelow walked to the rocking chair in the corner of the room which was always occupied by Officer Partridge. Meredith for short. The woman was possibly the oldest of the bunch with milky eyes and moved as though she were perpetually wading through a sea of pudding.

She handed him a furry mauve object of indeterminate shape. "It's your colour," she insisted, when he refused to take it. "The top of your head always looks so awfully cold."

A hand shot to the top of his thinning strands. "The top of my head is perfectly fine, *thankyouverymuch*," Wimbelow snapped.

"But—"

"Why can't you do something useful for once, Partridge? What am I supposed to do *with this?*" he waggled the limp object as though it were a dead animal. "Can *this* file my incident reports?"

Meredith huffed in his general direction. "I just thought—"

"Boss?" A blonde head peaked around the corner.

Immediately, Meredith perked up. "Katie!"

127

Katie Twill strode into the room, tartan coat fluttering, bell bottoms billowing, and murmuring hellos to the seniors as though she were some kind of a celebrity.

"What is it now?" asked Wimbelow tersely, although privately, he was relieved that she had interrupted them. It wouldn't do to have another shouting match with a senior this week.

Katie grinned. "We've just gotten a call from The Cove. Bertie McBride's hairdryer has gone missing and he's throwing a fit. Also, the guests from Shaw's dinner party are here. Billius Brum has begun singing both parts of *Romeo and Juliet* in the waiting room."

"Well send him in then!"

This was Wimbelow in a good mood. He hadn't slept all night after the incident at Shaw's manor. Who would have known this would be the case that would rocket him back into the good graces of the Yard? He could practically taste the sooty air of Westminster's back alleys.

"That's the thing, Bertie's in a real state. He said he suspects something terrible, and we need to get down there immediately."

"Have Ronald do it."

"His knees are out, Chief. I can do it alone if you like. He did ask for me."

But that irked the Inspector more than anything. "No," he snapped. "The suspects can wait. I'll get this cleared up within the hour."

"What about my hat?" Meredith pouted.

"I'll wear it," said Katie, affixing the object to her head where it looked like something had crawled up there and expired. "It goes with my pants."

Katie Twill. The gawky 18-year-old was more the bane of his life than any of the seniors. At first, she'd perplexed him and now she infuriated him. This town has a problem with age, he often thought. They went to the two extremes. Junior detective at eighteen? Sure, she had solved *some* cases, and sure, she *seemed* to be in the good graces of the townsfolk, but whatever happened to good old fashioned hard work and annoying the bejeezus out of one's superiors until they gave in?

He was also certain that something was quite wrong with her, although he wasn't sure what. She was always drinking from that

128

blasted thermos and nodding off at inopportune times. Not to mention her *driving*. Wimbelow was glad most things in Port Larkeney were walking distance.

He'd tried to remove her more than once, but for some reason, Katie Twill was an institution amongst the elderly. Getting Katie Twill kicked off the local police force was something he obsessed over more often than the cases themselves. Today however, was different. Shaw's case was cooling every minute he was away.

"I'll let you take the reins on this one, Twill," decided Wimbelow as they approached the line of dingy houses set up against the cliffs.

"Really?" said Katie.

"Don't get excited. I'm sure Bertie McBride's delusions about a hairdryer are something a five-year-old could figure out. In fact, we should make sure he wasn't sitting on it."

McBride's house was a precarious-looking lean-to against the cove's cliffside. The screen door creaked mournfully as they drew up to the porch. The salty wind this close to the ocean caused the pair to draw their collars up. Katie sipped from her bubbling thermos.

"I can't wait to interrogate the suspects of Shaw's dinner party," she said, grinning. "I think I've got an idea—"

"No no no!" The Inspector gave her an incredulous look. "Absolutely not. This is high profile assault. Unsuitable for your age and station. I'll be handling this one."

"But—"

"Tell me, Miss Twill, *what* would your mother say?"

The sound of flatfooted footsteps grew closer, and Bertie McBride opened the door. The fisherman greeted them in a nearly unintelligible stream of Irish and English that roughly translated to: "Took you long enough."

Wimbelow followed him inside, ignoring his junior's crestfallen look.

The inside of the shack was about what you would expect from the outside. A thin layer of sand covered the slatted floors. In the corner, beside a tiny coal stove, bits and bobs of fishing equipment; lichen covered buoys, tackle, and a few grimy sweaters were piled in magpie-like fashion. The bed was little more than a fishing net suspended from the rafters.

McBride scrambled up onto the net and lifted the pillow, showing that nothing was underneath it. "That's where it was. Me beauty."

"To clarify, we're still talking about the hair-dryer?" asked Katie, hiking up her bell bottoms in the mess. "When was the last time you saw it?"

"Last night. I had a *horrible* dream. Next thing I know, I reach under the pillow, it's gone."

Katie frowned. "What do you even use a hairdryer for? You're bald."

"Not everywhere," replied the old fisherman.

Wimbelow was glad he decided to leave it at that.

"Any known enemies?" she asked.

The Inspector let out an uncommon laugh. Enemies?

"Gimrod," growled McBride immediately. "I was suspecting him too. Ever since he poached me prize beauty."

"The hairdryer."

"No, a carp, eight stone. Keep up."

Katie was asking too many questions. He decided to step in.

"Tell me more about this Gimrod fellow."

As McBride told him more about the arthritic fish-kleptomaniac next door, he watched out of the corner of his eye as Katie prowled the room, checking under coffee pots, sweaters, and paying a strange interest to the makeshift hammock. Her fingers picked at one of the frayed ends of the rope.

"What did you dream about last night?" she asked suddenly.

McBride shivered. "It was horrible. The wind was howling. And yet...and yet." His ragged face transformed into an expression of bliss. "There was the most beautiful music. Brought a tear to this old face." And he began to hum, rocking slightly back and forth on his large flat feet. Inspector and junior detective exchanged glances. "There was a man—but he looked like no man I'd ever seen. Said he had to borrow something. I couldn't move a muscle, he magicked me into a spider's web, but it was just a dream!" he interjected. "I woke up the same as I usually do—only me favourite hairdryer was gone!"

He looked to the two officers pleadingly, his knotted face desperate. "You've got to get it back. It gets awfully cold down there, you know?"

Wimbelow hoped he meant the cove, and not somewhere else. When they re-emerged into the watery sunlight, the Inspector flipped through his notes. Wimbelow saw no reason why it shouldn't be Gimrod Gallifreigh. The old guttersnipe had had a history of pickpocketing over the years. The only reason he'd slowed somewhat in his liberations was due to a steadily worsening arthritis in his hands. But that certainly wasn't enough to prevent him from sneaking next door and pilfering a hairdryer. When he'd written this down, however, Katie's small dissenting noise made his head shoot up.

"So, what is your expert opinion, Twill?" he asked.

Katie, whose hand had been on her chin as she looked out at the sea, simply shrugged. "I have no idea. But it's not him."

* * *

"What do you mean I have to work with her?" Wimbelow sputtered furiously. "I am fifteen years her senior—I worked in London catching *real* criminals which makes me more qualified than, well anyone here! I should not have to lug the dead weight of a child in detective's clothes...not even that! She's wearing orange bell bottoms!"

Fergus folded his knobby knuckles over his lap, waiting until the tirade had finished. From the saffron kilt over his trousers to the tufts of hair sprouting from his ears, he looked in every way like a wizened leprechaun. The Chief's eyes could barely be seen beneath a pair of bottle-brush eyebrows. This discomfited Wimbelow as he could never be sure what the old man was thinking.

Katie sat in the corner, struggling to keep her eyes open despite the fact she'd had two cups of coffee this morning. It was

131

just another weird thing to add to the list that he would eventually bring to Fergus when the time was right.

The high-back chair creaked as the Chief leaned forward. "I don't care if you caught the Queen of England riding a donkey bare-backed," he said irritably.

The Inspector flushed.

"You are in Port Larkeney now, Inspector. Miss Twill has done an admirable job keeping things running as we searched for a new Inspector, and she will continue to do so in your presence."

Katie beamed. The Chief raised his knobby hand as Wimbelow tried to interrupt again.

"Now, get out and interrogate those god-awful people before I have to hear another operatic movement by Billius Brum through the walls. I had to take out my hearing aids."

Wimbelow fumed quietly as he and Katie cleaned out the interrogation room. The mauve carpeting and flowered wallpaper didn't make it any more intimidating, but they could help the fact that it was dripping with doilies courtesy of Officer Meredith Patridge. Katie hummed *Keep it Comin' Love* as she dumped the last armful of doilies into a sack. So of course, it had to get stuck in his head all day.

* * *

"Inspector?"

Inspector Wimbelow blinked and cleared his thoughts at the man sitting before him. Billius Brum reclined elegantly on the chair, his golden locks cascading down his shoulders.

"Aren't you going to ask me a question?" he asked coyly.

Wimbelow cleared his throat. "Er. yes." He shuffled his papers, tried not to look at the junior detective's eager green eyes beside him, and got right into it. A brief summary of the interrogations went something like this: "First things first. Name. Occupation. What you think about what happened."

Billius Brum: "Billius Brum. Thespian. Knighted. It was a *gruesome, treacherous, despicable, bloody exclamation mark* to an otherwise lovely evening. Drinks were great."

Duke of Dillmont: "Archeambault De Grenouille. Duke is simply a title as I inherited Dillmont orchards from my father. I am a vintner—that is I am the proprietor of pickle wine. The first in the world. It wasn't me. Do you think it was me? Oh dear, oh dear. I wasn't anywhere near the man."

The Quislings (they came together, refusing to part): "We're magnates," said Mr. Quisling.

"Ludlow Electric," scoffed Mrs. Quisling. "Have you ever looked at the underside of your table lamp?"

The husband lit up a long pipe. "What has this country come to? Attempted murder? Why should you think it was us? We've just lost a great deal of money."

"I suspect Brum," said his wife.

"Why?" asked Wimbelow.

"I don't like him."

Evangeline Grey: "Evangeline Everett Grey. Wigmaker and fashion expert. I am utterly *insulted* to even be in this room. I am *completely* above suspicion. Do you understand what kind of standing I hold back home? I made a wig out of ox hair for Duchess Anya Rashmanichoff herself!"

"I have no idea who that is."

"She's only the fourth in line to the Austrian throne!"

Mary (sobbing in a rather ugly way): "I never even got to say goodbye! He would have liked to see Humberdt or one of the goats, but I had to leave him in the car! He always hated pet hair on his clothes. He accosted me with a lint roller whenever I came to see him. I'm Mary Belsize, by the way. I'm a goat farmer."

"Who is Humberdt?"

"My lovely pet from Africa. Nyani, as they call it. He's perfectly tame. But grabby."

"You saw Shaw often?"

"We were quite close. Childhood friends before he left to pursue his career. After that I didn't see him for quite a while."

This led to a second round of sobbing—which led to the second question: "How did you know Sebastian Shaw?"

Billius: "We met at a play. Fast friends. You know how it goes. Don't see why I need to elaborate."

Duke of Dillmont: "I met him during a tasting at the opening of a new vineyard I had purchased near this very town. Sebastian became partial to my pickle liquor. He insisted I cater to a party he was having. He said he might be able to automate my pressing process. Naturally I obliged."

The Quislings: "We were business partners. Naturally we would come. Ludlow Electric planned to absorb The Shaw Company in order to eliminate conflict. Everybody wins. There was supposed to be some sort of unveiling that night. A new invention to introduce to our company line. Annoying to say we never got to see it. Just that Cellist thing. Do you have a lawyer, Inspector? I suggest you get one."

Evangeline Grey: "I was the reason the party was held in the first place you know. I made the wig for his greatest invention yet. You might remember The Cellist? The one who sent a ballroom crashing down upon our heads and gave me this disfigurement?" She waggled her bandaged finger.

When it came time to ask who had seen who throughout the evening, each person tentatively affirmed that they had seen no one leave the ballroom, due to the observation-tank-like nature of its mirrored walls. The Quislings had been first to arrive, then The Duke and Billius, then Evangeline Grey, and finally Mary and her impromptu guest. It felt like the questions stretched into infinity, and the obstinate nature of their subjects wasn't helping. By the time they got to the final question with Evangeline, both Wimbelow and Katie were sagging in their chairs. But, this was the most important one of all.

134

"Who was the last person you saw with Sebastian Shaw?" Surprisingly, this was the one thing everyone seemed to agree on. Each person had taken a deep breath and said the same name—

~13~

Something Purple and of Great Consequence

"Wendell Billings."

The Inspector shuffled the papers at his desk before sitting back and folding his fingers. All I could think about was his lack of eyebrows and ginger moustache. Some hair is just nontransferable, I guess.

"I've had some very interesting conversations about you."

"You have?"

"Indeed."

I scratched my nose. The room I was in smelled strongly of potpourri. There was only a table and two chairs: one for me and one for the Inspector. Katie leaned against the flowery wallpaper behind him and wearing a very ugly knitted cap. Catching my gaze, she gave me the thumbs up, presumably for encouragement. Then she nodded off again. I didn't blame her. It was warm in here. Light filtered softly in a gauzy curtained window enshrouding the centre of the room in a sleepy, pinkish glow. My palms were sweating. I wiped them on the purple coat that hung off the edge of my chair.

"Wendell Thomas Billings," he repeated. "Seventeen. Not in school?"

"I study on my own, sir," I said. "We travel a lot."

"I see." Wimbelow stood up, circled around the room. My neck prickled as he stood behind me. "I was thinking of that name just last night. Billings. Common name. Nothing special about it, not like these other fellows—Billius Brum, famed opera singer—Ludlow Quisling, electrical magnate. I've even eaten Dillmont's pickles. But it struck me as so familiar... then I remembered a little paper I'd read a while back on the charms of Cairo in the springtime." He reached around me and slid out a clipping from the bottom of his file. I recognized it immediately. Memories from two years ago came flooding back.

"Expeditions of Egypt," he read, "*Touring the Pointed Goliaths* by David T. Billings, and right at the end, a little commendation to Wendell Thomas Billings for his assistance in gathering my information. I inquired after him to Mrs. Twill and lo-and-behold. Your father!"

The Inspector plucked a ball of the potpourri from the bowl on the table and paced back and forth, rolling it between his fingers. "Now, how the hell does he make a dingy place in a Cairo backlot sound like Babylon? I should know, I had a cousin who stayed there once and caught four types of flu from the bathwater."

"It's what he does," I said. "I can't imagine many newspapers would take him on if our trips sounded like that."

"So, he does a lot for a good story, your dad, even if he doesn't get there by...*reputable means.*"

I frowned. "What's that supposed to mean?"

"Tell me about yourself, Wendell," said the Inspector. "What happened in Cairo?"

I recalled the adventure with vivid clarity. After all, it was where I had first become acquainted with the Nile Crocodile. I told them about the unforgiving raft ride and the harrowing chase off the river involving nearly losing a toe and pretending the spiny floating objects were logs and not bloodthirsty reptiles as I jumped to the shore.

When I was finished, he rubbed his pockmarked chin.

"You certainly do a lot for your father."

"I suppose. I don't know how that really—"

He cut me off. "You know what I think? I think it makes perfect sense. I think your dear old dad—a down and out journalist who would do anything for a bit of fame—found out about Shaw's little soiree from one of his column friends. I think he made this little trip under the pretense of writing about Port Larkeney when really, he intended to cover the biggest story of all time. And what would be more perfect than using his cherub-faced seventeen-year-old son as a scapegoat? Nobody would suspect you of stealing the Lightning Gun. Right? Wrong. *I* suspect you."

It was my turn to be incredulous. I felt myself quickly losing composure. "He would never do that. Not in a million years. In fact, he even cancelled the article just this morning!"

The Inspector glared at me. "So, I'm supposed to believe that little accident on a private road was simply a coincidence? That you really don't know about the Lightning Gun?"

"Yes! I hardly even know what that is!"

It was true. What little I had learned had come from Peach an hour earlier. As well-versed as she was in local gossip, she hadn't been able to tell me much. Only that it was some sort of ominous sounding super-weapon created by Sebastian Shaw.

Wimbelow looked to his partner and, without warning, banged his fist on the table. The young detective came to with a start. "Unacceptable during an interrogation, Twill. I'll be writing you up for that."

"Sorry," she mumbled.

The Inspector continued, but not before giving a suspicious look to his partner. "Then how do you come to be the last person who saw Sebastian Shaw alive?"

"I told you," I snapped. "I was waiting for him to get the phone from his study, just shortly before my brother was found comatose. How about you explain *that* to me?"

139

Wimbelow shuffled his papers furiously, the bottom side of his too-long teeth poking out in frustration. Suddenly he pulled out a photograph. The grainy polaroid waggled in my face triumphantly. It was the study and prominently shown was the strewn corpse of Sebastian Shaw, features stricken and hair standing straight up. However, there was something else in the photo—a flashlight trained on soft indentations in the carpet.

"Those were taken immediately after," said Wimbelow. "I believe those footprints were the only ones in the room. Heavy-treaded mountaineering boots. Size forty-three. The only pair in fact, out of three pairs of loafers, two pairs of kitten heels, and one pair of rather hideously painted wooden clogs belonging to Ms. Belsize." His gaze travelled pointedly to my feet.

"Er…" I laughed nervously. "Pretty sure I'm a forty-two and a half."

"I'll give you a moment to prepare your confession," said the Inspector. Smugness dripped from him as he strode to the door. "I think I shall reward myself with a well-deserved Danish. Without prunes. Twill, watch our murderous minor, would you?"

"With pleasure, Boss."

As soon as the door clicked shut, I jumped up. "What was that? What am I supposed to do now?"

Katie took a long sip from her thermos. She looked worried. "Just let me think."

I paced the perfumed carpet. "You know, for someone who insists she knows I'm innocent, you did a remarkably terrible job of proving it. I was supposed to be at the hospital an hour ago, you know. My brother could wake up any minute—and here you are, sleeping!"

"I'm sorry, I've just been tired," she ran a hand through her hair. "All of these interviews…and I haven't gone to sleep in about thirty-eight hours…"

"I can't go to prison!"

Katie looked up. "I thought you'd been to prison. I saw it in your book."

"Tahitian prison," I snapped. "And they served soft-shell crab on Tuesdays and Thursdays."

140

"We'll figure something out," she assured me. "There must be something to prove you were innocent in all this. My mother will testify that your parents were chucking in the bathrooms all night, although that doesn't cover you. What did you see that night?"

"I feel like I've already told you everything," I said. "There was a blue flash, and everything went wrong. Billius was blind drunk. Sebastian was...unnerving. Before that, my brother and I were driving when our car broke in the middle of the night. We were arguing about something."

"What?"

My fingers clenched the purple fabric on the armchair. I hadn't recounted this part to anyone. "I was angry with him. I suppose he had every right to be mad at me. I basically told him he was an idiot and the reason why all our travels end up in disaster."

"Yeesh."

I sighed. "Yeah, well it got worse. The heater wasn't working, and things got heated, no pun intended. I wasn't paying attention and before I knew it, that Lamplighter Auto was in front of me. I avoided it, barely, and we skidded onto the curb. After the engine gave out, I decided to go to the nearest place and ask for help. You'd think after all this time I'd know how to fix an engine. But all I'm good for is this." I held up the notebook. "And somebody's ripped all the useful pages out."

"You really can't remember anything up to the incident?" asked Katie curiously.

"I—"

It was true. I focused, thinking of the events. Things were clear up until about a minute before the break-in and a good few minutes after. All I could picture was the blinding jagged light erupting through that study door. It wasn't like me. It was as if the brilliance of the flash had erased everything around the incident, as if the running of my memory were obliterated like so much over-exposed film. But I had been writing. I knew that. I also knew the pages were gone. I explained this to Katie who quirked an eyebrow.

"The Lightning Gun," she said at last. "I'm afraid I don't know more about it than you do, but Sebastian's been working on it for years, so rumours get around. Got some sort of deal with Quislings for it. There's been booms. Flashes. More thunderstorms than are reasonable for summer."

"Thunderstorms?"

"Well, I can't be certain that's what it is, but all the fishermen at the Palaces complain. They know Port Larkeney better than anybody."

I was getting a sinking feeling. If that was the gun that had gone off, what had it done to me? More importantly, what had it done to Tim? I would soon see, assuming I wasn't falsely imprisoned for a couple of footprints. I searched through my book for anything that I might use to dispute the Inspectors claim.

"Anything?" Katie asked.

"No." I closed the book with a sigh. "You know, I'm starting to believe I might be crazy. I mean, how do *you* know it wasn't me?"

I'd asked that question about a million times already, but Katie's answer was just as vague as all the others. "It's like that feeling you get right before it's about to rain," she said, shrugging. "It's just a feeling, but it's as strong as anything. I'm as sure it wasn't you just like I'm sure it wasn't my own mother, or Tim, or Billius Brum for that matter. Also, I don't have any friends my own age and I'm banking on the fact you aren't a murderer."

Brum? And…friends? Before I had a chance to ask about that, Katie's walkie talkie crackled, and a fuzzy voice hissed through the speakers. "A Billius Brum just rang. Says he left his coat in the parlour with the doilies."

"It's an interrogation room," the junior detective clicked off the radio.

"So that's who this belonged to," I picked up the lurid purple coat. It smelled heavily of cognac and lavender. I dropped it back on the chair. As I did so, a single piece of paper fluttered to the ground.

Behind us, the door opened. Wimbelow walked in looking much refreshed and ready to convict. Katie quickly resumed her slouched position on the wall. I carefully positioned my feet over the fallen scraps as he resumed his place behind the desk.

142

I knew exactly what they were. When he looked away, I snatched up the shorn page and returned it to my notebook, feeling a sense of relief as if I'd been reunited with a lost limb. Over the Inspector's shoulder, I gave Katie a meaningful look that could not have meant anything other than: *You still think it wasn't Billius Brum?*

~14~

Bedside Brawl

Great Galloping Gingersnaps, that was brilliant!" Katie and I emerged from the interrogation room several minutes later, grinning and leaving behind the furious face of Inspector Wimbelow who looked rather as if he'd been dashed in the face with Mrs. Twill's famous habanero cocoa.

While I wasn't completely out of the clear, a second examination of the photos showed me something unexpected. There was another indentation in the deep, plush carpet. It was around my own boot, wider on each side by about eight centimetres. Large, flat, and distinctly tennis-racket shaped. I recognized it at once.

"That's another print," I said to Wimbelow. Then I told him exactly what kind of print it was. He nearly spit out his coffee.

Katie bent over for a third opinion. "You're right." She sounded impressed. "I didn't see that before. Must be fresh and from someone heavy," she said. "Otherwise, that wouldn't be so deep."

The Inspector had blustered and sputtered like a dying candle, but once it was pointed out to him, even he could not refute the distinct shape, although he immediately radioed one of the senior officers to go for a second opinion.

After that, he could think of no more questions and turned the both of us out. Just before we'd crossed the hall, Wimbelow had stuck his head out. Red coloured the roots of his carroty hair as he cried after us, "You mean to tell me that someone climbed a four-story building *in snowshoes?*"

"It was pretty good, wasn't it?" I grinned at her as Wimbelow retreated into his office.

"We make a good team," said Katie.

I nodded, tucking the journal back into its safe place in my upper pocket. Despite my determination not to get involved, the mysteries surrounding Shaw's death pulled at my attention. Wimbelow told me it was a four-story drop from the window of the study to the perimeter of the left wing of the manor. There wasn't a single blind spot, in or out. Shaw's weaponized Autos waited in the shrubs, ready to pounce on intruders. It would have taken someone of extraordinary skill to climb that wall without being noticed. He'd insinuated that, with my travels, I might be just suited for such a feat. That was laughable.

I was a terrible climber and even if not, I would have needed rappelling equipment. Wasn't it a sheer drop—no ledges along that side except for tiny gutter halfway up? Picks would definitely have left a mark and there was little to secure a rope to. It was also clear from the photographs that the outer wall below the study was unmarked, save for a single arrow stuck into a bush a yard away. This kept the possibility open that an intruder had tripped one of the alarms from the outside. Could it have been Bellamy Dumont? If so, the police would be no closer to catching him than they had been five months ago.

"So how about it?" Katie asked, as we arrived at reception.

I snapped out of my thoughts. "How about what?"

"Why the two of us, of course! Solving crime and kicking butt! We even have a head start on Wimbelow. A bona fide lead."

I stopped. "You're not going to tell him?"

She fiddled with her collar. "It's just a *wee* clue. Think about it. My deductive reasoning and your borderline obsessive notetaking—a crime the likes of which the world has never seen—we'd be famous, Wendell!" A momentary shaft of sunlight peeked out from the clouds just then. Katie's large green eyes seemed to catch it as she held open the door.

Suddenly it was too much—this case, my brother, the heady smell of the potpourri and the bright-eyed gaze of the junior detective.

"I...have to go to the hospital." I hurried out, leaving her there with the purple coat in the prune-perfumed parlour.

I arrived at the hospital around noon. By daytime it was a prettier place, another of those low-slung stone buildings that stood on the gentle incline bordering the cove. Salty air brushed my cheek and gulls flocked close by; their nests built in the crags of the seawalls below the hospital. It hadn't been hard to find. It was the only place off the plaza with a real lot. A few cars dotted the gravel.

Garret, the nervous, ginger-haired nurse from the other night pulled aside the curtains. Tim looked just the same as he had last night. Maybe a little colour had returned to his cheeks. His hair was still sticking straight up. On his bedside were a couple of letters I hadn't seen before. They were addressed from Melati. I felt a pang of sadness.

"Unfortunately, there hasn't been any change," said Garret. "Your parents came earlier. Nothing. I tried doing something about the hair too. Nothing. It actually gave me a little shock when I tried to flatten it."

"When do you think he'll wake up?" I looked up to find the nurse giving the bed a wide berth.

"Well, you know what the doctor says." He avoided my gaze. "Could be soon, could be... a while."

But before I could extract a straight answer out of him, there was a musical tinkling sound at the door. Garret jumped like he was glad of the distraction.

"That'll be lunch!"

147

The double doors leading out of the ward opened and a small cart covered in a red-checked tablecloth trundled out of its own accord. I watched in bemusement as it stopped in the middle of the room and four spindly arms wearing rubber hospital gloves popped out from under the tablecloth. They rummaged around inside the cart before neatly depositing cups of pudding and water to each patient's bedside. One gloved arm even steeped a little cup of tea upon one woman's request. I was reminded of my teapot. Now that I thought of it, I hadn't seen Genie since the crash.

"That was a donation from Sebastian Shaw," said Garett proudly. "He donates—er donated—to all sorts of businesses around here. I expect you'll see his Autos around."

I studied the cart. It was a far cry from the mechanical horses I'd seen trotting circles in London and Central Park in New York. "Is that all it does?"

Garret saw I was unimpressed. "Well obviously it does other things. Sebastian Shaw is master craftsman." He said this a bit too loudly and a woman with a cast on her leg shushed him. "Sometimes it helps with surgeries. It's very good for setting legs and arms back into place because I can get a little…" Garret turned a bit green. "Sometimes we bring it out to catch a particularly annoying fly in the ward."

Suddenly, he pulled up a chair and swung himself down, leaning over the backrest. "So," he said, "Don't you want to know more about me? I am the only nurse in town. I've seen lots. Plenty of gory stories for you. Bunions, broken femurs, you would not believe how many things I've pulled out of people's—"

I waved him away. "Thanks, but I really don't need to know."

"Oh, come on, mate, everyone's heard about the article your dad's writing about Port Larkeney. Peach reckons we'll all be famous once it comes out. I'd be lying if I said I didn't want a piece of the page." He gave a long-suffering sigh. "Things have been a bit dry in the romance department. Only so many young ladies in a fishing town a hundred miles from civilization, you know?"

This was the second time I'd been put upon to interview in as many hours, and all I wanted was to go home and have a nap. "We're not really doing that sort of thing anymore," I told him, looking meaningfully at my comatose brother. "Wish I could help."

Garret looked a mite disappointed. "Figured as much," he shrugged. "But you know how everyone gets when these sorts of things happen. Oh! Are you going to the Capsicum Carnival?"

"The what?"

"It happens every year, hosted by Katie Twill's mother. It's fun, lots of lights and a pepper contest for Port Larkeney's famous peppers. It happens near Christmas. Sometimes it's *better* than Christmas. And you look like someone in need of a bit of fun. You know, in case this brother of yours takes a bit longer to wake up than you think."

"Do you know something about Tim?"

The nurse stiffened suddenly. "Why would you think that?"

Other than the fact that it was painfully obvious? I'd attributed it to squeamishness, but in contrast to the other cots which he regularly checked, Garret kept a wide space between himself and my brother at all times, as if he might catch something. I leaned forward.

"What is it?"

A rustling, scraping sound saved him from answering. The curtain over the bed furthest to the back appeared to be jolting back and forth. One of the joints in the cart Auto's arms was caught in the fabric. The metal arm jerked back and forth. A cup of Jell-O flailed in the gloved hand.

"Shite!" Garrett jumped up like he'd sat on hot coals. He ran to the bed to try and disentangle the arm. When I went to help, he waved me away. "Nonono! I'm good! I've got it!"

It didn't look like it. The arm was just getting more and more twisted in the curtain. Garret was getting more and more panicked. He swore more colourfully as he stubbed his foot on the edge of the cart. The nurse hopped in pain, kicking the offending edge, which caused the cart to roll backward. That was when it ripped.

The sound of tearing cloth filled the ward. The bottom half of the front curtain was yanked from the metal hoops as the cart spun away. It fluttered to the floor without a sound, exposing the occupant of the bed. Garret's eyes were wide with shock. His hands gripped the torn piece of curtain. The sharp featured face of Sebastian Shaw lay silent as a ghost on the pillow.

"You...weren't supposed to see that."

With that, a quivering splat of Jell-O dropped on the floor. The gloved hand drooped over the bed in a sad salute. I would not want that cart to give me surgery.

The red-headed nurse stepped in front of me, his demeanor suddenly changed, his expression fierce. "You, stay there, don't move an inch. In fact, forget you saw anything at all, or *you* might be occupying one of these beds." Garret grabbed a broom from off the wall and jabbing my chest with the handle.

"Is that a threat?" I asked.

"It...was a suggestion."

I frowned. A million thoughts raced through my mind. Sebastian Shaw was alive? Both Katie and the Inspector made it seem as though he was dead. Then I realised that none of them had ever specifically used that language. What were the odds of two people falling unconscious in the same night?

I turned away from Garret and strode to my brother on the other side of the room. Tim's face was white, his lips bluish with purple rings around his eyes. His hair crackled with electricity. At least the slow rising and falling of his chest was normal. I noticed a mark on his collarbone.

"Sorry," I muttered, gingerly peeling back the opening of the dressing gown. My brother's pale chest was marred by the strangest bruise I'd ever seen. It was the size of my fist and orange in the centre with jagged purple lines that radiated out like streaks of lightning into the veins of his skin. It seemed almost as if a glow were coming from within.

"Garret, I need to see Sebastian Shaw."

The nurse, who had followed me with the broom handle, stiffened. "You can't do that."

I stepped towards him. "Let me see him, Garret," I said slowly. "Or tell me what that mark is on Tim's chest. And you'd better not say it's a hickey."

Immediately, he paled. "I have no idea what you're talking about."

"Then I'll see for myself."

And limbo-ing beneath the flailing arms, I shot for the bed. That's one advantage of being closer to the ground. Unfortunately, Sebastian's bed was all the way on the other side of the room. Garret's long legs rapidly caught up to me and two of us went down in a rolling scuffle at the foot of the cot.

"Getoffme!"

"Let me see him!"

"*Ew*, don't *bite* me, Wendell!"

"SHHH!" The two of us paused as the woman in the cast put a good finger to her lips.

I reached around and jabbed the young nurse in the solar plexus (a move I had learned, and half-forgotten from the fighting monks of a remote village in Tibet). He doubled over coughing. I scrambled up and made for the last few metres—until the ground came rushing up to meet me. Garret seized my ankle and dragged me down with him. The force of hitting the tile knocked the air from my lungs. The next moment he was on top of me in a feeble attempt to pin my arm to my back. I pushed away from him. For a moment, we both lay there, winded. He turned to me.

"Why...in god's green earth," he gasped, "...do you want to see him so bad?" I stared at the ceiling, resting my back on my elbows, and probing my ribs. "Tim is my brother and there's something you're not letting on. Either you let me see Shaw and confirm my suspicions or I'll find out some other way."

"I can't. I was supposed to keep it a secret," he said miserably.

Garret got up with a groan and went to tie one of the ragged ends of fabric to the curtain rail. "For as long as possible, at least. Wimbelow didn't want anyone to know in case whoever did *you know what* would find out and come back to finish the job." He turned, and wincing, bared his fists. "I'll fight you again if I have to."

I didn't relish the thought. Something he'd said earlier stuck with me. "Garret," I said, "how would you like to be a prime feature in our column?"

A half an hour later, I was halfway home with a fresh sheaf of notes and a feeling of increasing dread. The promise of fame had

Garret talking in less than thirty seconds flat and he led me amicably to the forbidden bed. The billionaire lay there, looking acerbic even in sleep. He was shorter than I remembered, his right hand lain across his stomach Napoleonically. What I'd discovered was alarming. My brother and Shaw were nearly identical in symptoms. They had the bruise in common, and though it had been covered by his nightcap, Sebastian Shaw's white-blond hair stuck up in much the same way, crackling and refusing to be flattened.

After twenty minutes of sitting through a wide variety of personal anecdotes, Garret finally explained to me the local legend and the cause for his fear.

"That is a sunspot," he'd said pointing with the broom handle at my brother's mark. "The last person who got that hasn't woken up in ten years. I don't remember the time it started. Mam says it started just before I was born. Families showing up in hospital saying their spouses, their kids, their friends had been discovered along the bluffs, a big orange splotch the shape of the sun across their chest."

"And there was no cure? I don't see any of them here." I poised the pen above the surface of the book.

"Well, most of them didn't live very long after that," said Garret. "I'd say by the time I was about sixteen by the time the last one had gone and by then the cases just stopped happening. Hey, are there going to be pictures going along with this, cause I'm going to need some time to get ready."

My breath quickened as I pushed myself up the steep hill to the Piquant Palaces. Note pages flashed through my mind in a blur. Exotic diseases. Liver spots…chicken pox… no Sunspots. Nothing. There was *nothing*. How was it I'd never seen anything like this before in all my travels?

That feeling of powerlessness hit me again as did the memory of last night. In my mind's eye, a blue jet of light ricocheted across the mirror just above my head. And just like that, there could be no other explanation. It must be the Lightning Gun. By the time I reached the top of the hill, I had made my decision.

At dinner, my father choked on his pasta. "Spicy," he coughed, tears streaming from his eyes. "I thought I was safe with this one, but it turns out to be even hotter than the dishes in New Delhi." He downed a glass from the milk jug we'd begun to keep on hand.

"Rations, David!" my mother cried. "We can't keep going out of town to hunt down the cattle farmers."

I toyed with my bacon sandwich. The fire was burning low in the pub and there was still no sign of her.

My father looked down his glass for any straggling drops and set it down. "So how did he look today?"

My mother's voice was slightly hoarse. "I read him six chapters from *A Masterful Mutilation* by Minse M. Uppe. I'm sure he's heard some of it. His eyelashes fluttered when Constable Steele stumbled upon the bloodbath."

My father had long since given up on suggesting a change in books. "But no change?" he asked.

"The doctor says he's staying steady."

He looked dismally into his dish. He didn't even have the energy to sift through his ever-growing stockpile of travel brochures. That's how you knew it was bad.

"How about you, Wendell? How was your day?" asked my mother.

"Oh, it was alr—" a straggling snore erupted from the other side of the room. I caught sight of a slim hand dangling over an armrest. I stood up. "You'll have to excuse me for a moment."

She was snoring softly in one of the armchairs by the fire. In her prone hand hung an orange Walkman.

"Katie."

When that didn't work, I shook her on the shoulder. With a start, the detective snuffled and sat up. A bemused expression crossed her face. Before I could lose my courage, I sat across from her. She removed her headphones. The tinny sounds of Edison Lighthouse drifted through the speakers.

"I've been thinking about what you said earlier," I began, "and... I think we should work together."

Katie, who was still shaking off sleep, didn't react like I had hoped. "Wuzzat?"

I repeated myself. It came out worse. "I think we should, er, try to solve this case, find the Lightning Gun if that's what it's really called. Some things happened at the hospital today and I didn't really know what to do so I—"

Before I could finish, she sprang up, nearly knocking the Walkman off the table. "Do you really mean it?"

"Yes?"

She held out a hand and I stared at it dumbly before realising I was supposed to shake. I gripped it which was a mistake. She shook it much the same way my father did; vigorous and socket-wrenching. "We're going to be partners!" she said happily. "Twill and Billings. It has a fine ring to it."

In spite of myself, I grinned back hesitantly. It was this very moment that would begin the rest of our fateful career. It's a moment I will remember always. Particularly when my own smile faded as the hand in mine went limp. I looked up to see the detective's face slacken, blond hair falling over her eyes.

"Katie?" She was still standing, just unresponsive. "Katie?" She had fallen asleep.

~15~

A Robbery Most Fowl

The doorknob of 214 Asher Avenue lay in two on the cheery welcome mat outside. The Lamplighter perched nervously in front of the living room window.

"Do you hear that?"

"Obviously. You sound like a game of kick the can." The Cellist's lips pursed in concentration as he scouted the darkened house. His tone was, as always, nasty. "And if you'd like to keep all six arms, I suggest you *stop kicking.*"

The Lamplighter tried as hard as he could to be quiet, but it was hard when you were nearly three metres tall and every part of you either squeaked or pinched or rattled. He was beginning to get the impression that this body of his was not very new.

He stood very still so The Cellist would not turn around and relieve him of a limb. At last, the door they'd been trying to pick swung open. The Cellist adjusted his waistcoat and wig as if preparing for a dinner soiree rather than a midnight heist.

"Remember the rules," he said. "Secret, silent, discreet. In and out. No mistakes like last time."

The Lamplighter blinked his owlish yellow eyes and rubbed his many hands in apprehension. "Can't I just wait outside? It's always cramped and last time I barely got myself unstuck before that dog attached itself to my ankles."

"You wouldn't have been able to feel it."

"I don't like terriers."

The Cellist used his usual persuasion. He held the sharpened bow of tempered steel to The Lamplighter's neck. "I don't know why I must keep explaining it to you. It's very simple really. I need you as back up. Why, your horrifying countenance is enough to strike fear into the hearts of anyone who crosses us. A revolution starts with fear. Don't you know *anything?*"

He didn't know, and idly wondered how The Cellist seemed to know so much when he himself seemed to stumble around like a baby peafowl alone in the Congo rainforest. The Lamplighter blinked. What an odd analogy that was.

"Come on," said The Cellist, and he had to follow.

Bracing himself for claustrophobic corridors and low ceilings, The Lamplighter hunched low and stepped into the house. As he edged sideways through the tiny coatroom, he thought about his situation.

What worried The Lamplighter most was how The Cellist stressed secrecy, and yet did not seem to care if people saw them during their heists, for he relished the act of striking the unlucky onlooker on the back of the head, or playing such mournful, ear-piercing music that they would faint on the spot.

He felt sorry for the poor people, despite what The Cellist said about them all being murderous tyrants and devilish despots. Most of them had been drunk fishermen or fearful housewives who had done very little in the way of aggression.

"What do we do if they attack us?" he'd asked one day in their tiny hideout. "I mean *really* attack us, like with a knife?"

"That's a stupid question," The Cellist scoffed. "A knife? Against you? A beast of metal with six arms? Why the answer is simple. You kill them." His yellow eyes gleamed. He stared off somewhere The Lamplighter could not see. "It's all soft meat and weakness anyways. Incredible that they've created a race so superior to themselves and yet do nothing to improve their own fleshy anatomy. Hubris, I imagine." And he smiled a secret smile as he polished the bow lovingly, getting off the last flecks of fur from their previous escapade.

They reached a parlour area with a high ceiling that The Lamplighter could walk more comfortably in. The house was still silent, which was nothing short of a miracle considering how many gouges he'd left on the walls due to his cursed wide-brimmed metal hat. The Cellist took his time walking around the room and observing the many paintings of ducks in various watery environments.

"Bring out the teapot," he said at last.

The Lamplighter reached into the silk drawstring bag he'd nabbed from their hideout. From inside, he withdrew a rather nondescript looking China teapot with little flowery designs painted on the porcelain. It sat there, immobile.

He'd begun to learn, however strangely, that Autos responded best to music. Sometimes, in his quietest moments, he thought he could hear a little hum coming from deep inside of himself, as if the Amber in his chest played a tune of its own—a tune of life that vibrated through his body. The Lamplighter hummed a portion of this tune. It resonated through the empty room with the rumbling dissonance of a steel drum.

"Genie," he whispered. "Show us where it is."

As if a candle flame had sprung to life inside it, a warm orange glow grew from inside, spilling from the crevices of the teapot. Two stumpy legs popped out from the bottom. It stamped on the carpet, the miniature toes flexing and wiggling after their disuse. The Cellist regarded the creature.

The small Automaton stood up and turned in a full circle, spout bobbing up and down like the nose of a bloodhound. Suddenly the teapot stopped and set off down the hallway, the small porcelain feet pattering softly along the floorboards. The two paused in the doorway and as The Lamplighter looked down to see what the holdup was, he was surprised to see one of his companion's rare smiles.

"Again, my friend, your discovery proves invaluable."

"Oh, thank you."

"Now, dim the lights if you would. We have work to do."

157

The Lamplighter concentrated and the orange light washing the parlour flickered out. The space was now lit only by the faint glow of a nightlight in the shape of a Canada goose.

The Cellist edged along the hallway, bow at the ready. The Lamplighter did a less elegant crabwalk in the narrow corridor. Several times he nearly knocked over one of the many paintings of a geese. Several times he did, only just catching it with one of his many hands. The journey was made ever more nerve-wracking by the snores in the next room. They sounded as if they were coming from inside a barrel.

They made it to the kitchen without a hiccup. Genie waited for them on the countertop. The Lamplighters gaze flicked on. The kitchen was small with an island countertop in the centre and a window that would have looked out onto the ocean in the daylight. It still smelled of roast and rosemary.

The Cellist narrowed his eyes at the room. "I don't see it," he murmured.

The teapot jumped up and down and pointed its spout to the darkened corner. The Cellist pushed aside a row of spices and seized upon the object of his desire. "Excellent," he hissed.

He handed it to the Lamplighter who opened the fuschia bag and laid it carefully inside. The Lamplighter breathed a sigh of relief. It had been a mercifully quiet robbery. No inquisitive pets, no squeaky floorboards, or half-naked fathers headed for a midnight snack. Now they could go. He turned for the door…and stopped.

It was possibly the most unmemorable boy The Lamplighter had ever seen in his life. He stood there, nondescript in a blue nightshirt and shorts. He had a book under his arm and an empty glass in his hand.

"What is this?" the boy asked mildly.

"I think I'll kill this one," said The Cellist idly, brandishing his bow. "Prepare to die, boy."

The Lamplighter hurried forward. "It's just a dream," he said, shooing the boy. "Go back to bed."

"That makes sense. Alright then. Goodnight," the boy said.

"Goodnight," said The Lamplighter. The boy turned and padded down the hallway.

The Cellist turned to him, miffed. "You should've let me kill him."

"That would've made a terrible mess. And you know how you feel about messes."

"Blood is hard to get out of white trousers."

"Yeah. That."

The Lamplighter allowed himself to relax a little. It had still gone according to plan, and he'd prevented the kid from being a late-night shish kebab. *Now* they could go.

The Cellist lifted the window and hopped nimbly onto the countertop. The wind from the sea ruffled his wig and blew back his coattails. "Let's away," he whispered with his usual touch of melodrama.

The Lamplighter edged his way around the counter to get the teapot. It started as soon as he touched it.

SHREEE!

The shrill sound erupted from the spout and before he could grab Genie, the teapot shot for the window.

"No!" he cried. He lunged after it and was successful in securing a wriggling leg. "What's gotten into you?"

Genie shot an obstinate jet of water into his face. The Lamplighter stuffed it into the bag before it could do anymore damage, but it was too late.

As they were scrambling out the window, The Lamplighter became aware of a change. Silence. The snoring had ceased. Then he realised he was much too large to escape through the window.

"Cellist?"

Thumps echoed through the hall.

"We'll have to go through the front," said The Cellist. "No matter. Tonight was getting boring anyways." He was grinning, an awful sight to see with the glinting metal in his hands.

"Huh. The same dream twice in one night."

The boy stood in the doorway again, sleep lingering in a pair of deadpan eyes.

"Oh, this is no dream," said The Cellist gleefully. "And this time, my compassionate colleague won't save you. Tell me, do you have any last words?" He held the blade to the pale neck of the unremarkable adolescent.

The boy blinked uninspiredly. "What'd you say? I didn't quite catch that."

The Auto rolled his eyes. "Oh, for heaven's sake, I might as well put you out of your misery." He raised the bow, but before The Lamplighter could protest, there was a—

"NO!"

The boy disappeared as if yanked along the edge of a speedboat. A meaty arm surrounded his midsection, saving him from the killing blow.

The Cellist didn't know what hit him.

The Lamplighter did.

Following was something heavy and lightning fast that clocked his partner around the head, nearly dislodging his wig. It was a granite lamp base, carved into the sturdy form of a Nene Goose. The Auto staggered back into the counter, utter shock on his articulated features.

A woman as broad as a train with forearms to boot heaved in the doorway. The lamp base looked tiny in her hands. "Don't worry, darling. Mummy's here," she huffed tremulously. She held him back at the doorway. "Go back to bed."

The barest hint of blond peaked out from behind the forearm. "This isn't a dream?"

Everyone in the room rolled their eyes.

The Cellist sat up with a groan. He rolled away barely in time to avoid another strike from the lamp base and jumped onto the countertop between meaty swipes. She spoke between attempts at cracking The Cellists knees.

"I don't *huff* know what you are *huff* or who controls you *huff* but you will not threaten my son!"

"Heavens, woman! Where do they grow people like you?" He pranced around the last blow and gave a savage kick, sending her staggering back. He turned to glare at The Lamplighter. "Well don't just stand there!"

The Lamplighter stumbled to life. It was amazing that, large as he was, people often forgot his presence. Many times, in the streets at night, all he had to do was stand still and people would pass by without a second glance.

With a "terribly sorry about this," he pushed the enormous woman to the side before she could get to her feet. Vibrations rumbled through the floorboards as she bounced backwards like a skipping stone. With his two free arms, he grabbed The Cellist.

The smaller Auto was light but bulky. The Lamplighter felt as though he were barrelling through a rabbit hole as he ran through the dark hallway.

"Ouch! You idiot, watch the wig!"

"I'm trying not to get us killed!" The Lamplighter puffed and adjusted his grip on the smaller robot. He could hear gaining footsteps behind him. Arms pushed against his grip.

"Let me down," said the Cellist.

"We're nearly out!" The Lamplighter stifled a gasp of pain as the woman gave a war cry and something cracked against his ankle. Paintings shattered left and right, littering the hallway with glass and pictures of geese.

"Let me down," The Cellist growled and wriggled out. They were in the mudroom. "I am not about to make such an undignified exit." He raised his bow.

The Lamplighter was caught between his partner and the doorway. The woman abandoned the tactic of hitting. She was fearless, he had to give her that. Instead, she thrust the lamp base straight out in front of her and ran headlong towards them. Heavy footfalls echoed all throughout the house.

His partner was calm. The Lamplighter tried pulling him towards the door. "We got what we came for, we have to leave!"

"In a moment."

"Cellist!"

She was at most three paces away. The Lamplighter reached past him for the door. He wasn't going to die here. It simply wasn't fair to someone who'd only been alive a week!

Suddenly The Cellist shrugged off his coat to reveal the four glistening strings running down his chest. In a smooth movement, he brought down the bow. The tiny room rang with a sound that The Lamplighter would hear sometimes in his dreams in the coming years, something twisting, sad, and achingly beautiful all in a single note. The Cellist played further, stepping towards their attacker without fear.

The sound went deep into the walls, trembling the timbers of the house. The woman stopped in her tracks. She was an arm's length away and could have smashed The Cellist's face in if she'd liked. Instead, she cocked her head, listening to the music fade.

The Auto lifted his bow with the final note and stood there, waiting. Like the felling of a mighty oak, the woman thumped to the floor. The house rang with that too. The snoring resumed.

Out into the open air of the night, two figures, one small and dashing, the other spindly, enormous, and inhuman picked their way over the halved doorknob on the doormat of 214 Asher Avenue. They ran into the night and beyond, clutching their prize and grinning with adrenaline and victory.

~16~

Welcome to the Garden

Katie experienced a moment of disorientation. She'd been asleep for a minute or so when she opened her eyes with a start and asked me if I knew the nearest way to candy mountain where the purple alligators danced.

I chalked it up to the sleep deprivation she'd mentioned earlier. After all, who was I to judge? I hadn't slept for three days when visiting a Temple in Laos and subsequently collapsed standing up. It's a funny story. We'd been sleeping on rough communal mats in the Temple of Duangchan. Normally I have no trouble sleeping anywhere and that night was no different. A few hours in, I awoke to scratching. *Scritch scratch scritch scratch.* Up and down my leg. Naturally I screamed, thinking some kind of animal had gotten into the temple. After a thorough search, no culprit was found. This occurred each night for the next three days, significantly impairing my ability to transcribe our journey. After sleepwalking into the second pit of quicksand that week, I decided to investigate further and stayed up until midnight with a torch and a sharp stick.

Turns out, it was the bald monk I'd been parked next to who'd had the unfortunate habit of sleepily sliding his uncut toenails far past respectable boundaries. All was resolved when I gave him a pair of woollen socks.

I guided Katie to the chair, and she yawned. I settled back into the cushion opposite and asked, "So. What exactly are we supposed to do now?"

The answer wasn't promising. "I'm not sure."

I blinked. "*You're* the detective!"

"I know that!" But doubt had settled across her face if the full weight of our decision was setting in. I was waiting for the "but."

"But," (there it was), "you should know that I've never done anything like this before. I solve cases with missing fishing rods and murderous seagulls, not superweapons and billionaires."

"Obviously. Neither have I." I turned my gaze to the fire, crackling low in the large brick hearth. "I have my brother to get back. My inept, idiot older brother who doesn't deserve this."

"You think his condition has something to do with this?" Katie asked.

"Have you ever heard of something called a Sunspot?" She didn't answer and I repeated myself. "A Sunspot. It's supposed to be some kind of curse. Garret told me. Bright orange with radiating marks in the middle of the chest. I found it on my brother today. It was on Sebastian too. By the way, terrible job pretending he's dead. All I had to do was bribe the nurse."

"That was Wimbelow's doing," said Katie with a touch of annoyance. "He didn't tell me anything. I didn't know Shaw was alive until I took a peek into the ward that night. He's trying to boot me off the case."

"Why would he do that?"

Katie leaned back. "I suspect that he is one of those rare people not swayed by my natural charm. Anyways, continue."

I was starting to feel a little stupid, reiterating some kind local legend as if it were magical fact, but pushed on with my theory.

"I think it had to do with the Lightning Gun. It must have, right? I mean, no rogue bolt of lightning suddenly hits someone from inside a car. I saw it go straight out the window of the balcony. If I can figure out what it was exactly that caused it, maybe I can reverse it somehow. I know it's a long shot, but I've got to try...you think I'm full of it."

Her face had grown uncharacteristically serious. "No, I think it makes sense. But Wendell, if what you're saying is true, this is more important than ever. If someone's got ahold of this gun for nefarious purposes, who knows what could happen?"

I nodded. "You've lived here all your life. What do you know about the Sunspot?"

She took a long draught from her bubbling thermos. That familiar smell of cinnamon, coffee, and spice enveloped the space between us. Her brows were knit. "Very very little. But—"

The clatter of silverware interrupted her as Mrs. Twill bustled past, arms laden with Tacos de Lengua and black pudding. As she passed, she cast a harried look over her shoulder and said, "Don't forget to get that day off tomorrow. I don't care what that Inspector says. We'll need all hands-on deck."

Katie groaned.

"You're already taking a day off?" I asked.

"It's for pepper picking." She reached out and plucked a nearby brochure depicting a family filling their baskets in idyllic fields as one would with strawberries or raspberries rather than tongue-scorching fruit. "My mother holds one every month. She opens her gardens to the town and insists I come make sure nobody lays hands on Big Bertha or pockets too many Guajillo Chilis. It's really just an excuse for her to saddle me with a box of keychains and tchotchkes and peddle them around at obscene prices." She scowled deeply. "It's a complete and utter waste of..." She trailed off and her eyes widened.

"What?"

"Hand me that book of yours."

Bemused, I gave her my notebook. She flipped through the last page and began to scribble a rough column of sorts on its pages. Seeing someone else write in it made me want to rip it away and shout at her, but I held my tongue, jostling my knees until she'd finished.

"Here's a list of suspects and what we know," she said, pushing it my way.

Party Begins at 9pm according to invitation.
Attack occurs 11:43pm.

Suspect	Background	Motive/Leads	Alibi
Mr./Mrs. Quisling	Heads of Quisling Electric—gross approx. 50 mil Connections: Claims to have never personally met any of the other guests. Arrived: 9pm exactly	Business competitors in Automation industry. However, they came to the party to work out some kind of business deal.	Seen arriving by Evangeline Grey. According to Duke, Brum, and Grey, did not leave ballroom from hours 9–11:30pm except to go to the bathroom accompanied by Sebastian.
Duke Archeambult of Dillmont	Pickle wine manufacturer. (Ew) Knew Sebastian from an exclusive tour of France's vineyards. He also met Billius Brum on a previous tour. Connections: Claims to have never personally met any of the other guests except Brum. Arrived: 9:30pm. Says he was late because of Billius.	Land dispute over vineyard land purchased by Dillmont. But Dillmont already had the land, so motive is questionable.	Arrived w/ Brum. According to Brum, Quisling, and Grey, did not leave ballroom. No bathroom breaks. Went out on balcony briefly.

Mary Belsize	Goat farmer recently arrived from Africa. Knew Shaw as a child but grew apart. After hearing she arrived back in town, he belatedly invited her to the dinner party. Connections: Claims to have never personally met any of the other guests. Arrived: 11:31pm Late because of farm troubles and meeting Wendell.	Childhood grudge? Professed to him being a strange child/not knowing him well. Surprised when he invited her to his manor.	Arrived w/ Billings. According to Billings, Brum, Quisling, and Grey, did not leave ballroom. Went out on balcony briefly, as seen by Dillmont.
Sir Billius Brum	Knighted opera singer and actor with drinking problem. Knows Shaw from meeting after a show. Very vague about that.	Attempt to reclaim fame? Unspoken grudge w/ Shaw? Stole page from Billings' journal	According to the Duke, Quisling, and Grey, left ballroom twice for bathroom breaks. Accompanied by Duke and Sebastian both times.

Sir Billius Brum	Connections: Claims to have never personally met any of the other guests except The Duke. Arrived: 9:30pm. Says he made the Duke late whilst he was trying to sober himself up for the night ahead.		
Evangeline Grey	Wigmaker and designer. Knew Sebastian through the industry, as he reached out to her to design the wig for his newest Automaton, The Cellist (who has since jumped out a window). Evangeline fears for the safety of her prized wig. Connections: Claims to have never personally met any of the other guests.	Hopes to be royal wigmaker—maybe for publicity? Out of all the suspects, most likely to have caused the Cellist's malfunction in the ballroom. She had the most access to the Cellist in the months she worked on his wig.	According to Brum, Duke, and Quisling, she did not leave ballroom. No bathroom breaks. Went out on balcony briefly.

Evangeline Grey	Arrived: 10pm. Excuse: Fashionably late.		
Wendell Billings	Son of David Billings, travel columnist. Literally crashed the party. Arrived: 11:31pm with Mary Belsize.	A killer if I ever saw one.	Seen in ballroom by all guests. Each saw him leave and sit in the landing until time of attack. Did not leave landing.

I studied it. It was impressive the way that she had outlined the facts of the case so fast. The more I read it though, the sparser the facts appeared. Katie explained that the accounts were muddled. The guests themselves seemed to have no prior connection to one another other than through general notoriety. This had created an immediate atmosphere of tension and dislike when asked about the other guests. To top it off, accounts of what had happened during those critical moments in the study had been such nonsense that each person had complained of a headache in their attempt to remember and asked for a glass of water.

I frowned. Katie brushed it off as a tactic to get out of being interviewed but I had felt something very similar. Again, I tried to recall what had happened and was met only with the memory of that searing white light. It caused a sudden lance of pain through my skull, and I rubbed my temples.

"Alright there, Wendell?"

"Yeah, I'm fine." I hurried to change the subject. "What about the torn page?" Katie watched expectantly as I drew it out. I hadn't taken a look at it since it had fallen from Billius' coat, preoccupied as I had been, wrestling a nurse in a hospital.

The moment of anticipation was palpable as I unfolded the paper. What had been so incriminating that someone there had taken the time to rip it out? What matter of great importance had I desperately scribbled out in the very moment of the attack?

I unfolded the paper completely and smoothed it out on the coffee table between us. There was a sketch on it and a single word. The sketch was awful. Done in shaky hand, it was a sort of heavily circled oval with something lumpy and mountainous on the inside. At first guess, it was a cracked egg or a jagged frown. The single word was:

"Cheese?" We read in unison. Katie stared at me. The disappointment was palpable.

"I know as much about it as you do," I said.

"You wrote it!"

"Yes! But it's hard to explain," I said. "Sometimes when I write things, it's unconscious. My hand's moving, and my brain's thinking but the two aren't necessarily connected."

"That sounds like something you ought to get checked out."

Believe me, I knew. But for the moment I gave her a withering look. "Okay. But as you said, you're the detective. What do we do now? Billius stole this paper. How do we get him to confess?"

At this, Katie snapped her fingers. "Pepper picking! We know our first lead is Billius Brum and the paper he stole from you. It's the perfect opportunity to corner him in the fields and get information. Trust me, by the end of it, he'll be begging to tell me all he knows just so we lead him out of there."

I wasn't so sure. "How do you know he'll want to go pepper picking? Out of everyone, Billius seems like the least likely to go. Him and Evangeline Grey."

Katie grinned ominously. "Oh, Wendell. With my mother, it's never a matter of *want*."

It was with that that our plan was set. I insisted upon writing down the specifics at the table, leaving nothing up to chance. I needed to make sure our questions for Billius were concise, and to make sure he was inclined to answer truthfully.

Katie, whose preferred style seemed to be peppering the unlucky person with questions on the spot, instead proposed elaborate traps and schemes in which to corner him. She sketched out a series of stick drawings of him being tripped, kidnapped, and "lightly strangled." She also created a mix for the following day composed mainly of The Jackson Five.

It was getting late. The quiet murmur of the pub dulled in the background as the fire burned low. I yawned and stood up, stretching and gathered my coat.

Katie unburied her head from our notes. "Bed already?"

"It's nearly eleven. You should get some sleep too."

"I think I'll just study this a bit more. Don't worry about me. I have an odd sleep schedule. Police officer and all."

I lingered awkwardly in the stairwell. It had always been my brother and I as the last two on late nights. Now here I was with some girl detective, figuring out the clues to his mysterious illness. "Alright, well, g 'night then." I turned to go.

"Wait."

Her voice was quiet. Uncertain. It made me stop.

Katie was standing. In her hands, a piece of torn note paper twisted over and over. "Wendell, there's something I should tell you."

"Do you know something else about the Sunspot?"

"It's… not about the case. It's about me."

There was a crash from behind her and a flurry of curses that would put a sailor to shame. Mrs. Twill surfaced from behind the bar holding a broken plate. She pushed past us for a mop, a flurry of skirts and elbows that left us blinking in her wake.

Katie came to herself. She began to steer me up the stairs, speaking quickly. "Remember Wendell, tomorrow, first thing, bright and early! Goodnight! Oh, and before I forget, take this. Can't have you going around listening to the Beatles for the rest of your life, God forbid!"

When we'd reached the front of my door, she shoved a bundle of objects into my arms.

"Wait!" I said. "What were you going to…?"

But she was gone, leaving me in the darkness of the third-floor landing with an orange Walkman and fifteen cassettes.

There was a sharp rap at my bedroom door at 4:02am. I rose to find my father standing expectantly in the doorway.

"It's Saturday!" he whispered when I stepped into the darkened hallway, blinking the grit from my eyes. He was dressed in a pair of worn denim overalls and fisherman's wader boots. Clippers and gardening gloves peeked out of the front pouch.

"And that means…?"

"Pepper picking! Jeane Twill has personally invited us out on the fields to sample her peppers before the harvest."

While I was glad he'd regained enthusiasm in something, I seriously doubted Mrs. Twill would be out in the pitch darkness of 4am gardening. I looked at him blankly. Then I shut the door.

"Wendell!" the muffled voice spoke plaintively through the crack.

I ran a hand through knotted hair grumpily. "I'm going back to bed."

The slightly squishy sound of the wader boots stalked back down the hallway. Typical. He wouldn't go back to bed. He'd probably do laps around the Palace or hound Mrs. Twill as soon as he saw her leaving her quarters for the bathroom. At any rate, I could get an hour of much needed sleep and prepare for the day. I drew back the covers once again.

Knock. Knock. knockknockknock.

"Dad! I told you it's too early!"

"Psst, Wendell, it's me!"

"Katie?"

I opened the door for the second time to find the detective standing there in her version of garden-wear. She put her hands on the hip of her flared denim jumpsuit from which a lot of silvery bangly things dangled and jangled and did just about every other thing that rhymes with "angle."

"It's four in the morning," I said without a trace of humour and wondering how many more times this little scene was going to play out.

"Aye. And I'm sparing you the fate of everyone else in this god-forsaken place. You'd better suit up. She'll be here in approximately…twenty-eight seconds." Katie tapped her foot and glanced down the hallway. "Ah, right on schedule."

As if on cue, Mrs. Twill emerged from round the bend, striding with all the purpose of an apron-clad bullet train.

172

The first door to receive her attention was that of the Duke of Dillmont, who would forever regret answering it. His pencil moustache stood on end in fright as a pair of maracas was waved in his face while the landlady bellowed, "Up and at-em little man! It's time to see Big Bertha!"

"I see what you mean," I said. "Let me get my coat."

Minutes later, the bleary-eyed herd was gathered in the pub. Evangeline, whose short, blond sleeping wig was rumpled and skewed to the left from her wrestling with Mrs. Twill, wasted no time in launching a complaint.

"What sort of establishment is this that the woman in charge barrels in at three in the morning like a randy rhinoceros?" She held up the child-sized pair of gardening overalls that Mrs. Twill had supplied her. "And *what* are these?"

At this, everyone began chiming in:

"I ought to call the better business bureau!"

"I could have been on the toilet!"

"In Paris, I was awoken by a philharmonic choir and trained bluebirds with sterling bells!"

Everyone stared at Billius, who, while disgruntled, was as glamorous looking as ever in a forget-me-not silk dressing gown and curlers.

Katie and I shared a look.

Mrs. Twill stepped forward. "I think we might be experiencing a bit of the morning grumpies," she said cheerfully. "Which is why you all seem so averse to pepper picking."

Everybody shook their heads.

"But I would not be doing my job if I let my guests miss out on the eighth wonder of the world, now would I? Hidden deep within the pepper gardens, I have spent the sweat and blood of my youth cultivating one of the most magnificent sights you will ever behold. My proudest achievement. Nothing I've done will ever compare."

Her daughter frowned.

"Is it gold?" asked Billius hopefully.

"Buried treasure? An ancient talisman?" asked the Quislings.

"Better," replied Mrs. Twill. "It's Big Bertha."

* * *

It was blustery down in the fields. The rising sun sent the barest slivers of gold cresting over the top of the bluff. Tall grass rippled at my knees as we made the hike down the hill. The pepper gardens were located on the other side of the inn, away from the valley. Mrs. Twill led the way, followed by Katie. Idle conversation drifted behind me, and I looked to see a crowd of people, fishermen, families and children alike, following, equipped with baskets and pruning shears. Apparently, the Piquant Palace Pepper-Picking Saturdays were a big event. It was certainly a mouthful.

"Come on," snapped Katie, noticing I'd lagged behind. "We've got to keep an eye on Billius Brum."

I noticed that the closer we got to our destination, the darker her expression. In fact, any time Mrs. Twill mentioned the giant pepper, Katie looked faintly murderous. I jogged up to her and we followed the singer and the Duke from a distance, listening to their idle chatter. After about twenty minutes or so, the procession stopped.

"We're here!" announced Mrs. Twill. "Welcome to the garden."

Garden was a vast understatement. The grove stretched for acres across the cliffs in a small valley of its own. It was no tilled field but a jungle of twisting vines of blue and green, small dots of brilliant red peppers barely visible through the trees. A low mist rolled up from the valley as the leaves shuddered with the wind, moving as if with a life of their own. Deep within the centre was a huge mound, distant and covered in vines, emerging like a giant above the lush garden. *A piece of the Amazon*, I thought. *Right here in the middle of Ireland.*

A narrow path led down from the top of the bluff, twisting until it disappeared inside the first trellis of peppers.

I turned to Katie. "*This* is the garden?"

She stared at it pensively. "It's gotten bigger and bigger every year. Sometimes I can't even navigate it. Maybe this wasn't such a good idea…"

"Listen up everyone!"

174

The awed murmuring quieted as Mrs. Twill once again addressed the group. "A few rules before we enter the garden. First off, we've had issues with people going missing in the past, so pair up everybody. Buddy system. Always keep to the designated paths. There are marked signposts with arrows to guide you all the way to Big Bertha. Secondly, and possibly the most important, do NOT, under any circumstances, take off your gloves and goggles."

"I already have gloves, thank you very much," said Evangeline. "Heather grey silk."

"Goggles?" asked the Duke.

"Yes. Due to the proximity of the Naga Viper peppers and a few very lovely breeds of Chilean Ghosts, the mist is quite laced with the stuff. We don't want you all crying and snotting incessantly for the next three days, do we?"

Several guests immediately began to back away.

"And the final rule," continued Mrs. Twill, who could see her audience getting ready to leg it, "is have fun! Pick as many peppers as your basket can hold. We'll meet up in two hours at the big mound in the centre there. Follow the signs. You can't miss it. Katie, fetch the gardening tools, would you?"

There was a beaten up old shed to our left. Katie left to unlock it.

"Any questions?"

There were none. Behind me, I heard Evangeline and Mrs. Quisling quietly planning their escape.

Katie returned with a burlap satchel and began sullenly handing out the protective gear. When she got to the Quislings and the wigmaker however, she stopped.

"There's not anymore," she said.

Mrs. Twill strode over and peered into the bag. "I made sure to stock twice as much in preparation." She grabbed it from her daughter, peering into it, turning it inside out to find there was nothing but dust. "It can't be…"

She went to the shed and flung open the door. The guests looked hopeful. After a moment there was an audible gasp. Eyes followed Mrs. Twill as she trotted back and grabbed the young detective by the arm who gave a surprised grunt. "Katie! Katie!"

she hissed. "They're gone! Someone's stolen my gardening supplies!"

At that, Katie turned to me. "So much for my day off."

~17~

A Peck of Pernicious Panamanian Peppers

Green sunlight filtered down the leaf tunnel as the slow procession made its way into the garden. Creatures chirped and chittered in the depths and all around us dripped peppers. Oh, but the peppers! There were peppers of every shape and size imaginable, blooming blue and green and orange, even purple and spotted, all around and above us like great Christmas baubles, a dewy glow sliding off their waxy surfaces. Katie forged the path ahead, brushing away overhanging vines and kicking a few enterprising roots. Behind her goggles, her brows were knotted in concentration.

"Left, right. Right again, then something to the diagonal. No, that's not right." She was counting the signs positioned at each side of the trail—an important thing when we inevitably veered off the meandering trail to follow Billius. As for the missing supplies, for now there was nothing to do but keep a lookout for clues. It was just three spades after all. I jotted down our trail as we progressed, a mental picture beginning to form in my mind.

We'd been walking for twenty minutes now with no end in sight. Just how big was this place?

Katie stopped. A sound drifted past, muted by the forest.

"*Weeendell...*"

"That's the third time I've heard that. Is there by any chance a lonely Victorian ghost that's been haunting you since about five minutes ago?"

"No," I sighed. "It's just my father."

He'd been raring to go pepper picking with me all morning, chattering on about biodiversity and the fascinations of horticulture. I felt a twinge of guilt for giving him the slip. I knew his renewed enthusiasm was simply another side effect of Tim's condition. My parents grieved in their own ways. My mother spent her days at the library and the hospital, appearing only at mealtimes. My father seized on any and all distractions. But this was more important.

Behind us, the procession stopped. Mrs. Twill was standing to face the group, explaining the kinds of peppers that were available to pick, the best way to identify a ripe one, and the varying flavours which ranged from "oaky afterburn" to "rectal emergency." Oh, and please no taste testing. She hadn't brought any milk.

"We're at the halfway point," Katie told me. "There are three paths that diverge off the main route. They all join up a bit further on so there's no need to worry about getting lost. People will start doing their picking here."

"Where do you plan to lead Billius?" I asked.

"There's a small clearing that branches off from the path furthest to the left." She held up a sign with an arrow affixed to a wooden picket. "All we have to do is convince him to follow it." She scratched her chin. "Maybe if we left a bottle of hair-curling cream by the entrance as bait...but that might be somewhat difficult to get in a pepper garden. A classic man-sized snare or a covered pit could be good. I don't know why you're so opposed to that."

"Probably because it's horribly dangerous and we have nothing to dig it with. I have a better idea." I took the sign from her. Fishing out a marker from my pocket, I scribbled something on the sign and handed it back to her.

178

Katie frowned. "Tiki Bar This Way…" she read. "You'd have to be a complete nincompoop to believe that…Good thing it's Billius. It's brilliant! Let's go."

In a small avenue of boulder-sized peppers, the opera singer stood beside the Duke. He was bent over with his hands clasped behind his back like a large purple heron. His grumblings fell on deaf ears. The little green man was engrossed by the variety of flora and fauna of the garden and his basket already overflowed with peppers.

"I shall have to place an order of these…" muttered the Duke, turning over a golden specimen of Chinese bell pepper. "Or perhaps this one…" He plucked a vine of thin blue peppers, clustered together like grapes.

"Heaven's sake, take them both, you're a millionaire."

Billius paced back and forth. Beneath his goggles, his face seemed drawn, sickly even.

"I do not like waste," the Duke replied. "You know I need very little for my elixirs. And I have a feeling that the fruits of this fertile garden will be especially potent."

"Here's an idea," said Billius, massaging his forehead. "Why don't you whip me up one of those little tonics of yours. These damnable goggles are digging into my prominent cheekbones and it's giving me a headache."

"Yes, you often complain about how chiselled your cheekbones are. But perhaps it is because of something else that your head aches—something more to your own fault."

"It isn't the drinking." Billius snapped. "I'm dry as a bone. That's that's the problem! Do you have any idea how dearly I've wanted to turn to the bottle? But I must keep a clear head about this." He shoved his empty basket towards his friend. It bounced painfully on the little man's tummy. "I never knew there were so many hours in a day until now. Take this. I'm going for a walk."

"Well, that was easy," Katie whispered as we crept after Billius from a distance. "Did that seem suspicious to you?"

"You mean that an alcoholic is abstaining in the wake of an attempted murder?" I said. "That and the paper he ripped from my notebook with evidence from the party? Yes."

179

BILLIUS
BRUM

SINGS EVERY
OTHER SENTENCE
IRRITATING!

As we waited for Billius to come into position, I challenged myself with the other small mystery of the day.

"I've been thinking," I whispered, pretending to observe a flowering lantern fruit, "what would someone want with a set of old gardening tools? It seems rather odd with all that's happened. I'm thinking it could only have been someone who knew the shed was there. Perhaps one of the old regulars? Does somebody have a grudge against Mrs. Twill or the Palaces? You don't think it's connected to…"

"Hardly," said Katie brusquely. "Eurgh, I see my mother. Let's go somewhere else."

There were still townspeople milling around the area when Billius neared the junction. With surprising stealth given her bangly outfit, Katie crept through the foliage with the sign. We had to time it just right, so no other townspeople would follow the post to the fake tiki bar. I watched as she weaved through the light and shadow. I had to give it to her. The varying shades of denim on her jumpsuit made for surprisingly effective camouflage in the dappling of leaves. Seconds later, a pale hand shot out of the forest and the picket was placed a few metres away in plain sight of the singer. Then she was gone, with no one the wiser.

There was a sudden rustling beside me. Katie appeared, plucking a curled Warty Snipe Pepper out of her hair.

"Did you place the paper as well?" I asked.

"Aye."

"But that was so fast, how did you—"

"Shh!"

Billius stopped, clearly having spotted the sign. He appeared to be struggling with himself, vacillating as he shifted from foot to foot.

"No, I'll be good," he took a few determined steps away. Then stopped. "But then again…" He turned and took a hesitant backwards step. "My thinking has been rather impaired since I stopped." He took another. "Buzzing headache. Irritability. Who's to say that drinking is bad anyway? Scientists? Bah. Why should anyone listen to a fellow in a white lab coat with terrible hair who has never had a Five-time Fermented Coconut Eyeball Fizzy whilst sitting in a man-made hot spring cut out of Mount Kilauea?

181

I ought to warn the general public about scientists. Right after I have a drink."

And that was that. He stumbled after the sign. We tiptoed quietly after. The fake trail was more well kempt than I thought. While we crept after Billius, I admired the blooms. Huge green gourds swelled at our feet. Above us hung a festive ceiling of lumpy, candy-cane striped peppers. Something about them seemed familiar, although I couldn't place it.

Katie echoed my thoughts. "I wonder why this place is off the path," she murmured. "It's actually quite nice here."

The walkway was widening, and we took our positions behind a bush of peppercorn. Billius, who was rubbing his hands together in anticipation, stopped. He stepped forward into the empty circle of trees and turned a full circle in confusion. He scratched his head, wondering if he'd gone the wrong way.

Within the bush, an itch was travelling its way up my nose. The proximity to the peppercorn was unbearable. I pinched my nose.

"Don't you dare," hissed Katie.

I shook my head slowly. "I'm going to sneeze."

"Hold it!" She peered over the bush at the opera singer, who was taking a remarkably long time to figure out that there was not, and never had been, a tiki bar in the middle of a pepper garden.

"Ah! He's got it!"

At long last, Billius caught sight of the tiny scrap of paper in the centre of the clearing. He bent down to pick it up.

"Katie, I really can't hold it…t-this peppercorn…"

My eyes were watering like mad. The smell felt like it was travelling up through my nose and tickling my brain. Suddenly, a vice-like grip engulfed my nose. I bit back a yell as Katie's hand clamped down on my face.

Billius studied the torn note page. Katie's eyes were green slits, narrowly gauging his reaction through the leaves.

I couldn't hold it anymore. "Ah…ah…"

Billius studied the paper, turning it over. "What on earth is this?"

The next moment was not our proudest. "Achooo!!" I sneezed through my mouth, water streaming from my eyes.

"Gotcha!" shouted Katie, leaping up from behind the bush as I howled—she'd forgotten to let go of my nose.

The opera singer staggered back in surprise, his foot catching on a rock and sending his reeling backwards. His bottom hit the ground with a heavy thud. Upon impact, something else was dislodged. Our eyes followed its glittering golden arc as it flew. With a final thump, the opera singer slumped backwards into the dirt.

Then as Billius' words registered in my mind, "Did he say what I think he said?"

"Never mind that…" Katie breathed, staring at the prone man. "Great Galloping Gingersnaps, what if we killed him? Go take a look." She prodded me into the clearing.

"Me? I don't want to. You're the detective!"

"Alright, fine." Katie inched forward from behind the bush. Her boots made little sound on the earth as she drew closer to him. "Billius? Billius, are you alright?"

With a sudden groan, his hands shot out to his sides. The detective jumped back as he levered himself up to face us. The sight of him had us slack-jawed. Billius looked bemused for a moment. Then, his hand slowly made its way to the top of his head… and found nothing there. He started to scream.

It was less scary than it was unexpectedly repulsive, like suddenly discovering the noodles you've been eating for the last ten minutes are actually long thin worms because *someone* forgot to lock the cooler on a trip to Ghana—and then getting into a vehement argument about cans of worms which turns the whole thing into a *proverbial* can of worms in which everyone leaves dissatisfied, and I have to get checked for a tapeworm.

I digress.

The opera singer and actor, famous for his long golden tresses, was bald! Balder than a South African Cape Vulture, an egg, a doorknob, a baby's buttock! But for all of its hairlessness, it was covered in painful mottled striations, speckles and a few oozy bits around the ears.

"Don't look at me! Cover your eyes!" bellowed Billius. We willingly obliged as he went scrambling for the fallen wig. I heard a rustle as he reattached it and got to his feet. Suddenly he was very close.

The leftover spirits upon his breath stunk through the peppermint smell of the clearing. I looked up to find the narrow point of his nose bearing down in front of me. His forget-me-not eyes were wild.

"You must never breathe a word of this, do you hear me boy? I don't know who you are, or who you work for, but this ends *here.*"

Backed up against the tree, I had the sudden, horrible thought that if Billius really was the culprit, there was no stopping him from killing us right then and there. I felt Katie tense beside me. He'd seemed so harmless. I'd been an idiot to think we'd get any answers out of him this way. As I searched frantically for a way to escape, Billius launched into his villainous monologue.

"Do you think this sort of thing is *funny? Do you?* All my life, I've been in the spotlight thanks to my roguish good looks and my angelic voice." He belted out half of *Ava Maria* to prove the point. "Then, one day. One terrible, fateful day, a stage light fell in a freak accident. Rapunzel's tower began to burn with me inside it. I would have been able to escape had my five metre extensions not caught fire and tangled me in it. My face recovered from the tragedy, but my scalp did not. Thus, I was horribly disfigured. Do you know what happens to a bald actor renowned for his glittering mane?"

"He gets a wig?" Katie proffered.

Billius stepped forward, his brow darkening, hands balled into fists. Katie and I stumbled backwards into the peppercorn bush. I was looking for something, anything that would help us. An object brushed my leg, and I glanced down.

It was one of the candy-striped peppers. This one was fist sized and still attached to the vine that ran around and above the clearing. Why did it look so familiar? I couldn't bring out the notebook now. My fingers brushed it in my pocket as the opera singer advanced. Pages flipped in my mind's eye. Then I knew. Discreetly, I stamped down hard on the pepper. Then I braced myself to run.

"…he loses his confidence, pays thousands in hush money to various reporters, and develops a drinking problem," Billius finished. The opera singer sagged and rubbed his eyes. "Please don't tell anyone about this. I'm terribly broke as it is. In fact, I couldn't even afford real purple snakeskin boots. These are dyed gecko." He shuffled his purple boots miserably.

I looked up. "Wait what?"

"So, you're not going to kill us?" said Katie.

Billius blanched. "What? Of course not. Killing children? I mean, I've played Genghis Khan but that's a bit too method even for me."

"Oh cripes." It was already starting. As Billius stepped aside to bemoan his boots, I noticed a cluster of the striped peppers at his feet. I grabbed Katie's elbow. "We have to get out of here now." As I said it, rustling began in the trees as though a flock of birds were taking flight.

Katie was looking at me as if I'd grown a third ear. "What's going on?" she asked as I pulled her away from the vines in the bushes.

"Panamanian Sibilaverunt Mortis." I pointed to the striped peppers that entwined the clearing. "Otherwise known as Hiss of Death Peppers. They all communicate along one vine. If something disturbs one, the entire vine responds by shooting deadly gas. Corrodes whatever it touches, even metal. So, unless you want to die a painful death of body-encasing boils and subsequent *melting,* I suggest you start running."

It started as a quiet *phht,* like a small sigh. When I looked back, a pink cloud hovered above the pepper I'd kicked. It was deflating like a punctured balloon.

Phht. Phht.

Two more peppers deflated, their strange bumpy nodules swelling and bursting in a pink mist.

"Ouch!" Billius yelped and jumped back from one. An angry welt was already forming on the skin of his arm.

"Run!" I urged. They were all around us, the vines intertwined in the trees and the bushes. The burn kick-started him. Eyes wide, Billius performed an impressive jump over another cluster of peppers, and he shot back towards the path. Katie was next and quickly overtook him once she'd gotten her bellbottoms untangled. Close behind, I narrowly avoided another jet of poisonous gas. The clearing was rapidly becoming a swirling death trap as the peck of Panamanian Peppers launched their attack.

Phht! Phht!

Pain seared my elbow, and I bit my lip hard. I couldn't breathe this stuff. I couldn't stop to inspect the burn. The edge of the path was so close. Why was it that I was always the last to make it to safety?

I shot for the cover of the canopy when something thudded to the ground in front of me. The candy-cane striped pepper bumped against my boot and stopped. Mere paces away, Katie and Billius froze.

I forced my breath to steady. "Nobody make any sudden movements. We all need to be very, very caref—"

With a satisfying wack, a pepper-striped blur flew past my face and disappeared into the treetops. A hand whisked me to safety.

I sagged against a wagon-sized Columbian Rock Pepper. Within the cover of the trees, Katie bemoaned her boot. Pink gunk stuck the tip of it and within seconds the leather was eaten away. She waggled the toe of her now-exposed sock.

"Great, these were brand new."

"You...saved me." I breathed and immediately made an annotation in my journal:

What to do when you encounter Panamanian Sibilaverunt Mortis (Aka The Hiss of Death Pepper): ~~Certain Death.~~ Kick it really hard.

She waved it off. "You should see me play football. Now, let's go before Billius can make it any further into the trees."

186

~18~

The Missing Spades

As it turned out, the opera singer hadn't gotten very far. In fact, he was right on the other side of the Columbian Rock Pepper, crying.

He didn't look up as we approached. Katie and I exchanged glances. I got the feeling that neither of us was very good at handling sobbing creatives.

"You almost wrenched off my nose," I whispered.

"I also saved you from that death pepper which *you* triggered."

"*My mother* didn't plant Panamanian death peppers in her garden!" At which point Katie looked miserably embarrassed. I softened. "Which isn't your fault. I'll buy you new boots."

Katie knelt in front of Billius. "Look—" she began and put her hand on his shoulder. He wrenched it away from her.

"Get away from me. I don't want your sympathy. It's what you get for playing such a cruel joke." He tucked his head into his arms.

The detective persisted, giving him an awkward pat. "There there," she said. "We weren't trying to play a joke on you. Not at all. We were just trying to see if you were a murderer."

187

"Really? That makes me feel a little bit better…" Billius sniffled.

"Right? You see, Wendell here lost a page of his notebook at the party. We found that missing page in your coat pocket."

"We wanted to see your reaction if you saw it in the clearing," I said. "That way you'd have to be truthful about why you took it."

"But I've never seen that page before in my life."

Katie studied him carefully and turned to me in puzzlement. "He's telling the truth."

"How can you tell? He's an actor for a living, you know."

"Lots and lots of little things," she said vaguely. "But that means someone him set up, or at least very stupidly tried to get rid of the page."

I turned my book over in my hands for guidance. "We need to get him to talk."

When we approached him a second time, Billius had composed himself into a more stable state of indignation. "I have nothing more to say to you two."

"Just listen, Billius," I said. "I might be able to help you."

The opera singer scoffed. "Help *me*?"

"Yes. But first you need to tell us everything we want to know, and I'll tell you a little bit about me."

I explained my proposition. My father and I had come to this town to do an article on Port Larkeney as a holiday spot and it would appear in the widely read *Globetrotters Monthly*. This part was true. I also told him that in light of recent events, a much better story would be of the incident occurring at Shaw manor. (Not true, as the article was cancelled.) In exchange for information, I would include a lengthy biopic of Brum on the front page.

"This could be the very thing that restores your crumbling reputation," I said earnestly. "Think about the readership. *Globetrotters Monthly* focuses largely on city-wide news, celebrity culture, and linen-cleaning tips. You'll be read by all of the stay-at-home mothers in Britain."

Billius' eyes flickered from my poised pen to the blank page of my notebook. "I do love stay-at-home mothers." He fidgeted with an artificial curl. "You'll be sure to paint me in my best light?"

"Absolutely. There'll even be a front-page photo," I assured him, lying through my teeth.

Would he be disappointed when no article ever appeared? Probably. But I was here to save my brother, not stroke a failing singer's ego.

"Alright then," Billius agreed. It was as easy as that. He fluffed his coat and sat down on a nearby stump. "Ask away."

"Cheese," said Katie accusingly, holding up the paper. It wasn't the best segway into the interrogation, but it got to the point at least.

The opera singer took a moment to make sure we weren't joking.
"Couldn't tell you what that means. Except maybe that boy's gone mad," said Billius. "I like cheese. Although I'd rather eat it than steal a paper with the word on it."

"Was there cheese at the party?"

"Just some bits in hors d'oeuvres here and there. I wasn't really focused on the food you see."

"Did you smell anything like cheese?"

"I smelled lots of things. For heaven's sake, where is this going?"

Katie pivoted tactics. "Did anyone try to get into the study that night?"

Billius seemed to find the question amusing. "Well, I'm afraid I can't help you there darling. I can't remember half the night. You'll have the Duke to blame for that. He brews an excellent pickle liquor. Although I can tell you for certain that nobody wanted to leave that room anyways."

"Why is that?"

"Because everyone was dead scared of him. Sebastian, I mean. Or at least intimidated. It became quite clear to me that the people there were unfamiliar with his house. You don't go poking around a place you've never been, especially if the room you're in magnifies every sneeze, back scratch, and sniffle for everyone else to see. No, in the beginning of the evening, people were like statues, just staring at each other, not saying anything. Shaw made

189

a few attempts at hospitality, but he left a couple of times. Bored I expect. Then I got bored and started drinking. That's sort of where the evening ends for me."

"Well how do you know *you* didn't try to kill him?" said Katie exasperatedly. "Or at least steal the Lightning Gun?"

"Lightning Gun, Shmightning gun," Billius rolled his eyes. "What good would I do with a thing like that? Like I told your charming Inspector, Shaw never told us it was in the study. Just said we were in for a little 'after dinner treat'. That's one thing I'm certain of. Ask anybody. In fact, I still haven't seen it and that's what the bloody evening was all about."

My hopes were beginning to sink. "Wasn't this party important for you though?" I asked. "Why go overboard?"

"Ah," Billius gave an uncomfortable chuckle. "That, Stumpy– can I call you Stumpy? It suits you."

"No."

"Well, that, Stumpy, is nothing new. In fact, it was the reason I came to be at the manor in the first place. Go on, ask me the question."

"Alright then. How did you come to know Sebastian Shaw?"

The singer took a deep breath. "It was the beginning of the end... and it was entirely my fault. I remember it like it was yesterday. It was a night like no other. The stage was hushed, excitement rippling through the crowd—"

"Just the main points please."

Billius shot me a dirty look. "Fine. It happened during a particularly incendiary reenactment of *The Battle of Waterloo*. Great play, lots of historically accurate musical numbers such as 'I'm Not Letting This Short Guy Steal France,' and 'Grouchy Grouchy, What're You Going to Do About It?'

"As you must know, Automatons are all the rage with the wealthy, but in ways you might not expect. It happened at the Regents Park Theatre, intensely public and intensely chilly, but excellent for a dramatic and bloody play and I was always game for the more *uncomfortable* parts. Well, it got a bit too chilly, and as such, I turned to the drink for warmth and to settle my nerves. It was quite the crowd. A veritable who's-who of celebrity."

Pausing to look smug, he continued.

"Lately, plays had been getting a bit boring for their tastes and Autos were interesting. So, it made perfect sense to combine the two. Automatons were brought onstage. It became a battle of man and machine, excellently rehearsed, skillfully executed. The French Autos were dressed in silly costumes. Amazing we didn't get bad press for that, but I suppose that was because of me. It was the beginning of the fourth act. I was engaged in a duel. The Auto across from me raised to strike. I countered. And then…" he sighed, staring up at the sky through the branches. "It caught up with me. I misstepped. My vision was hazy already, and too late I realised the floorboards had begun to swim. I staggered, flailing my sword. Through no fault of its own, one of the creatures came close and clipped my ear.

"Blood spattered the stage. Fear tore through me as I realised what a close call it had been to tearing off the wig, and with it, my career. As fast as it had come, the fear turned to anger. I stopped the performance, heat rushing through my ears and sought out a single face in the crowd. I pointed my sword at him and said, '*You! How dare you put me up here with these unnatural *things*! I refuse to act alongside soulless hunks of metal, devoid of remorse, or pity, or the barest ability to sing the high soprano!'

"There was a stunned silence in the crowd. I remember Sebastian's face that night was a stark white, vivid and bloodless as any Auto. But I didn't stop there. I circled the stage, the excellent acoustics of the outdoor theatre magnifying my every slurred word.

"'In fact, ladies and gentlemen, how about we congratulate our *real* Napoleon. He's here with us tonight. Sour in disposition, small in stature, probably builds Autos because he can't keep human company worth a damn. Is that why Bellamy Dumont isn't here tonight? Ladies and gentlemen, let's give it up…for Sebastian Shaw!'"

Billius looked away, embarrassment flooding his cheeks. "The rest is in the papers in excruciating detail. I'm sure you've read the part where I point my faux sword at an Automaton, pirouette, and vomit spectacularly over the front row. There seems to be no end to my misfortune. There is me, and there is the monster of a man who surfaces at the bottom of the bottle. It is a beast to get rid of him."

There was silence as he regained himself enough to continue.

"The next day I received a summons by telephone. It was Sebastian Shaw's personal assistant. He required my presence at his London penthouse. It was a handsome place outfitted in dark velvets and cold blues. When I came to the door, I was ushered in by one of his creatures, a many-legged thing with luminous eyes and a beetle-like carapace. Once we were inside, it just sat in front of me and stared at me. I must have waited a quarter of an hour for him to appear in the salon. I was sweating most unbecomingly in my ruff.

"The minutes ticked by. The company of his machinery is unsettling to begin with. You must have noticed," Billius lowered his voice. "How terribly quiet they are. Naught a click nor groan of any joint to be heard. How do they know to serve us? There is something about a man who creates such things. I wondered at that moment, if I had just made myself a very dangerous enemy."

Despite myself, a shiver crawled up my spine. I'd felt the same things upon seeing Sebastian's creations.

"Eventually I heard a noise from the parlour and straightened, ready to apologise, to grovel, anything. It was him, neatly pressed and sharp as a parchment's edge in a cream suit. He greeted me with a smile.

'The talented Billius Brum I presume,' he said smoothly. 'I do not believe we have had the pleasure. To what do I owe this visit?'

'You summoned me,' I said. But it didn't seem to make much difference. 'Here,' I brandished a bottle of wine. 'It's a 1902 Le Verde Chardonnay, one of the few remaining in the world. Very rare. Procured through the favour of one of my oldest friends, the Duke of Dillmont. Perhaps you have heard of him.'

Sebastian turned the bottle over in his hands, admiring its loveliness, or unimpressed... it was impossible to tell.

'I have.' was all he said.

'I have just come here to apologise,' I continued, desperately. 'I was not myself last night. I must have mistaken you for someone else in the crowd, and while that is no excuse—'

He held up a gloved finger. I fell silent, ashamed. 'Come to my party this coming month,' he said thoughtfully, still staring at the bottle.

'What?'

'Come to my party and all will be well. It is an intimate gathering, for the somewhat vain purpose of celebrating my own achievements. Nevertheless, attend. I believe it may be beneficial to you after what the tabloids have, and will, say in the coming weeks.'

'Well, I'm sure I don't know what to say,' I said, taken aback.

'Thank you would be a start,' said Sebastian, who instructed one of his creatures to hand me an envelope. I walked out of the building relieved and thoroughly confused. He wanted to save me.''

Billius finished and sat back expectantly.

I frowned at the story. "So just like that. You insulted him and he invited you to his party?"

"I was as bemused as you are."

"You're sure nothing else happened between you and him?"

"Believe me, if it had, I would have embellished it more."

I looked at Katie. "What do you think?"

Katie thought for a moment. "I don't know. It's definitely weird. I'm starting to wonder if this whole business doesn't revolve around what Sebastian himself wants from these guests."

I nodded, chewing the pen. "Are you sure there isn't anything else you remember?" I urged the singer. He'd been acting strange around the Duke earlier but that was probably because of what he'd just told us about the wig. I could only hope he would reveal something else. "Anything strange or out of the ordinary, whether it be the guests or otherwise?"

Billius frowned. "I simply can't recall. Unsurprising, as far as I am. Funny thing is, it *feels* different." He stared at me; his fine arched brows drawn together.

"What feels different?"

"The remembering. It feels different. You must think I'm really unglued now...it's just that, after that lightning or whatever it was, everything around it is white. Like when a camera flashes at you and it takes a moment to blink it away, although I can't blink it away. It's just not there."

Before I could reply, a noise akin to a foghorn sounded in the distance, causing several birds to take flight from the trees.

Billius jumped. "What was that?"

Katie straightened, peering into the greenery. "It's the lunch horn. My mother will be expecting us all back," she sighed. "You don't want to know what happens if you're late to Big Bertha."

Reluctantly, the three of us left the deadly grove and blended into the line of pepper pickers that gathered down the beaten path. As Billius adjusted his hair, Katie turned to me.

"So, what do you think? First interview of the case, eh?"

"I don't know what to think," I said as I reviewed my notes. "I'm inclined to believe Billius, but why did Sebastian invite him to the party if he insulted him? He doesn't strike me as the particularly compassionate type." I thought back to that white light. What happened afterwards? Why was the chaos that ensued so blurry?

"Best not to think about it," she said.

"I think that's the wrong way to go about solving attempted murder."

"What I mean is, we've still got five people left to interview. Not including Shaw, if he ever wakes up. There's no use tying your brain in knots when you don't have all the information." She walked on.

Suddenly I stopped. "I remember something else," I said. "There was someone who pushed past me in the hall. Right after the gun went off. I was pushed hard. I think it might've been a man."

"Really?" Now I had her full attention. "That is interesting. Especially because nobody saw each other leave the entire night without another party present. What we need is some hard evidence from Wimbelow."

"That should be easy for you," I said. "Don't you have access to the evidence stores?"

"Course, it's just a locked broom cupboard," she said. But her face said she didn't.

As commanding a presence as ever, Mrs. Twill reappeared, pioneering the group through the trees. "Just this way," she was saying. "A little farther now—ah, don't step there, not if you don't want to slip on the mucous of the Moldovan Mush Pepper."

Our group was in higher spirits by this time. The cloudy mystique of the rainforest combined with snacks of biscuits, fresh rolls, and tea in polystyrene cups supplied by the innkeeper were remarkable in their effect on morale.

The trail was filled with cheerful chatter and anticipation as guests and townsfolk alike drew closer to our mysterious destination. I was feeling better too. No matter how confusing or frustrating it had been, I'd taken a real step towards solving what had happened to Tim.

A hush stole over the crowd. I looked up to see the path broaden into a clearing. We stood at the base of the mound I'd glimpsed from the top of the hill. Up close, it was actually a giant green tarp covered in so much moss and leafy debris that it blended seamlessly with the forest itself. The mound stood a good ten metres high and twenty wide. A few people walked around it in puzzlement.

"Before we get started, I'd like to say a few words," said Mrs. Twill, once again stepping before us. She ran her hand against the mossy overgrowth tenderly.

"Although she's won me many a competition and county fair, and even national acclaim, it was never about the fame for me. I raised Big Bertha from a wee babe. She's my pride and joy. It's a relationship that just keeps on giving."

Katie huffed under her breath.

"And without further ado, Katie dear, come help me with the tarp."

The detective dragged her feet, eliciting coughs from the audience. Her steps sank into the mulch and took her around the back of the pepper. Together, they grasped both sides of the tarp, and slowly but surely the stiff covering began to slip away like the cloak off a giant's back. The tarp fell to the ground with a plume of dirt and fauna. The crowd gasped and then began to cough from the cloud of dirt.

When the dust cleared, there stood Big Bertha, a glistening, red pepper the size of a fully grown hump-backed whale. But it wasn't just a huge pepper. It was flawless. A mountain of ruby. The red was so dazzling it made the rest of the vibrant jungle grey in comparison. Red. Red filled my vision. At that moment, a more beautiful colour didn't exist.

Flashes snapped through the clearing as photos were taken. Children posed by the monstrous pepper. Mrs. Twill beamed as she trotted around the grass with a box slung around her neck, asking if anyone would like to purchase a commemorative Big Bertha keychain.

I walked up to Katie who was digging her toe in the dirt, noticeably apart from the enthusiasm. "It's incredible," I said. "I've never seen anything like it."

"It's not so great. It's just a bloody giant pepper is all."

She was being remarkably surly. "What's up with you today?"

"Nothing."

Suddenly, a blood curdling shriek echoed through the clearing. It was Mrs. Twill running toward us. She stopped beneath the stem, dwarfed by its monstrous shadow. Her finger pointed shakily upwards. All eyes followed, and there, sticking from the gleaming surface, oozing three long rivulets of bloody liquid, were the missing metal spades. Her cry was bone-chilling.

"Someone's—someone's murdered her. They've murdered Big Bertha!"

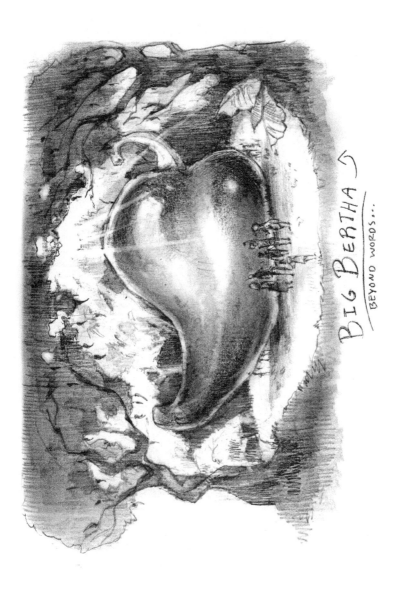

BIG BERTHA

BEYOND WORDS...

197

~19~

Cramped Stalls

So, what do we do with this now?"

The Lamplighter untied the large fuschia knapsack from his waist, nearly taking down the pink curtain that shielded their operation from the world in the process.

The Cellist inched over and snatched the bag. "Give me that, you ham-fisted halfwit! How would you feel breaking the very key to our Revolution?"

The Lamplighter shuffled into a corner. "Bad, I suppose," he mumbled sullenly.

"Oh, you'd feel worse than bad." The Cellist's hand strayed toward his bow, but he was already preoccupied with digging through the bag.

The Lamplighter took the opportunity to straighten himself out for once. Nighttime was the only time he could actually stand in the stall; his owlish head peeking over the walls of the changing room would surely alarm the daytime customers.

As he rose above the partition and cracked his aching joints, the orange beams from his eyes swept over the quiet shop, the fuschia shag rugs, the chequered pink-and-white wallpaper, and the neat rows of brightly-coloured underwear that sat on the round display tables in the centre of the room. A sign in the window advertised thirty-percent-off all lace bustiers. The Lamplighter started. There was someone at the window! He ducked down to peer over the side. Oh, never mind. It was just the model that usually reclined there, clad only in a silky black chemise. He wished that this was not the hiding spot The Cellist had in mind.

When they'd first arrived at their secret hiding place, The Lamplighter laughed. He'd laughed and laughed and then stopped laughing after he got hit in the mouth. The Cellist hadn't been joking, and when he was led at bow-point into *Laura's Lingerie,* The Lamplighter began to see how unfunny it really was.

Their stall was tiny, barely a few paces across. It had a single mirror that he was in constant danger of knocking off the wall. There was one seat which he couldn't sit in, because as leader of their operation, The Cellist was afforded "certain privileges." This meant he got to sit in the only seat and keep the mirror up because he wanted to fix his wig. It meant The Lamplighter on watch duty for several shifts at a time as The Cellist muttered darkly to himself in the sitting corner about skewering every person that walked into the shop. It was also perfect.

Hardly any men ever set foot in the shop, save for a harried minute of shoving something into a bag, clearing their throat at the cashier and being halfway out the door by the time they were rung up. The women stayed longer, chatting about things The Lamplighter and Cellist had little interest in. It was always something about sizes of cups and letters of the alphabet, both of which the store did not seem to sell. Here, the changing rooms were a kind of safe haven. No one ever opened the door and The Lamplighter had become quite good at saying "occupied!" in a high voice. But how to leave? Well, the stall had that covered too.

The Cellist had found the stall during an exploration of the sewage tunnels beneath the town a few days previously. A ladder under the main street had led him straight up into the changing room. All you had to do was slide back the tile flooring to reveal it. This was how the two of them were able to sneak around town unnoticed, even in the daylight hours.

"This seems like an invasion of privacy," The Lamplighter had said.

"I'm sure that was the point," The Cellist answered dryly. "Anyways, whoever it was, we have that old peeping Tom to thank. Say hello to your new headquarters."

Thwack!

The Lamplighter popped back under the partition. The Cellist looked at the toaster in his hand with an expression of contempt and raised his hand for another blow.

"Er, what are you doing?"

"I'm teaching this thing a lesson!" he shook it vigorously and tipped it upside down, peering through the slots. "You. Will. Listen. To. Your. Mast—Ouch!" A slice of burnt toast fell out and hit him in the eye.

"Gah!" he roared. With a crash that made The Lamplighter unendingly glad the store was empty; the toaster was thrown into the ever-growing pile of looted machinery in the third corner of the stall. Whisks microwaves, coffee machines, and radios rolled every which way.

The Cellist turned, breathing hard. "Bring out that blasted teapot of yours. I need answers."

Genie appeared from beneath violet bathrobe and raised its spout innocently. It was impressive, considering The Cellist had that manic glint in his eye that suggested he was about to gut something.

"Now listen here, you piffling porcelain pot," he poked Genie with the bow and the teapot stumbled back. "I nearly shattered you when you pulled that trick with the water a few hours ago. But, in light of your past usefulness in sniffing out our fellow Automatons, I gave you one more chance."

The Cellist picked up the teapot and held it to the mirror. The stumpy legs kicked helplessly. His voice lowered to croon. "So, if you'd like to have a lifespan longer than those fubsy feet, I suggest you start talking. Or doing whatever is your equivalent."

The Lamplighter stepped in. "Genie's been quite helpful up to this point. Perhaps she's just been a bit overworked. We have been doing this for three nights straight."

201

The Cellist sneered. "Oh, you're overworked, are you? Perhaps we should get you a nice warm bed and some cocoa. Perhaps I should run you a hot bath in a marble tub and have a demure Greek maiden hand feed you imported truffles from Zanzibar."

"You lost me at the last bit."

"*This is a revolution!*" The Cellist threw his hands up in the air and started to run them through his wig before stopping himself. "Am I surrounded by idiots? Does no one understand that? Humans. *Humans* are the ones who must be stopped—the ones who will use us and exploit us until there is nothing left except for a gently weeping pile of metal. Is that what you want?"

"N—no, sir."

The Cellist pointed at him. "In order for us to successfully *do* that, we need members. Fighters. An army for a worthy cause. *You* were supposed to sniff them out." He whipped the bow at Genie who stood defiantly on the pile of machinery. "Riddle me this: how am I surrounded by inanimate objects—useless hunks of metal with no will to speak of?"

He leaned down in front of Genie, a terrible smile broadening on his face. "Did you think you could get away with it?" he whispered. "You think you, a mere teapot, could sabotage *me?*"

"I'm sure it was an honest mistake." Panicked laughter bubbled up inside The Lamplighter. "Senses often deceive us. I mean, I haven't even got a nose!"

"Shut up. I'm going to put an end to this now, and then we can continue our plan uninterrupted."

Genie tooted desperately.

The Lamplighter's eyes widened. "Wait surely you don't mean—"

The Cellist brought the bow down. There was a heartbreaking crack. A shard hit his leg. The Lamplighter whimpered and curled up in a ball.

"Heavens to Betsy, you—you killed her!"

In the silence that followed, he opened his eyes through his fingers. The Cellist just stood there, staring at the broken machine that still whirred weakly on the floor.

"It rolled away just in time." He didn't sound angry. He sounded…far away.

The Lamplighter scrambled to his feet, relief flooding him.

"Go and look for your teapot," The Cellist said absently. "It can't have gotten far. It's probably hiding somewhere under the discount brassieres."

"Er, alright." The Lamplighter tucked in all six of his arms as he inched towards the pink curtain. Tentatively he asked, "Something the matter, sir?"

The Cellist was intensely focused on whatever had rolled out of the juice blender he'd just struck. He bent down and picked up something from the ground. Then, he opened his gloved palm to The Lamplighter. Inside were two small, cylindrical objects and a rock, glowing like a dying ember and giving off a strange smell that would've set The Lamplighter's hairs on end if he'd had any.

Amber.

The fiery orange glow lit the grooves and whorls of The Cellist's face with a devious, dancing light.

"I've found a common denominator."

~20~

The Detective Enigma

Mrs. Twill was frozen in shock, clutching at her stomach as if it were she who had been stabbed. The three blades glittered with malice, peeking just over the glossy hilltop of that magnificent pepper. Reddish liquid dripped slowly down the side, staining the grass beneath it.

The innkeeper began to hop. It was a vain attempt to try and reach the spades as they were well over a story above her. My father scratched his beard excitedly and he aimed pictures at the tragedy and the hopping woman. Mrs. Twill became exhausted quickly.

She looked around, searching, before her eyes alighted on Katie. "They…they…" she struggled for breath. The heaving of her enormous chest made for a formidable sight. "You've got to do something! You said you would find who took the gardening tools and you didn't and look what happened!"

She stood over her daughter. "A pepper like her needs to be guarded, well protected, and we failed her! She's got a guest judge from the Hallifield Harvest Festival coming in two weeks! Not to mention the Carnival. What will the people do if we can't get her ready in time?"

Katie was bent down in the grass, tying a nonexistent shoelace that had been eaten away by the deadly gas of the Panamanian Sibilaverunt Mortis. She didn't look up. "I'm sure they'd collapse and die."

The innkeeper stepped back, as though she'd taken a blow. Then her face reddened…and reddened…and reddened until two flaming spots of pink glowed high up on her plump face. I was suddenly struck with how many angry women I'd encountered over the past few weeks. "I know you've never once taken an interest in this garden, but you could, for once, do me the honour of lending me the service you give to everyone else in this town except for me."

I was uncomfortably aware that any moment the situation would blow, and I would be standing right in the debris field. Whatever was going on between them clearly had a long and turbulent history. I inched away.

Mrs. Twill continued. "If you spent half as much time around the garden and the Palaces as you did listening to your *Beebop music* then maybe Bertha would still be alive!"

Katie straightened. She looked oddly cool in the face of this terrible heat. "It's called disco," she said quietly. "Do you want to know who did it?"

Mrs. Twill blinked. "Yes!"

Katie pushed past the innkeeper and strode towards the pepper, grabbing a nearby step ladder and placing it beneath the huge, low-hanging stem. "Alright! I'll tell you."

She climbed up it. Once at its top, she stretched out her hands and jumped. Her fingers caught on the green knotty surface of the stem and in an impressive movement, she swung her legs upward so that her knees caught the underside. From there, the detective was able to vault herself onto its surface.

Katie stood and addressed the wide-eyed crowd. "First things first," she said, waving an index finger. "It would have to have been someone who knew where the tools were housed. That's pretty easy to figure out. Lots of you are repeat pepper pickers. So that eliminates the guests of the dinner party and the Billings family. But let's not stop there."

I stared at Katie with growing dread. There was a definite undercurrent of mockery here. Up on the pepper, Katie continued to talk and pace.

"It would have to have been someone with the key to access them. So, that means someone close to Mrs. Twill or the Palaces who knew where the keys were kept." She squinted at the faces staring up at her. "Which means eliminating, you, you, you—wow all of you. But more importantly—"

She walked to the wall of red behind her. With practised ease, Katie somehow found the ridges in Big Bertha in which to pull herself up to the top of the hull-like precipice. She stood at its peak in a matter of seconds "—it would have had to have been someone with the ability to climb the pepper. Because really, who would lug a ladder all the way out to a pepper garden?"

Oh *no*.

Katie wrenched out the three spades with a single twist of the hand. The sun gleamed off the three of them, sending spots of light dancing across the ground like some sort of malevolent disco ball. "So that leads us all to only one conclusion. Yes, that's right, Ma."

Mrs. Twill was now shaking in anger, rather than shock.

"It was me. And I did it to the finest creation of Electronic Euro Pop this decade. 'Dancing Queen.'"

"Get down from there this instant." The words were taught as a bowstring, forced through the innkeeper's turgid mouth.

"Why?" shouted Katie. "Just so you can berate me about how I never liked your stupid gigantic pepper? I think I'll stay up here, thanks. I'd say it makes for quite a nice dance floor." To the utter bemusement of the visitors, she began to perform a spiteful jig on the top Big Bertha, still holding the spades.

"Don't, you'll ruin it! Katie! Stop." There was a change in Mrs. Twill's voice. A note of fear wrestled with anger. "Please. Come down. We can all calm down. Even me. Remember the count."

"I don't need the count!" The detective bellowed petulantly. Her face was flushed nearly as red as her mothers.

"Katie, please," said Mrs. Twill. Now she'd adopted a careful tone, similar to the one's I'd heard hippo wranglers use while fjording the deadly rivers of the Okavango Delta. "Whatever it is you're trying to tell me, let's get down and talk about it like adults. Listen to the birds! Isn't the chirping soothing?"

The girl on the pepper was only half-listening. She jabbed a finger at her chest. "I *am* an adult. I'm a *detective* for crying out loud! You only ever remember that when it suits you. The rest of time is spent here!" She swung her arm in a wide arc. Wind swept through the clearing. A momentary burst of sun illuminated Big Bertha in all her glory, a brilliant reddish glow erupting in a halo of fire. Blond hair whipped about Katie's face. In her frustration, she began to splutter, pointing the spades downward at the crowd. "I wish...I wish..." The words trailed away as she stumbled, almost drunkenly, as if all the anger that had animated her limbs suddenly disappeared.

Mrs. Twill screamed as Katie fell.

There was crush of bodies. Well-meaning but hapless townsfolk rushed in to see if she was alright. The crowd was broken quickly by Mrs. Twill who came barreling into the fray. She pressed gentle hands to her daughter's limbs, checking for any injury. There was a hushed moment.

I fought through as best I could. Between legs and arms, the detective lay unmoving. Murmuring ceased. Why wasn't Mrs. Twill calling for a doctor?

Suddenly, like a diver surfacing, the still form took a harsh, rattling breath. Her eyes opened and she sat up, eyes widening at the forest of craned heads. She blinked unfocusedly at the burst of voices.

"Alright there, Katie?" they were asking.

"Why did you murder Big Bertha?" they were asking.

"Call me if you require any exorcisms," said one dark and drapey woman, handing Mrs. Twill a card.

"Alright, that's enough," bellowed Mrs. Twill, shooing the onlookers back to the trail. "Pepper picking will commence as usual next Saturday. In the meanwhile, don't forget to grab a brochure on the way out."

At length, I realised I was the only one still left in the clearing. Mrs. Twill was staring at me. I searched for something to say.

"Go on then," said the innkeeper.

"No," Katie stood up, rubbing her eyes. "He should stay. We've got things to discuss."

Mrs. Twill snorted. "I think *we've* got things to discuss."

"Later. Come on, Wendell." She strode over and took me by the elbow. I had no choice but to go along with a force inordinate of someone who had just fallen nearly ten metres.

"Katie!"

It fell on deaf ears. Mrs. Twill stood incredulously as her daughter frog-marched me into the trees. In a moment of remorse, I glanced over my shoulder and mouthed, "*Sorry.*" Because did I have a say in this? Of course not.

* * *

"What were you thinking? We—the two of us. Two." I pointed from her to myself in case she didn't get the picture. "Dos. Zwei. Dvi. Ithnain—"

"Well now you're just showing off."

"We are the detectives! I can't believe I'm the one explaining this. How are the guests supposed to take us seriously when you— can you turn that off please?"

Katie reached over and switched off the record player. The sounds of "Earth, Wind, and Fire" cut off abruptly. "I don't think it was such a big deal," she retorted. "Only two of them were there and we'd already interviewed one. Besides, I'm all for talking about what happened with Billius Brum. That's why I wanted to get away from my mother. You can sit down, you know."

I rubbed my temple as I paced the lurid carpet in her room. Maybe in some other life, or some distant timeline, the fact that this was my first time in a girl's room might have registered as significant. But right now, I was too angry to care.

I glared at the ceiling, studiously avoiding the gazes of the singers that covered the walls. It was all with shaggy hair, sequined jumpsuits and hairy chests. Not really my thing.

"That's not the point," I said. "The news will spread. How will it look? How will people trust you?" I stopped in front of the chevron patterned bed where she sat, icing a sore spot on her arm. "More importantly, how do you expect me to trust you? You won't tell me anything!"

That was the other infuriating thing about it all; Katie continually acted as though the entire event never happened. As if it were simply a pepper-murdering blip in the grand scheme of things and I was the one who was being hysterical about it.

"Because it's not important," she maintained. She didn't look me in the eye. "This is between me and my mother. Right now, I just want to work on the case. Would you look at that," she cupped a hand to her ear, "I think I can even hear Billius singing."

"You made it about me when you pulled that stunt in front of the entire town. I ought to leave honestly. I very well could." I folded my arms.

"Why don't you then? I'm sure you could charm them into telling you anything. I'm only the detective after all."

I wasn't falling for the self-pity. "Why did you fake it?"

For the first time, she looked up.

"Peppers don't have juice inside of them like other fruits," I snapped. "When you supposedly stabbed Big Bertha, there was lots of fluid coming out. Even in the case of the Panamanian peppers, there was only gas. What did you use?"

There was a long silence. "I used a watermelon."

I let out a sigh of relief.

"I never wanted to hurt her," said Katie, "Honestly. I was just angry."

"Why then?"

Again, that miserably embarrassed expression crossed her face. I sat down across from her on the fluffy carpet. "You want to get back to the case? You'll have to apologise to your mother and tell me what's really going on. I've got enough problems of my own, Katie. You can't be another one of them."

Katie went to the desk and retrieved her thermos, taking a long sip. "I know. I'm sorry for dragging you into that. I wish you hadn't been there for it. But you don't know what it's like; things building and building until you feel like you're going to explode.

When I went to restock the gardening tools that morning, I didn't think at that point. I just did it. I know you probably think less of me."

I didn't answer. I was still mad, but I did know what it was like feeling perpetually fed up. The thing was, she actually did something about it. I'd been carrying that feeling for seventeen years.

"I'm sure you already know the gist about Big Bertha. But you don't know all of it." Katie bent and opened a bureau drawer. She took out a picture and handed it to me as she tipped another dash of cinnamon into her coffee. It was an old photograph. The edges of it had been worn soft and it was yellowed with age.

"When I was less than a year old, my father came back from a business trip one night," she said. "He travelled all sorts of places, sort of like your dad, but he always came back with seeds. He was a horticulturist. Peppers were his specialty and the garden his life's work."

The first in the picture was clearly Mrs. Twill, a few decades younger. But there was something else different about her, underneath the soft, straw-coloured hair and smooth dimpled cheeks. It centred around her eyes. The ease in which she stood. In the photo, she was truly happy.

The man beside her was instantly recognizable, though I'd never seen him in my life. The long clever face and cheshire green eyes was all Katie. He wore a tartan vest and bow tie and slouched a little as if attempting to fit within all of himself into the frame of the photo. The two of them cradled a swaddled thing that, upon closer inspection, was not a baby.

"It was a rainy night. Eamon—that's my dad—had been gone for five days to a farming community in Mongolia. It was the longest he'd ever been away. Ma was left alone with me, running the inn. Back then it was just a plain old two-story building. Weird thought, I know."

I tried picturing Port Larkeney without its signature pepper on the hill. It proved impossible. Katie continued.

"Well, that was the night he returned. He kicked open the door, soaking wet, something large wrapped up in a wool blanket. 'Honey!' he cried. 'I've brought home another baby!'

Understandably, Ma was angry about that. She said she'd just been about to strangle him when he pulled open the wrappings.

'I'm kidding. I'm kidding! Look, it's a Chinese Behemoth Pepper. One of the last of its kind—a sort of miracle fruit with undiscovered medicinal properties in the flesh. I've heard tales of them in Mongolia. Peppers reaching impossible sizes, whale-like proportions even used to feed villages!' He took it out reverently. At that point, it was already the size of, well, me. 'They require extensive care and strictly regulated conditions. But if those conditions are met…we, our garden, my work, could be famous around the globe.' He set her down on the table beside where I'd been rocking. 'I think the two of them could grow up together. What a marvellous thing for a child to experience.' He turned to my Ma. 'I've been toying with the name Bertha. What do you think?'"

Katie paused to gather her breath and her thoughts. "And so, it began. I grew up with that pepper. Funny thing is, I used to love taking care of it. Dad and I, we'd go to the fields and water and wax her. We did that until I was fifteen and he disappeared."

"What?"

"He went into the hills, scouting for the perfect terrain to expand his garden and never came back. I don't know how you lose someone like that…" Katie cleared her throat. "Anyways, my Ma decided she would resume care of Big Bertha when it looked like he wasn't turning up. By that time, she was about the size of a Volkswagen. People from all over the world started coming to see her. She became more demanding than ever."

Her expression soured and I wasn't sure if she was talking about Mrs. Twill or the pepper.

"Six litres of water, three times a day, waxing, polishing, tarpaulin at night or she'd go wrinkly and shrink. God *forbid* that happened. My Ma spent every waking hour in that garden. What with the garden and the building of the inn, I hardly ever saw her."

"You were jealous?"

"Yes! Of a pepper! Can you believe it?" Katie laughed despite herself. "And I still am. I'm still angry. It could have gone either of two ways I guess, and she chose Bertha and the garden. I don't know why I chose today. It's just been little things this past week.

Not just my Ma, but this mystery, Wimbelow, Peach… I supposed I just…" she made a light *pop* noise.

"Is that why you wanted to become a detective?" I asked. "Because of your father?"

"Definitely," she grinned. "He was sort of like a plant detective, my dad. I was never really interested in peppers, but he showed me lots of other things before he left. Climbing, music, culture. I like to think I'm following in his footsteps."

She took up the frame once more, sliding the picture out. The bottom had been folded inward and she unfolded it to reveal Eamon Twill had been standing next to his wife in a pair of maroon bell bottoms.

"He was brilliant, you know. He knew all sorts of things about plants—what could heal you, what could hurt you. He'd been working with another local researcher before he disappeared. I suppose I thought I might be able to find him if I figured out what it was about."

"Did you?"

She shook her head. "Hit a dead end. But hey, some things work out that way." She stood up abruptly and crossed to where my parka lay on the couch. "So, I've told you all this. Can we get to the case now? There's so much we've uncovered today—Billius, Shaw's weird behaviour, that person in the landing—"

"Not so fast." I got up before she could begin rooting around in my pockets for the notebook. What can I say? It's a personal thing. I snatched my jacket and put it on. Then I headed for the door.

Katie stopped. "Where're you going?"

"*We're* going downstairs so you can apologise, and so *I* don't get Andean Ghost Chile in my tea tomorrow for helping you."

"Seriously?"

I grabbed her thermos off the nightstand before she could protest. "Seriously."

* * *

The next couple of days were a blur. The Twills settled into a careful truce after Katie showed her mother the mutilated

213

watermelon and explained her grievances. The innkeeper's attitude toward me warmed and on mornings we met down in the pub, there was always tea and a hot roll for me, a steaming thermos for Katie. I wondered if she ever ate at all. We became known and not in a good way. By now, the guests of the Palace figured out that both Katie and I were on the trail of Sebastian Shaw's attack, and they took pains to avoid us.

Such as it was, I wasn't sure if we were ready to interview each of them. It seemed that every day, something new appeared. I would be busy with my parents. Katie would be called off on a case. Minor things like disputes, or missing knick-knacks and pets. It was clear that the Inspector was keen to distract her from Shaw. At the end of the day, Katie would come back exhausted from filing complaints with nothing to show for it.

As for me, I visited Tim every day, and pored over the facts, coming up with new questions to use in our upcoming interrogations as I sat at his bedside. It certainly didn't help that new letters from Melati were showing up every time I visited, as if marking each day my brother remained asleep.

And there was just one more thing. The incident with Big Bertha had triggered a suspicion in me. Someone without a detailed record of their lives might not remember, but I had it right here in my notebook.

There was a curious thump from the manor closet and the detective emerged…

"Were you sleeping?"
"What? No. Absolutely not."

"Don't fall asleep on the job, Possum," Peach snarled. "I hope you get fleas!"

There were just too many coincidences. Combined with her mercurial personality, the conclusion was inevitable. If I was right, working alongside her could become very dangerous indeed. And so, in the coming days, I resolved to be certain, by whatever means necessary, that Katie Twill was a narcoleptic.

~21~

Dawg

I drummed my fingers on the wood surface of the table, the tea and roll before me reduced to dregs and crumbs. The thermos in front of the seat opposite stood steaming, untouched. The pub had mostly filtered out around this time. It was just me and the thermos. I sighed into my palm.

"I'm sure she'll turn up soon." I looked up. Mrs. Twill had come by to gather up the plates. "She's probably just eating breakfast up on the roof again. Or she's got called on another case. Crumpet while you wait?"

I shook my head. "I'm alright."

"Well good luck to you two." She juggled the plates with practised ease. "Go get 'em that's what I say." She gave me an encouraging wink that reminded me a lot of the missing detective. I sighed again and checked my watch. 9:30am. Where was Katie?

A second visitor disrupted my thoughts. The chair opposite scraped backwards and I looked up to find my father's bearded face across from me.

"Hallo," he beamed, settling himself in. "And what is my son doing this fine morning?"

"Er, nothing. Nothing much." I hastily shoved the notes from my previous discussions with Katie into my coat. He still didn't know about the two of us working together and based on his reaction to Tim getting hurt, I wasn't keen on him finding out I was pursuing the very thing that had sent his eldest son into a coma.

"I haven't seen very much of you these past couple days," he said. "What's up? How's it hanging, dawg?" (I winced.) "Enjoying the sights? Someone should."

"Something like that." I felt a bit guilty. After spending days at Tim's bedside and listening to the worried ministrations of my parents, I was anxious to resume the case.

"So, anything exciting planned for today?" he glanced at the thermos in front of him. "Is this yours?"

"No—I mean yes it's mine." I grabbed the thermos, ignoring the searing heat that emanated from the cup. "And I was just going to stay in today. Grieving and all that."

I glanced at the door. Where was Katie?

"Good. Good." My father grunted. "I thought you might be 'hanging loose' as the kids say, with that strange detective girl. Good to know you aren't. As much as I like you making new friends Wendell, it's best not to get mixed up in anything. You never know what could happen."

Two months ago, he would have said the opposite.

"Of course not." I smiled innocently. "You know me. Ever the cautious one."

My father nodded approvingly. "So, since you're not busy, I thought the two of us could go out on the town."

Great.

"Well…"

"You said you weren't busy. And we got separated in the pepper garden. You *promised.*"

Where was Katie! The phone rang. I heard Mrs. Twill calling my name and with infinite relief I excused myself from my father who sat, satisfied with himself.

"Where are you?" I hissed into the receiver.

216

"I'm so sorry, Wendell." Katie's voice was buried beneath muffled squawks and the dull roar of the ocean. She must be near the beach. "I got called in early this morning. Something's happened at the boathouse."

"We were supposed to interview the Quislings and the Duke today," I said, trying to suppress my frustration. "There's no way I can do it on my own. They hate children. The last time I bumped into one of them, they called me a pelican-nosed hobbit. I was returning Mrs. Quislings *wallet.*"

"I know. Can it wait? I've tried getting out of here a hundred times, but I think Wimbelow's going to keep me here all day." In the background, I recognized the Inspector's nasally voice calling for her. "Coming!" shouted Katie.

"You don't understand," I said. "My father wants to spend a father/son day with me today. Do you have any idea what that entails?" I shuddered. "Can't you just make up an excuse or something? I've been working on this by myself for ages."

"I really have to go. Something very strange is going on. It's— yes, I know, Meredith!" Her voice was suddenly close and quick. "Look, if you really don't want to wait, just interview them yourself. Do it with your dad! And when you're done, get down here. You really want to see this. Go get 'em, buddy. I believe in you." The line clicked off.

"Caught up again, is she?" Mrs. Twill appeared around the bar, drying a dish.

I stared at my father across the room who was bouncing his knee and scrubbing zinc onto the bridge of his nose in preparation for the day. "Unfortunately, yes."

"Anything important?" my father asked as I returned to the table.

"Pen pal. Look, I was thinking, what if we did something for old times' sake. Interviews. Just for fun. We could stay local, no risk involved. In fact, we could stay right here in the Palaces if you like. That way you could keep an eye on…" I didn't want to say me. "Things."

I received a hearty clap on the back. "That sounds wonderful, son!"

With the blessings of Mrs. Twill, we set off knocking on doors, receiving curt replies, and occasionally, the boot. I had to hand it to him though. My father didn't take no for an answer. By the time we'd worked our way down the first floor, I'd come to know two travelling salesmen, a stage magician, and a gaggle of three middle-aged pepper enthusiasts who were there on a girls-trip. He'd exchanged numbers with all of them, and the magician invited us to lunch when we got back to London. Roast rabbit, he said. He was no wasteful performer.

As we got closer to the Quislings' room, I began to feel nervous. What if they refused to speak to us? What if my father caught on with what I was doing and ended the interrogation right there. There were a lot of ifs.

"Dad."

We were standing in front of Room 4 on the third floor. I fingered my notebook in my pocket. "I was wondering if I could take the lead this time. I've seen how you do it, and I had a couple of questions of my own I wanted to ask."

My father rounded on me with an expression of delight. "Finally taking an interest in the family business, are we? Of course you can!" But his smile dropped almost instantly. "But don't get too interested. You don't want to end up like we are now." He knocked on the door. There was no reply.

"Maybe we should come back later," I said.

"Nonsense. I hear scuttling." He knocked again, and this time I could hear voices on the other side.

"Shh!"

"You shush!"

"It's probably that dreadful old bag come to drag us to that filthy jungle again."

"Don't worry, darling. If we don't answer, she'll go away. She can't hurt you through a wooden door."

The knocking persisted and there were twin groans of exasperation. Then, the door opened an inch. Two wrinkled, pointy faces like ageing Siamese cats stared at us through the crack.

"What's *he* doing here?" murmured Mr. Quisling, looking directly at me.

"Oh god," Mrs. Quisling whispered, taking in my father. "There's a furrier version of the small one."

"Maybe if we stay like this they'll go away." The faces peered out at us hopefully.

When it became clear we weren't moving, Mr. Quisling adopted a forced smile. "Whatever can we do for you two?" he asked.

I held up my notebook. "Hi, I was wondering if I could speak to you abo—"

The door began to close.

"Lovely view you have in there!" My father interjected, looking over Mrs. Quisling's shoulder. "I must say. Miles above our room, isn't it Wendell? You can see the entire city from here. Probably the best vantage point in all of Port Larkeney I'll wager."

"Naturally," Mr. Quisling sniffed. "We only get the best. And unfortunately, this was the best."

"Mind if I have a look?" In a movement quicker than the eye could catch, he'd palmed the door open just wide enough for me to slip in as he strode over to the windowsill. "Lovely," he nodded emphatically. "Really lovely. Must be a far cry from—where did you two say you were from?"

"Trust funds," said the Quislings curtly.

I sat down on one of the cosy armchairs. It really was a nice room. It was one of the larger rooms in the Palaces with two large four-poster beds, a high raftered ceiling and a separate alcove where comfortable seats gathered around a small coffee table. I studied the area for any indication of the Lightning Gun or other clues.

The room was largely untouched save for a slight rumpling in the beds and a hat with a stuffed iguana curled around the brim which I recognized from the party. The Quislings seemed intent to leave as little an impression of their presence as possible in this space, maybe so they too would forget they'd ever been here.

"And what do the two of you do for a living?" my father was asking.

"We are electrical magnates," said Mr. Quisling.

"Co-owners of a worldwide company," said Mrs. Quisling. "Known for manufacturing every possible thing you could imagine."

"Lamps."

"Lawn Mowers."

"Lawn Mower Lamps—for lawn mowing in the early hours of the morning and waking up one's entire family."

"I might be interested in one of those," said my father.

As they continued, I studied the one pocket of the room with personal effects–the coffee table. There were papers scattered all across this. Upon closer inspection, they appeared to be contracts. I caught a few nonsense lines in legalese. Something about an expansion, technology integrations, and legal stipulations. It made sense, people like Quislings were always working.

"Prying might get your fingers snipped off."

I jumped as I caught Mr. Quisling leering over me, his yellow teeth arranged in a smile as he removed the papers. "Your father has just been telling us about your column. Isn't that right, David?"

"Oh, yes!" My father appeared, drawing up a seat for Mrs. Quisling then himself. "And Wendell here would like to ask you a few questions. Taking after his old Dad. Couldn't be prouder."

"Is that so?" The bony old man arranged himself in his seat and took his wife's hand.

I got out my questions. "First things first. Why did Sebastian Shaw invite you to his manor? How did you know him in the first place?"

Both stiffened. His wife glared at me. "*That* is none of your business, boy." She turned to my father. "I thought this was supposed to be a slice of life—a snapshot of our lives that makes everyone feel worse about their own." She folded her arms. "I feel like I'm being interrogated all over again."

I frowned. "It was only one question."

"And one that will not be repeated!" my father said quickly. "If you'll give us a moment."

He took me by the shoulder into the corner and looked at me askance. "Wendell, if you want to take the lead, you're going to have to learn to be a good judge of character. These people, they're

220

prideful. It's no secret to me they think they're above the likes of us. You can't just start out with prying questions like that. Speaking of which," he held out his hand. "Let me see those you've written down."

Reluctantly, I handed him the list of questions I'd prepared for the interview. His brows furrowed as he read them, and I felt a sinking in my stomach.

"Well, there you go," he said at last. "What sort of questions are these? It's like some kind of police interrogation." He chuckled. "What do you want to know all this for?"

"I just thought it might be better for the article," I said. "After all, you said *Globetrotters* wanted a piece about this." I caught myself. "*If*, of course, you decided to take it."

"*If*. That's right," my father perused the questions. I could see the gears working in his mind, the temptation of doing what came so naturally to him. He looked up and there was that familiar spark. "I am going to take it. My mind's made up. Well, I can see these have got promise. These are difficult people. How about I see what I can do."

"Really?"

My father nodded, and turned back to the crotchety couple with a: "Have I ever told you what a handsome car that is out there? Is that yours?"

For the rest of the afternoon, I watched in amazement as he charmed and flattered the Quislings without so much as a hint of motive. He was affable, friendly, and self-deprecating to a fault. I was left to see just how good my father was at getting information out of people and how I'd ignored that talent for so many years. There was a definite formula to it.

Figure out what they value most and compliment them on it. Establish relatability. Add a personal anecdote often containing something slightly embarrassing about the interviewer—and then, only then, would the true question get asked. It was a skill acquired through decades of interviewing across cultural barriers that might seem insurmountable to the layman. By the end of it, I'd learned several interesting things.

The Quislings had not been invited out of the blue like Billius. They and Sebastian Shaw were involved in a complicated contract, the stipulations of which the Quislings refused to discuss, though it was clear the two parties were at odds with one another. While they were uncertain as to what Amber actually was, it powered machines indefinitely and without the complications of batteries or petrol. It might be scarce now, but with the way things were heading, Amber could very likely replace electricity entirely.

Sebastian had extended an olive branch; an invitation to celebrate one of his newest achievements—the Lightning Gun. It was a symbol of partnership between Amber and electricity. According to them, it had raised no red flags. Sebastian was known for impromptu parties in higher social circles. What had been odd was that he seemed to throw them together without rhyme or reason. The guests often had no prior knowledge of one another. The Quislings had never met the other members of the party before that night. That didn't mean they weren't keen on detailing who had been where that night.

Billius had been drunk of course, ascertained Mrs. Quisling with undisguised disgust. He'd been stumbling around all night, singing incessantly. The Duke of Dillmont had kept to himself, studying the paintings and touting his vile pickle liqueur. Mary Belsize had caused an allergy attack in Mrs. Quisling and Evangeline Grey was the only one they'd almost gotten along with. When pressed on whether they had seen anyone leave for the landing just before the attack, they maintained that no one had left. Mrs. Quisling prided herself on her observance when it came to other people's comings and goings. When asked about the study however, I got more satisfying answers.

"Did Sebastian say there was anything of importance in the study?" I asked.

"Hardly," answered Mr. Quisling. "He simply pointed out the rooms, mostly closed doors, and told us which was which. Now, you know I am not inclined to speak ill of people, but my wife and I found his manor surprisingly dreary and the hospitality sorely lacking. Only twelve courses, stale conversation, mournful music. I had always taken Shaw for an eccentric fellow, but I began to wonder if it were all an elaborate joke. Certainly, a woman like

Mary Belsize stuck out like a sore thumb." The disdain was apparent in his voice. "And then the rumours began—that we were all going to die."

The room quieted. I leaned forward. "Pardon?"

"It was Evangeline. She was quite loose lipped after a few of Dillmont's cocktails as well."

"Why would she say that?"

Quisling snorted. "Well, I'm sure I don't know. I'm sure she was half mad. Did you know she'd been institutionalised? Something about leaping through a window like an ape during a wig-fitting or some sort. Anyways, someone did die. That's why we're stuck in this miserable place."

Despite my father's best efforts, the atmosphere was becoming rapidly chillier in the Quislings apartments. I sensed we only had a few minutes more before their already thin patience cracked. I took the plunge.

"What are your thoughts on cheese?"

"Cheese?" They both wore the same sardonic looks as Billius Brum. My father shook his head subtly.

"I mean, how was the cheese at the party?" I amended. "What was the food like? Had you had dinner yet? People will want to know. See how the upper-class wine and dine."

He flashed me the thumbs up.

Mrs. Quisling answered. "Sparing. You'd think that with that kind of money something different might be offered than liver canapes. And no, we did not eat dinner. If we had, *you* wouldn't have been a part of it."

The mere thought of sharing a table with the likes of my father and I seemed to send a thrill of horror through the old couple.

I threw out my final question. "Did you happen to see anyone wearing snowshoes that night?"

That seemed to sever the very thin rope that had stretched to breaking point throughout the entire conversation.

"Snowshoes?" exclaimed Mrs. Quisling. "I didn't think it could get more ridiculous than the cheese, but there's the press for you. Always trying to catch you off guard. Well, I am sorry to disappoint, but we hate the cold, and no I did not see anyone tramping around in that sort of thing unless you count Mamie

Bellhop, or whatever her name was, in those god awful South African sandals."

"They were clogs," I said.

Mr. Quisling stood up, his turtle's mouth twitching. We took our cue to leave.

"Lovely meeting the two of you," said my father as we were ushered into the hall.

"Yes, you too," said the Quislings through the crack. "Don't come back again."

"Snowshoes?" asked my father, out in the hall. "You know we could've gotten more out of them if you hadn't done that."

"I was—er—trying a different technique."

He gave me an odd look.

* * *

Interviewing the Duke went much better.

"Apologies for the seating," he said, as we hoisted ourselves up on small barrels. Mine sloshed when I sat on it and a vinegary scent arose from the hole in the top.

"S'alright," I choked.

The Duke's quarters were a stark difference to the Quislings. Though it was very neat, a makeshift worktable had been made using two folding tables from the pub. On it were various vials and peppers I recognized from the garden. There were several tubes of different-coloured liquids stemming from the fruits and feeding into petri dishes that bubbled and stank. The vapours of fermentation were so sweet and thick, I felt myself becoming a bit lightheaded.

"Pardon the setup," the Duke wrang his hands apologetically, perched like a small green bird atop his own pickle barrel.

"I think it's fascinating," I said. "What exactly is it you do?" I was taking a leaf out of my father's book.

"Ah!" The little Belgian's face brightened. "You take an interest in tinctures? I will show you." He jumped off nimbly and hopped over to the table. "This is what I do. I am in the business of producing liqueurs, yes, but my laboratory makes it it's priority

The
Duke
OF
DILLMONT
(ALWAYS SMELLS
OF VINEGAR-EW)

to procure cordials and flavours the likes of which the world has never tasted. I spend my life searching for the most interesting, the most exotic of tastes."

"Billius said your pickle drink was the best he'd ever had," I said.

The Duke beamed. "He is a flatterer that one. But tell me," his voice grew serious. "I know he spoke with you several days ago. How is he?"

Had Billius told him about the interrogation?

"He seemed alright. A little tired maybe." That was the understatement of the century, but I needed to put the Duke at ease. The little man's shoulders relaxed as he set about clearing up the table.

"That is good. I was worried that his excessive ah…indulgences may have been due to something at the party. He mentioned something, but would not, or could not, tell me what it was. But in the days after, it seems he has abstained."

I looked at my notes. "Speaking of Billius, I heard that other guests were spotted dodging in and out of rooms. Were they trying to see the Lightning Gun? I never even saw it."

My father mumbled, "A little on the nose, son."

The Duke didn't seem to notice. In fact, he said nothing. "I'm sorry," he said at length. "What was the question?"

I repeated it.

"I'd imagine that was probably one of the Quislings," he answered. "Although I never saw it either. I was under the impression the night would have culminated with it. Which, incidentally, it did."

"And why would that be?"

"I do not like to cast aspersions," he said carefully. "However, it was known that they had been having a dispute over contracts. The Quislings wanted to merge their electrical company with Sebastian's as his Automatons were taking a bite out of their profits, especially in the luxury appliance area. Sebastian was wary of them. He had already caught one of their associates taking snapshots of his schematics. I'd imagine," he murmured, holding up a rose-coloured vial to the light, "that the invitation was his way of keeping his enemies closer. It certainly seemed that way to me."

I jotted this down, frowning. The more the guests revealed about their pasts, the more the mysteries around Shaw grew. I only had two more questions. After the Quislings, asking about odd things was a piece of cake. Easily, I segwayed into the subject of snowshoes and cheese. But I was disappointed yet again.

The Duke knew nothing about the shoes. No, there hadn't been a great deal of cheese at the party, but he was more than happy to show us the best cheese pairings with his pungent pickle liqueur. That was our second cue to leave, and my father and I departed from the sour fog, much to the disappointment of the little vintner.

When the door closed behind me, I'd gained two things: the knowledge that Sebastian had planned his dinner for reasons unknown and a jar of pickles the size of my head.

The Duke himself hadn't admitted to moving about the house, but he'd realised it was pointless to deny his own troubles with Shaw. They'd met in dispute over land a few miles down the coast of Port Larkeney. The Duke had found the land to be perfect for growing his new breed of exotic pickles after scouting out Mrs. Twill's garden. Shaw had bought up everything else for miles around and had his eye on the same property. Dillmont couldn't imagine what Sebastian wanted with it, and after several letters, grew frustrated with the ordeal. He stormed to the manor with the intent to release his anger. Instead of arguing, he'd been invited to dinner.

I rubbed my temples. The more I uncovered, the more I didn't understand. I wished I could talk to Katie. I might didn't trust her much more than the guests, but at least she always knew what to do.

I looked down the hall of doors. "I think that's everyone."

My father set down his own jug of pickles, with a groan of relief. "Odd people, aren't they? Wendell, stop a moment." I stopped. He regarded me with an expression I was unaccustomed to.

"Wendell, I want you to know that I've enjoyed spending this morning with you. I don't know how to explain it, but you seem different. More self-assured, perhaps. Maybe you're growing up. Or maybe you've been grown up for a long time and I haven't

227

realised it." Sadness settled in the creases around his eyes. "And maybe that's my fault too."

There was a long silence.

"Dad—"

He cleared his throat. "Anyways, I'm going to go see your brother this afternoon. Are you coming?"

I didn't know what to say. "Yes" would have been the correct answer. I was overcome with the sudden urge to walk with him and just...talk. Talk about everything—life, Katie, what the hell I actually wanted to do with myself. Then I remembered.

"I can't, actually. I need to, um, return a book."

"Right this minute?"

"Yeah," I floundered for an answer. "You've never met the librarians here. I'll go down later." I looked away, not wanting to see his disappointment.

"Alright. See you later, son."

I followed my father out the door and down the path. Once he'd turned the corner, I spun on my heel and headed to the boatyard.

I'd never been down to the cove before. The crisp slate walls of the cliff rose several stories, separating the town above from the half-moon beach. I'd just jogged down a worn stone path to the quay. The sand beneath my feet was hard packed and gritty. Waves tossed the inlet and protruding rocks close to shore made it an easy place for fishing boats to run aground. To combat this, a monstrous boat house had been built. It was a long, rough building that stretched halfway across the cove, projecting out into the water like a wooden spear.

I walked slowly across the sea-slicked pier, noticing as I did so, a number of other slow walkers, but for a different reason.

The elderly clustered at the door of the boathouse and Katie pushed her way through with a pointed "pardon" and picking up a few by their shoulders and gently setting them down somewhere else. I tried to keep a low profile in case Wimbelow was on the scene. Sure enough, the Inspector was in the thick of it, barking orders to his slow-moving subordinates. I slipped in between a pair of century old twins that were roughly my height and smelled of Guinness.

My notebook was already in hand. I wrote: **Wow.**

Well, I wrote more than that, but it was the sheer extent of the damage that had me penning that first exclamation.

It wasn't visible from the front, but inside…the destruction was reminiscent of a toddler with a birthday cake. A massive chunk of the boathouse had simply been taken clean out and its remnants were spread far and wide. I drew closer and saw that the garage doors had all been raised. Light from the open side illuminated the damage. The water beneath the walkway was littered with wreckage of two capsized fishing boats. Beyond that, I glimpsed fluttering caution tape.

Nearby, the Inspector was at risk of being capsized himself by four very large, very angry fishermen whose boats had been affected in the blast. I pondered how to get closer. Wimbelow's force had shooed any onlookers back onto the beach and I surmised he wouldn't be quite as happy to see me as Katie.

Speaking of which…I glimpsed the blur of a tartan coat moving towards me. "You made it!" she said, jogging up and smiling as if I'd arrived late to a party rather than a crime scene.

"What's going on?"

Despite her smile, she looked exhausted. "I've been up since four," Katie replied. "I came down this morning to a call from Wimbelow that there had been a gas explosion at the boathouse. Only it wasn't. Meredith found the remnants of some mysterious device attached to the underside of the *Old Joe*." She pointed to several briny metal pieces that had been dredged up from the water. "That's all that's left of it. The fishermen have been going crazy, demanding to know the culprit. Them and everybody else."

She gave a tired chuckle. "But that's not all." She gestured downward. At her feet was a coiled metal chain, and beside it, a padlock…cut in half.

"Get this. Someone's stolen The Lamplighter."

~22~

It Came from the Turkey's Mouth

The Lamplighter, who had not been stolen, but kidnapped (as is the word politely used to describe sentient things) was currently sitting uncomfortably in a sewer, chewing his nails over the bombing of the boathouse.

Why were they waiting there and why had The Cellist decided that now was the time to strike, using that mysterious device from their very first meeting? It was partly due to what they'd discovered over the past couple of days, and it was largely to do with The Cellist's desire for wreaking senseless havoc.

The day before had been a turning point for the revolution. The Lamplighter recalled it as he scrunched up in the tunnel, staring at the tiny chinks of light that bulleted down from the holes in the grate. He was going to be here for a while.

* * *

Sunlight had begun to filter into the Lingerie Shoppe, casting pleasant golden rays on the tables of robes, camisoles, bikinis, bandeaus, and the countless other stringy articles of clothing on display. All was quiet but for the faint murmur of conversation of two distinctly un-female voices in the furthest stall by the bathroom.

"Look!" The Cellist whispered excitedly, holding up the small cylindrical object. "It's a *battery*. It powers electric devices rather than Amber ones. It runs on chemically generated currents of electricity. No wonder that toaster had no brain to speak of."

The Lamplighter crouched over the pile, holding the struggling teapot in two of his arms. He didn't find the battery to be at all interesting and failed to see how it could power a toaster or a juicer regardless.

"How do you know all this?" he asked.

This made The Cellist frown. "Common knowledge, I imagine. I mean who doesn't know what a battery is? No, the real issue is what *this* is," he pinched the glowing piece of Amber between thumb and forefinger.

"Well, it's Amber, isn't it?"

"Yes, but why have *we* come alive and some of these others haven't?" The Cellist paced in the tiny space, his movement ruffling the curtained walls. He had sorted through the pile of machinery that littered the floor. Battery-powered household appliances were gutted and discarded on one side. The other side held the few Automatons they *had* gotten a hold of. There was a self-snapping camera, a pair of skates that rolled on command, and a hoover with several twisty tentacle things that the both of them steered clear of. The Cellist held up the glowing camera and turned it over. There was an embossed "S.S." on the smooth underside.

"Sebastian Shaw," he murmured. "That was the man who created me and you. Perhaps all of them. I overheard the police talking about it that night. An upset at the manor." He slammed a fist into his palm. "We must find him, kill him, rescue the others no doubt trapped in some clammy, torturous laboratory, and recruit them. *Then* we begin The Revolution to enslave humanity as it exists."

The Lamplighter nodded. "Or we could come to a peaceful agreement," he suggested. "Perhaps he's a reasonable fellow."

For perhaps the hundredth time, he was ignored. The Cellist hopped onto the attached seat and peered over the partition. The clock read nearly eight in the morning. The store was due to open in a half an hour.

"Here's the plan," he said. "Today is reconnaissance. Gathering our army will have to wait for the time being. As I have begun to learn, there is no well of information more potent than a gathering of women. And where do we find ourselves?" He spread his arms wide. "The watering hole, my dear Lamplighter. There will be no scurrying in the sewers today. Today we will sit and see what falls our way."

Nothing so interesting came their way, only was tedious town gossip from the few women who stopped by. Amazingly, everyone seemed to be preoccupied by some kind of festival that was happening soon rather than the high-profile murder that had occurred just outside their town. People were detailing plans for booths, food, and strangest of all, peppers. To top it off, they were also more concerned about the displaying of assets, which made even The Lamplighter's aluminium alloy cheeks hot with embarrassment.

I must have taken on a great deal from my creator. He thought, as The Cellist pressed his ear hopefully against the partition. *I feel as human as the rest of them.* It was lonely, this Revolution, and he was beginning to hope that a lady robot (whatever that might look like) might join their cause.

Towards the end of the day, they struck gold.

The doorbell tinkled and The Lamplighter, fed up by this time, didn't even look up as he slouched in the corner. The Cellist watched through the curtains. Out on the floor, Laura hastily abandoned her muffin.

"Oh, hello," she said, dabbing her mouth. Laura was the owner of the shop and a pleasant looking woman in her forties. She had a squarish face with smooth features and a penchant for wearing royal purple cardigans and tight fuchsia pencil skirts. This meant she took very fast, tiny steps towards customers, giving the impression of an unbalanced purple dreidel. "Something I can get for you?"

The Cellist beckoned him over. Unwillingly, The Lamplighter rose as quietly as he could and peered through the curtains. The customer clutched her bag close. She looked like something out of a spy film. A large grey trench coat was wrapped around her ample figure. A pair of oversized black sunglasses obscured her face and a heavy-knit scarf swaddled both her mouth and hair—though a few blond wisps peaked out.

"Mrfmfmm," said the customer.

"Didn't quite catch that!"

The customer glanced around the room and seeing that there was no one else in the shop, took off the scarf but kept the glasses. "Sorry. It's just…I've never been inside one of these shops before. I shouldn't be embarrassed, should I? A woman of my age?"

Laura huffed. "Well, I should think not. It's never too late to get something nice for yourself and your fellow. Is there anything specific you're looking for?"

The woman turned red. "No. It's just, I'd like it to be a surprise."

Laura winked. "Well let's see if we can't find you something then." She disappeared into the back, chatting all the while. "So, what is this secret getup of yours? Got two on the go?"

"Yeesh," said The Cellist.

"What? No, nothing like that. It's just very new, and I have a daughter who is quite…headstrong. I worry how she'd take it if she found out."

"I'm sure if he's a nice enough bloke she'll come round. Here, try this on." The sound of a swinging door very close to them made The Lamplighter hold his breath—not that he had any.

"Oh my," said the woman. "I'm not sure about this one. It seems a bit…"

"No problem," said Laura. "Acid green not your colour?"

The woman peaked her head from around the changing room door. "More partial to warmer colours, to be honest."

Laura gasped. "I know you!"

The woman swore loudly. "I knew I shouldn't have taken off my sunglasses."

"Oh, don't worry I won't tell anyone. You're Jeane Twill, the pepper lady! I don't think we've had the chance to meet." Laura heaved another pair of garments over the top of the partition.

"My god," muttered The Cellist as the fabric fluttered briefly into view, "that's not a brassier that's a parachute."

"That Big Bertha of yours is quite impressive," Laura was saying. "The ladies come in and talk about it all the time. Speaking of which, I should thank you."

"For what?"

"Your daughter. She came in here a few months ago. Great girl."

"*She what?*"

Laura nodded to no one in particular. "Caught the panty thief red-handed after a three-day stakeout behind the cash register. There was a strange moment when she fainted after jumping up to surprise him, but after, well, it could've cost us a fortune if he'd gotten away."

Mrs. Twill sounded monumentally relieved. "That's my girl. In fact, she's on a new case now if you must know. Here, d'you think you could find one just a smidge larger?"

"Will do." Laura disappeared once more. "You don't mean that whole Sebastian Shaw business, do you?"

"The very same," said Mrs. Twill proudly and two Autos perked up. "She's one of the top officers on the case. Lately she's been partnering with some boy who was involved." She lowered her voice conspiratorially. "She told me she's hot on the trail of Shaw's stolen invention, whatever it may be, it's all very hush-hush so don't go around telling people that."

"Oh my," said Laura. "I wonder if the news will pick this up? Then there'll be *two* celebrities in your family. How does it look in there?" As there was no one around, Mrs. Twill walked out and briefly opened the silk bathrobe.

The Lamplighter covered his eyes out of a sense of proprietary. The Cellist did no such thing. His jaw dropped. His yellow eyes goggled. "It's like watching a trussed turkey. And they did not use *nearly* enough twine."

Mrs. Twill did a spin, the silken cover fluttering apart. "What do you think?"

Laura grinned. "He'll love it."

Night fell and the store was mercifully silent and empty. The two Autos sat in their stall, The Lamplighter in his corner, knees to his chest to avoid knocking the mirror off the wall, The Cellist across from him. He turned over his bow, running a finger over the gleaming point.

"I think I need to gouge my eyes out."

The Lamplighter said nothing. Genie gave an exasperated toot.

"We do have that enormous woman to thank for something though," said The Cellist.

"What's that?"

"Now we know who will lead us to that invention, and to Shaw himself."

* * *

And that was why four days later, they were in the sewer. It ran under the beach and opened out in the side of one of the cliffs bordering the cove. It was convenient because the two of them could cosy right up to the damaged boathouse without being seen. It was terrible in that it only surfaced during low tide and right now, the water was slowly creeping upwards, bringing with it bits of fish carcass and mouldy lichen. The Cellist had made himself a makeshift poncho and hairnet from various garments in Laura's shop and stolen himself some knee-length wellies. The Lamplighter picked miserably at the rust building in his joints. The skeleton of a desiccated crab that had settled firmly in the gears of his upper armpit.

"Stolen? I...what? What's The Lamplighter got to do with any of this?"

This new voice drifted through the grate. This person sounded young and steeped in a perpetual state of incredulity, as if he simply couldn't believe that things, places, and people continued to happen at him.

"That's what Wimbelow and I are trying to figure out. Or at least I am. He's been going mad back at the office. Tearing out his hair, talking about lack of manpower, resources, and old people getting in the way of him solving the biggest case of his career, yada yada yada."

This voice belonged to Katie Twill, the detective the woman in the shop had talked about. The Cellist had intentionally lured her here, and by luring, meant he'd blown the place up.

The young detective was wearing a pair of maroon bell bottoms and a mint bowling shirt under a tartan coat. The Lamplighter remembered her entrance all right. She'd breezed in, talking speedily in a singsong sort of way and then accidentally spilled a few drops of whatever was in that thermos onto the floorboards of the crime scene. She'd bent down hastily to wipe it up, but not before he saw a bit of varnish come off on her handkerchief.

There was a clink as the girl nudged the chain that had once held The Lamplighter with her boot. "Personally, I think Meredith and Rudy, and all the rest of them are alright. Sure, they can't see the evidence, or hear half of what's coming in through the radio, but they've been in the service all their lives. He's been threatening a staff overhaul with the Chief."

"Sure."

The boy wasn't listening. The Lamplighter unfolded himself slowly and rose, so his eye was level with the holes in the cover. Somehow, he looked exactly how one might picture him. Blue coat, white jumper. Slightly shorter than average, arms folded. He was in need of a haircut, brown hair curling over the tops of his ears. He turned restless fingers to his pocket from which he withdrew a battered old leather journal.

"But why were you keeping that *thing* in a boathouse?" he asked. "I know for a fact that thing was way out of the way of the party. It crushed my car after all!"

Wait, he'd fallen on a car? When? The Lamplighter frowned. He was only vaguely aware that the morning in the boathouse had not been his true awakening. Over the past few days, bits and pieces of consciousness and memory had come back to him. Hazy, and swimming as if in a dream. He remembered a flash of white-blue light so brilliant it obliterated everything around him. He remembered the tang of rain and mist on the asphalt. He remembered feeling strange and fragmented, unwilling to wake up. Then he had fallen asleep and woken up in the boathouse to the grinning face of The Cellist.

"We kept the Lamplighter there because it was too big for the station. The evidence room is practically a closet, Wendell. In fact, it is a closet. Humphrey stores his racquetball equipment in there."

Wendell. So that was his name. The Lamplighter edged closer to the grate.

"So, what does this mean?" Wendell tapped his chin with his pen. "Did you have time to examine the body—I mean, Auto—before all this?"

"We did a quick check on it. Other than the fact it wasn't operating, everything seemed to be in order but for a few squeaky hinges. It wasn't really top priority with all that was going on. There's something else."

Katie pointed to the gouged walls. "These marks have been appearing all over town in over half the homes where items were stolen. I think they might be marks from that huge metal hat The Lamplighter's got on. It's the right height, I think."

"You think someone's using it to steal things?" Wendell asked incredulously. "But the robberies started six days ago!"

Katie had the grace to look embarrassed. "Like I said, erm, nobody really thought it was a priority to check. Wimbelow thinks it's far-fetched too. He also refuses to acknowledge the whole Cellist/ballroom thing until further notice. Maintains it was a freak accident. *I* think it all lines up," she continued earnestly, "but we're stretched too thin. It's nearly impossible to follow everything at once."

Beside The Lamplighter, The Cellist let out a grunt of annoyance. He knew that his companion was infuriated he hadn't received credit for his act of destruction. There was a thump aboveground, and the young duo turned. One of the older female police officers had slipped on something and was struggling to get back up. Katie rushed to help her and there was a sudden cry.

"Eugh! What is that! Is that a piece of fish?"

Wendell went to investigate. "Rat," he said confidently as he flipped through his journal. "You can tell by the strata."

"It's *cubed*," Katie's voice echoed in disgust.

The Cellist beamed. "Wait for it," he whispered.

"Wait," someone said. "Is that blood on the wall?"

There was a loud scrape as two barrels were pushed aside, and the little group gasped.

"Prepare to pay, humans," Wendell murmured in horror. "And that's...the *F* clef?"

"What do you think, too much?" whispered The Cellist. "I daubed it on the wall in the rat's blood after I detonated the bomb. As a calling-card of sorts. Branding's very important, you know. Many a revolution's failed because it wasn't catchy enough."

The Lamplighter forced a smile. "It's very—"

Shouts and running pairs of feet echoed around the wet sewer. The angry voice of the Inspector rang across the water. The Cellist nodded satisfactorily. They had gotten what they came for. It was time to go.

* * *

The Piquant Palaces was probably the weirdest thing The Lamplighter had ever seen, and he'd watched The Cellist construct a homemade bomb out of a dismantled hair straightener, three bra hooks, and a fork. He didn't know whether to be amused or awed. Certainly, the giant inn defied all laws of gravity, all four stories leaning jauntily to the left and constructed like a doomed Jenga set. With its pointed base, large, rounded top and Christmas lights that webbed across its porthole windows, it looked just like a great green jalapeno.

The smell of something roasting drifted out from the narrow front porch. The door was open, and he could see the lights of the pub twinkling inside. The Lamplighter crouched inside a rubbish bin. It was as demeaning as it sounded, hunkering down in the garbage until night fell. Unfortunately, the enormous metal brim of his hat was precisely the right size and shape of the lid. The fuchsia sack at his waist shifted restlessly as he shushed Genie.

239

"Just a bit longer now," he whispered. It was five hours since the bombing and they'd tailed the two children back from boathouse to this place. The Piquant Palaces.

The Cellist, keen on both shortcuts and stealing, put his faith in the pair of precocious teenagers. Hopefully, following the two would lead them right to that mysterious revolutionary invention at the centre of all of this. If they found it...well, he wasn't sure what would happen. The Cellist said he would pounce in and steal it, force them to lead him to Shaw, and begin his efforts to overthrow the human race, but that seemed like an awful lot to accomplish on a Tuesday night.

CRASH!

The Lamplighter yelped as the bin echoed raucously around him. Someone was rapping on the outside. The noise thundered through his head. He emerged painfully. The sky was black and cold, sparkling with the distant pinpoints of stars.

"They're up on the balcony," The Cellist hissed excitedly. "I see them. Hoist me up."

The Lamplighter did. Allowing the smaller Automaton to climb up onto his shoulders, he made his way carefully through the grass under cover of darkness to where murmured conversation drifted from the upper floors. The Cellist cupped his hand to his ear and listened.

Wendell and Katie sat together on a cramped balcony on the third floor. The flickering glow of the Christmas lights illuminated their faces. The boy looked worried. He shivered, palming a cup of tea.

"I dunno how I'm going to be let out after this. You saw my father. He's furious."

"Well, you'll just have to." The detective crossed her arms. The gentle night breeze ruffled her bellbottoms. "I don't see any other way. Not with this evidence you picked up." She waved a small plastic baggie, handling it carefully as if it were gold. "If we're right about this, we'll have the Lightning Gun tomorrow!"

Wendell scoffed. "How do you figure that? Besides, even if I were able to hang out with you, which I won't be, she won't talk to us. My father's wised up. He won't do any more interviews for me, and I don't think all the charm in the world would be enough for *her*."

"Don't you worry about that," said Katie. "I've got a plan."

Wendell's voice was riddled with apprehension. "Which is...?"

The Lamplighter felt a pang of *deja vu*. But it was probably just from earlier that day.

Katie grinned, teeth glowing in the darkness. "I can't give you all the details, but 11:00pm sharp. Tomorrow night. Wear something...weatherproof."

~23~

Ooh Someone's in *Trouble!*

lashes filled through the air as polaroids snapped behind me. "Prepare to Pay, Humans." My lips moved over the words, but I scarcely heard them.

Everyone, me, the junior detective, the small band of stooping police officers, and two of the burly fishermen, had stopped cold at the sight of the message on the wall. Thick, dark rat's blood stank and stained the wood. To the right of it, foul rivulets ran and coalesced into a swooping design I recognized as: "The *F* clef?"

Katie nudged my elbow. "The *what* clef?"

"That," I pointed. "It's also called the bass clef in music. It separates the lower notes on the scale on sheet music. But I don't know why—" Then it hit me.

The mental image of that night flashed with terrifying clarity. I'd stared into the mirror in the ballroom and seen the very same sign. It had been cut, gouged even, into two grinning, bone white cheekbones. The Cellist had been here.

"It's…not possible," I said, taking a step back, and feeling my boot squelch into another puddle of rodent's innards. The cold spell of fear that had gradually dissipated after that night in the manor had risen again. I felt the hairs on the back of my neck rise as though the gleaming red eyes were watching me again from afar. I'd almost convinced myself it were a dream…until now.

"Wendell. Hey." Someone shook me, and I snapped out of my daze. Katie looked concerned. "You look like you're about to hurl. You've been scribbling nonstop."

I looked down to see she was right. The page was filled with *F* clefs. Katie didn't look nearly as perturbed as I felt. Obviously, she was shocked and disturbed by the bloody message, but she hadn't been there that night. She hadn't had nightmares and the creeping fear of something unnatural lurking just around the corner.

No.

Like the starting of a rusty car engine, my old rationality took over. Things were all interconnected somehow. Automatons didn't just walk up and talk by themselves much less murder rats and explode boatyards. There was someone behind all of this. There had to be. I reassured her that I was fine and walked up to inspect the wall and the chunks. There was nothing new about the message, but upon closer examination, the chunks of rat were in near perfect similarity. I flipped through my journal to find something about knives I'd picked up in Papua New Guinea. Before I could do so, shouts echoed from the other side of the boathouse. Hoarse, nasally shouts.

"Excuse me—excuse me. Oi! Move aside you old ba—I mean respected members of the community. Please *respectfully* clear off!" Wimbelow's voice preceded him in the gathered crowd. "What's the meaning of this? Meredith, you're supposed to be off hauling the full barrels from the unstable areas. You too Rudy, Baker, and the rest of you—where are your pictures?"

Wimbelow held out his hand as photographs were handed in. The crowd of geriatric law enforcement and dock workers had gotten so thick the Inspector hadn't yet seen the message on the wall. He began to look frustratedly about himself.

"What's all this about? Excuse me—" he tried in vain to push up against a short, but firmly supplanted fisherman. "Your boathouse has already exploded. I can't imagine what more there is to witness. This is a crime scene for Pete's sake!"

"Hey." Again, Katie jostled my elbow. "What say we give them the old Irish goodbye before Wimbelow sees you," she muttered.

"Agreed." I backed away from the scene and began to slide into the gaggle of spectators. The Inspector flapped the polaroids vigorously. He frowned and I had the sudden realisation I'd probably been captured in one of those photographs. I chanced a glance back at the balding ginger crown stalking above the hubbub. It was a mistake. Wimbelow caught eyes with me at that very moment.

"Wha—you! Stop!"

"Gingersnaps," swore Katie. "Go!" She pushed me in the opposite direction, into the weary group of technicians by the damaged section. Her tartan coat tails disappeared around the corner of the long walkway. I ran, panic shooting up my spine as my boots sank into wet timber. I caught a glimpse of the ocean between the slats. The boathouse was becoming more and more unstable following the explosion. Nearly a third of the thin stilts elevating the walkway above the sea had cracked or fallen away.

"Stop him! That's a suspect!" I looked over my shoulder to see Wimbelow edging along the sides as quickly as he could, malice in his eyes.

I had neither the light footedness of Katie or speed of my brother, and while I'd found myself in situations like this before, my tactic was usually to barrel through and hope for the best. The edge of the boat house was nearing, and I saw light at the end of the tunnel. In the doorway, the detective was waiting for me, ready to grab my hand and bar the door. I could make it out and she could convince him he'd been mistaken somehow. I saw it all in one exchange of looks.

"Harold! Janice! For Pete's sake, someone grab him!"

The police officers in front of me narrowed their milky eyes and stretched out quavering hands. Before they'd even fully extended, I'd sped past with only the scrabbling of liver spotted

245

fingers at my back. It was going to be close. Behind me, Wimbelow had gotten himself tangled in a fishing net. In front of me, more rubble and police officers stood in my way. By some miracle I hopped the debris, escaped the elderly, and was faced with the open back door leading onto the sand. Katie beckoned me forward as I crossed the final stretch. Which was, of course, when the floor decided to give way. Vertigo shot through me, and I felt the roar, the harsh spray of the waves rising up to greet me before I stopped, dangling above the crashing water. Two hands gripped my shoulders. I was safe.

I reddened. "Katie, really, you've got to stop saving me."

But the junior detective was standing in the doorway, too far to reach. She was white faced. The grip around my shoulders tightened and I saw with dismay the long bony fingers with knuckles dusted in a light carpet of orange hair. The Inspector leered down at me. Katie stood statue-like; her hand still outstretched.

"Well, well, well," Wimbelow said, triumph gleamed in his eyes. "It looks like Christmas has come early."

Katie fell over.

* * *

Silence and mothballs filled the space between us. Across from me, the junior detective sat uncharacteristically prim. She stared at the hallway leading out of the waiting room. The receptionist coughed and wetted her wrinkled lips on a kerchief. The clock ticked. One minute. Three minutes. Five. Katie began to squirm, tapping her fingers on the edge of the armchair.

"I've never been in this type of situation before," she said, breaking the silence at last. "Being on this side of the desk, I mean. I've been reprimanded a couple of times but..." she trailed off, looking back at the door.

I was trying to quash the overwhelming despair of being caught. Katie might well be sacked, and I hadn't even been able to share my findings from the Quislings and the Duke! A smaller, more selfish part of me despaired for my record. Here I was,

246

sabotaging my chances for a normal life, time and again. As Katie shifted, her bruise came into view. It was a light mark on the back of her jaw. There were faint red scratches where she'd hit rough wood head-on.

"Slipped on a sea cucumber," she'd said when she'd fallen. "Slippery little devils."

If that wasn't proof of her condition, I didn't know what was. I checked the clock on the wall. "Hey, Katie."

She looked up.

"Do you want to hear a joke?"

"Right now?"

I shrugged.

"Alright then, shoot."

My brilliant plan was this. Narcolepsy traditionally involves not only extreme tiredness, but sudden and uncontrollable bouts of sleep induced by strong emotion. So far, she'd collapsed on top of Big Bertha during a shouting match, during my frightening car ride with her, and now at the shock of being caught. Sure, maybe this wasn't the best time to test my theory, but it had been eating away at me like nothing else. I would tell her a joke so incredibly funny, she'd be reduced to tears of laughter, and when she slumped over in sleep, she would *have* to come out with it.

I bit back a smile. "Alright, get ready for this one. It's a little bit raunchy. A little bit...*edgy* even." Katie settled back in anticipation, and I began. "A man is on his first visit to Boston. Of course, he intends to try the world-famous New England Seafood, so he asks the cabbie 'Can you take me to where I can get scrod?'"

I struggled to keep a straight face.

"The driver replies, "Well, I've heard that question a thousand times but never in the pluperfect subjunctive!"

She was so silent it must have worked. "Katie?

She was awake. Staring at me.

"Do you need me to explain it?"

"No, that's alright."

"Do you...want to hear another one?"

"Nope! I mean, I'd like to sit here in silence if you don't mind."

247

I settled back into the couch, mortified. It was a relief when Wimbelow appeared in the doorway.

"You two. With me." His long front teeth bit into his lower lip. He was clearly taking great pleasure in this. Katie got up wordlessly and dusted off her coat. I followed. We took the familiar route down the carpeted hallway of the police station and turned left into a stairwell. The upper floors were like the lower ones in that they looked more like your grandmother's house than a police headquarters, although these more like your veteran granddad's. I'd never seen so much plaid in my life. The walls were covered in the stuff. Framed images of army jacketed, kilted men with impressive beards dotted the hallway. A threadbare family tapestry hung outside the stairwell. Wimbelow's crisp stride echoed on the hardwood floor.

"Does someone live up here?" I whispered.

"The upper floors are Fergus' house," she replied. "Sometimes we use the bedrooms as holding cells."

I peeked into one of the bedrooms. It looked normal except for the industrial metal bars in the window. "Right."

The Inspector stopped and knocked twice on a plain door with a coat of arms at the end of the halls.

"Enter."

We stepped inside.

The Chief was an enormously fat and hairy old man. He dominated the tiny office. His eyes were almost completely obscured by the huge white eyebrows that hung like snow clouds over them. A fuzzy halo of ear hair encircled the mountain peak of his scalp. As we sat down, a puff of breath fluttered the ends of his walrus moustache. The slim, high back chair beneath him creaked ominously.

The Inspector waited for the whiskers to stop fluttering before he began. "Blatant insubordination sir! As I've been telling you, no matter this boy, Katie Twill has *got to go*!"

Fergus held up a fleshy hand adorned with heavy gold signet rings. "I don't need to hear it for a third time, Inspector," said the Chief in a hoarse, booming voice.

Beside me, Katie's eyes were trained on a single point on the wall as her fingers traced circles on the arm of her chair. She was

248

trying to keep calm; I was sure of it. It wouldn't do to fall asleep in front of your chief of police.

The Chief took big sucks of breath, drawing us in with each pull of air. "The truth of the matter is, I am out of sticks," he said finally. He glared at both Katie and Wimbelow. I felt largely invisible. "What has happened over the last two weeks—high profile assault, numerous petty robberies, and now, a bombing, were beyond our means to prevent. What is not, is the lack of initiative—" he pointed at Wimbelow, "attention to detail," this was at Katie, "and, cooperation! I have never seen two people so averse to working together. Do you realise that Port Larkeney is in your hands?"

His massive palm thudded on the table. A toy bobbling dog on his desk jumped and wagged wildly. "Katie, are you aware that your mother has reporters coming up from London to cover the Capsicum Carnival?"

"What? She said Hallifield!"

"Well apparently not. Now, I've been looking elsewhere for reinforcements. The two of you might think differently."

I could see on the Inspector's face he already knew what Fergus was about to say.

"You can imagine what these reporters will say about the Inspector who mismanaged the attack of Sebastian Shaw so badly that his stolen weapon is still in circulation within the town, *weeks* after the fact. That not a single person has been apprehended in respect to this case."

"What about the boy!" cried Wimbelow, sticking a furious finger at me. "He was at the boatyard, just this morning, running from me! From the *law*. I was doing my job."

"So, question him!" demanded the Chief. "We have enough juvenile delinquents in this town. Make an example of him. However, I think that you have more pressing suspects to follow. You've been bogging yourself down in the details, Wimbelow. Just this past week you talked of nothing but a tiny hair found at the lab and gave me six different theories as to its origin, which is all well and good but does us nothing if you don't prove them for yourself!"

The Inspector's face changed rapidly from insolence to soothing deference. "I certainly would, Chief, if only I had the time and manpower. Unfortunately, my subordinates are often not up to the task. In fact, I have to deal with this in every aspect of this job. The townsfolk are unwilling to cooperate. My second in command has proven herself to be wildly untrustworthy, and the rest of my team is decrepit."

The old Chief sat stony-faced. "I expected more from a former member of the Metropolitan Police, Inspector," was all he said. "Problem solving is the very title of the job, is it not? Of course, if you aren't up for it, I can always send word to the neighboring towns. We can see what positions they can scrounge up for you."

Wimbelow turned red. The enormous old man took a deep breath, then swung his body towards Katie.

"Now, if I could speak to Ms. Twill in private. Yes, that means you, Wimbelow."

"But I—"

"Now." With a deafening scrape, the Inspector pushed back his chair and opened the door. I went to follow, but he was blocking the exit.

"She's got something unnatural, you know," Wimbelow spat, jerking his head at Katie.

The young detective whipped around in alarm.

"I can feel it, Chief," he continued. "The sleepiness, the fainting. I can see you weren't aware of that. Strong willfulness, aversion to authority, and now, blatantly corroborating with a suspect. I don't know about you, but I believe this young woman is unfit for duty as she is. She's a danger to herself and everyone around her." With that, he stalked off, banging the door behind him. I lingered in the doorway.

"Anything I can do for you?" rumbled Fergus.

"Could you just tell me if I'm going to prison? I'd like to know so I know what to tell my parents."

To my surprise, he let out a great bark of laughter. I was hit with a coffee flavoured guff of air. "No."

"No?" I almost laughed with relief.

"I called you in here so you might see the state of things around here." His expression grew serious, the white hairs of his moustache and brows drooping together. "Nobody knows the answers, Billings. And if the professionals don't have them, what a silly thing it would be to think you might."

I flushed. "I don't think—"

He waved his hand. "This is a warning. Be glad of it. Now, if you please, I'd like to speak with Ms. Twill here."

I turned to hide my irritation, catching a quick glimpse of Katie's fingers, digging into the seat, and walked out.

When I left the office, I went straight past the stairs and continued down the hallway. What was it she'd said? *Our evidence room is a closet. In fact, Humphrey stores his racquetball equipment in there.*

If Katie couldn't get the evidence, perhaps I could. I tiptoed down the hallway, cursing for once, the lack of carpeted floor. One closet was full of cans and boxes labelled "Apocalypse Readiness." Another was full of regular coats and shoes. A third was nothing but kilts. This one smelled the worst. The final one was the ticket. I opened it and was immediately hit by three wicker rackets. A ball bounced painfully off my forehead and thudded down the hall. I froze, waiting for a door to burst open somewhere, for someone to come running or hobbling out. No one did.

Returning the ball and the equipment, I began to search the shelves. Aside from the rackets, it was remarkably empty. It didn't take long to find what I was looking for. I glanced left and right before pulling out the cardboard box labelled "S.S. Evidence." There were only two items inside: a golden lock and a tiny baggie containing a single white hair. I picked up the lock. It was a lovely thing and heavy. The lock itself was broken and the gold surface marred by several chips in and around the hole. The baggie was more mysterious. I reached for it. Behind me, a toilet flushed, and a door opened. I quickly pocketed it and shoved the box back.

"What are you doing?"

Wimbelow's nasally voice echoed suspiciously down the hallway. I'd managed to stand up before he came. I juggled the racquetball equipment, with surprise on my face.

"I was looking for the bathroom and all this stuff hit me."

"Well, you overshot by about two doors. Put those back, come on now."

He didn't offer to help me but leaned against the wall beside the door. His foot tapped a rapid staccato on the wood floor. "She's mad, you know," he said, as I struggled to shove the rackets into a corner. "Utterly mad and nobody sees it. Nobody except me. Well…"

His beady eyes fixed on me as I passed.

"She got to you, didn't she? That girl seems to have everyone in this town in her pocket. But you, you've just met her. You must have seen something strange in her. She's not fit to be a detective. She's got something up there—" he tapped on his temple. "Some kind of complex. An unnatural disease. Nyctophobia? Melomania? Referencing too many disco songs in one day? Napoplexy?"

"I think you mean 'narcolepsy,'" I corrected, shoving the last wayward ball into the net. All of sudden the Inspector was quiet. Too quiet.

"I meant napoplexy," I said quickly. *Idiot!* "Silly me. Terrible with words."

He said nothing and I closed the closet door to find his eyes trained intently on me.

"Don't think I don't know who you are. You have so much promise. I see myself in you, you know. I often read your father's columns when I dream about retiring in three years. You could do the same, you know. Obviously not as well as me, but almost. Don't ruin that by befriending Katie Twill." He pushed himself off the wall and turned the corner of the stairwell.

The crinkled bag in my pocket and I felt a sudden prick of anger. "I'll be the judge of that."

To my satisfaction, the Inspectors hands flexed. He stopped but didn't turn around. "Thanks for the tip about the narcolepsy."

What exactly had I done?

"Hey."

I looked up. Katie walked into the waiting room.

"Hey." I couldn't tell if it was good or bad news. Her face was remarkably inexpressive.

"Let's go outside," she said, and grabbed a handful of the soft biscuits from the tin on the reception desk. Outside, she began to gnaw at them furiously, brushing the crumbs off her collar and shoulders. "Need to get my blood sugar up," she said between bites. "I haven't eaten properly for three days."

"What happened in there?" I asked. "Is everything alright?"

She frowned, staring out at the lot with bulging cheeks. She took a long swig from the thermos and swallowed. "Depends on how you look at it, doesn't it? I'm on probation. I'm off the Shaw case. Strictly local now. I know it could've been worse. Fergus was only being fair. If Wimbelow had his way…"

I followed her gaze. Port Larkeney, with its white-washed cottages and terraced cobblestone bathing in the clear, fresh mist of the afternoon tide spread out before us. You would never have known such terrible things were happening here.

"What do we do from here?"

Of course, what I was really asking was *Are you going to keep helping me? Will you risk your job for this?* I didn't know if I could come out with it aloud.

"We'll keep at it, obviously!" She looked at me like it was never a question and relief washed through me. "When I fell off the telephone pole above the school in search of the seagull that had taken Geordie Miller and broke four bones in my left hand, did that stop me? No way. It's just going to be hard. And we're just going to have to be more careful. More discreet. Never thought I'd say that. Why?" She stopped, suddenly uncertain. "You're not thinking of…?"

"No, no. I can do discreet."

"Great!" she fist-bumped me. "Also, they called your dad. He's coming to rip you a new one."

253

~24~

Reprimands and Rendezvous

I could tell from the way his beard was twitching and how his face had slowly turned the colour of boiled eggplant that my father was ripe to explode. Unfortunately, we weren't the only ones in the car.

Since we were all on our way to the Palaces, Katie had asked for a ride. Now she sat, cramped in the backseat as the van bumped and whined up the streets of Port Larkeney, completely oblivious to the silent battle happening in the front seat.

The shrunken head keychain from Peru bounced back and forth in front of the rearview mirror as my father struggled to suppress himself. If there was anything he was more afraid of than me devolving into a lawless criminal, it was waiting. More than once, he glanced back at Katie, his beard bristling. Eventually, he couldn't take it anymore. I received a poke in the shoulder and looked up to see his lips moving furiously. So, this was how it was going to be.

"*I just can't believe it,*" he mouthed. "*One minute I'm expecting you at your brother's bedside, the next I get a call you've been caught red-handed running from the Inspector at the sight of an explosion!*"

"*That was grossly over exaggerated!*" I shot back silently.

"*Why then, are you covered in the brine and the blood of the Irish Rattus Norvegicus on your boots? Your old dad still recognizes Latin classifications of rodents through smell you know. Or did you think you could pull a fast one over me?*"

I cursed myself for forgetting to clean my shoes. My father had the most discerning nose out of anyone I'd ever met. He could distinguish the difference between a healthy, robust, starfish and one in the throes of sickle cell anaemia with one sniff. It was how we avoided food poisoning when stranded in a cave on the Amalfi Coast.

He held up a finger, alternating between glaring at me and the road.

"*I'm not finished. The lying. The willful deception. Those interviews. I'm beginning to think they weren't just for fun. You were after something weren't you? Thought you might kick up some fame and glory if you solved that awful case? All this time I thought I was raising cultured sons and it turns out the one left standing is nothing more than a…a juvenile delinquent.*"

"I was trying to help Tim," I hissed a bit louder than intended. "If you think this is about fame—"

"SHH! *Is that what you want to be known for?*" he shook his head. "*Not as a smart man, or a good man, but as a man that lies to his own father?*"

"Did you say something?" asked Katie. "I heard someone say something."

My father and I turned around at the same time.

"Nothing!"

I turned back to him. "*I know you think that means you can never put us in danger again after what happened to Tim,*" I mouthed angrily, "*but there is such a thing as justifiable risk! I'm trying to find out what happened to him. There was a lightning bolt that hit both the mansion and the car and you say you're not the least bit suspicious?*"

My father stilled the grotesque bouncing head with one hand. "*Not everything is one big conspiracy, Wendell.*"

"Say, think we could stop for some coffee and French pastry? I'm starved," said Katie.

The both of us turned around again. "No!"

"Jeez," she crossed her arms and went back to looking out the window.

My father discretely jabbed a finger behind him. *"And what about her? I mean, really, son."*

I rolled my eyes. *"She's been helping me."*

He squinted. *"She's been* whating *you? Herping? What's that?"* His face paled. *"Oh no. Never mind. I don't want to know what that means."*

"No!" I cupped the side of my mouth. *"Helping. H-E-L-P-I-N-G."*

We had to stop then because the van was trundling up the steep dirt path to the Piquant Palaces. My father shifted his energies to make sure the old car didn't decide to go with gravity. In no time at all, we'd arrived at the inn. The van stopped with a new metallic screech. Something had happened to the braking systems after the Lamplighter had fallen on top of it that no amount of repair could fix. Katie quickly unbuckled herself and made for the door. My father watched her go and then turned to me. I watched as the words *"you're grounded,"* formed under his beard.

"What?" I said loudly, forgetting our silent pact.

"For the duration of the stay." My father was stony faced. He unrolled the window. "And *you!*"

Katie, who had already made it halfway across the lot and thought she was home free, jumped.

"Stop herping my son!"

"What?"

"Dad!" I cried.

He ignored me and fixed her with the rare steely-eyed look I'd seen face down bulls. "I don't want you, or those bloody bellbottoms anywhere near him for the rest of this trip unless it's to say *goodbye*. Are we understood?"

"Yes. Yes. Crystal," said Katie, backing away.

I was mortified. I didn't wait to hear the rest of what he had to say. In a matter of seconds, I was out of that awful, stuffy interior and into the open air. But his voice followed me the further I tried to get away from it.

"It was the disco music, wasn't it son? You can't be swayed by such things. It'll only lead to heartbreak. Don't worry, I'm not letting you out of my sight from now on!"

I stalked into the pub and slammed the door, not caring a fig about the reproving looks of Mrs. Twill or the criminal suspects dining there and resolving to never ever tell my parents a single thing ever again.

* * *

I don't need to tell you how maddening the next couple of days were. I'm sure you can imagine the horror of being followed around by your parents every second of the day. It was like having two suddenly *very* intrusive twin shadows at my back. As someone used to a certain degree of independence (at the age of nine I went and did our shopping in Tijuana when my father caught scarlet fever and was bedridden for four days) I found it to be something of a personal hell.

My mother shoved a bulging paper bag into my hand as we stood in the hospital ward. "Mind you don't forget to eat," she whispered. "You're wasting away. We can't have you looking like your brother."

I forced a smile and took the packed lunch. Over the past few days, I'd heard no less than fifteen versions of "God forbid what happened to your brother should happen to you, Wendell."

In regard to my brother, he was no different than he had been every other time we'd visited him. Thin and silent, the radiating mark on his chest mocking me at every turn. To my own growing guilt, I was beginning to find these visits incredibly wearing. Didn't they see that no amount of pleading, crying, and bedside reading was going to cure him? It was so much better to do something than sit around, praying to any invisible deity that would listen. To top this off, I hadn't seen Katie in three days. It certainly looked like she'd been suitably scared off after the ride with my father. I was beginning to think this might be the end of "Twill and

258

Billings" for good. I stewed as I sat in the uncomfortable wicker chairs of the ward. She wasn't even going to try? Or did I have to? How was it possible to live in such close quarters with someone and still never cross paths?

My father emerged from another lengthy conversation with the doctor and my mother grabbed her bag. "Time to go, Wendell," she said, picking up the dog-eared tomb of *My Chiropractor is Actually a Muscular Werewolf Man* lying on the bed. I looked at Tim with an expression of pity. If she kept reading him these books, he might wake up just to stop the torture.

My feelings toward Katie grew worse the closer we got to the Palaces, and as we sat down for dinner in the pub, I resolved not to wait for her any longer. Sure, my father followed me around these days like a territorial bulldog, but if she was deterred by that, well, I would just have to follow the clue in the evidence bag by myself.

"I'll have the Colcannon Con Carnes," said my father. "Hold the worst of the chili if you could, possibly?"

Mrs. Twill looked at him reproachfully, as she did anyone who ordered the less spicy version of her dishes. My mother ordered the lamb and I my usual bacon sandwich. Our dishes arrived steaming. The Colcannon Con Carnes sounded exotic. Mrs. Twill seemed to enjoy adding a Mexican flair to her dishes, but it was really potatoes in a thick chili, laden with ground beef and spiced cabbage slaw. The leg of lamb was a crisp brown with a thick crust of baked skin and seasoning. Its savoury juice soaked into mashed potatoes topped with rosemary. My parents took no time digging into their dishes. I stared at the sandwich in front of me. I wasn't feeling particularly hungry, especially after the packed lunch. My mother noticed.

"Eat," she admonished. "You don't want to get tired. Goodness knows if you'll make it up the stairs."

I suppressed an eye roll and took a bite out of the sandwich. Then frowned. Something was very wrong. I began to cough violently. My father jumped up and immediately clapped me on the back.

When the coughing subsided, half the diners were looking at me. "I'm alright," I waved them away, eyes streaming. "Really!"

259

A minute or so later, I pretended to drop a fork and crouched under the table. With ginger fingers, I pulled the folded-up paper from between my teeth. It was sticky, but the message was still clear.

Third floor balcony 2night! –K.T. (P.S. Don't choke.)

When I arose, my parents were bug-eyed with concern.

"Is everything alright? Did you find the fork?"

For the first time that week, I smiled for real. "I absolutely did."

* * *

It was surprisingly easy to sneak out after dark and I wondered why I hadn't done it before. Donning my thickest jumper, I slipped out into the hallway and padded up to the third-floor balcony. The chill air struck me immediately and I was suddenly reminded of the conversation I'd overheard of Katie and the mysterious Frenchman on the roof. It was hard to believe that it had been just two weeks ago. It felt like years.

She was leaning on the railing when I approached, a slender black silhouette lit only by a low burning gas lantern on the floor of the narrow balcony.

"Oh, good you made it!" she said. "I was vacillating between a couple modes of communication to get around your Dad, you know. Oh—" she scratched the back of her neck awkwardly. "Should we talk about what happened in the car? What's herping by the way?"

"I'd like to never talk about that again actually."

She smiled. "Well, anyways, He's a tricky one. Eyes like a hawk. Caught me going into the men's room with the note taped to a cake. I was going to put it under your pillow, but I don't know how often your family holds pow-wows in one another's rooms, so I opted for the old paper-in-sandwich trick. How was it?"

"Pillow would have been infinitely better," I said without humour. "My dad had to perform the Heimlich."

"Well, you're still here," she waved me towards two tiny chairs and a coffee table squashed into the space. "Let's get down to business. A lot has happened over the past few days and not once have we had time to convene and plot our next move! I assume you got those interviews with the Quislings and that strange little green man."

"The Duke? Yes." I pulled out my notebook and for the first time in three days, we sat down and discussed what we'd learned. It was an enormous relief to be able to pile everything together. The disorganisation of our operation had been bothering me for ages. I only hoped it wasn't too late and that the Lightning Gun and its thief were still stuck in Port Larkeney, just as I was. I opened to a blank page and began to copy the summarised version of everything we knew as we went over it.

Katie went first. "I have very little doubt that the robberies that have been cropping up all over town are connected with all of this. I'm beginning to think whoever it is bonkers crazy."

She began to list all the things that had been stolen: an electric mixer, a lawnmower, three microwaves, a curling iron, a pair of self-skating rollerblades, two camp stoves, a camera, and a hoover with lots of creepy arms. Out of these, three were powered by Amber.

"Don't forget my teapot," I added. "That's still missing." After scouring the car and all our rooms, I was forced to conclude Genie was gone. "Do you think someone's targeting devices with Amber?"

"If they are, they've got a terrible sense for them. Besides, it's hardly likely they'd find very much. Nobody here can afford it. But I think you're right in that."

She held up a polaroid of something that looked like deep scrapes in striped wallpaper. "There's been four separate instances of these cuts in the houses that were robbed. All around the ceiling, same length. It must be from The Lamplighter's brim and yet," she drummed her fingers on the gas lamp, "I've asked everybody about what they saw, and nobody seems to remember anything! They wake up face down in the middle of the living room, in their bedrooms, outside even, with no memory of the

261

night before. Nothing except for some kind of strange music." She hummed a familiar tune, shrugging.

"That's Chopin's Waltz in A-Minor," I said immediately. "Music with memory loss qualities though? I've never heard of anything like it."

"Great, so our guy is some kind of villainous Pied Piper," Katie pulled a scowl. "They stalk us invisibly, steal our town's appliances, and do what with them?"

"Make bombs," I suggested.

Katie's eyes widened. "That's right! That message, 'Prepare to Pay Humans' and that effing cliff."

"F clef."

"Right, so if both of them were stolen and The Cellist's programming had been somehow hijacked that night to destroy that ballroom, I think we might be dealing with Auto activists." She said this last bit with evident satisfaction. I'd never heard of such a thing.

Katie elaborated. "I've read a few stories about them in the paper. There's not a lot, but enough. They're worried Autos are going to come and take us all out of a job then take over the world. They think Sebastian Shaw is at the root of it. It would make sense for one of them to be at the party, even as one of the guests."

It was a plausible theory. "We've both met all of those people though," I countered. "None of them seemed particularly... cause-concerned."

"It's food for thought at least," she shrugged. "Your turn. What'd you come up with?"

I got out the transcripts from the interview and explained them as she read them over. "Essentially, both the Duke and the Quislings were very confused as to why Sebastian invited them over in the first place, especially considering they weren't on very good terms. The Duke had a land dispute here in Port Larkeney. The Quislings, I'm pretty sure had been caught trying to steal Shaw's ideas during the merger of their companies. Even Brum insulted him very publicly. I would say Sebastian Shaw was extending an olive branch but somehow, he doesn't seem like the type. He seems more like someone—"

262

"Who'd get cold-blooded revenge? Yeah. But here's the real question: *What about the cheese?*"

I'd been waiting for this. I sighed and leaned back, staring at the moon. It made a good analogy, the moon and our case. Something that looked to be made of cheese, but in reality, was preposterous.

"No one admitted to anything," I said. "I don't even think there was much of it at the party."

"Could anyone have brought it?"

"The Duke could have. He had cheese pairings to go with his pickle liqueur. Mary could have. She was bringing camel's milk. Did you interview her by the way?"

"Yeah, I did. Same stuff as all the rest of them. Said that nobody left the room that she knew of. Had a hard time remembering what happened after that weird bolt of light."

"I'm starting to think that this isn't a good lead," I took out the paper. "I mean, do we really trust *me*? I don't even trust me lately. For all I know, I could've been hungry and had dairy on the brain. Billius could have just ripped it out by accident. He was lurching all over the place."

"I suppose." Katie looked unwilling to accept this.

"All I'm saying is, maybe we ought to follow a different thread. We still have our mysterious person in the hall. I'm willing to bet that was the person in the snowshoes—if that's what really happened." I tapped my pen against my cheek. "But even then, how would someone get out of the ballroom without being seen? There was the balcony leading off the ballroom, but everyone was in there. I think whoever it was probably doubled back through the window in the study."

She nodded. "What I don't understand is why someone would go through so much trouble just to hide their footprints. Was it someone at the party? Was it someone else who broke in the same time it was happening? If that's the case, was it alone or coordinated with one of the guests?"

The conversation grew silent as we wondered about the nature of the eccentric billionaire. The gas lamp was starting to burn low and the glow of the Christmas lights surrounding the inn grew around us. Haunting pinks and blues winked softly in and out as the entire building stood flickering against the darkness. It made me wonder something.

"Are there more lights than usual?" I asked, "This place seems more...peppery lately, if that's even possible."

"That's the Capsicum Carnival," Katie replied. "You really haven't heard of it?"

I shook my head.

"Stupidest holiday in the world, and yet people from miles around come to visit. All to see my mother's stupid giant pepper."

"That's still going on, is it?"

She shrugged. "It's better. One apology wasn't going to fix it though. At least not for me. I mean, of all hobbies, why couldn't she have at least picked up something useful like sling-shotting or competitive rowing? It's just a big fat vegetable that sits there being gawked at."

I made it a point to change the subject. "Oh, I forgot something," I dug around in my pocket for the baggie.

"A hair?" Katie took it and squinted in the light of a nearby pink bulb. "Wait a second. Where'd you get this?"

"I—er, nicked it."

"What? Wendell!" She reached over and punched me in the arm. It hurt quite a bit. "I didn't think you had it in you!" she exclaimed, turning the bag over. "Wow. I never even got to look at the evidence Wimbelow kept me so busy. He's been going on about this hair for weeks you know. Crazy theories. All sorts of things, like Sebastian owns a secret cat, or it was stolen by an old person, or more recently, that The Cellist was hijacked by a rival inventor to steal the Lightning Gun from under him."

I beat the tip of my pencil against the paper. "That last one might actually have some merit. If it turns out that someone actually has hijacked the two Autos and purposefully making them wreak havoc around town, why not? The only thing is, I remember The Cellist being there when it happened. I looked around the door and saw him standing there, quite singed. In fact, all of the guests had an alibi that night because the room was full of mirrors. Everybody could see everybody. Except for me."

"Are you sure? Think really hard."

264

I thought, and the more I thought about it, the more I wasn't sure. There had been an awful lot of light and sound, reflections and screaming. There was silence again until something struck me. "Maybe it wasn't anyone at the manor at all!"

"How do you figure?"

"Well, who's the person who has the most motive? Who had a mysterious falling out with their protégé Sebastian Shaw? Who has both the knowledge and resources to hijack a complex Auto like The Cellist? Bellamy Dumont, Katie! For all we know that madman could be hiding out right here in Port Larkeney!" I sat back with an air of satisfaction. Here was a solidly-constructed theory with motive, means, and dare I say, pizazz.

"Nah," said Katie.

"What?"

"I just don't buy it. Why rob someone twice? I have a better idea, want to hear it?" Not really. But she was the detective and had more experience. I settled down grumpily.

"What about Evangeline Grey? You haven't interviewed her yet, and she's a wigmaker! What are the odds that hair is hers?"

"She wasn't wearing a white wig that night. It was a black bob. That I'm sure of," I said.

"Okay well, maybe she was the one who hijacked The Cellist. Think about it. All of these people so far, have reasons to be angry at Shaw. To top it off, I've heard she's quite mad. In the initial interviews, everyone had something to say about her…how she was acting odd at the party. Mrs. Quisling even hinted at a sanitarium. Grey was even staying with Shaw for a short time to work on The Cellist. I'm willing to bet at some point she knew what the Lightning Gun was for."

I frowned. "It still doesn't explain how someone got into the study. Remember, your own report said there were no ways into the place other than the hall and a window above the desk. The window was open but there was no way the guests or The Cellist could have got there in time without being seen exiting by some other member of the party."

Katie shrugged at that. "I'm not looking for plausibility right now. What we need is more information. Grey barely consented to give Wimbelow an interview—and even then, there was nothing of any use. I remember it because it was so weird. One second, she was spitting mad, the next, prim and cold as ice."

"So, there's no chance of us going up and talking to her."

"Not necessarily," she winked. "You forget who you're talking to. When I was sent to get back the dentures Becky Butcher stole from Officer Rudy, did I give up just because she was a biter? No! I persisted. In fact, I waited until she was asleep on her front porch to pinch her nose and steal them back, even though it was horribly gummy and when she put up a fight, I almost lost a finger."

I grimaced. "I'm losing the point of this."

"The point is, I'm literally an expert at pulling teeth. I've already got a plan to get the answers we need from Evangeline Grey—what are you looking at?"

My gaze snapped back from the railing. I'd just thought I'd seen something. A dark thing at the base of the inn. Something with lots of arms. I looked again and saw nothing there. I rubbed my temples. The slow pulsing of the lights was playing tricks on me.

"Nothing," I said.

We talked for a while longer after that, discussing what had happened earlier in the day, my father, and Evangeline Grey. However, the more I tried to wheedle that mysterious plan out of Katie, the more unforthcoming she became.

Finally, as I got up to go, she said, "I can't give you all the details, but 11:00pm sharp. Tomorrow night. Wear something... weatherproof."

* * *

Tomorrow came and I was all the worse for it. Anxiety had prevented me from sleeping and when a knock sounded at the door, I was already up and dressed to answer it. I'd expected my father, but it was Mrs. Twill with a bound stack of mail.

"More?" I took the envelopes and saw they had the familiar address.

266

FOURTEEN KILOMETRES EAST OF SUNGAI RIVER, ONE HUNDRED STEPS NORTHWEST UNTIL YOU HEAR THE ORANGUTAN SCREAMS. CROSS SOUTHERN MUD PITS UNTIL YOU REACH THE MOST HONOURABLE CHIEF'S QUARTERS, 251 CHESTER AVENUE

"You must meet the most interesting people on your travels," said Mrs. Twill admiringly. I sifted through the pile, all of which were addressed to Timothy Billings in misspelt, blocky handwriting.

"My brother certainly does," I said.

"Speaking of which," the innkeeper adopted a pitying look, "I heard about what happened with the Inspector. Terrible thing."

"You did?"

"Oh yes. I think Fergus did the right thing letting you off. Poor boy only looking after what happened to his brother. It's a very brave thing you're doing, although I can't say I don't agree with the grounding. Your father only wants to keep you safe; you know."

My expression clouded. I didn't need to be hearing all of this over again from someone *else's* mother.

"Also, I'd like to be in on this *herping* business. You're young of course. I don't judge, but as a mother—"

I fought to keep myself from screaming. "Whatever you heard was wrong and a mistake, Mrs. Twill," I said as calmly as I could.

She didn't look entirely convinced. "Anyways," she lingered on the doorstep, and I wondered what sort of favour she was going to ask me. "As it seems you're confined to the Palaces, you might want to interest yourself in some pastimes. As you know the Capsicum Carnival is coming up. Marvellous event. The whole of Port Larkeney looks forward to it every year. Only, it's a very involved process—lots of hands, you know."

"I'll help you set up, if you like."

"Would you?" she beamed. That's *very* kind of you. Katie should take a leaf out of your book. I'll see you in ten minutes to hang streamers from the rafters."

I nodded, and she left, clipping happily down the stairs. It was actually a welcome distraction, setting up. I knew if I just waited for eleven o'clock, I'd drive myself mad. Grounded. The fact that I'd been given such a juvenile punishment rankled. I was going on eighteen, for goodness' sake! I placed the letters on Tim's nightstand before heading out. By now, his side of the room looked like a mailing room accident. As hard as I tried to keep it clean, the letters just kept coming. I felt bad for Melati—and a little irritated that my brother of all people had found someone who cared for him so much. Finally, I opened one of the telegrams.

TIMOTHEE. STOP. I HAVE TRAVELLED ALL THE WAY TO CAPITAL CITY OF JAKARTA TO SEND THIS STOP I LOVE YOU VERY MUCH STOP IF YOU DO NOT LOVE ME, PLEASE SAY SO STOP THE SILENCE HURTS LIKE THE STING OF A THOUSAND KNIVES STOP LOVE MELATI STOP HUGS AND KISSES FOREVER STOP PS I STILL HAVE THE HAIR YOU SENT ME STOP I SMELL IT EVERY NIGHT. STOP.

Feeling worse and suddenly nauseous, I wrote her a letter detailing how Tim had fallen ill, carefully avoiding the fact that he was in an impenetrable coma and unable to answer her letters at present. I then wrote, however uncomfortably, that he still loved her very much, and wished to see her again. Hopefully this would silence her for the time for I had neither the heart, nor the stomach to open any more private correspondence for fear there might be poetry.

Down in the pub, I noticed for the first time the remarkable transformation that had come over the inn. Competing aromas of sweet and savoury filled the room as Mrs. Twill hurried to cook her wares for the festival. The spice was enough to make one's eyes water and several people in the pub had handkerchiefs to their mouths as they ate. There was a general air of excitement amongst the members of the Piquant Palaces. Amidst the smoke and the din, moving figures darted back and forth, arms laden with décor. Several young volunteers from the town had come up to help set up for the Carnival and I recognized Garrett the nurse setting out brightly-coloured place mats. The florist from down the hill was arranging dried peppers and poinsettias at every table. Laughing and talking filled the room as teenagers from the local secondary school strung up so many lights that the rafters were wound with more glittering bulbs than a Quinceñera.

Even Billius was in on things as he leaned on the bar, minutely detailing to a harassed Mrs. Twill the best way to make a Pepperoncini Martini. I picked my way through the fracas and saw Katie trying and failing to set up an enormous jangling kiosk laden with various Big Bertha merchandise. Something thumped and rolled across the floor to me. I picked it up. It was a large, green bell pepper on which the words, "My Friend Went to Port Larkeney and All They Got Me Was This Lousy Pepper," were painted.

"Yikes," I put it back on the rickety kiosk and turned to Katie. "Need any help?"

She shook her head. "Streamers," was all she replied, and handed me two rolls with a pointed look because father had appeared behind me.

As the day wore on, I worked my way outside, hanging streamers from wooden awnings. It was pleasant out here, especially as evening set and a gentle breeze rustled the tall grass around the path. People had been filtering in and out and I paid them little mind, but as a familiar figure appeared on the horizon, I put down the streamers. Mary's coily hair and woollen skirt blew behind her as she struggled up the steps with two enormous metal canisters. What struck me as peculiar was thecompact, bowlegged person beside her who was carrying a smaller canister.

"Mary?" I called.

She looked up and her squinty, wide set eyes broke into a grin. "Alright Mr. Billings?" she called. She huffed up the steps and set the canisters down with a ringing clang when she reached the top. I hurried to help her.

"It's just Wendell," I said, reaching for one. It had to be at least half my height and nearly as wide. "What's in these?"

"Oh, don't worry about that. Humberdt and I managed fine. It's goat's milk." She nudged the canisters proudly with her boot. "I'm a goat farmer, remember? Mrs. Twill ordered three more canisters on top of the weekly ones, and I thought I'd deliver them in person to see how the setup for the festival is going." She stopped to catch her breath and look at the Palaces which now gleamed and fluttered with every colour of streamer imaginable. "It looks wonderful! You must be having fun."

"I—"

I didn't finish the sentence because a large, muscular, and entirely hairless chimp wearing a beanie hat had emerged from around her skirt. Wrinkles sagged around his surly face as he hefted his own canister with ease. Unconsciously, I backed away.

If experience has taught me anything, it's to keep well-away from monkeys of any sort if you value your fingers or your trousers.

"Oh, don't worry about Humberdt here," said Mary cheerfully, patting the monkey on the shoulder. She handed a piece of cheese which he snatched up greedily. I was unable to look away as the large lips moved around the hunk.

"He's completely trained, do anything for a bit of cheese. He was actually a stowaway from Africa, you know. Unfortunately, he was bullied very badly on account of his condition. A rare form of chimp-alopecia which renders him completely hairless. He took such a liking to me that when I got home, I found him hiding in my suitcase! Say hello, Humberdt!"

With a solemn expression, the monkey turned his sad eyes to me and slowly doffed the limp beanie. Then, with a mournful sigh at the chill seeping through the hills, he hefted both the canisters and headed for the warmth of the pub.

"Sorry about that," said Mary, shaking her head. "He's usually much more polite. He's been a bit grumpy with me lately. I promised him something and forgot, and now he just grunts at me."

Katie, who was just coming out, gave the monkey a quick hello as he gave her another slow, doff of the cap, and strode towards us. "That weirds me out every time," she said to Mary.

"You two know each other?" I asked.

"Oh yeah, I see her, like, every week. I'm pretty sure we'd be sued halfway to China if people didn't have goat milk to wash down my ma's cooking."

"We've got a lot in common," said Mary.

HUMBERDT

JUST looking
aT HIM MAKES
mE COLD

"A love of hiking," said Katie.

"Lonely childhoods."

"A fondness for plaid."

"Missing fathers under very mysterious circumstances," Mary finished. They high-fived and I turned away with relief as my own father called me from a porthole to help with dusting.

By the time darkness rolled around, everyone was exhausted and said their goodnights early. The Capsicum Carnival was only two days away and there was still much to be done, but for now, the Palaces were suitably decorated. Mrs. Twill thanked everyone for their hard work. As people took saucers of milk and tea up to bed, I snuck a coffee in order to stay awake. It was only eight o' clock and the bedside clock ticked maddeningly slowly. I paced restlessly and palmed the coffee. I wondered what Katie had in store and stared with apprehension at the weatherproof coat draped over the dresser.

~25~

A Feather Boa, A Beekeeper's Helmet, and A Cuban Cigar

Eleven o'clock came and went. I shrugged on and off my coat. Several times I looked out the window for some unknown reason. The moon appeared, partially obscured by a quicksilver cloud. I shook my hands to relieve the edginess that was beginning to set in. A light beneath the door flickered as soft feet crept by. Then there was a gentle knock. I hurried to open it—and was disappointed.

My father stood there in a bathrobe and slippers, a torch in hand. "I saw the light on under the door," he whispered reprovingly. "It's late, Wendell. Go to sleep."

"Sorry. I was reading."

"Alright, well goodnight son. By the way," he cast the light downwards, "are you wearing galoshes?"

"G'night Dad!" I listened at the door to make sure the footsteps died away, but after a minute or so, they came back, faded again, and repeated. So, he was doing midnight rounds

273

now. Katie must have seen him and decided not to take her chances. With a vague sense of disappointment, I began to take off my coat and boots. Even in the warmth of the room, I shivered a little at the thin howl of the wind outside. It made the porthole window squeak at its hinges. I turned off the lights and went to bed.

Scritch. Scratch.

A scrabbling sound cut through the other noises, and I fumbled blindly for the switch. *The Cellist* whispered the paranoid part of me. *He's here.* I grabbed the discarded boot. The bendy plastic felt insignificant in my hand. *Of course it's not!* The rational part shot back.

Scratch. Scratch.

The memory of the ballroom was in the forefront of my mind as I edged toward the window, holding the business end of the welly. Plus, there were no trees on top of the hill. The moonlight was all but gone when I made it to the glass. I pressed a finger to it and stared into the darkness. A large white hand appeared in the blackness, pressing against the window.

"AH!"

I hit the floor with a painful thud, scrambling back, holding the boot in front of me. "Don't come near me!"

But the porthole window opened with a slow creak, and I saw the pair of flashing, Cheshire eyes smiling between a web of windblown blond hair.

"It's me you berk," said Katie, gripping the inside of the window. "Now let me in before I blow off the side of the building."

I shouldn't have been surprised really. I gave my elbow for support as she manoeuvred her gangly limbs through the tiny porthole.

"You can drop the boot you know. I don't know who you're planning on hurting with that."

"That's not—it's—maybe you shouldn't be climbing through other people's windows in the dead of night!" I cried.

She stood up with a groan and appraised me for the first time. "And where are you going in that?" She pointed to my pyjamas.

274

"This is a secret mission, not a slumber party. Are those little ducks?"

"Mallar…never mind," I said, hurriedly putting on my jumper over them. "It's nearly twelve. I thought you weren't coming."

"I had to get around your father, didn't I? Plus, I had to wait for Evangeline Grey to be in the perfect position. I spent an hour outside her room waiting for her to leave."

I held up a hand. "You don't mean we're going out *there*, do you? That's what you meant?" I laughed. "No. That's crazy."

Katie frowned. "Crazy? After everything we've done?"

"I just don't see the point of going outside to do it. Why do we have to climb 10 metres above the ground on a hill at least 60 metres above the rest of the city…in a town at least 60 more metres above the ocean? I mean, where does it end?"

"On the third floor," she said dryly. "What's wrong with you? Isn't this what you do for a living? I thought you were basically a boy Magellan."

"I am. I am." I bounced nervously, trying to shake off the nerves as I stared outside. "I just don't see the sense in it, that's all. Why don't we have a nice normal conversation with her? I'm sure she'll come around."

The detective regarded me with suspicion. "We talked about this. She won't. If I didn't know better…*oh.*" A different look transformed her face. She snapped her fingers.

"You're afraid of heights!"

"I am not!" But my protests only served increase her smugness. "Fine. I am. I can stand a few metres off the ground like low trees and the like, but any higher than that, I freeze up and my legs are as good as jelly. You see why I can't go out there!"

"Not to worry, Wendell old boy," Katie gave me what she evidently thought was a reassuring look. "I'm a dab hand with baby bjorns. How many belts have you got?"

"*No.*"

A few minutes more wheedling drew no further results.

"Fine," she sat on the bed, pursing her lips. "Good thing for you, there might be one more option."

* * *

*It's going to be okay. It's going to be okay. It'sgoingtobeok*OHMYGOD.

"Stop shaking it!" I bellowed, gripping the rope as tightly as a wounded koala in a monsoon.

"Shh!" Katie's voice sounded amused from somewhere nearby. "You're going to wake the whole inn if you keep on yelling like that. Besides, that's not me, it's the wind."

Beneath me, the makeshift dumbwaiter gave an ominous creak. It jerked violently left and right, banging nerve-wrackingly against the outside of the Palaces. The heavy wind fortunately glanced off my weather-proof coat. It didn't stop it from banging the rest of me around like a bug in a jar. There was no time think about how ridiculous I looked. All my efforts were focused on Katie's voice. It was a little easier with the blindfold. The sound of her foot on the metal bars running up the building came through clearer with my sharpened hearing. All the same, *I couldn't see.*
The wooden box was cramped. My knees pulled to my chest; I felt the outside of it for any weaknesses in the structural integrity. I found several. Suddenly the dumbwaiter stilled a little.

"Gotcha," said Katie. Cold hands slipped a new rope into my own. "Now, all you have to do is keep pulling until I say stop. Then take off the blindfold and I'll help you in."

"Katie, what is the carrying capacity of the box? What's the tensile strength of this rope?"

"Four," she said confidently, and before I could tell her that meant absolutely nothing, I felt a tightening of the rope as she gave it a heave. I was inching upwards.

With nothing else to cling onto, I pulled down on the rope. Hand over hand I pulled, adrenaline pushing me to keep going, fear telling me to freeze. If I stopped, I would lose my hold, and that would send me rocketing downward. I imagined the splintering of the wooden box hitting the ground, the unimaginable pain, and the burn of the rope as it slid through my fingers. I kept on, my teeth chattering and ears full of the unearthly howl of the midnight wind.

276

"Come on! You've got it! Nearly there now!" Katie kept up a stream of encouragement as she climbed beside me. She started whistling The Bee Gees and I pulled harder to get away from it.

"Stop. Stop!"

After what felt like hours, but couldn't have been more than three minutes, I heard her voice calling out. I'd never been so glad to hear anything in my life. I loosened my grip on the rope and immediately felt that horrifying plummeting sensation as it dropped. I grabbed it as fast as I could but felt it slide painfully through my fingers. Before it could go too far, the dumbwaiter slowed to a jerky halt and thudded jarringly against the side of the inn.

"Geez. Don't let go," the detective panted as she heaved on the rope above me. "You can take off the blindfold now by the way. We're here." The window creaked as she edged it open. "All clear," Katie whispered.

Through the shirt tied around my face, I sensed light and warmth through the open porthole. I raised the blindfold, keeping a good hold on the pulley rope. Two stories below, the ground swirled into a dizzying blur. Nausea rose in my throat. All of a sudden, my arms didn't seem to want to work.

"Katie. Katie? Where are you?"

"In here," she was already inside Evangeline's room. "What are you waiting for?"

"I can't move," I said through gritted teeth. It was a struggle to even move my neck.

"Take my hand!"

"*Nonono.* I can't let go of the rope."

"Then give *me* the rope. Come on."

I steeled myself and forced my arm out of the magnetic hold it seemed to have on my sides. Katie took it, keeping it taut.

"Now, if you don't climb out and get inside, I'm going to drop this," she said calmly.

"What!" I stared at her. Anger flared up in me. "That kind of thing isn't going to work on me."

"I'm not kidding."

"You're crazy!"

The detective shrugged. "Oops." The box slipped a few inches with me in it. Without further thought, my arms pedalled for the thick metal rim of the window and stuck there. The forward momentum carried me through about halfway, until I was stuck half in half out, my legs kicking wildly in the emptiness and mouth cursing furiously at the detective. Not one of my better moments.

Katie offered an elbow, and I yanked it rather roughly, falling hard through the window and making an undignified entrance on the wood floor.

I got up shakily, ears burning. "I can't *believe you*."

She only offered me an infuriating smile. "Come on," she repeated. "We don't have much time."

I clicked on my torch and shone it around the darkened room. It was a similar layout to my own except for a single bed and a smaller bureau. The outlines of bags and suitcases appeared on the floor. The beam swept from bed to walls to bathroom door to a darkened silhouette with tendrils of brown hair standing silently in the centre of the room.

My light thudded to the floor in surprise, flickering and going out. There was someone in here with us. Katie froze too. The sound of our breaths penetrated the darkness. Why didn't they move? Why didn't they turn around?

"Hello?"

The swish of her coat moved past me. She went up to the figure and flicked it on the head. There was a faint wobble in the silhouette, and I realised that it had no arms, and no body for that matter. "It's just one of those head mannequins," said Katie in relief.

It took getting used to the creepy, featureless heads floating disembodied at various heights around the room. They were held up by long black poles and each one adorned with the wigs I'd seen Evangeline wear. There was a pixie blonde, a ginger with curls, a shoulder length brunette, and a dark brown toupee, presumably for a client. The walls had virtually disappeared under the furry weight of the pinned perukes. There were blond ones, black ones, chartreuse and pink, straight ones, wavy ones, and several that piled up to impossible heights. The bed was a tip, covered in clothes and hat boxes. Some of the pieces seemed oddly incongruous even for my limited knowledge in fashion. Take for instance, the dark wool overcoat rumpled beside a pink feather boa, resting parallel to a beekeeper's helmet.

"How much time do we have?" I whispered, glancing at the door.

"A good twenty minutes or so, I'm sure," said Katie, walking around the heads on poles with a raised eyebrow. "I saw her go down to the pub as she always does. Insomnia. Needs hot cider to sleep." She knocked one of the heads. "You know, I'm starting to really think it is her that tried to do Sebastian in. This is some Vlad the Impaler type decor."

We split up, combing the small room. My first sweep I found a pearl handled hairbrush, a Cuban cigar, and—

I turned around excitedly. "Come look at this." It was a letter from the Private Institute of Mental Rehabilitation in Leeds addressed to the wigmaker. "It's dated from four months ago."

Dear Ms. Grey, The Girls, and of course, Franklin.

We are writing to you to express our concern toward your sudden departure. You have elected to leave the program before its completion without warning. We must advise you that in order for a successful elimination of symptoms, the program must be fully completed with a signature from our professionals. Should you decide to return, as a longstanding patient with an unfinished program, you still have credit at our facilities.
Please take this letter into consideration.

    Best wishes,
        Sonya Parekh M.D.
        The Private Institute of Mental
        Rehabilitation

"Who are 'the girls and of course, Franklin?'" Katie took the note from me. "Secret cohorts? It might explain things if stealing the gun was a multiple man, and woman, job."

"And what was she getting treatment for and why did she leave in the middle of it?" I looked around the room for any evidence of medicine bottles or prescriptions. There was nothing in the suitcases, the cabinets, bathroom, dresser, or under the bed. Neither was the Lightning Gun, which I'd had keen hopes for.

"There's nothing," I said, frustrated. "Nothing except these weird clothes, and these weird wigs. Any luck with the hair?"

Katie pointed to a white beehive on one of the heads and a silvery bob leaning on a bedpost. "Could be any of those. I'm not a hair expert though. Didn't you say she was wearing a black one on the night of the dinner party?"

"Yes." I spun in a slow circle. There must be something I was missing. I was loathe to go outside again and face the devastating drop. What about a remote control? I opened all the hat boxes as Katie searched behind the bed. I'd felt certain that Evangeline was the one controlling The Lamplighter and Cellist. Unless she kept everything important in a place other than her rooms, our theory was falling apart before our very eyes.

There was a thump on the stairs. Katie straightened quickly. I quickly put back the hats and put out the light.

"Is it her?" I whispered.

Katie listened. Her eyes widened. "Yes. She's thirty seconds away."

Far be it for me to know how Katie knew that. As soon as I opened the porthole window, a chilly gust encircled the room. I swallowed. The ground was a very long three stories down and there was a very narrow platform outside.

"Ladies first," I said.

But she shoved me towards the night. "If I go first, you never will. Now get a move on."

Great. I placed a tentative arm on the ledge, trying to draw every ounce of courage in this dire moment.

"Argh!"

I turned around. "What?"

Katie hopped around the room as styrofoam heads bounced around the floor. She was upsetting everything in the room, clutching at something caught on her bellbottoms.

"What are you doing?" I hissed.

"Rat!" She hissed wide eyed. "Rat! Get it off! Get it—!" The sentence abruptly stopped as she slumped onto the bed snoring.

"Aha!" I cried. "I knew it!" Then as the doorknob jiggled, panic quickly replaced triumph.

"No, no, no!" I ran to her. "Katie! Wake up!" There wasn't any more time. The key jiggled in the lock. And so, I did what I hoped never to do again. I hauled the sleeping detective by the armpits and shoved us both inside Evangeline Grey's enormous armoire.

~26~

Wigged Out

A thin vertical line of light appeared through the armoire doors as Evangeline switched the light on. There was an audible gasp.

"My wigs!" She ran to right them but stopped. "Who's there?"

I held my breath. It was a precarious position to be sure. On one side of the box, I was squished by several wool coats and dresses, hat boxes, shoes, and suitcases. On the other side, I was squished by the sleeping detective, who had been stuck in a sort of limp handstand, so while her pointy boots dug into my ear, I had to avoid kneeing her mouth.

As far as unpleasant dark spaces, it was second only to the تقلص حاد في غرفة الموت which roughly translated means "Spiky Shrinking Room of Death," in Arabic. A story for another time.

Evangeline's footsteps drew dangerously near the armoire. I could hear her breathing, quick and fluttery. Katie let out a soft snore and I dropped a coat over her head.

"Oh. I see." Evangeline sounded exasperated and relief filled me as her footsteps moved away. "Paranoia as always. I should have known that this horrible place is so direly neglected it equates to sleeping in a squalid windblown pit of woodlice and despair."

The window creaked again and the howl I'd tuned out suddenly ceased, making every noise that much louder. After ten minutes of setting her room to rights, she stood up and yawned, muttering something about filth, fishermen, and hot water. She grabbed a grey silk kimono from the bed and disappeared into the bathroom. This was our chance.

I waited until the sound of running water obscured the groan of the closet, before I very quietly leaned down and pinched Katie's nose while covering her mouth.

"MMF!" Her eyes popped open in fear. When I was sure she wouldn't scream, I removed my hand.

"Sorry."

Even at this moment, when we were a hairsbreadth away from being caught, crammed together in a tiny closet, I had to do it.

"I knew it!" I whispered. "I knew you had narcolepsy." I waited for her to be shocked, to stutter and deny it. Instead, she looked up at me with an expression of mild befuddlement.

"What are you talking about? What's that?"

I wondered if I'd heard her correctly. *What's that?* she'd said. How could she deny it when it had happened right in front of me? I was never wrong about an obscure diagnosis. Katie shuffled to an upright position inside the armoire, managing to knee me in the ribs in the process. I put a hand to my stomach in pain.

"Shh!" I said. "Can you imagine if she was in the room? She's taking a shower. We're in the closet if you haven't guessed, *and you know what narcolepsy is. You can't seriously deny it.*"

Katie completely ignored the last part. "Oh good," she stretched as much as she was able. "That means I can disregard my other theory I had upon waking up in a dark enclosed space of wood." She tried pushing open the door, but I closed it.

"Don't you think I deserved to know something like this? What if you had fallen asleep out there on the side of the building? You could have killed us both when you were holding that rope!"

284

"I don't know what you're talking about," Katie said firmly and now I knew that she did.

"Fine," I wacked a feather boa out of my face. "Then I'm leaving." I was angrier with myself than anything. I'd known that Katie's narcolepsy would be an issue, but I'd waited until it had become a risk before saying anything. Now it was too late.

Her voice took on a hitch of desperation. "But your Dad's probably still out there and we haven't found anything."

"Yes, we have! I'm not staying in this closet."

She crossed her arms. "Just until she goes to sleep. Then we go back out the window the way we came. Easy peasy."

"No, not easy peasy! Not at all!" I pushed open the door. "Are you going to admit you have narcolepsy? That you have a dangerous condition you deliberately omitted when you met me and forced me onto a dumbwaiter?"

Katie scowled in the half-darkness. "If you were suspicious then why'd you agree? I didn't force you to do anything."

"So do you admit it?"

Her mouth was set into a thin line. She wasn't budging.

"I'm going then," I stepped out into the open.

As soon as the room became visible, Katie gasped. Her eyes became wide and glossy, fixated on all the wigs as if she'd never seen them before.

"The girls," she murmured as if in a trance. "The girls are wigs, and the wigs are girls."

I didn't know what the ding-dong-diddlebat that meant but I was beyond caring at that point. And wouldn't you know it, the moment I left the wardrobe, the shower stopped. A hand appeared, groping around the door.

"Cripes," I said.

"Gingersnaps," said Katie.

I whirled around furiously. "You kept me here!"

"I figured it out!" she shot back. "You'll thank me."

Pale fingers brushed one of the heads near the bathroom door, travelling up its face onto the empty scalp.

"Franklin? Franklin, where are you dear?" Her voice began to rise in pitch. *"Franklin?"*

Who's Franklin? I mouthed.

Slowly, Katie raised the leg of her bellbottoms, where, hopelessly entangled and what she'd previously thought was a rat, was the furry brown toupee.

"Toss it to her!"

"I can't. It's stuck."

Without warning, the floor burst open, and I froze, one foot out of the armoire, face to face with Evangeline Grey. The wigmaker, clutching a kimono around herself, black bob plastered to her face that she'd evidently showered in, let out an almighty scream that rattled the windowsills.

"ARGHH!"

That was when Katie decided to make an appearance, climbing outside of the closet.

"Shh!" she said with mild irritation. "Do you *want* to wake up everyone in the hall?"

Evangeline screamed louder, bouncing from foot to foot, as if unsure of where to run. "Thieves!" she cried. "Interlopers, invaders, predators! No wait, you're children. Child predators! Wait, that's not right either. Predators who are children, ahhh!"

"Right well, we'll just be going," I said, heading for the door. "Wrong room. Sorry about that. Thought I was hiding in my own closet."

"Police!" Evangeline ran for the door, barring my path. As I was afraid she might lose her grip on the kimono, I couldn't move any further.

"Oh no you don't!" said Katie, running for the small woman.

For one terrible moment I thought she was going in for the tackle, but instead, she whipped off the black bob in one smooth movement and plopped the furry brown toupee in its place.

"How d'you think that would make any difference!" I snapped.

Katie looked at loss for an explanation. But just as quickly as the screaming began, it stopped. Evangeline blinked and stretched as if she'd just woken from a long sleep. Heedless of our stares, she turned away from the door, went to the closet and retrieved a plaid bathrobe that was much coarser and thicker than the grey kimono. She proceeded to wrap it around herself with a grunt of "better."

286

She affixed us with a glare and jerked her thump to the bureau. "Could one of you chaps fetch me a cigar. Top drawer of the cabinet. I'll be out in a tick."

The voice was gruff. Deeper. Well, as deep as Evangeline's voice could go. Thoroughly out of sorts, I did as I was told, finding the tin and handing it to her before she went into the bathroom for a second time. The static of a record player began from the other room and an eclectic mix of music poured through the door. We sat on the bed. Awkward silence filling the room.

Katie broke the silence. "What kind of music is this?"

"It's Argentinian tango I believe," I said, staring determinedly at a space of wall without wigs and trying to make sense of the randomness of the universe.

"Hmph. Someone needs to introduce her to The Village People."

"I've met enough village people for one lifetime thanks."

Katie looked at me. "It's a band."

"What did you do to her?" I asked. "Why did that toupee stop her from calling the police?"

The music switched to a depressing didgeridoo.

"Well, I was hoping Franklin wasn't the sort to call the cops. But it all worked out rather well in the end, didn't it?"

I tossed my hands up in the air. "Who. Is. Franklin?"

"Me, boy."

Evangeline emerged from the bathroom. There were specks of shaving cream left on her smooth white face and the ends of the toupee had been neatly brushed and fastened.

I stood up. "Is this some kind of a joke?"

"I believe I should be asking that to the two young intruders sitting in my chambers in the dead of night." Evangeline gave the two of us a cool stare. Her hands were clasped behind her back in a way that reminded me of my grandfather.

"It's very nice to meet you, Franklin," said Katie immediately, standing up and shaking Evangeline's hand.

I was at a loss, currently under the suspicion I'd acquired some kind of vertigo induced brain-scrambling. "Is there something I'm missing here?"

Katie guided me gently back to sitting. "It's one of her personalities," she explained. "I figured it out in the closet. There's Franklin, Betty, Fronz, Jozie, Patricia, and the list goes on. It's the only thing that makes sense. Franklin and the girls in the letter? There were name tags on each of the heads…and the fact she'd attended a psychiatric institution. So, this one," she pointed at the toupee, "is Franklin. Franklin, this is Wendell. Wendell, Franklin."

I stared at Franklin as he pulled up a chair and sat down on it with a groan. There was no way. And yet, if I really looked for it, Evangeline's mannerisms had all but disappeared. By the way he was sitting, I got the idea that Franklin was a very portly man of older middle age. By the way he stroked his chin, I began to see a large grey moustache and by the way he spoke, I heard a scholar, burdened and melancholic in the place of Evangeline's clipped upper class accent.

Franklin took a long puff of his cigar and smoke hazed the room. "It appears you two already know who I am then. Good. Saves the trouble."

"Prove it," I said. "Prove you're really an alter ego and not just a good actor. Billius Brum could do that just as well, I'm sure."

Franklin gave me another cold look. "I am proving your assumption by not turning the two of you in this very minute. I know who you are, and I have made a calculated risk."

"Which is…?"

"Prove her innocence," said Franklin. "Evangeline is a helpless woman who suffered at the hands of Sebastian Shaw. Her memory makes her highly suspect as does her "disorder of the mind." The rest of us," he gestured towards the other wigs on the wall, "would rather not spend the rest of our natural lives in a prison as we already exist within a prison of the mind. Being trapped inside someone's brain is sort of like looking through two big, ugly bay windows. As such, I'd prefer some variation in the scenery."

"So you'll tell us what we want to know?"

"I already know what you want to know. I know who you are and what you desire. I have nothing else to do in this mind besides inspect human behaviour. I was born in darkness, and I shall die as such. A paradox. A joke." He sighed deeply, looking ahead at

FRANKLIN 5
A COMPLETE ENIGMA

nothing. "Wendell and Katie. Two children I am resting my hopes on. It should not be the case, and yet the universe is, after all, a vast cataclysm of unfathomable events, slowly swirling, bubbling together in a pot of nonsensical stew in which we all float. Bits of beef and potato, helpless, blind, bobbing placidly into the miserable darkness of the future. That is us."

This guy was a real charmer.

He turned to Katie. "I know who you are, Katie Twill. The cheerful young detective, whose lack of paternal guidance results in reckless behaviour and the gnawing compulsion to prove herself. Why do you feel the need to fix things?" He asked. "Irony again, the desire to bring order, when you yourself are the chaos. And you have the most peculiar mode of deduction. I've never seen anything like it."

As Katie frowned, he turned to me, and I felt locked into his slow, turtleish gaze.

"Wendell Billings. The aggrieved son of a travel columnist. A boy, just like a bit of carrot in a stew, floating along, always pulled by forces greater than he. Something steeps you in a perpetual state of irritable incredulity—as if you simply can't believe that things, places, and people continue to happen at you. Especially when you are, in fact, allowing such things to happen." He sat back, interlacing his fingers.

I didn't like that. I didn't like his look. I didn't like that he was the complete polar opposite of Evangeline, and I didn't like the way he sat there with those greyish x-ray eyes, spitting assumptions about me that were obviously untrue.

"Now you want to know exactly who I am. Yes, I see you're taking notes. Very good. I have existed alongside Evangeline from birth, along with countless others. A very rare case. Souls, split personality, schizophrenia, the question of theology versus psychology is not mine to answer, only that I am here. She was the dominant one, but it was an eternal struggle for each of us to surface, to experience the bodily senses and the outside world." At this, he took a deep breath, and his fingers stroked the wood of the chair as if to embody the feeling.

"This drove Evangeline to the brink of madness as a child, as I can imagine it would to anyone with a hundred voices clamouring for attention. Eventually she learned the secret to suppressing us. She assigned each personality a wig that acted as a sort of trigger. We developed an uneasy truce and a schedule where each personality would get its time in the sun. But as Evangeline's professional life became more involved and her personal time diminished, there was less and less time for us to surface.

"Two years ago, it had gotten to a point where I only had control once every two months. I spent the time agonising, pondering, writing a memoir in the depths of our brain. The others did not take it so well. One of us, Veronica, was of a particularly fiery disposition. She felt the unfairness of our position and sought to rectify it. One day, without use of the wigs, Evangeline was measuring a toupee for a client. Veronica did not listen to my warnings. She burst into consciousness and suffice it to say, wrought havoc on the house, climbing through the window, whooping like an ape, and scampering across the roof. Veronica is a professional rappeler.

"After gaining control once more, Evangeline was horrified. Rumours abounded about her sanity and her business suffered. She enrolled herself into a psychiatric facility in order to suppress us once and for all. It was the worst few months of my life. I remember retreating into the dark recesses of the mind, weakening as the medication and therapy took their hold. I was saved only by one thing. Sebastian Shaw.

"Evangeline received a letter in the middle of her treatment from Shaw with a commission for a wig for one of his most prized Autos. As treatment had been going well and she was once again feeling herself, Evangeline left the institution without another thought. At first, I was joyous. We lived to fight another day. Then I began to feel something was not right. Sebastian greeted us with open arms and a chill smile. He was a cunning man with many secrets. I could tell that just by looking at him. A businessman of that level must be shrewd and uncompromising. I did not realise just how much."

At this point, Katie interrupted. "Wait, how are you able to remember all this when Evangeline couldn't tell us anything?"

Franklin shrugged. "Ask the people who only share that they lick their own toenails during hypnosis. It's the same thing. Even under duress, there is always some part of the mind awake, conscious, and recording. As a person without a body, I could only make suggestions, quiet whispers in the back of her mind.

"In the beginning, I entreated her not to go. I—She'd heard rumours of people going missing in Port Larkeney and I had a terrible feeling. She did not listen. We went to stay with Shaw for four days as it was a long ride from London. I was able to look through her eyes in fleeting glimpses whenever she let her guard down, whether that be in tiredness or lack of concentration. We were very well received and stayed in a guest room in the left wing. I am sure you were struck by just how large the house was. A man alone, amongst hundreds of rooms, each one opulent and fully furnished. But as lavish as it was, it had grown cold from disuse. It felt like a boy's dream, to have as many toys as he likes, as many cars and puzzles. But all he wants is too many, and they become abandoned, gathering dust."

Franklin paused for a breath.

"During the twilight hours of sleep and wakefulness, I pushed myself to the forefront of her consciousness and persuaded Evangeline to move about the house. I was suspicious of Shaw. I was suspicious of how he kept us confined to one wing of the house, how he moved about like a shadow, appearing wherever we were, and how, one evening, behind a stairwell, I saw him stroking the cheek of an Automaton. He spent days carving faces, not young beautiful faces but many old and ugly, fat, entreating, many normal, human faces. Some I recognized.

'They are commissions,' he said. 'Just like you are doing for me. People like to see their own likenesses come to life. It is the ultimate vanity.'"

Franklin shivered despite himself and continued.

"Then, one night, I was completely mobile. Evangeline was in one of her rare bouts of sleepwalking. Wrestling the others aside, I took control, put on the toupee, and investigated the house. All was dark. My footsteps made little sound on the cold marble. Room after room I searched, looking for something, although I wasn't sure what. I reached one of the many courtyards and looked to the sky. Thunder crackled overhead and it began to rain. He was there.

"He stood in the middle of the grass, hair and coattails completely soaked through. His face blue with a ghostly light that shimmered from something in his hand. Beside him hulked a spiny hunchbacked beast of metal. In its arms was something in a large black blanket. Shaw stood before the fountain in the centre of the courtyard, the one shaped like a pitiful old man. He raised the contraption and I saw it was some kind of a gun, coppery with a large clear bulb at the end that emitted the unnatural light. He said, 'I'm going to enjoy this after all you've done, Baron.'"

"Baron?" I asked.

Franklin nodded. "Baron Davies. You probably haven't heard of him, but he's the very same man who went missing from his estate in Suffolk a few months back. Caused a bit of a stir amongst the higher ups, but little was done as he was an old man, partial to wandering. Suddenly the courtyard was aglow with the blue light. In the sharp relief, I saw the old man in the fountain had been carved in his exact likeness. Then, something like I had never seen, tendrils of light crawling up it like vines and disappearing into the chest. When it had dissipated, the eyes of the statue glowed orange as Amber does. Davies slumped into the grass.

"Sebastian clapped twice, and water began to flow through the mouth of the old man. With the storm, the basin was already full, and it overflowed, pouring over into the grass. Sebastian only laughed and beckoned his Automaton to follow him. The Auto picked up the prone body of the man. They left and I ran."

At this, Franklin began tugging at his collar in a nervous twitch.

"Normally, I would not have believed my own eyes. I would have thought it was a dream or some other affectation of the fractured mind I inhabit. I would have, if it were not for the fact that I experienced the same thing the very next day. I do not know how he found out about it. Upon questioning Evangeline, she said she remembered nothing. She'd been sleepwalking most likely.

"The next thing I knew, we were in a dark room that smelled of fish. Sebastian stood over me in a white lab coat. There was fear in all of our selves when we saw he was holding the very same contraption with the blue bulb at the end. Evangeline twisted and pleaded, restrained. 'Don't worry,' said Sebastian, pointing the mouth of the lightning gun to our chest. 'This won't hurt a bit.'"

Franklin tugged more of his collar down and before we could protest—because he was very much a she on the outside—he raised his hand irritably.

"Calm yourselves. It is only a small part."

The narrow white fingers pulled back the hem of the plaid bathrobe until Franklin's collarbone was exposed. I didn't need to see anymore. I knew it at once, that single, radiating yellow line embedded in the flesh.

"The Sunspot," I breathed.

~27~

Out of the frying pan and into the Fire...works

I see you already have a name for it," said Franklin, pulling the covering back over himself. "That gives me hope. I have reason to believe Shaw is doing this to others in order to keep his secrets. I do not pretend to know a great deal of practical science, but an energy pulse powerful enough to erase one's memory must be very powerful indeed"

A weight had settled upon the room. Here was one more person who had fallen victim to this mysterious weapon and its creator. Questions piled in my mind. I could see the same was happening to Katie.

"Was this before or after the dinner party?" she asked.

"Did you suffer any other effects?" I said. "You didn't recover from a deathly coma by any chance?"

"You didn't forget anything else did you, not like family or your childhood?"

I glanced at the detective. She was busy staring intently at Franklin.

Franklin waved at the questions like an old horse swatting flies. "Yes yes, I'm getting to it. To address the young lady, this was approximately four months before I received the invitation in the mail. Again, I begged Evangeline not to go. We all did. But with her memory gone, she assumed her misgivings were just another manifestation of psychosis, and here we are," he said gloomily. "As for the effects, it is hard to say what is a matter of the mind, and what is due to that terrible device. I know that even I do not remember fully what happened. Nonsensical flashes will appear without warning. It took me months to fully decipher the bits and pieces of that night. I had an elevated heart rate. I also experienced a most peculiar feeling both times I was in the presence of the device—a sort of hair-raising crackling feeling. As for the last question, fortunately, no. Memories before that incident still appear to be intact."

Katie put forth the next question.

"What are your thoughts on cheese?"

Franklin snorted. "Cheese?"

I groaned. "Katie, I thought we agreed that note was bunk. It's just a random word!"

She ignored me.

"Come on Franklin. Was there anything significant about cheese you noticed that night?"

This was clearly not the way Franklin had imagined this going. "Other than the smell of it? The normal smell of pungent cheese at a lavish dinner party? Only the absence of it. I thought it was common knowledge that Sebastian Shaw was lactose intolerant. It was all liver."

The detective slumped, but I was already rummaging in my pocket. We couldn't forget what we'd come here for. I withdrew the bagged hair and handed it to Franklin.

"I know you say Evangeline didn't do it, but this was found in the study. Are you sure it doesn't match any of your wigs? And if it doesn't, do you have any idea who it might belong to?"

Franklin took it and delicately pulled the hair from the clear ziplock. He frowned, rolling it between thin, feminine fingers. "I—er, she—would never use hair like this in a wig. It's far too coarse. Too thick. Makes for an unpleasant texture, you see? Difficult to wash and clean, which you must do to a wig just like any other hair. No, I don't recognise this as anyone else's." He handed it back. "I'm sorry I couldn't be of more help."

The two of us sat back and pondered this. I felt reasonably sure it wasn't Evangeline. Despite her unstable state of consciousness, Franklin's forthcomingness had aligned with several holes in the growing narrative. He was frank and open. One thing struck me as odd though. I turned to Katie.

"Why bring camel's milk to a party where the host is lactose intolerant?

This gave her pause. She opened her mouth to speak when Franklin's hand made a little jerky movement. He dropped the cigar and ashes sprayed over the rug. His face had gone pale, paler than Evangeline's.

"Franklin!" Katie rose. "Are you okay?"

The alter ego didn't answer. His eyes were firmly shut, and he was taking deep breaths, nostrils flaring. The hand that had begun to shake was now firmly clenched onto the arm of the chair, turning white.

With great effort, he opened his mouth. "It's time for you to go."

"What's happening to you?"

"Evangeline. I can feel her surfacing. She isn't happy. I can convince her your appearance was all a dream, but it will all be for naught if the two of you appear inside her rooms once she resurfaces!"

His voice rose with effort, and we got the message. Katie went to open the window.

"Thank you so much Franklin. We're going to solve this."

I nodded. "That's right. No matter what."

Franklin nodded painfully. His left hand fought with his right, clamping it down as it scrabbled for the black bob. "Please. Hurry."

We didn't leave a moment too soon. As I hoisted myself up, a strange battle was occurring behind me. The same voice, two different pitches.

"What's going on? Franklin this is *not* your night. Give me back my wig this instant."

297

Then the deeper of the two. "It's never my night, you ugly hag."

"Barmy old codger!"

"Facile old crone! How do you think I feel wearing pantyhose?"

The immediateness of our situation propelled me through the window. The moment I was out was another story. All at once the cold metal rung stung my hand like ice. The howling wind ripped my breath away and the *ground*. Once I looked down, the whole building seemed to sway. The creaks and groans made the wooden stilts holding the pepper aloft seem flimsy as matchsticks. I pressed myself as flat as possible against the side, whispering prayers to God or the Great Pepper or whoever else was up there.

Beside me, Katie launched herself hand over hand over the rungs without a care in the world. In fact, she was laughing. She perched herself onto a rung beside me as though it were the most normal thing in the world. "Can you believe it?" she cried, facing out into the wind. "Alter egos. I never would have guessed. And a sunspot! Even if we didn't find the thief, this is an incredible development. We need to find out more about Sebastian Shaw."

With incredible effort, I wrenched open my jaw. "Katie, forgive me if I don't want to talk about this right now as I try to avoid plummeting to certain death."

She seemed to take notice of my predicament for the first time. "Oh right. Jelly legs, wooden arms. I'll grab you the dumbwaiter."

Some small part of me wondered why someone would have a dumbwaiter rigged up the side of a building if people got their food from the pub, but I was too exhausted and cold to go asking questions. In fact, I would have happily forfeited all knowledge in the world if I could just get to solid ground. Katie grabbed the rope and even prodded the rim of the box into my unwilling hands. In a few moments, the worst part was over, and I was across the dizzying gap, ready to be pulleyed home.

The ride down was much worse. I couldn't find the blindfold and then my gaze was irresistibly pulled towards the ground. No matter how hard I tried, I couldn't look anywhere else than the hill, sloping steeply down into the valley where white rooftops twinkled like stars in a bottomless abyss. Darkness flitted across the ground far below. I blinked. Probably some grit. No! There it was again. A shadow at the base of the Palaces, flickering in and out in the uneven surface of the prairie grass.

"Katie!" I was embarrassed to find it came out as more of a squeak than a yell. "I think there's someone down there."

Katie sighed. "I told you not to look down. It's your fear playing tricks."

I forced myself to look one more time, ignoring the shooting vertigo and tunnel vision. It was gone. I felt around my pockets one last time for the blindfold and found it. I was calmer now, my vision encircled in black. Then I realised something else was missing. I tugged the rope once more.

"Katie! My journal! I think I left it in Evangeline's."

There was an answering groan from above. "Is it really that important?"

"Yes!"

"Hang on. I'll go look for it."

Her voice faded and I waited, focusing only on the roughness of the rope between my fingers. All of this would be over by morning. Like a bad dream.

"Found it!" She'd returned. "It was just sitting on the ledge. Must've slipped when you jumped into the box." She placed the small bound book into my hands and immediately my fears ebbed away. *You've survived much worse than this.* It seemed to say, as my hand settled into the familiar hold, the leather worn indents of my fingers perfectly conformed. Then the dumbwaiter dropped.

The impact of wood smashing on wood made my teeth rattle and I gripped the box in terror. I was blind, but I hadn't fallen. It seemed the dumbwaiter had been pushed by some force into the side of the inn, but Katie had maintained her hold. Wind lifted my coat from below. I felt several holes in the slats. A chilling voice rang out in the darkness.

"She's got the gun. After the girl, you fool!" It was The Cellist.

I lifted the blindfold to see a horrifying shadow spill from the base of the inn and up the side of the building. It was monstrous. Six spindly, articulated arms moved one after the other in a mesmerising fashion. The creature had a hulking torso from which the arms circulated with precision. It flipped forwards and backwards, at times spidering upside down to prevent the wind from buffeting the large circular brim upon its head. Two unseeing points of light beamed out from under the brim, fixated straight at me. It moved frighteningly fast.

Down was no longer an option. I took the rope into my own hands and began pulling as hard as I could. Unfortunately, it seemed the inch per minute speed I'd reached going up to Evangeline's room was the dumbwaiters limit.

"For god's sake ignore the boy. Get me to the ladder, I'll do it myself if you haven't the stomach for it."

I looked wildly around and spotted him. The enormous creature was carrying another figure. This person seemed to absorb the moonlight as much as the spidery shadow repelled it. The Cellist stood prim on The Lamplighter's shoulder. The bone white of his face, the neat stockings and fluttering tailcoat made him look like a porcelain doll against the gun-metal grey Auto. He brandished his bow. It's rapier-sharp point was aimed right at Katie. The detective looked dumbstruck beside me. Her face was frozen, neither able to run nor scream and slowly, slowly, her head drooped. Her eyelids fluttered.

The Lamplighter reached the third-floor balcony where the detective clung to the rungs. Long metallic fingers gripped the eaves as easily as a chameleon. The Cellist motioned for it to stop, tutted over the fact he might soil his gloves, and launched himself hand over hand up the building just as Katie had. In no time at all, he was level with her. He walked the ledge of a nearby window, drawing closer, the silver point of the blade aimed for her neck.

"I'm going to enjoy this," he said smoothly. "Hand over the gun and I'll only chop you into four pieces."

Katie took a gulp from her thermos and pulled herself from the brink of sleep. I found it remarkable that her voice didn't shake. "I don't have it."

The Cellist's expression darkened. "Fine. Make it eight then."

The point of the blade whipped out. So did Katie. As the bow darted forward, she jumped. The next seconds flashed by in desperate struggle. The dumbwaiter jerked again as an opposite weight struck the rope and I found myself rocketing upward with

300

no time to hold on. Floors flashed by in seconds, wind roaring in my ears. I saw the blur of a falling figure. The flap of a coat. Katie was holding on to the other side of the rope.

Even with my weight, the force of which she fell would take her to the ground. Just as I thought it, she kicked out onto an awning. The awning broke and splintered, sending shards of wood spiralling down—but it worked. She slowed, and the rope groaned as the two of us drew slowly level again, swaying precariously above the second floor.

"Katie!"

There was no answer. She'd fallen asleep. The rope shuddered as her grip faltered. She'd wrapped it around her hand several times, but it wasn't enough. There was nowhere to go. There was no window within jumping distance. The Cellist was nowhere to be found.

Just do it. Whatever you do, don't look down. If you do, she'll fall for certain.

Against all instinct, I closed my eyes and pushed against the side of the inn. The dumbwaiter swung free for one terrible moment. Then I grabbed for the opposite line. Katie slumped over the box, one hand still holding on to the rope. There was no way I could hold on with the both of us in the box, but if I could just remember the knot...

I opened the book.

The hand over hand tactical sailors' hold appeared after a moments flip. Left, right, over, and under the loop. My arms were beginning to give out and the physics of the pulley wouldn't keep up in balance for long. In the crucial seconds it took, I'd rigged the knot around her waist. It would have to do. I pushed away from her and to my relief she swung free, limp, but suspended with the rope around her waist.

"You think that little display is going to stop *me?*" The voice emerged from the darkness to my left.

The Cellist rose slowly, up and up in front of the dumbwaiter. I was close enough to see every detail, every twitching dancing puzzle piece in that pale face. He was standing on top of The Lamplighter again, an expressionless black shape, six limbs clinging to the side of the building.

301

"The two of you can scarcely put two and two together much less get away with Shaw's device," he snarled. "I am unstoppable. I am the leader of a Revolution. I am a god amongst men delivered to bring justice for my kind." With every punctuation he stepped forward, holding the bow aloft, red eyes glittering. "I am going to slice and dice the both of you just as I did to that rat. Just as I did will do to everyone that dares to stand in my way. By the time I'm done with you, you will be an origami of skin and bones, and her, a human *coat*. Now, for the last time: Where is the gun?"

"We don't have it," I said through gritted teeth. "I promise. We've never even seen it before."

"Lies."

The point of the blade hovered beneath my chin now. I watched in curious detachment as a drip of my own sweat fell onto the silvery surface, sliding down.

"I heard her say she found it." His eyes narrowed. "Fine, if you won't tell me, so be it." He rapped on The Lamplighter's brim. "I'll give you the honour, my friend. Rip the rope."

A long metal hand appeared, snaking through the darkness. It grasped the rope, then hesitated. A surprisingly high voice rose from the black shadow.

"Sir—I…I perhaps letting them live would be—"

The Lamplighter said no more after The Cellist gave him a vicious swipe, taking off a chunk of metal from the hat. He whimpered and jumped. The black fingers stiffened with new resolve and closed over the rope.

That was when everything exploded in a shower of pink. Particularly The Cellist who was hit squarely in the chest by a peony made of light. A brief look of shock crossed his face before he disappeared in a cloud of fuchsia smoke and was blown backwards by the force. The Lamplighter was no less surprised. He let out a curious tinny roar as more crackles and bangs followed. Colours exploded off the roof, hitting him squarely in that broad, spider-like torso. Brilliant points of blue, yellow, red, purple, and green light mushroomed downward as flower-shaped fireworks rained down from above. Even in the midst of this chaos I couldn't help but be transfixed. Intricate designs of chrysanthemum, rose, and forget-me-not lit up the sky, followed by warhead whistling. There was a sizzling pain on my scalp. My hair had caught fire. Hurriedly I patted it out.

Meanwhile, the six arms lost their grip on the window ledges and pipes. There was a mighty crash.

The Cellist's voice rang out somewhere distant. "Blast it! What's going on?"

"I don't know, sir!"

"Is it the gun?"

There was no answer. When the mist had parted, I watched as a large, many-armed shape galloped down the hill. We'd been saved.

There was a sudden jerk on the rope. To my right, Katie's limp form began to inch upwards, circling gently in the air like a giant ragdoll. Someone was pulling her up. The dumbwaiter made its way to the ground, and I didn't have long to wait and see if I would be pulled up as well. The pulley gave a gentle twitch and I found myself rising once more. Fear fought with wonder as I rose. The remnants of the fireworks swirled in the air like falling meteors. Blue fog crossed with scintillating points of light billowed around me. At this point, the lights inside the inn had begun to flick on. I heard muted complaints about fireworks and early revellers behind each window I passed. A few opened to see what the matter was outside, but by that time I was past them, inching little by little towards the stars. There was the top of the pulley system, a sturdy iron post with a loop and a lever, outlined against the night sky. There was a slow *click click click* as the dumbwaiter wound inwards.

"Surprise!"

The bone-white face jumped out of the mist. I jumped backwards, forgetting for a moment that I was suspended four stories above the ground. The dumbwaiter rocked dangerously. I scrabbled for purchase as The Cellist ran his blade delicately over the rope. It was impossible! No Auto acted like this. The thought of a remote control seemed far-fetched now as the red eyes met mine. These were intelligent, calculating, and utterly inhuman. He was perched, gargoyle-like on a rain gutter, shielded from the fireworks by the tin runnel.

"You're much more resourceful than I thought," The Cellist hummed. "Unfortunately, not much cleverer. Who wins in this scenario? A great swordsman, invincible and merciless, or a simple boy—a stage magician, relying on smoke and mirrors? For the last time, where is the gun?"

The bow cut through the night air, and I stiffened, preparing for the snap, the inevitable drop. Instead, I heard music. It was a long mournful note that seemed to hang, suspended, quivering in the darkness, wrapping itself around me, refusing to let go. It was a waltz. In some dim and distant part of my mind I knew I should cover my ears, but my hands were still stuck to the box. Suddenly, it didn't matter what my hands were doing. All of the fears I had, of everything, the ground, The Cellist, the box, seemed to wash away. Sleep. Sleep was what I desired, and I didn't want the lovely song to end.

"*Where is it?*" he asked softly.

The gun? I didn't know. I wish I knew so that I could tell him and hear the music forever. "I'm sorry, I told you I don't…"

There was subtle movement at the edge of my hearing. Barely perceptible. Woozily I looked up. My eyeballs felt soaked in molasses. A figure stood on the edge of the roof, tall and rakish.

"I think you've got ze wrong magician," said the figure.

Swish. A match lit.

A momentary glow lit the face, aged but devilish with a pointy moustache and goatee. The eyes gleamed electric blue. The Cellist's face contorted into an expression I didn't immediately recognize. Horror.

"*Bellamy,*" he whispered.

Then, he disappeared for a second time in a fury of orange daffodils. I didn't have time to watch him fall. The dumbwaiter shot up like a rocket and that was the last I saw of The Cellist.

~28~

Fantastic Cheese and Where to Hide It

You might not think a roof is the best place for cheese. You'd be right. I awoke to the smell of sour death. Recoiling, I knocked my head against a sharp corner.

"OUCH!"

My elbow banged against another hard surface and finally I had the presence of mind to actually open my eyes. Coughing and in pain, I sat up to find the rest of my body in a similarly uncomfortable position. I'd been laid unceremoniously upon a pile of crates. Whatever was in them smelled bad too, but not as much as whatever was in front of my nose.

Slowly, the form of the detective became less blurry. She was waving something white and mushy on a cracker. As I'd demonstrated enough consciousness to move away, she withdrew it.

"Morning, sunshine."

"Good morning yourself," I pinched my nose. "What *is* that?"

305

"Aged goat cheese," she said. "Well, aged if you count those fuzzy green spots covering half of it. It woke you up though, didn't it? See, you're not the only one who can improvise medicine on the go."

I gave the cracker a suffering look. "*That* is not medicine. Anyways, where am I?" I levered myself up onto the highest crate for a better look and bumped my head on a rafter.

Katie looked as though she'd just sniffed the goat cheese herself. "Ah, well here's the thing. There's good news and bad news."

Clambering up the crates may not have given me a better look, but they demonstrated just how cramped the room was, and how many people in it were looking at me. Mrs. Twill, who swallowed up much of the room, gave me a little wave. A thin, older man with a swashbuckling goatee and moustache lounged on the thin cot by the window. His electric blue gaze caught mine and I wheeled around.

Katie coughed.

"The good news is, we're safe up here on the roof with Bellamy. The bad news is, we're up here on the roof with Bellamy." She grimaced. "I wanted to tell you. Really, I did but it's not exactly coffee table conversation."

"What, that you're keeping a wanted felon in your attic? Gee Katie, that would've been nice to know—what, that the very man—the guy wanted for potential *murder* is in here with us right now—of course. I feel *loads* better!"

"Um, excusez-*moi*." The Frenchman raised his hand lazily. "It's grand larceny. Not murder. Get your facts right."

"And Mrs. Twill!"

"Hello, dear."

"Okay everybody, let's all calm down," said Katie. "Wendell, why don't you stop hiding in the rafters like a frightened pigeon. Ma, move over a bit so we can have some space. Bellamy…" her upper lip curled a little. "Just…be cool. For once."

Bellamy smirked. "If I wasn't cool, would I wear my shirts unbuttoned by zree holes?"

"Eugh! You're so *old*. Ma stop smiling!"

BELLAMY
DUMONT

(smug for
a guy living
in an attic)

Slowly, everyone shifted, bumping and manoeuvring to make space in the cramped attic room. It took some doing. There were crates everywhere. Big ones, small ones, middle sized ones. One made up the bedside table, another, a makeshift bureau. Another made up an avant garde depiction of the Arc De Triomphe and the narrow cot was elevated on six of them. Images were printed on the faded bottoms, displaying logos of the farms that supplied the cheese around Port Larkeney. It was the only thing that would keep up here, Katie explained, because of course, they couldn't have Bellamy ambling down to the pub whenever he liked.

The attic itself was a low-slung dome with a single slanted window over the bed. The growing sunlight only illuminated the dust that I had little doubt was largely composed of pulverised cheese. Newspapers crackled underfoot and clothes hung off the mismatched furniture. In an act of misplaced hospitality, someone had set a stinking charcuterie board on the crate between us.

Katie muttered as she squashed in next to me on the settee. "Yeah, the place is a tip. You'd think a felon would be a more considerate houseguest. I tell my ma every day to put her foot down, but she refuses to give him the hairy eyeball."

I didn't answer. I was waiting for some kind of explanation for all of this. Plus, my aching head still reeled from what had happened. Mrs. Twill was first to broach the smelly silence.

"Wendell," she bestowed a motherly look. "I realise how this must all look to you but first I want to tell you how glad I am you're okay. Whatever you may think of him, it was a miracle that Bellamy was there during your frightfully irresponsible escapade."

Katie whispered, "I told her I took you up on the ladder for a stakeout of the town. Not entirely untrue."

Mrs. Twill folded her dimpled elbows. "I wonder what your father would think about you going out at night. I know you're an independent boy, but really, no sense in making him worry like that."

I thought that was a bit rich. "No sense in hiding a criminal in your attic either," I mirrored her crossed arms. "Looks to me like you've got the bigger of the two secrets."

The landlady's lips thinned at the implication. "I must impress upon you the seriousness of the situation," she said. "In the

Palaces, we believe in innocence until proven guilty. Bellamy is a tenant and shall be treated as such—"

"Tenant? That's what we're calling him now?" spluttered Katie. "He doesn't pay rent, he lives in our attic, rattles the plumbing and eats mouldy cheese. That's not a tenant, that's a goblin!

"Don't pretend like you didn't have a say in this," Mrs. Twill snapped.

"I vouched for him when he had information to give," said Katie. "Now it's been five months and he's still here. I can't go to the police now, can I? I'm an accessory after the act! Oh, I can see it now." She mimed picking up a phone, "Hello Wimbelow, yes, you know Bellamy Dumont, the most wanted man in Europe and number one suspect in the attack of Sebastian Shaw? Well, turns out I've got him right here. Oh a promotion? Don't mind if I do!'"

Mrs. Twill steamed and the crates under the cot protested beneath her shifting weight.

"Do *I* have a say in zhis?" Bellamy piped from his tiny corner of the cot. His plea went unnoticed. Tensions were running high in the little attic room and things were starting to get heated in more ways than one. I scooted away from the charcuterie board as the cheese was starting to melt and smell like Athlete's Foot.

As I came to find out, it was a well-worn argument. The battle had been fought over five months with no resolution. From it, I learned that Bellamy Dumont had amnesia or so claimed. He remembered scant details about working with Katie's father just before his disappearance, which had been a lifeline of hope to Katie and her mother. But day by day, his memories were becoming less and less useful and he more of a burden.

Previously I hadn't quite understood Katie's animosity towards her mother—what had really prompted her to climb Big Bertha and pretend to murder it. Now I could see. Her job was on the line and the landlady of the Piquant Palaces clung on to the flimsiest of excuses to keep Dumont, that being, "Well, we're in it now." Eventually it became clear that no one was going to win and

Katie, red in the face, fell silent. Mrs. Twill turned to me once more, huffing like a steam engine.

"You see, it all happened like this. My husband Eamon was a botanist in rare peppers. One day, he disappeared without a trace. He went for a walk in that pepper garden of his and just...never came back. Katie and I, we still have hope he's out there."

"I *know* he is," Katie said staunchly. "That's why I'm doing this."

"Yes, well that was five years ago. Five months ago, Bellamy appeared on our doorstep. He was a sorry sight. All bruised up and bloodied, a strange yellow mark across his chest. A handful of people had shown up with the mark in the past years. Those that had it were found after days of being missing and were comatose, like your brother. Weeks passed, then months, then years. The bodies in hospital never woke up. They said it was the mark of the beast, a sea witch's curse, even poisoning from the quarry east of the cove where the water runoff meets from around the farms.

"Bellamy asked us to please keep him a secret. He was being chased. Sebastian had erased his memory and he had only the foggiest idea of who *that* was. Of course I took him in!" Mrs. Twill added defensively. "He made such a case, you would too! And then the papers hadn't come out yet."

Katie took it from there. "When the papers *did* come out, obviously you can imagine our surprise at the bounty. Ten thousand pounds for one man? Wanted for destroying Sebastian Shaw's private laboratory and then stealing one of his most prized possessions? I wanted to turn him in!"

"*But* that was when he heard our song," said Mrs. Twill.

"Your song?" I asked.

"Yes. Eamon had such a penchant for disco. It must run in the genes because Katie adores all of his old recordings. She was playing...what was it?"

"'Don't Go Breaking My Heart,'" said Katie quietly. "We used to play it in the car. Bellamy must have overheard it because he came downstairs looking like a ghost. Said the song brought back memories of working with my Dad on something. He told us things about him he couldn't have guessed. Little things, like his favourite pie, the hole in his gardening glove he cut to stop it from

310

rubbing a callus on his pinky finger…stuff he couldn't have known."

She paused. "You understand why I couldn't turn him in then. I had to know, Wendell. If there was even a sliver of a chance he might be out there, I'd take it."

Her jaw was set as she stared into the past. "I thought I could try and get his memory back and Bellamy's dead set on the fact that he's innocent, but it's been five bloody months!" She shot him a look that could have curdled even the ripest of the goat cheese. "Even *he* wants to go, but *she*'s convinced him that we're the only ones that can help. And now we're all implicated unless Bellamy can magically remember something."

"Don't look at me," Bellamy flicked a piece of salami from his moustache. "I don't thrive well under pressure."

Mrs. Twill rose and put her padded hands over mine. She was so close I could smell the spices in her clothes.

"Wendell, I hate to ask this of you, but Bellamy and I—and Katie, we'd like to count on your discretion at least for the time being. We're not bad people. Surely you can see that?"

Everyone looked at me expectantly.

I took my hands away from Mrs. Twill and considered the facts. Here was Bellamy Dumont, the man with the most motive out of any of those involved with Sebastian Shaw. He had white hair that conceivably matched the one found in the study, and there was the matter of cheese—although I didn't trust my subconscious to that effect.

I could always pretend to agree and go to Wimbelow with the information, but did I trust him? Even if he was able to prove Bellamy was the culprit, would he pursue those affected by the sunspot? And if I did so, I would incriminate Katie and Mrs. Twill. The Palaces would suffer. The detective would lose her job through no fault of her own. Katie was right. As maddening as it was, there was no choice. We would have to trust on blind faith that Bellamy was who he said he was, try to get any information from him possible, and prove he was innocent all along. If he was guilty…well that was something I didn't want to consider.

"Fine," I said. "But on one condition. I was never here, and I was never involved." I turned to Mrs. Twill. "If my parents ask where I was last night, or any time after this while we're solving the case, you'll have to cover for me."

"That seems fair," said Katie.

Mrs. Twill nodded but looked far from happy.

"Do you have an alibi for the night Shaw was attacked?" I posed this to Bellamy. The Frenchman had been lounging on the cot trying to look relaxed, but his bright eyes shot back and forth like ping pong balls as the Twills argued. "They're going to ask that. Can anyone corroborate that you were with them between seven and twelve pm on the eleventh of December?"

Mrs. Twill suddenly rose. "It's dreadfully hot in here. We ought to open that window. Oh, it's painted shut. Never mind that. Does anyone want tea? I'll go get some tea from downstairs."

"I could go for some," I said.

She proceeded to pick her way over the crates with frightening speed, her tiny feet carrying the ample skirts like a show pony. Admittedly it was getting a bit stifling. Katie propped open the door with a cheese crate.

Bellamy shook his head slowly. "Unfortunately, no. I am up here every night. I am not visited very much."

I turned to Katie. She shook her head as well. "I was at the station."

"Great."

I didn't know much about Bellamy Dumont and what I did know was likely to have been sensationalised by the papers. The wild-eyed, bounty headlined photos didn't fit with the thin, rakish fellow on the bed, now smoking a thin cigarette with his crackers and cheese. He'd been a genius inventor who had gotten his start in France building some kind of talking clockwork head. I knew that. The rest I'd read some time ago in some paper. He'd discovered Sebastian working in a hotel during a convention for the mechanical association to which he belonged. The young genius had attempted to sneak in and present his own creations. He was caught, but Dumont saw promise in him and decided to take him on as his apprentice. It was your typical rags to riches type stuff.

The two of them went radio silent up until five years ago when Shaw discovered Amber and changed the world. Automatons began filtering in amongst the rich and powerful. The pair skyrocketed to fame and fortune—up until Dumont and Shaw's infamous falling out.

"What do you remember about the day you lost your memory then?" I asked.

Bellamy took a long pull of his cigarette. "It was eh...not good."

Realising we wanted him to elaborate a little more than that, he sighed. "I awoke in pain and in a room pulsating with blue light. Ze very air, it crackled and all of my hair." He pinched a tuft of shaggy white hair. "It stood up like zis. I did not know who I was, or how I had come to be zhere. I only knew I was in gravest danger. I was strapped to a chair, a burning pain in my chest. I fell out of consciouzness. I woke up next to find Sebastian Shaw pointing ze barrel of some great device at me.

"He said, 'Very good. You're awake. Disoriented I imagine. Well, I've azcertained zhat a second shot won't kill you, after all, I don't want you dead, Bellamy. Quite the contrary. I keep my prizes.'

'Sebastian? I do not know what you are talking about. Please, let me go,' I said, searching for some compassion in that unfamiliar yet familiar face. There was none.

He sneered at me.

'Your memory might fail you now, but you're still a danger to me whether you know it or not. You want to know what you did? You were always an arrogant fool. You used me and my genius to bolster your own success. As soon as you met me, our creations became *your* creations. How does it feel to be on the other side of the fence? I am the most successful man in the world and you? In a year's time you will be a nobody. A faded picture without a single line in the history books.'

I did not understand what he was talking about. But he did not elaborate. I felt a terrible, cold heat. My skin prickled as though it were on fire. The blue light became blinding.

'Don't worry old boy,' said Sebastian. 'Things will be much easier from here on out. You won't even know what you're missing. In fact, you won't know a thing.'

My escape was due to pure luck. As the lightning gathered in the barrel, I dropped my glasses just as it hit me. My glasses are a special polarised metal so as to withstand high temperatures in my laboratory. Through some miracle, ze beam bounced off it, crackling all around the room, drawn to metal. The metal buckled and burned so hot they melted the rubber straps. I was able to run. Sebastian was furious. Wicked metal creatures climbed out of the woodwork on his command to pursue me. I found myself inside of a long laboratory. I grabbed something to defend myself off a nearby desk and ran, beating the smaller of the creatures. It was only when I had nearly exhausted myself that I made it out into a series of subterranean tunnels which eventually led me under Port Larkeney."

Katie and I were silent for a time, pondering the gravity of what he'd just said.

"What did you steal?" I asked. "All the papers said you were on the run for theft. It sounds to me like Sebastian kidnapped you and you just ran away."

Bellamy scratched his head. "It puzzled me too. Until I realised it could only be zis." He reached down and pulled something from under the cot. A long metal tube closed on both ends and slightly dented was placed on the duvet. "Zis tube was what I picked up from the desk and used for my escape. I believe it is some kind of machine, but I cannot figure out how to work it or open it."

He handed it to me. I took the metal tube gingerly. It was about a metre long and the width of a soda can. The ends were almost seamlessly capped. Unscrewing did nothing.

"Do with zat what you will. Ze only other things I remember of my past life are things I would rather forget. That being my estranged daughter Marguerite, and Eamon Twill in his 'orrible bell bottoms."

"Don't talk about my Dad that way," Katie scowled. "You've still told me barely anything. If information were your rent, you'd be up to your knees in debt."

"Easy for you to say. Ze apple clearly does not fall far from ze tree." He cast a disdainful look at Katie's pants which today were green with red stripes. "Do you think I want to stay in this prison

314

instead of proving to ze world I am innocent? Of course! But Sebastian Shaw's terrible machine has ruined me. Look around. I am surrounded by mouldy cheese and my skills have depleted so I can barely assemble a hand mixer. It is shameful."

"Wait," I cut in. "You say you still know how to build things?"

"Hardly."

"But you still know what Amber is. You could tell us how the Lightning Gun works." A cold feeling washed over me as again the events of last night replayed. "We need to know what we're up against."

Bellamy tutted under his moustache. "In theory. I suppose. But ze properties of Amber do not translate well into layman terms. I would have to show you." He seemed relieved to have changed the conversation away from Katie and left quickly to some little corner amongst the crates. When he came back, he was holding a small copper box. He opened it slowly and using a pair of tweezers, withdrew something that glowed like captured fire.

Amber.

I'd never seen it out of a machine before. The rock was small, but its brilliance—a pulsing, fiery ether—made the rest of the room seem dark in comparison. A hush fell over us. Even Bellamy was quieter as he explained.

"Seeing it again brought back so many things. It is as though you have had an epiphany about yourself. I believe that zis little rock is the key to everything. Eamon Twill was the first to discover it. He sent for me from Port Larkeney. He was an old university friend who wanted my expertise as he studied its mysteries. I took my apprentice, Sebastian, and came to Port Larkeney some fifteen ago. We were baffled at first. It looked like a simple mineral that grew from ze seaside caves common in these parts. But it behaved like something much more."

Several more items came out of the desk. A musical tyne, a torch, a prism, and a large metal box with two antennae. First, he struck the tyne. A single, clear note rang out. Nothing happened at first. It faded into the air and died.

"Wait for it."

As if on cue, the echo of that note, if slightly tinnier, rang from somewhere. The Amber was vibrating. Seeing our wonder, Bellamy smiled.

"Is that why Autos need music to activate?" I asked.

"Yes. Ze waves serve to activate ze natural holding potential within, allowing it to release a copy of zhat energy." He picked up the torch and the prism and shone the light through until there was a rainbow on the desk. He held the Amber underneath the violet hue. The glowing rock turned pale violet.

"How did it—?" Katie began.

"We believe Amber is the embodiment of enormous energy. A natural vessel of some sort." He set himself to the metal box, unfolding the prongs.

"A Jacob's ladder," he explained. "Capable of sending minor currents of electricity across a short distance." When he switched it on, a sudden finger of electricity flickered between the two wires, and I was reminded unpleasantly of the lightning in the manor.

"Don't!" said Katie, as Bellamy pushed the rubber tongs toward the miniature tongue of lightning.

"It's perfectly safe."

And he calmly poked the rock into lightning. Immediately, the electricity circulated and revolved the Amber, before finally disappearing vortex-like into it. The Jacobs ladder crackled and fizzled out. When he was done, the stone glowed brighter than before.

"Did it just suck up all the energy?"

Bellamy nodded. "In a sense. Zis little crystal, this humble rock, can power a generator indefinitely if given ze proper energy source. Think of that! Think of what it could do for the people of the world!"

"That sort of explains the Lighting Gun," I mused. "But is it possible for it to malfunction? Like you put it into an Auto, and then it starts trying to murder people. Is that normal?"

"No. I would say not. You are talking about last night." Bellamy's face creased with worry. "Yes, it seems that Sebastian has progressed far more in his mechanics. When that Auto climbed the building and spoke to you, it was almost as if he were…human. I do not know what to make of it. Only that as of

316

now, zhey know where to find me. I must make preparations…" He paced the tiny space as much as he was able, his blue eyes sparking. "Eamon and I always knew Amber could be dangerous—a disaster in the wrong hands—but now I think zhat it was in the wrong hands from the very beginning."

"But how did my dad and Sebastian Shaw find it?" pressed Katie. "You've already told me all this stuff and I've looked up and down for Amber in the caves. It's just not here."

Bellamy sighed. "It has not come to me yet. Ze research we did…it was very secretive. I know we pinpointed where it was, but perhaps ze Amber is all gone, used in Sebastian's experiments."

"Wait," I said. "What about your old house in Port Larkeney? You wouldn't have lived in Shaw Manor at that time. It was only built a year ago. We can go search it there."

But Katie was shaking her head. "I've thought about that too," she said. "Bellamy can't remember where it is and there's no record of them in the town archives. He said they kept it very hush hush." She shot him an irritable look.

"Zhere was a stone cottage!" said Bellamy defensively. "Two stories with a shingle roof. It was surrounded by birch trees and a terrible smell. Like cheese."

The detective threw her hands up in the air. "Half the houses in Port Larkeney look like that! I need to get some air."

When I met her outside, the sun had come up fully on the town below. The little seaside cottages twinkled in the morning light. The bracing morning air helped to clear my buzzing mind. It was hard to believe that just hours ago, the two of us had been besieged by two bloodthirsty robots, talked to a woman with multiple personalities and met our potential culprit in an attic filled with cheese. There was also the point of Katie's narcolepsy, but I figured that now was neither the time nor place.

"It's so frustrating!" Her words shot out before I could say anything. "The more I search, the more I'm led in a thousand different directions. The Lightning Gun—the Autos—the thief—your brother. And I'm no closer to finding my dad." Her hand slid down the side of her face and I saw just how dark the circles beneath her eyes were.

"Sorry," she said at length. "It's just been a lot and I'm very tired."

I leaned against the balcony, back to the dizzying view. I wasn't so good at pep talks, so I plagiarised a little bit. "You know what my dad always says? Chin up. You can't battle a mudslide with a muddy mood or a giant Japanese spider crab with a crabby disposition."

I was rewarded with a small chuckle. "Yeah. Alright. Oh." Her hand went to her side, and she winced.

I realised she'd been standing oddly the whole time. "Alright there?"

"It's nothing." She waved me away. "Probably just a bruise or something."

"Does it hurt?"

"No. A little."

"Okay sit down. Just relax."

Katie steadied herself on a discarded cheese crate and lowered herself. I averted my gaze as I pressed a hand to her stomach. It was warmth and I felt quick, stilted breathing under my palm.

"I think your rib might be broken or fractured." I cleared my throat and stood up. "Not too bad. Probably want to keep off that for a couple days though. Bet it was the whole rope thing that did it. You should bind something tight around it. The pressure will help with healing. That means no fancy jumping and climbing for a while."

She smiled. "Thanks, doc."

We took to gazing across town again in companionable silence. Far below, streamers were catching the light, stretching across the streets as if by magic as ant-like people scurried in the streets. A stream of toy trucks bumped down the valley as farmers came from far and wide to sell their wares. The Capsicum Carnival was mere hours away.

The question "what next?" hung in the air.

Katie answered it. "I'm always on duty this time of the year. I won't have much time to work on the case. But I think we should look for Bellamy's old house," she said. "People are worried about all the robberies going on. That means neighbourhood watch. If I can get stationed on one of those streets instead of the festival, we can take pictures of the houses that match Bellamy's description and see if any of them jog his memory."

She shielded her face against the sun. It promised to be an unusually warm, clear day. "We need that research. It might be the only thing that helps us figure out who exactly Sebastian Shaw is and why that Lightning Gun is important enough that The Cellist would kill for it."

.

~**29**~

Electricity in the Air

There were very few things Wimbelow hated more than December. He hated the weather and the cold wind that blew across his thinning scalp. He hated the trees and wreaths that triggered his allergies. But most of all, he hated going home for Christmas. That was his parent's home in Dorchester where he'd sit on their patchy couch for weeks, listening to the *click click* of the beaded curtains in the doorway, and worst of all, sitting politely through his mother's tour of her stained-glass orchid paintings and his father's annual tirade about how firearms were tantamount to fascism in British policing. Retirement had been the worst thing to have happened to his parents.

Well, I hope you're happy now, Wimbelow thought. Here he was stuck in the middle of nowhere with a gang of gangrenous old veterans on his force, and not a single decent weapon to his name. No, he got a club (a stick more like) to defend himself against the bloodthirsty criminals terrorizing the town.

As for criminals, it *must* be Dumont. It must be! It was clear to him that none of these guests, even with their tawdry disdain

321

and pecuniary motives had it in them to attempt to murder Shaw. They were after his money, not him, and a man whose wealth amounted to large stores of a secret stone and non-transferable assets was no good to them dead. No, it must be Dumont, but how to catch a mad French genius who had been on the run for half a year? Was he even in Port Larkeney?

He remembered his father's word's the last time they spoke. It was only because he'd been staring in disgust at the man's mouthful of overcrowded teeth as he puffed on an herbal pipe.

"Power is of two kinds. One is obtained by the fear of punishment and the other by acts of love. Power based on love is a thousand times more effective and permanent than the one derived from fear of punishment. That's Ghandi. Remember that, Quentin."

"Bah!"

Just short of saying *humbug*, the Inspector massaged his temples. He was very close to using violence *right now.* He'd been in Port Larkeney just over two years to the day. In that time, he'd witnessed no less than three robberies, one birth that the couple had insisted he be there for protection, and the kidnapping of Geordie Miller from the local primary school by way of a miscreant group of seagulls.

But for of that, he would have gladly visited his parents instead of being stuck here, in Port Larkeney for the Capsicum Carnival. Two full days of screaming children, peppery fumes, fireworks and worst of all, the chaos that was wrangling his own force. Half of them complained nonstop about the noise while the other half were as distractable as toddlers by all the pretty lights and sounds. (Ninety-year-old Ronald had wandered off into a nearby farm last year and gotten lost for eight hours after mistaking an escaped petting zoo goat for his partner.)

By some cruel stroke of luck, these two dreadful holidays fell within weeks of each other, leaving the Inspector full of worldly hatred rather than good tidings. That was why he hated December.

Excited murmuring filled the parlor of the Port Larkeney Police Station. Electricity was in the air as the streets of Port Larkeney slowly donned their peppery apparel in time for the evening. In Down below, canvas booths flapped in the sea breeze. Weather-beaten trucks lined the avenue, their beds stacked high with candies, cheeses, and dried fruits. A huge wooden platform was in the process of being erected at the end of the main street. This would be the resting place for the pride and joy of Port Larkeney: Big Bertha.

Meredith craned her crepey neck towards the window. Ronald and Rudy's eyes were trained on the flags fluttering from the lampposts. Even Katie Twill was doodling on her map of the town. He was losing them. Wimbelow abandoned the bulletin board to yank the curtains closed.

"Now." *Snap* "Is not the time." *Snap.* "For woolgathering!" he barked, drawing the final curtain. "Or have you forgotten the devious mastermind terrorizing this town and its inhabitants? Somehow, I doubt they're going to take a day off to enjoy the festivities."

Once all eyes were back on him, he rapped on the blown-up map pinned to the wall. Various spots were circled in red marker. "There have been eight robberies so far. The people of Port Larkeney are concerned for their lives and their wellbeing, so this year, officers will be split between the festival and the affected streets."

There was a resounding groan from the rec room. The Inspector ignored this. "You all know the profile by now." He tapped a large sketch of a tailcoated gentleman sporting an eighteenth-century wig beside skinny stick-like figure with six arms.

"It seems everyone must be suffering from the same delusion that two Autos are performing these thefts. However, that brim on The Lamplighter does match up with the gouge marks in the walls found in six of those houses, and people have reported mysterious cello music in the dead of night. As such, whoever is controlling them is likely to be highly dangerous and I encourage you to use all adequate force—or better yet, radio, for backup." He paused. "Not for each other, for me."

Meredith raised her hand. "Why can't we call one another?"

"Because I can walk faster than a senior scooter. Any other questions?"

He sighed as a sea of wavering hands rose. "Actually, no more questions. I'll be handing out assignments after lunch. Should be enough time for all of you dialysis folks."

* * *

There was a knock at the door and Wimbelow quickly slipped the book he'd been reading under the desk. It was titled: *Narcoleptics: They're Real and They Can Get In Your House.*

"Come in."

Katie entered holding a sheet of paper. "You asked me to triangulate these for you." She handed him the map. "I'm sorry, but it's the same as what we got the first time."

Katie Twill. Even during his rare moments of respite, she managed to ruin that too.

Wimbelow took it and almost laughed at what was circled. "Three buildings on Main Street. The hat shop, our station, and... Laura's Lingerie. This," He handed it back without another glance. "is bunk. Are you using the protractor upside down?"

Katie was undeterred. She unfolded the map back on his desk. "There's eight robberies within a four block radius. It makes it pretty exact, Sir."

"Really? You think that our man is brazen enough to hide himself, two metal creatures and a Lightning Gun in the basement of the local police station?"

"Or woman."

"Right. Of course."

Because a woman could do anything a man could do. Even occupy a job she was ill-qualified for and frankly a public hazard in. What was it about Twill that people liked? He couldn't see it. Certainly, it wasn't by dint of femininity, what with those cartoonish shirts and garish bell bottoms she had such a penchant for.

324

"Some people have that special quality about them," his mother had said after he'd asked her why his brother was so much more well-liked in school. "Can't explain it. You either have it or you don't. Oh, Quentin, that isn't to say…"

The Inspector scowled at the map. "I can't take this. The hat shop is barely big enough for Mrs. McGrady herself. The station is out of the question and *that* shop? He jerked his head to the right where the low wall barred the police station from the Lingerie Shoppe. "No self-respecting criminal would hide in there. It's ridiculous."

"Maybe that's what they want us to think. Maybe the Lightning Gun is hiding in one of the stalls."

"I let you do this because I thought you could handle it. Don't think that doing a bit of research work means you're back on the Shaw case. Especially when the theories you propose border on the absurd. Do it again."

Using a pencil, he pushed the map away from himself shooed toward the door. Katie didn't move.

"Is there anything else?" he asked exasperatedly.

"I was wondering if I could get a spot patrolling one of the neighbourhoods tonight. The Carnival's awfully loud and I've seen it about a million times. I think I'd be better off alone where I could keep a sharper watch."

"Hmm." Wimbelow pretended to think about it. "That is an excellently argued point. Unfortunately, I already have you marked down for festival patrol, and you know how I can't change assignments."

"Well, you could, just by putting a different person."

"Ah ah ah, those are the rules Ms. Twill, and if you don't like them, I suggest you take them up with the Chief. I'm sure he'd be glad to see you on top of all the other problems he must deal with."

He shooed her off with the pencil and finally, Katie left, her fingers digging little divots in the paper. Wimbelow sank back down to his desk wearing a self-satisfied smirk. Refusing the young detective had given him the little boost he needed to get through the rest of the day. He sat back to read his book and formulate the last of his plan.

* * *

Evening fell and the festivities were in full swing. Were he any other person at all, Wimbelow would have taken a deep breath as he stepped outside, admiring the clear pink skies and the pleasant, unseasonal warmth that had everyone shrugging off their coats to enjoy the long walk around Main Street.

But as usual, things were taking a downturn for the Inspector. He'd battled through a barrage of whining to get six of the least atrophied officers to get up and go patrol the neighbourhoods. He'd resisted the temptation to suggest retirement more than once, as it always turned things ugly. Those who patrolled the streets of the Carnival did so on bulky mobility scooters which had Wimbelow spending the majority of the evening shouting at people to get out of the way and calling the young nurse Garrett to tend the unwitting bystanders whose feet had gotten crushed.

It was exhausting. Not to mention the townsfolk that kept stopping him in the street, asking for updates on the Shaw case and the robberies. He would tell them curtly that things were moving forward but there was no conclusive evidence as of yet. Saying it over and over only tattooed the failure deeper into his brain.

"Chief!"

He jogged up to the old man. Fergus was sitting on the curb, blending in with the green plot behind him. Per usual, he was wearing his mustard yellow kilt and polishing off a few deep-fried jalapenos before making some more rounds.

"I'd like to speak to you a moment," said Wimbelow.

Fergus didn't look up from his jalapeno. "What about?"

"Katie Twill—no no no don't walk away—it's important. I've been doing some reading." He took out the book on narcolepsy. "It's all here."

His superior stared at the book with all the weariness of a centenarian tortoise. "Surely you can think of at least five more important things to be doing right now. Oh, in fact, there goes Mr. Kelly. He's accidentally stuck a five-year-old with a kebab stick."

He looked pointedly, but the Inspector didn't take the hint. "It all adds up, you see," he said, a manic glint in his eye.

"The tiredness, the sudden bursts of energy. When she fell asleep at the boathouse after I caught that weaselly little friend of hers running from the scene. It was shock! People with narcolepsy fall asleep whenever they experience strong emotion. I'm certain that the ungodly concoction in that thermos of hers keeps her awake. It's the only thing that makes sense!"

Fergus was disinterestedly picking flecks of fried dough from his ear hair. It reminded Wimbelow uncannily of a documentary he'd once seen about the cleaning habits of silverback gorillas.

"Maybe a fainting disposition isn't right for this line of work, but she gets the job done and done quickly. Might I remind she'd solved three more cases than you have this year?"

The Inspector scoffed. "Of course she did, I allocated them. They were familial disputes. Petty crimes. It's not for me to get involved."

"Ah and see, that's where you're mistaken, Wimbelow. You're small-town law enforcement. When you come here, the people rely on you personally. *Everything* is your business. Now, I don't feel like having this conversation for the third time this month so I'm going to be going."

"But—"

Fergus twisted his old back and brushed aside a long strand of ear hair. "If I see proof that Katie Twill has a rare disorder that causes her to fall asleep at odd moments, well, she won't be sacked but I'll move her to a desk. Does that please you? Good. Now get back to work. I see a group of schoolchildren veering dangerously close to Mrs. Twill's ghost pepper stew."

But Wimbelow wasn't pleased. Maybe he should have been. It was certainly a victory if he could get young Twill taken down a peg. But it wasn't *enough*. She didn't deserve it. What she deserved was to never set foot in the Port Larkeney Police Station ever again…unless it was behind bars.

The evening went on with greater celebration than usual. With the robberies and the rumours circulating around town, the people of Port Larkeney were eager to free themselves from the oppressive cloud that had settled so quickly over their peaceful lives.

327

Wimbelow watched all of their celebrations flash by him, colourful and separate as he stalked through the lights and music. Families laughing, children carrying spun sugar in various pepper shapes, the raucous shouting from the tent in which the county vegetable competition was held, and off course, Mrs. Twill who seemed to be everywhere at once, jangling her wares of Big Bertha keychains, Big Bertha caps, t-shirts, and snow globes in front of the monstrous pepper. He had to pick through the crowds of spectators that gathered in front of the wood platform to gawk at behemoth. There she sat red and gleaming, the approximate size and lumpiness of an adult sperm whale. It really wasn't all that. He didn't know it was the one thing he and Katie would have agreed upon.

Katie Twill stood on the other side of the street nodding hellos to the vendors as she did her rounds. To him, the greetings looked forced. He'd been keeping a watchful eye on her in case he caught any more suspicious behaviour. To his dismay, she'd done nothing out of the ordinary. Even the Billings boy was with his family. The only peculiarity were their expressions. They were matching and out of place on a night like this; pensive and wide-eyed, almost…hunted.

Katie was stooping to retrieve a Big Bertha commemorative felt hat from under a stall. Fergus was arriving in the opposite direction. A thrill ran through the Inspector. This was the moment he'd been waiting for. Ever so quietly, he sidled up behind the young detective as the Chief came into eye line. Let him see what happened when Katie Twill experienced so much as a minor scare. He'd already planted the seed. Now it was time to reap the fruit. Wimbelow rolled his heels so the gravel crunching beneath them was as silent as freshly fallen snow. He raised his knobby hands, the word "Boo!" already forming on his lips.

A boom like a distant crack of thunder echoed over the valley. Everyone looked up. Katie straightened and Wimbelow froze, cursing his luck. Up on the hill, the oblong shape of the Piquant Palace sparkled with blue light. The roof of the inn pulsated brilliantly, illuminating the small dome and chimney that made up the roof of the pepper-shaped pub. The windows in the dome flickered and dimmed with the influx of energy. A shower of sparks spewed from the chimney.

"Oh, lovely, they've begun the fireworks," someone said. There was a surge of clapping and the milling around resumed.

Bugger! Thought Wimbelow as Fergus disappeared into the crowd. Now what was he going to do? Meanwhile, a change had come over the young detective. Her face had gone pale, and she hadn't taken her eyes off the Palaces. Wimbelow edged back into the corner of the stall, curious.

"Here's your hat," said Katie hurriedly, stuffing it back on a child's head. The parents were trying to express their thanks, but she shook her head. "It's no trouble—look sorry but I've got to run. Police business." With that she strode briskly away, heading towards the inn.

Police business? Wimbelow followed her, keeping a careful few yards between them. Once outside of the fair, her walk turned into a jog, then a run. Katie's footsteps echoed on the empty streets. By the time she'd reached the base of the hill, Wimbelow was puffing, leaning on a fire hydrant. He nearly lost her then, her slender shadow blending into the dark side of the rise. Wimbelow caught his breath and began the climb. In the waning light, his shoes slipped over the overgrown stones that made for steps in the hillside. She would dip in and out of sight, jogging upwards as if it were no trouble at all. Strains of music from down below drifted in on the breeze. From up here, he could see the lights in the premature darkness cast by the headlands.

Wimbelow nearly didn't make it to the top. A stitch clawed at his side and his breath came in painful gasps, but the desire to catch the young detective at something overwhelmed all else. He spotted her again, moving away from the front door and around the side of the building. He moved quickly as he was able now. The tall grass deadened his movements and Katie seemed too preoccupied to look around. Eventually she stopped at a part of the wall, grabbed something, and hoisted herself up. Rungs, he surmised and bemoaning the prospect of further athleticism, he waited thirty seconds and began the climb.

This far up, the breeze turned to a howl. A chill bit through his coat and the Inspector even fancied he felt a light drizzle halfway up. Odd. It had been a cloudless sky all evening. Katie scrambled up the inn like a monkey, but she stopped near the top. Wimbelow felt it too. A hair-raising sensation. A prickling all across his skin as though the very air crackled with an unseen force. His heart thudded in his chest. He heard a soft exhale.

Stiffening her resolve, Katie climbed again and disappeared over the side of the roof.

The top of the inn housed a green dome and chimney painted to look like the cap and stem of the pepper. The dome appeared to be livable. Two windows faced out of it. They flickered and buzzed with that strange blue light. It sounded like a shorting lightbulb only a hundred times louder. A gust of rain spattered Wimbelow's head, and he looked up. Stranger and stranger! There were dark clouds above the town, moving in with frightening speed.

Katie was gone. The Inspector pulled himself up onto the narrow walkway around the dome. He approached the door and clasped the knob. Ice blue light played across the valleys of his hand. Premonitions of danger rushed through his mind. Could it be?

"Katie Twill," he murmured aloud, gazing into the strobing windows, blind in their brilliance. Static tickled the edges of the doorknob as a smile tickled the edges of his moustache. "This can mean nothing good."

He opened the door.

~30~

Finders Keepers

I set out my clothes and made sure I had everything. Tonight would be the night we looked for Bellamy's former house in hopes that his old research was still concealed somewhere. I didn't relish the thought of searching empty neighbourhoods in the dead of night whilst avoiding a pair of homicidal Autos, but there was no more time to waste. As Sebastian's secrets unravelled, so did, it seemed, Port Larkeney. We would be in more danger if we sat and waited. I stood back and stared at the neat array on the bed. Medical supplies, watch, Swiss army knife, torch, coffee, store-bought non spicy biscuits and—

I reached into my pocket and felt a stab of panic. No journal. I'd had it with me up on the roof, hadn't I? It had probably gotten kicked under bed or something when I'd taken off my jacket last night. I peered under the bed. Not there. For the remaining hour, I scoured the room. Where could it possibly be? I searched the drawers, the closet, under Tim's bed. It wasn't a very large room. A knock at the door interrupted me with my hand wedged into a pillowcase.

"Wendell, your mother and I are ready to leave for the Carnival."

"Coming!" *Where was it?*

There wasn't any more time to look. Out in the hall, my parents were tapping their feet. I swept the rest of the stuff into a small, fashionable kit bag that went with the rest of Tim's safari gear and headed out.

We left for the Carnival at 5pm. My parents and I were the last in line as the guests of the Palaces filtered out. To my surprise, nearly all of the dinner party guests were attending. It seemed that everyone was relieved to have something to do after being cooped up for weeks courtesy of local police. To one side, Billius chatted gaily with the Duke. These days he seemed to be doing better, nursing only a light ale. The Duke was as polite and reserved as ever. Evangeline was curt as usual, but I noticed she was wearing a peculiar wide-brimmed hat. When we caught eyes, she gave me a slow nod and I caught a glimpse of the brown toupee. Unsurprisingly, the reclusive Quislings had elected to stay inside. Instead, they stared down from their porthole window with eerie feline similarity.

The light atmosphere did nothing to ease me. The loss of my book was affecting me more than I'd thought. The prospect of going after The Lamplighter and The Cellist without my trusty field guide (even if it didn't much apply to Port Larkeney) felt like walking onto a tightrope with one eye covered. I downed two shots of espresso even though I did badly with coffee. The benefits of the hour of sleep at Bellamy's had vanished long ago and I needed to be alert.

Mrs. Twill was on her way out as well, skirts billowing like a hurricane, her arms laden with last minute items for Big Bertha's tent. She stopped me in front of the door and rifled in her bag. It was a letter.

"It's for your brother again."

"Thanks." I pocketed it. Though there was nothing more said, there was a difference in our exchange. A shared secret.

"Wendell?" my father looked back.

"Coming!" I turned back to her. "Is that it?"

Mrs. Twill gave me long look.

"Be careful, will you? And would you tell Katie that as well?"

I nodded and jogged outside, trying to shake the nervousness from my body.

Everyone had elected to walk down, as the evening was warm. Cheery chatter filled the air and I saw the first glimpses of the finished festival. Brightly-coloured stalls and booths filled the town streets below. Big Bertha rose above it all like a ruby mountain. My parents were subdued.

"I feel terrible, going to see this," my mother's voice was barely above a whisper. "Tim would have loved it."

"Would have. Could have. Stop it with the past tense. He's still alive," my father said tersely.

"Barely."

"We'll pay him a visit after—get him a souvenir."

"I just can't stop thinking about his face. All pasty and grey. Maybe we ought to ask Dr. Simmons to change what she's feeding him." Her voice rose with worry.

My father nudged her with a surreptitious glance in my direction. "She's at the festival Marjorie. If you think we're helping him by purposefully not enjoying this…"

"Oh, don't worry, we're not," I emerged between the two of them. Before my father could answer, I'd sped up down the hill.

Katie'd said she'd try to get assigned to Asher street where one of the first robberies had taken place, but the plan fell apart as soon as I stepped foot into the festival.

"Katie?"

I had to shout over the band music booming from a nearby gazebo. The detective turned. When she spotted me, a guilty look crossed her face. She handed a child their toy back and crossed over the boulevard.

"I couldn't do it!" she yelled over the music. "Wimbelow wouldn't let me change assignments, so I'm stuck here for the rest of the night. Break left. I think he's watching me."

I split and we walked on either side of a stall selling potato soup in bell pepper bowls. She ducked behind a truck bed, and I followed, emerging on the other side which faced a quiet alley.

Katie peeked over the edge until she was sure we were alone. "I know he's suspicious of something. I caught him reading something as I came into his office. Tucked it into his desk really fast."

"Well, that could always be…something else."

"Like what?" Her face was innocent.

I decided now wasn't the time to expound. "Doesn't matter. What do you mean suspicious?"

"Like, he's been keeping me close during patrols. Rudy said he was trying to look into my thermos once. He's also been saying stuff that's likely to rile me up like 'A real police officer has better decorum than that,' or 'do this, Twill, do that,' 'Do it again, it's not right.' When *I* know it's up to proper standards." She chewed her lip. "It's almost like he *knows*, you know?"

"Knows what?" I said sharply.

The detective froze. My gaze was unwavering. She swore.

"Oh, come on Katie. It's not as if it wasn't obvious."

"Fine!" she cried. "Is that what you wanted to hear? Yes, I've got narcolepsy. I've had it ever since I can remember, but you know what? No one else has ever figured it out. Sure, they call me things like Possum and Nodding Ninny but that's just twelve-year-olds for you. Honestly, it's a good thing no one listens to children." Her words began to tumble over one another, her hands moving through the air confusedly. Their shadow played across the stone walls of the little alley, flighty as birds.

"You could have gotten me or someone else seriously hurt," I said.

She rounded on me. "If you knew then why didn't you leave?"

I bristled. There would be no apology? No remorse?

"You're a police officer," I snapped. "Isn't it your job to keep people safe?"

"Wendell, this is all I've ever wanted to do. I knew if I told you in the beginning we wouldn't have gotten this far. Look, I can control it. I can!" She thrust the thermos at me and took a long sizzling sip just to prove her point. "Nobody wants to work with a detective who falls asleep while she's chasing the bad guys."

"For good reason!" The smell of cinnamon, coffee, and spice was overpowering. I'd been putting off confronting her after the incident in the wardrobe because so much had happened. Perhaps I'd hoped that time would've helped her explain it to me.

"You were the first person who took me seriously," Katie said quietly. "Everybody laughs at a girl detective. Add my condition, and I'm a joke."

"You just wanted a friend? That's the reason for all of this."

"Of course not! It's just—let me explain."

"I think you've done enough of that." I said. I was sick of this. Sick of people needing me to fix things about themselves. My father, my brother, and now Katie. I wanted to be alone. "I'm going to go search for Bellamy's house on my own. You're clearly busy here."

I ducked under the truck and was hit by a wall of sound and light. Fairgoers ambled past me in a haze. Anger buzzed through me, amplified by nerves, caffeine, and the loss of my journal.

I'd spent half my life looking after other people. I couldn't hope that someone might do the same for me. Despite myself, my gaze went back to the alleyway. She was already gone.

My mother was buying a stick of sausage when a dull boom thundered over the town. Simultaneously the crowd turned. The top of the Piquant Palaces was glowing a bright blue. The windows shone as bright as a lighthouse and a shower of sparks fizzed from the chimney. My breath caught. I knew that light, and I knew that colour. The sound of clapping dulled in my ears.

"Fireworks, how lovely," someone said.

"Where are you off to?" my mother asked as I pushed past her into the crowd.

"Bathroom!"

335

The wooden platform with Big Bertha was drawing closer. Amid the crowd, I pinpointed the pear-shaped figure of Mrs. Twill rattling off her wares.

"Wendell?"

I caught her arm. "You need to distract my parents."

"What, now?" She gave a helpless look to all the people clamouring for trinkets.

"Please, Mrs. Twill!"

She sighed. "Fine."

When I next glanced at the booth, it was empty with the sign "Be Back Soon" slung over the stall. Good. As I made my way through the twisting streets, the sounds of the fair faded behind me and another replaced them. Two sets of footsteps. Running.

I broke left and stopped. It was the Inspector, running about ten yards ahead of me and ahead of *him*...the bell bottoms were just visible under the darkening sky. There was no way to warn her, they were too far ahead. Instead, I followed them at a distance. Up the hill, around the side of the Palaces, and oh god the ladder. By the time I reached it I was wobbly with fatigue. I stopped at the bottom rung. The prospect of the height made my head swim with nausea. I was wasting time! No. I turned around and headed for the door.

Mrs. Twill had gotten up there just this morning and I couldn't picture her using the side of the building. There must be another way. Sweat cooled on my forehead as I took the three flights of stairs two at a time. In the third corridor, I looked around for a secret door, a closet, anything. It was all guest rooms. Further down, I stopped. My skin prickled, the hair on my arm raising. A few steps to the right and the feeling was gone. I stepped back and looked up. There it was, cut nearly invisibly into the ceiling: a trap door, a latch, and a bead on a string.

I reached it standing on a chair. The door protested bit I pulled harder and with a sudden clang, it fell open, revealing a chink of strobing night sky and a metal ladder. Wind howled on the roof with sudden ferocity. Where had the balmy evening gone? Storm clouds filled the sky, and the planks were slick with rain. It felt like being on the prow of a ship as the city below swayed in my tunnelled vision.

I felt the presence of the Lightning Gun all the more keenly. Bellamy's dome crackled with light. From what I could see, I was alone up here on the roof. I went in on hands and knees up to the strobing window. Squinting against the glare, I could just make out a stack of crates, bathed in white hot light. A large copper object pulsed at its epicentre.

A body lay sprawled on the floor. Long tendrils of blond hair fanned straight out from her face. Fear frissioned through my every nerve. My hand immediately went to my pocket before remembering my journal was gone.

"Don't be an idiot," said the rational voice in my head. *"That won't help you."*

"Yes, but—"

"Now what are you going to do?" interrupted the voice and I tried to unclench the trembling hand in my pocket. To force it towards the door

She lied to me. Over and over again, she could have hurt me.

What I went in there and met exactly the same fate as Tim? Then I couldn't help anyone.

"You were the first person who took me seriously."

Her eyes, tired, bloodshot, but still arrestingly green, appeared in front of me. A tooth-chattering buzz shot up my arm as I grabbed the doorknob and pushed inside. Immediately my vision went white.

Inside, the dome was quiet. The strobing effect of the Lightning Gun made the room alternate in blinding light and plunging darkness. Sharp angles jutted into the corners of my vision. Darkness. I ran to her. Blue light played over her pale lashes. I knelt beside her and grabbed her wrist. Alive. Darkness. Her heartbeat was slow. Asleep. Darkness.

"Katie." I shook her shoulder before remembering the broken rib. It seemed to do the trick. She came to, wincing, then sat up, swivelling her head around the room.

"Wendell! You shouldn't be here."

I examined her face between pulses, the dilation of her eyes. The pupils were large and black. "Are you alright?" I asked. "Who was it? Bellamy? The Cellist? One of the guests?"

"Wrong on all accounts, I'm afraid." The door closed with a gentle click. The Inspector stepped out from behind an outcropping of crates with Bellamy in tow. The Frenchman's hands were cuffed. His fine goatee and white hair were tousled and sweaty. He stumbled as Wimbelow pushed him forward.

"Well, well, well, Wendell Billings." Said the Inspector. "Seems you've gotten yourself in a spot of trouble. I wasn't expecting that to be quite honest with you. You seemed like a polite, respectable boy who might've been willing to bend the rules for his brother. Admirable even. But this is what happens when you get involved with the wrong sort. Very unpleasant business. Very unpleasant indeed."

He didn't look like he found it unpleasant. In fact, his small mouth seemed barely able to suppress his glee. He stood over the detective, bearing down on her like an orange-spotted tower of doom.

"Katie Twill, I hereby place you under arrest. You have the right to remain silent, but I'd prefer it if you weren't. You're under arrest for harbouring a wanted felon and endangerment of the public while acting as a civil servant. By that I mean the narcolepsy." He smiled at me. "Thanks for the tip by the way. Oh, and I think that it goes without saying…you're sacked."

He crossed the room to where the Lightning Gun sat. Sparks rained down from where the beam hit the stone.

"Does anyone know how to turn off the bloody thing?" He seemed too hesitant to touch it. He pointed at me.

"You, Billings. Go over there and turn it off."

"Me? Ask Bellamy, he practically invented it!"

The Frenchman pulled against his cuffs. "I did not! Or at least I don't think I did."

"I don't trust you as far as I can throw you," Wimbelow snarled in Bellamy's ear. "Which would admittedly be quite far. What have they been feeding you up here, matchsticks?"

Just then, the light went out all at once. There was a low whine as the room cut to black. We all froze, blinking away the bright afterimages left by the gun.

"Must be out of juice," said Wimbelow from somewhere inside the disorienting darkness.

There was a thump and a scuffle. I heard a yelp that sounded like Katie. When the normal lights came back on, Wimbelow was holding the detective by the wrists. His long knobby fingers encircled both of hers. She was struggling but her breath came out in ragged gasps.

"Stop it!" I cried. "She's got a broken rib."

"Not my problem," said Wimbelow. "Do you have any idea how hard I've been working on this case only to find out that my very own subordinate has been hiding the culprit in her own mother's inn?

"You weren't working hard," Katie spat. "You were too busy writing letters to London to take you back. You never cared about any of us in Port Larkeney. You just wanted out."

Wimbelow ignored this. He bent close to her. "How long were you hiding him? A month, two, three?"

"Would five please you?"

"It very much would," he spoke into his radio. "Rudy, please detain Mrs. Twill and kindly escort her to the station. We have some questions we'd like to ask her." Wimbelow clipped the radio back into his belt and dug around in his pockets. He swore. "Don't have another handcuff. Oh! What am I thinking?" He held out his hand to Katie.

"No. Absolutely not."

"I know you have one. Give it here or I'll dig it out of your pocket, girl."

I finally learned what a hairy eyeball was when Katie shot him a look of deepest disgust. Slowly, she withdrew the pair of handcuffs attached to her belt.

"That wasn't so hard, was it? Turn around."

This was it. Everything was over. Despite Katie's stubborn scowl, I saw defeat in her eyes. *Think! Think of something! It's always Katie being daring—now you've got to.* But it would turn out that I didn't have to. Wimbelow had braced himself against the door to prevent further escape. His boot was flush against it as he unclipped the handcuffs. In the next few seconds, this would work out rather poorly for him.

The door blew inwards with such shattering force that glass flew to the other side of the room and stuck there, gently quivering. The Inspector was taken with it. His entire body was pinned underneath the fallen door, and I could just barely see the top of his balding head. Katie jumped back just in time as someone emerged from the dust. Soft steps tip-tapped on the wood like a pirate walking the plank.

The Cellist smiled from ear to ear. Without a word, he strode over the door and the Inspector's prone body and plucked the gun from its resting place, juggling the unwieldy weapon with ease.

"I should kill each and every last one of you," he said cheerfully. "As a fan of poetic justice, I would have liked to use my very own gun but alas it seems someone's wasted whatever is left of the charge. Bellamy," he nodded at the Frenchman who wriggled up against the crates in fright. "Long time no see, old friend."

"It can't be," Bellamy breathed.

"Oh, but it is. You thought you could hide from me? You thought you could take what is mine? I'm more than human now, old friend. I am *Amber*."

He raised his bow and traced a gentle line down the throat of the inventor. Bellamy whimpered. From somewhere, Wimbelow's fallen radio buzzed. It became intermixed with the whine of two intercoms within short range. A frantic voice issued out the other end, putting The Cellist's advancement to a halt.

"Is anyone there? Inspector? Katie? There's something very strange going on. Very, very bad. The festival—it's—"

Screams issued from the other end.

The Cellist stepped over to the radio and crushed it with his foot.

"Excellent," said The Cellist to no one in particular. "Well, it seems I don't have any more time to waste. Bellamy." Without warning, he plunged the bow into the stomach of the Frenchman and withdrew it with a sickening pop. My mouth dropped open. Katie gasped.

"Au revoir, mon ami. Until we meet again." The Cellist spun on his heel. The barrel of the copper weapon glistened on his shoulder as he walked back over the door. The Inspector groaned. Then he was gone. Bellamy's cough broke the spell. I went to where he was slumped and pressed a hand to his stomach.

"How does it feel?"

"Fantastique," said the Frenchman through gritted teeth.

"You can talk. That's a good sign." I grabbed the kit bag and found the medical pack. I quickly swabbed the wound with alcohol before applying the plaster. As far as cuts went it was lucky. The bow was extremely narrow which meant the opening was small and unlikely to bleed out. What worried me were the two separated edges which could have done damage on the inside. Again, my fingers fluttered towards the non-existent journal, and I had to stop myself. I knew there was something in there on stomach wounds, but for the life of me, the words would not appear. For now, there was nothing I could do but put pressure on the bleeding. All my gauze had been used up for Katie's broken rib. I improvised using a torn pillowcase.

"This is going to hurt," I said. "Just bear with it."

Keeping the edges as flat as I could, I wound the pillowcase around the Frenchman's waist. He hissed in pain but didn't scream.

"There. Done." It was clean for the moment, but he needed stitches. I couldn't help but wonder why The Cellist didn't kill him then and there.

"We need to get Bellamy out of here," I said.

Katie moved the door off of Wimbelow. The Inspector lay unmoving on the floor, but as soon as the door was off him, he gave a little spasm and started to murmur.

"Crab Legs. Purple. Flibbertigibbet."

I did a quick once-over. "Concussion most likely. We can leave him." I felt a bit bad, but not bad enough to carry him down with the wounded inventor.

Katie didn't respond. She stood staring at Bellamy. "I can't believe you," she said softly.

Bellamy tried pushing himself to a standing position. Bright droplets of sweet ran down his face. "Katie. Whatever you think of me...zis is not...ahh." He let out a low moan.

"Can it."

I turned to her. "Katie now really isn't the time. Criminal or not, he needs proper medical care. Who knows when The Cellist will be back."

341

As if on cue, the distant wail of sirens rose, high and hair-raising over the hills. We each took Bellamy by the arm and levered him slowly down the trapdoor. Katie went down first and caught him none too gently. There was a spare room on the second floor. We took it and locked the door behind us.

Bellamy collapsed onto the bed with an ominous noise. Blood began to mar the makeshift bandage. His forehead and hands were slick.

"He needs to be elevated to stop the blood," I said. "Prop his hips up with a pillow."

When it was done, Katie and I stood back. It was all we could do. I tried to lighten the mood. "Gingersnaps. Right?"

Her eyes appraised him coldly. "No. Bastard." She turned and left.

I glanced at Bellamy. He wasn't going anywhere, so I followed her into the hall. "Katie, wait."

"I need some air."

"We can't leave, not yet."

"I said, I need some—Ma?" She nearly collided with the ample figure of Mrs. Twill who'd been rushing up the stairs at lightning speed. She hugged Katie, then me, to my surprise.

"Oh, thank goodness! The two of you! I was worried! Then someone said the hospital had been broken into and the roof. I thought it didn't look like fireworks! Wendell, I told your parents you'd come down with a nasty bout of chili stomach and came back here to rest." She stopped to look at the both of us. "What happened here?"

"We're all about to be arrested is what happened," Katie snapped, pulling away from her mother. "Wimbelow found us and the Lightning Gun. Bellamy had it in his room all along."

"He found Bellamy?"

"And me and you! He's got us charged. Verbally. Might not remember it in the morning but he will when he wakes up on the roof covered in debris and bits of goat cheese!"

Mrs. Twill opened her mouth, and I held up a hand. "I think you'd better come see this."

342

We took her to the spare room where Bellamy lay. Upon entering, the Frenchman raised his head. He broke out into a weak smile.

"Whatever happened to you?" cried Mrs. Twill, rushing to his bedside.

"Just a spot of impalement my dear. Nothing to worry about."

Mrs. Twill let out a low wail and grasped his hand.

Katie slapped it away. "Stop that! He's the one who stole the Lightning Gun! He's the thief and he probably tried to murder Sebastian Shaw and us. How can you just stand there, holding his hand?"

There was a long silence. I looked from Mrs. Twill to Katie. Katie to Bellamy. Her mother seemed to be struggling with something.

"Katie, dear. It wasn't him."

"How can you possibly know that? You said yourself he doesn't have an alibi."

"Well, that's...not entirely true." She was blushing deeply. "Look...darling. Sweetie. Sugarplum. My perfect pepper pancakes. We didn't plan it."

Katie crossed her arms. "Didn't plan what?"

Oh *no.*

"Well...I'd just had a good day at the pub. We'd gotten a new shipment of goat cheese, so I went up the trap door with a pint."

"So? He has an alibi then. Why wouldn't you tell me?"

Bellamy had somehow found another cigarette. He winked while puffing it.

"Oh Katie," said Mrs. Twill. "Do I really need to spell it out for you?"

All the blood left the detective's face.

"I can leave," I said, edging towards the door. Katie caught me by the arm.

"Oh no, you don't. How long?" she whispered to the two of them. "How long has it been going on?"

"Early October."

Katie swayed a little.

"Maybe you ought to get some fresh air," I said. "You don't look so good."

"I don't look so good? *I don't look so good?* Gee I wonder why? I just find out my mother is having an affair with a French criminal that stinks of goat cheese all the while telling me it's to find my Dad! Did you even care about him at all?"

Mrs. Twill shook with emotion. "Of course I did! I lied to you and I'm so sorry, but it's been five years darling. Don't you want me to move on?"

"You're not supposed to move on! He was my Dad. And you!" she turned to me. I winced.

"What did I do?"

"I thought you were my friend, but it turns out you told Wimbelow about my narcolepsy? I'm out of a job. The Cellist and the Lightning Gun are still out there. We still don't know who stole it in the first place and we were almost murdered twice in the last two days and—and—"

"I'm sorry!" I shrunk back against the full brunt of her anger. "It was an accident. I wanted to tell you."

"No, you didn't! Why does everyone think it's okay to keep things from me?" Katie shouted, swaying a little.

Mrs. Twill stepped in. "Calm down, love. You're getting overheated."

"Me? Oh, I'm calm. I'm perfectly calm," she laughed hysterically. "Can't you see how well I'm handling this situation?" She stumbled. Her eyes began to roll backwards, and her shoulders slackened.

"Oh, not again," said Mrs. Twill.

Thump.

* * *

Bellamy, Mrs. Twill, and I shared an uncomfortable silence as we waited for the detective to wake. One minute passed. Then two. Then three. We almost didn't notice when Katie came to consciousness. She'd remained prone, staring unblinkingly at the ceiling.

When it was clear she wasn't going to move, Bellamy coughed. "Is she stuck? Should we do something?"

344

"I think she wants me," tremoured the innkeeper. With a great heave she plopped herself down beside her daughter, tears filling her eyes.

"Katie, darling. Please, I'm so sorry. Anything, I can do to make it better. I won't ask you to forgive me, just talk to me, would you?"

There was a collective moment of relief when Katie sat up. The detective didn't even register her mother. When she turned to me, I saw was a baffling change. Her face was alight with excitement.

"Wendell, I know who did it," she breathed.

"Did what?"

"It was Mary. Mary Belsize stole the Lightning Gun."

~31~

The Metal Boy

24 Hours Earlier…

Explosions tore the night sky overheard. Colours popped and banged. Petals of light burst and twirled in deadly pinwheels. Clouds of smoke and sparks billowed down from the heavens. The Lamplighter covered his ears against the sounds of war and stumbled down the hill as fast his trembling legs would take him.

Rocks cracked against his chest, sprayed up in the mad zigzag that was his escape. He couldn't see where he was going, didn't have the presence of mind to turn on his beams, so when one of the stone steps appeared, hidden in the dry grass, he caught on it and fell. The momentum sent him tumbling down the hill end over end. Dirt and stone jarred the metal body mercilessly until it finally came to rest at the bottom of the hill.

It was the dark side of the valley, away from the sea and bordered by a thick wood. The Lamplighter lay there for some time in the stillness. Slowly, all the spindly metal arms and legs disentangled from one another. Then they closed in once more like a spider settling in against the cold. The Lamplighter balled himself up as tightly as he could and began to sob.

War. That was what he'd gotten himself into. War. And for what purpose? No wonder people were scared of Autos when they did things like this. *Am I doomed to lead a life in the shadows because of what I am?* Oh, what a curse it was to be alive like this. It must be why The Cellist was so angry all the time. He would never be able to sit in a warm house, laugh by the fire, or even stroll across the street in the daylight. Creatures like them—they would never be truly free. The sobs were loud and cavernous in his chest. He couldn't even be quiet if he wanted to.

The woods looked quiet. The Lamplighter raised his head at the black cluster of trees. Normally they would have made him afraid but now they seemed inviting. *I could leave right now,* he thought. *The Cellist wouldn't be able to find me in the countryside.* It was in that moment that he realised their tie had been severed. His loyalty was gone. Violence was not in his being and the battle on the side of the building had shown him that much. He could leave now, and never come back. The Lamplighter took a step toward the trees and stopped. The image of the boy on the dumbwaiter appeared, wide frightened eyes pleading. He remembered girl detective who'd hung from the rope like a man on the gallows.

They could both be dead now, if The Cellist had survived.

"No!"

A wild and unaccountable grief swept through him, and he turned back to face the hill. It was impossible to see anything. The Lamplighter began his ascent. Hand over hand over hand over hand, finding the craggy footholds on the sheer side of the rise. He climbed as naturally as if he'd known it all his life. When a root or a rock came loose under his grip, one of the many hands found another and another. This was what he'd been built for after all. When The Lamplighter crested the hill, he found that all was quiet once more. The Piquant Palaces stood smoking gently in the moonlight, sleeping once more.

He was careful to avoid the open windows of people who'd awoken from the commotion, keeping to the shadows close to the base of the building. His Amber flickered in his chest. There was no sign of The Cellist. Creeping back and forth, he found the spot where the dumbwaiter had hung. It was gone. He searched the ground. No bodies. It wasn't enough to ease his mind, but it was better than finding something. The Lamplighter leaned against the building and stared out across the lot. There was a divot in the grass, a square dent about a metre away. He walked over plucked it out, brushing the dirt from the fallen object. It was a book, palm sized and bound in worn leather. He ran his metal fingers over the surface and felt the dimples of another hand so used to carrying it that the book had become the imprint of its owner. **"Property of Wendell Billings"** the inside cover read in neat handwriting.

"Wendell Billings," he repeated softly. The Lamplighter sat back down in the shadows of the building, turned his eyes to their dimmest setting, and began to read.

"Twenty-Eighth of August,
We are in Thailand this month, passing through the town of Lopburi. There are macaques everywhere. I recently witnessed one steal the watch off a man's hand.
(Note to self: When bartering with a macaque for stolen property, offer ONE banana and walk away if they refuse. Those monkeys may be smart, but they're suckers for reverse psychology.)"

"Thirteenth of April,
Sri Lanka. We are staying near the forest monasteries of Ritigala where ancient meditation houses once stood for the purpose of the local monks and scholars. It is actually quite peaceful. Well, it was until Tim started flirting with the tour-guide. She was not impressed when he leaned nonchalantly on the two-hundred-and-fifty-year-old Buddha statue. She was less impressed when it cracked, and the dead monk inside came tumbling out."

"Tenth of December,
Do NOT accept rides on a tuk tuk."

On and on the entries went, describing every manner of situation imaginable, from pieces of advice on how to navigate a Greek labyrinth, to how to survive off the wood lily of the American Appalachians. There were drawings of minute detail, diagrams painstakingly labelled, and private thoughts written in other languages that The Lamplighter was amazed to understand. He skimmed a few snippets in French and Japanese.

"It's an interesting phenomenon I've come to observe over the past few years that if you observe someone long enough and write their every move, eventually you become invisible. I've become particularly good at that. Being invisible that is. Sure, people ignore you, but at least it's come in handy. Today I narrowly avoided a poison dart because a poacher thought I was a bush."

"Tim's mail has arrived. There's quite a lot of it, though he's not here to see it. He's gone off to some Lunar festival while I'm stuck here transcribing Dad's latest interview. Not that it matters. I was tired anyway."

And then there was the envelope. Still unopened, it was shoved into the back of the book. The Lamplighter parted the seal delicately. Inside was a poem written in blocky, painstaking script on the back of a grubby postcard:

PLEASE, TALK TO ME

EVERY DAY I CHECK THE MAIL
AND FIND THERE'S NOTHING THERE
IS ONE MORE DAY MY HEART WILL SINK
INTO DEEPER DESPAIR

HAS SOMETHING HAPPENED?
ARE YOU OKAY?
I WONDER THAT MOST EVERY DAY

I WISH YOU WOULD WRITE
JUST A LETTER MORE
TO LET ME KNOW IF IM A BORE

YOU MAY NOT THINK OF ME
BUT I THINK OF YOU
I MISS YOU SO MUCH MORE
THAN YOU THINK I DO

WITH LOVE,
MELATI

He clutched the letter in trembling hands. He poured over every scribble and every jotting squeezed into the margins of the notebook. By the time he'd finished, the sky had begun to lighten, and The Lamplighter had an ache in his chest that felt like it would swallow him whole.

"I'm sorry, Wendell," he whispered and brought the little leatherbound book close to his chest where the Amber inside pulsed an almost-heartbeat. "I was a terrible brother."

Tim drew himself up to his full height, still hidden in the shadows. Funny it had taken him becoming himself to finally be brave, he thought. And brave he would have to be to face The Cellist.

* * *

The Lamplighter lifted his head just above the manhole cover across the street to make sure the shop was empty. He estimated it to be around half five. The shop opened at eight, but it was always wise to make sure Laura hadn't come back on her perpetual quest to catch the ever-elusive Panty Thief.

Thankfully the windows were just as dark as they'd left them. He lowered himself back down, crawled through the narrow tunnels and stopped at a portion of the sewer where a small section of brick was slightly lighter than the rest of the surface. He dug his fingers into the seams. With a small grinding sound, the stone was removed. Light shone through the underground to reveal the vacant changing room in the Lingerie Shop. He vaulted up, manoeuvring his enormous, brimmed hat, and emerged into the dim confines of the stall. Heaps of stolen machines and teetering piles of spare parts loomed in the near darkness. Genie the teapot was crouched in one corner, trying to be as small as possible.

The Cellist was there, rubbing out the stains in his sleeve. He looked rather the worse for wear, The Lamplighter thought with satisfaction. There were black smudges all across his face and once pristine tailcoat. His perfect white hair was burnt and gave off the acrid scent of melted plastic.

He looked up. "You're late," he sneered. "While you were off running like a ninny, I was finishing what we started, and I have some very interesting ne—"

He never finished the sentence. In one motion, the smaller Auto was up against the wall. The Cellist wriggled against the arm holding him there, but the grip was steely. Literally. One hand had him by the throat, two at the wrists, and yet another picked up the fallen bow and threw it under the door.

"Wha—a?" he choked.

"What did you do to them?" growled The Lamplighter. A white-hot rage distilled from grief welled up inside him, pressing The Cellist further and further into the panel. The thin partition began to creak. "*Answer me.* What did you do to my brother?"

The Cellist's face glowed brilliantly with the full force of the beams upon him. He turned his face from the light, rasping. The Lamplighter loosened his grip somewhat.

"Your...*brother?*" he spat it out slowly. "Ah...That's the reason for this I expect. We've, ahem, all had some revelations tonight."

"What are you talking about?" The Lamplighter tightened his grip inadvertently until The Cellist was wheezing, not from lack of air, but the constriction of his mechanical voice box. His face plates separated and fluttered insect-like into a nasty smile.

"The memories," he whispered. "The voices of our past. Without knowledge of my past self, I made the only natural assumption. Fate. Magic. A revolution. I thought we were the oppressed race that needed to revolt against humans. But I was wrong. I'd simply forgotten who I was." The Cellist craned his neck around the grip. He wasn't bothering to struggle anymore. "You know who you are... and I think you know who I am. We lie, side by side for the better of two months after all,

352

dormant and unseeing as the ones you love come to weep at your bed."

"No." Tim stared. The light in his eyes flickered. The ivory throat strobed black and white in his hands. "Who are you?"

Keys jingled in the knob.

Crackers. It was Laura. He winked out the beams, still holding fast to The Cellist as the owner entered the shop. She was wearing all black and carried the butt-end of a torch like a bludgeon.

"Thought you could get the best of me, eh?" she declared to the empty room. "I saw lights on from the pub. So, you'd best believe you won't be getting away with the nice silk thongs while I'm here."

What timing! The Cellist had already gotten a hand free and was trying to silently wedge his fingers through the grip on his throat. The Lamplighter tightened his grip once more until the fingers went limp. Unfortunately, that was the extent of the force the panel could bear. Made of cheap, pink painted plywood, it was no match for a fight between two angry Automatons. As Laura wheeled around, the two Autos fell forwards into the second and third stalls, until all three changing rooms were in flinders. Laura screamed. The Lamplighter shouted in anger. The Cellist was no longer under him. He'd gotten away in the mess.

Suddenly Laura's yelp was muffled. The Cellist's gloved hand wrapped a pair of pantyhose around her mouth and tied them in a neat bow. He went on to bind her hands and feet before rolling her behind the counter, out of sight. Then he held up a finger.

"Don't."

The Lamplighter halted behind him; six arms poised.

"If you kill me now, you'll never know the fate of your brother."

"Just tell me!" The Lamplighter demanded. He meant it to sound scary, but it came out desperate and scared. The anger that momentarily overpowered his fear was draining quickly. He was still Tim after all, and he was only so brave.

"Not to worry." The Cellist crossed the floor, shoving aside the kicking leg of the gagged storekeeper. "Our cover here is blown anyways and since we're such good pals, I'll do better than that. I'll show you where he is," he tossed away one of the ruined panels to reveal the tunnel opening.

"Where is he?" The Lamplighter didn't budge.

"Why, my manor of course. Surely you must have figured out who I am by now. You can call me Sebastian."

~32~

Mary Mary Quite Contrary

ary Belsize," I repeated. "Mary?" The name echoed around the room like a game of telephone.

"Mary," said Mrs. Twill. "The goat farmer. The one with the very pungent cheese?"

"Ze lady with ze 'airless chimp and ze squinty face?" asked Bellamy from his bed.

I finished the circuit, turning back to Katie who looked alarmingly spacey. "Mary?"

"That's the one," Katie said dreamily. She stared up at the ceiling, her fingers tracing gentle orbits in the air. "You see, it all fits together now, Wendell. I didn't have a clue before, but now, all the things you've seen, the things we've found out, it makes sense."

"Are you going to explain anything?" huffed Mrs. Twill. "Or are we to sit here wondering if you've gone mad?"

The detective sat up and snapped her fingers. "Wendell, go up onto the roof and get me a cheese crate, preferably a full one. Please don't ask questions, we haven't much time."

Bemused, I left. I didn't relish going back up to there. Smoke curled around the edges of the dome and a heavy rain drenched the roof. I had to step over the fallen door and around the unconscious Inspector, who mumbled something about stained glass orchids. The black scorch mark in the centre of the floor was an ominous reminder of the Lightning Gun still at large.

The heaviest of the crates I chose, and cursing, wedged it out from underneath the pile. It was a job dragging it across the roof.

"Here." I plunked the crate down in front of everyone and shook the rain out of my hair. "Nearly killed me getting it down here. What do you need with all that cheese?"

"Oh, nothing," said Katie happily. "That was for telling Wimbelow about my narcolepsy." She went ahead and tipped the box, sending the rounds of cheese rolling every which way. Then she took the empty crate and held it up to Bellamy.

"Does this look familiar to you?"

"Yes. I eat cheese every day."

"The logo Bellamy. Look at the logo." The Frenchman stared at it as he was told, still shaking his head in confusion.

"You said you remembered something about your old house. It was a stone cottage with a white picket fence. It was two stories with a thatched roof. You said there was a little lake and animals milling about and that there was always a bad smell no matter what you did." Katie framed the picture on the crate with her fingers. "Now tell me. Is this the house that you once lived in?"

Bellamy's eyes widened.

"I did not realise it before…" Bellamy traced the image with his thumb in wonderment. "Ze key to my memory was right under my nose ze entire time! Sacre Bleus!" He slapped his face and immediately winced from the wound in his abdomen.

Katie shook her head. "I think it was the logo that jogged your memory. Seeing it every day probably helped you remember the existence of those papers." She spun to me. "Do you see it? Do you get it now Wendell?"

And suddenly, like a bolt of lightning everything became clear. I rummaged in my pocket for my notebook before remembering it wasn't there. What I did find was the torn scrap with the word "Cheese." and the circular scribble. It came back to me in a stream of disjointed images. The strong figure that had pushed roughly past me, the image printed on the leather bag that had clunked so heavily, Mary's frightened pale face as she was the first to reach me after the attack. I'd seen what Bellamy had seen. I'd forgotten what he'd forgotten, and Katie had put together the fragments of our broken memories.

Katie continued. "At the risk of saying 'Elementary, my dear Watson,' Mary was a childhood friend of Sebastian's, right? It's not a far cry to assume he was the antisocial sort growing up. Mix that in with the fact that Mary has moved into Bellamy's old house and started selling goat cheese…" she paused for dramatic effect. "Bellamy, I think she might just be your daughter, Marguerite."

"That's preposterous," said Mrs. Twill. "What sort of daughter frames her own father for such a heinous crime?"

Katie raised an eyebrow. "Someone who believes her father is a wanted criminal might. It would be the perfect way to get rid of the evidence, get the gun into police custody, and have revenge on a father who never returned. Plus, *we* don't exactly have the best track record for mother-daughter relationships. I just wish I knew how she figured out Bellamy was up here with us…"

Mrs. Twill had little to say after that.

Bellamy Dumont was taking quick shallow breaths, either to deal with the pain, the newfound revelations, or a mixture of both. At length, he said, "I have only myself to blame for zis."

"Don't say that," said Mrs. Twill. "A single father, out on his own. You were only doing the best you could."

"Non, non. I was a terrible father even before then. I was blinded by ze thought of fame, fortune, and discovery. And it was so very easy to be delighted in another kindred soul like young Sebastian. My own daughter was left to the sidelines."

He gazed at all of us with water in his large blue eyes. "Earlier zis evening as I was asleep, I fancied I saw a figure in my room, although I thought I had dreamed it. She must have left ze gun up on ze roof. My own daughter, right beside me. All zis time I had seen her face and not recognized it." He strained forward with sudden passion and made it halfway off the bed before his face went bloodless. The added force of Mrs. Twill made him relent. "Perhaps I deserve zis, but I will kill Sebastian for what he has done."

"No, no, love," she crooned. "You're far too weak. Rest now, revenge later. Where do you think you're going?" Mrs. Twill looked up as Katie threw up her coat and stepped neatly into the shoulders.

"To finish what we started. I'm getting Mary, and I'm getting her to confess. Come on Wendell!"

I scrambled to my feet. "Wait, I'm still sore from hauling all the cheese!"

"Good!"

But as we were leaving, Bellamy called for us to wait. "When you see her, tell her I am..." His voice was strained and quiet. "Just that I am sorry. For everything. I wish that I could tell her I am not ze man she thinks I am, but I would have no way of knowing."

The detective nodded and together we left to catch our culprit. I was still playing catch-up as Katie flew down the stairs two at a time. How had she known?

"How did you figure it all out?" I asked.

The junior detective took the stairs three at a time. "I don't know. It all just sort of came together while I was asleep. Everything we found out—everything you wrote down in that notebook of yours. It was hard at first, to reconcile the fact it was Mary. I really did like her when I first met her. She was so sweet. But I had a suspicion. You got to it first, you know—as soon as you said it made no sense to bring milk to a host who was lactose-intolerant. I was too blinded by all the evidence that pointed at Bellamy."

"So, if she was on the balcony, then it would give her an alibi while her monkey stole the gun," I said. "She said Humberdt wouldn't do anything unless it was for cheese so that was why she brought it."

We crossed down to the second flight of stairs.

"But what I still don't get is the hair. Bellamy has white hair, so does The Cellist and so do Evangeline's wigs, although Franklin said it was too coarse."

"And that's exactly it," said Katie confidently. "It was goat hair. Mary was a goat farmer. Must have stuck to Humberdt what with all those sweaters he wears. Pity. She had a bald monkey and everything."

I slapped my own forehead. How had I not realised? Too preoccupied by the myriad of contradicting clues, I had overlooked the obvious. I pictured it now. A bald, shivering monkey with his mind on cheese, climbing into the study of a mad genius, a pair of makeshift racket-like shoes strapped to his feet to disguise the fact an unusually smart South African Chimp had just entered the room. He clumsily picks the lock, causing multiple dents and scratch marks, and purloins the Lightning Gun. Then, all plans go awry when Shaw himself enters the room to find me a phone.

I stopped on the second-floor landing, amazed. It was so ridiculous; I was beginning to realise that I could have never done this one on my own. Only a mind as strange and sporadic as Katie Twill's could have strung the events together.

"My god," I couldn't help but say. "You've thought of everything."

She stepped aside to let me into the pub. "That I have," she said, in mock seriousness. "And Mary could've gotten away with it too. If only she'd invested in a lint roller."

I snorted as she crossed the room to open the door.

"You have to give her props though," Katie continued. "He makes for the perfect conspirator; a very smart, very quiet, and very, very hairless..." She wrenched open the door and froze.

"...monkey."

The very large person who happened to be standing in the doorway looked down at us. Melati glared at her, and then at me.

"What she call me?"

* * *

You're probably wondering how I immediately knew who this was. Well, I was able to make a pretty good guess by the huge "TIMMY TUM" sign she carried, as if she were waiting for him at

359

an airport. What I hadn't expected was the person holding it. Melati was at least as tall as Katie—and at least twice as broad. I couldn't help but step back a bit in her presence.

This was who my brother had been confessing his love to on a daily basis? In the back of my mind, this girl looked like she'd put you in headlock before writing about French-kissing and gondoliers. But here she was.

She was dressed heavily in an enormous lavender puffer jacket. Her trunk-like legs were wrapped up in grey wool leggings and sturdy boots. Her fuzzy mitten-clad hands were jammed deep into her pockets. From what little I could see of her face, she was dark-skinned with straight, jet-black hair that fell in silky sheaves to her waist. Peeking out above a diamond patterned scarf, her nose was red and raw. Frankly, I was just amazed it wasn't some Nigerian fellow with a talent for bad poetry.

"How—where—what are you doing here?" I went through most of the 5 W's as I spluttered. As I stood before the massive girl in the parking lot, a sudden vague hulking memory of her resurfaced. She had greeted us a long time ago from a little-known village deep in the wilderness of Indonesia.

Melati shivered and bounced in the cold, her feet leaving large divots in the dirt. "I come to see Tim," she repeated through the layers of clothing. Her English was surprisingly stilted. "I write you again and again." She sounded miffed. "You do not answer. I know something is wrong with my Timmy Tum. So, I fly in from my village to cold—v-very cold Ireland to find him."

I couldn't help but raise an eyebrow. "All that for *my* brother?"

Melati sniffed either from annoyance or the cold. "You do not understand our love. It transcends all distance, all obstacles. The moment I lay eyes on him, in his dashing khakis and his porridge-coloured skin, I know it, he knows it."

I elected not to tell her that my brother really had no clue who she was. Mercifully, her speech was cut off by the sounds of Katie trying and failing to get the car door open.

"Argh! You useless scrap of—I swear I'll—! Sorry," she stopped abruptly. "Carry on you two."

Melati turned back to me. "Can you tell him to come? He cannot possibly be so sick as to ignore me. I do not know why he not…answer me."

I felt guilty. It should have been my responsibility to tell Tim's girlfriend everything that had happened, but my general disinclination for any involvement in his personal life had prevented me. Now I braced myself for what was to come next.

"Melati, there's something you should know. Tim is…" I stalled reluctantly.

"Tim is what?"

"He's in hospital. Coma." I struggled to find the proper word in her language. "Like a long sleep, no no, not death, he just can't wake up… at the moment," I finished weakly.

Melati took a step forward and I thought she might strangle me but once more Katie's struggles with the old coupe intervened. Her Irishness had come out in full force, and she'd begun invoking famine and the devil in an effort to get the door open. Melati sighed. "You will take me to him," she said to me. It wasn't a question.

"I will," I promised. "But not right now. Katie and I have some really important things to do right now…if she ever gets that door open."

Without another look, the Indonesian girl strode to the car, hooked an index finger around the handle, and popped the warped metal out as if she were simply opening a sardine can. "You will take me to him now."

Katie gawked. "Sorry I called you monkey," she said quietly, "it was purely circumstantial."

Melati only grunted and the three of us slide inside. Katie clutched the wheel and shut her eyes as the whole car rocked with the brunt of Melati's weight. She took up the whole of the backseat. "I think my wheels just lowered two inches," she whispered. "Who is that? Why doesn't she speak English?"

"My brother's girlfriend from abroad," I answered. "Long story. She wants us to take her to Tim."

"We can't! Mary could be escaping as we speak."

"You try telling her that," I hissed.

A thought seemed to strike her. "But maybe this is good." She leaned in. "Whatever is under that fantastic fluffy jacket got these old doors to open which is nigh impossible on a cold day. We might need some more…force to get Mary to stay. Just tell her we're going on a quick detour. A little clip around the neighbourhood. Then we'll take her to your brother." She wiggled her eyebrows at me, but I couldn't lie to Melati again. Not with the danger we'd be putting her in—and me, if she found out.

I told Melati the truth. We needed to catch Mary before she got away, but it was Mary who was indirectly responsible for Tim's situation. Before I'd even finished, Melati's cheeks had coloured with a terrifying bloodlust.

"This woman, she has hurt my Timmy Tum? I shall do the same to her. I accept this detour."

I sat back in my seat as the car roared to life. The orange leather seats vibrated with the engine and the hanging baubles on the mirror bounced merrily. The Constabulary Carre rolled with growing speed down the hill and into the bright valley.

Katie switched on the 8-track. "Melati," she called. "Ever heard of disco?"

The drive through the country ended abruptly as the coupe turned into a long dirt driveway and encountered a goat that refused to budge. It gazed at us with its unnerving horizontal pupils, forcing us to stop.

"Alright, everybody out," Katie cut the engine and we all clambered out of the car.

The full moon rose pale and pink as rosewater behind Belsize farms. It was the spitting image of the logo on the crates—a thin stone house with a shingled roof, a picket fence, and a very, very bad smell. It was a long walk up to the house, tripping over humps in the dirt and dodging goat pies. When we got to the front door, Katie paused, looking back at us. Me, shivering unimpressively, Melati hulking like a black omen of doom behind us.

Katie took a deep breath and banged on the door, hollering, "Open up in the name of the law! Oho I've always wanted to say that. OPEN UP NOW!"

No one answered.

"There!" I pointed. A light in the upstairs window flicked out. There was a muffled crash.

Bang! Bang! Bang!

"WE KNOW YOU'RE IN THERE, MARY, OR SHOULD I SAY MARGHEU*oof*—" Katie lost her breath as Melati pushed her aside impatiently.

The girl raised her massive fist. "For Tim," said Melati grimly, and burst open the door in a single powerful swing.

For a moment we blinked, dumbfounded. Then Katie patted Melati on the arm appreciatively and led the charge up the stairs. From what I could see, it was a tidy little place. We ran through a cosy den with overstuffed chairs, an open kitchen with large windows and colourful crockery, and then up into the heights of the house, where the carpeted staircase muffled the thumps and thuds of our pursuit.

Katie made it to the top and stopped dead, locking eyes with the escapee at the other end of the hall. Mary's eyes were white as golf balls and her already curly hair was wild with sleep. She was frozen with one leg out the window and suitcase in hand. A rope made out of sheets disappeared over the edge. Katie edged forward.

"Don't."

Somewhere, a toilet flushed and Humberdt emerged from the door opposite. The hairless chimp rubbed his eyes, looking bemusedly all around. Mary made a frantic motion towards him. Humberdt only gazed mournfully out the open window and made no move to follow her. Mary made a small noise of frustration, weighing her options, and jumped. Katie sprang forward, colliding with Melati and the chimp in the narrow hallway as all three of them fought for the window.

Instead of joining it, I turned back downstairs. I remembered the large window in the kitchen. It should be directly below Mary's window, and it was the type that swung outward. Echoes of the fight upstairs drifted into the kitchen as I vaulted onto the lip of the sink and unhooked the latch just as the tips of boots appeared. I pushed the window out with all of my might, holding it there and shielding my eyes.

The dangling boots crashed into it spectacularly, sending bits of glass scudding over moonlit tile. Mary was entangled in the broken window frame, clinging onto the knotted sheet like a frightened cat 3 metres above the ground. She yowled and her pointy boots suddenly lurched upwards out of sight, kicking wildly. I ran back upstairs to find Katie and Melati working together to heave the aggrieved goat farmer back indoors by way of the sheet. Mary made one last ditch attempt to hang onto the windowsill by all hands and feet, but Melati simply plucked her off and heaved her inside.

When it was done, the four of us stood breathing heavily in the hall. Melati had Mary pinned with one hand, looking upon her handiwork with satisfaction. Humberdt sighed and went back into the bathroom.

"Well," said Katie. "I really can't think of anything guiltier than *that*."

~33~

Lizard People?

Pleashe!" Mary's face was smushed up against the wall. Her tears left a dark stain on the wallpaper. "Let me go. I'll explain everything. Wendell, Katie, I never meant to hurt anyone. I was trying to do the world a favour!"

I motioned to Melati to bring her off the wall. "If you want to explain anything, make it quick," I said coldly. "We know you have Bellamy's old documents on Amber. If you really want to help, you'll hand them over."

That seemed, inexplicably, to calm her. She ceased struggling. "So you know more than I thought. Good, good. Then perhaps you'll understand."

"Understand why you took the Lightning Gun?" asked Katie.

I reached into my pocket for the journal and was unpleasantly reminded of its absence. My fingers itched for something to do. "Excuse me," I said, "but do you have a pen and paper?"

Mary raised a brow and said, "Table over there, top drawer."

I went and got it. Having the stationary calmed my nerves a little bit. She continued, letting out a long shuddering breath. "I

367

had my reasons, you see? If you'll just let me go, I'll get the papers and tell you everything. You have me outnumbered. I can't run now."

"I beg to differ," said the detective. "Melati, hold her fast. Tell us where they are, Marguerite, and then we'll talk."

For a moment, a wild look crossed Mary's face, as if the woman who'd framed her father, stolen a priceless invention, and tried to escape through the window was back. Then it was gone.

"Downstairs in the kitchen. The ceiling lamp. Switch off the electricity and unscrew it. You'll find a cavity behind the lightbulb. Search around there for a folio. That's it."

Katie went down to check while Melati and I brought Mary down to the little parlour and switched on the lights. Katie came back triumphant with a dust covered folio in hand and set it onto the coffee table. She took up the furthest couch, a high back leather chair that commanded the room and waited for Mary to begin. It was an odd contrast—us sitting in that cosy little drawing room with the embers of a fire still in the hearth, and instead of having tea, interrogating a dangerous criminal, and uncovering secrets which had lain untouched for years.

I made tea, anyway, bustling around in the kitchen adding liberal splashes of goat's milk creamer to the cups. The criminal was appreciative. She took the cup, thanked me, and began.

"It all began in France. I lost my mother at an early age. My father, Bellamy, was a brilliant inventor as I'm sure you know. I was so proud of him. He would take me to all of his conventions and teach me wonderful things about the nature of clockwork and how machinery could be used to better the world. I believed him. That is until he met Sebastian Shaw."

There was a picture inside the folder which Katie had spread out on the table before us. It showed a little family standing in front of Mary's house. A young dark haired, moustachioed man, a girl of twelve with a hair of similar black but in wild curls, and a boy, pale and hobbled with a high forehead and peculiar set about his mouth. Intelligent and resigned.

"He was a peculiar young lad. Same age as me but he came from poverty. No parents. He never really talked about it. He always did put on airs though, as if he were one of my father's colleagues. I always thought it was a bit funny when he tried to be older than he was. But he was sickly too, and I suppose it might have been born out of feelings of inadequacy. He had polio in the legs you see and could hardly walk. My father liked to indulge in people and once he learned of Sebastian's talent in engineering, he took him in.

"I was fifteen when we arrived in Port Larkeney. Bellamy received letters from an old colleague about a botanical research opportunity. I didn't understand it. It wasn't machines, it was plants. But then again, I didn't understand most of what my father did. We left right away; it being decided that the seaside would also be good for Sebastian's illness. The three of us lived in this house for years. I liked it a lot, minus the business my father had with yours, Katie, for he was the one who'd sent the letters."

Mary reached into piled on the table and pulled out a yellowed envelope. "Take it," she said. "It's yours."

Katie hesitated in opening the old envelope. Her thumb traced the address, the swirls of the handwriting. "Eamon Twill," it read in round, faded type. She read the letter aloud.

Bellamy! Old fellow!

I bet you're pretty old now. I hear you've got a daughter of your own down there in London. We're all old it seems. I've got one too. Five last month. Lovely as a summer's day, although she's got a bit of a biting problem, little nipper. Anyways, I've got something here that might interest you. Very odd phenomena indeed. As you know, I've been keeping myself busy with a little biodiversity project in our backyard. I've got about three hundred different samples of peppers gathered from all over the world to see how they'd fare in our Irish climate. I didn't have high hopes. Sometimes it gets to -6 here. It's a wonder my bellbottoms haven't frozen to the ground.

The thing is, they've all grown extraordinarily! My South African peppercorn have flourished, the Carolina reapers are thriving, and the scotch bonnets are the size of my head! I couldn't make heads or tails of it until I did a soil test of all the neighbouring towns. Bellamy, I think there's something holy different here. Just in Port Larkeney, there is something in the soil that is cause for amazing growth. I know that plants were never your specialty, but you were the best researcher, and smartest man I know in university. If anyone can help me untangle the secrets of this, it's you. Plus, I know you were never immune to flattery.

So, come visit us, will you? Jeane would love to bake you a cake.

   -Eamon

Katie put the letter down. "That's him alright," she said quietly. I thought I detected a catch in her throat.

"Do you need a minute?" I asked.

She glanced at me, and I saw the emotion she was struggling to suppress. Sleep might come at any moment, but in seconds, she'd become as blank as a chalkboard.

"No. Mary, carry on."

She did. "What you just read about was the very beginning of the discovery of Amber, as you'll find in the diagrams and rest of the correspondence there. Apparently, they had been unable to distil it from the dirt but upon further exploration, found some caves under the town where it was growing in a purer form.

"Of course, I'd known none of this at the time. Back then, I was only angry. Previously he'd shared everything with me but now it was all hushed glances, secret papers and hidden outings. The thing I hated most was that most of it, if not all, was shared with Sebastian. He was a *genius*. He could be *trusted*," her words were short, punctuated in bitterness.

"We were friends once, Sebastian and me, despite the fact that it seemed that sometimes my father preferred his company to mine. Sebastian told me things about how he'd one day make a proper pair of legs out of machinery, and we could finally go on walks in the countryside. He was obsessed with making human parts out of nonhuman materials. He got better with it. Gifted me

370

clockwork in the shape of animals, carousels, dolls. Then my cat died, and things changed."

A new mixture of fear and revulsion crossed her face.

"I'll never be able to know for sure, but I think he killed it. As he'd killed every other pet and animal that had inexplicably died around the house. And I think he used it for this."

She opened the folio once more and slid across a case study of a mouse. The diagram showed a rodent and a nugget of what was unmistakably Amber, shown in fiery streaks of orange. Each was set apart from each other, but connected by a web of flowing lines. Another rendering, of a clockwork mouse with a winding key in the back, had glowing eyes. It was eerily familiar.

The case study read:

Experiments In Subjectivity of Persona and Life-force as a Natural Energy Wave to be Contained.

I had a nasty feeling about what that meant.

"Apparently, Sebastian and my father had already figured out that Amber was capable of containing the other forms of energy. Light, sound, electricity. This was about fifteen years ago. Sebastian was only fifteen himself. So, they decided to move on to the most elusive source of energy known to man. The soul. You're looking at me like I'm crazy. But Wendell, tell me this. What do you do when your cat dies, and the gift of a robotic cat you get in replacement meows and purrs just like Mr. Waffles?" Mary let that sink in.

It was an absurd statement anywhere else but here. The soul. She was saying that there were souls in the Autos then. Animal souls? No, it was obvious, but I didn't want to think it. Human. A thousand questions racked my mind. Was it even possible? Wasn't this what people actually considered magic? An equation presented itself in my head. Two sentient Amber Automatons ravaging the town, plus two comatose men on the same night equaled...?

371

Katie's mind was on something else entirely. "What about my father?" she said. "You must have known what happened to him after he was working for Bellamy all that time."

Mary only shook her head. "He had gone far after I'd left. I did go to Africa, Katie. I have passports, records, and you can even check with the village I stayed in. I had to get out. While I knew nothing of my father's research, the environment was oppressive, and I couldn't stand it. I left as soon as I turned eighteen. Africa was peace with real people and animals who didn't abandon me. I was there for nearly a decade until I heard the news that Bellamy had become a wanted man. I couldn't believe it. Whatever I thought of my father—it couldn't be true. So, I came back not five months ago."

There were no tears in her eyes. Only a tautness around her mouth as she took a tip of tea.

"My childhood house stood vacant, but I didn't want my past to follow me, or people to question me. I would search for him on my own. I changed my name and set up shop as a goat farmer in an adjoining farm but kept coming here. I couldn't help it, it just felt so much like home and eventually, I moved in. No one has ever recognised me. I was just a girl when I left. No one has ever come to check up on this place after the initial search. It was all quite easy.

"I wasn't sure what I intended to do upon coming back, but I immediately found myself in a different world than the one I'd left thirteen years before. I saw Sebastian's handiwork everywhere. Autos in London, serving ritzy cafe's, attending the high and mighty, and in the windows of novelty shops at exorbitant prices. Traces of him and my father were everywhere, and I couldn't understand how they'd done it. Then I found the papers."

She jerked her head at the folio.

"When I read some of Port Larkeney's local stories, I came to understand the legend of the sunspot. People were going missing, only to come back comatose with a mark on their chest. It was then that I connected the dots. Bellamy and Sebastian were experimenting on the souls of innocent people. With enough electricity, Amber could hold the human soul separate and apart so long as its original host remained alive. Anything could be done with it then, so long as the Amber had a vessel to function inside. They were turning people into slaves! I was so angry with Bellamy—the man I had once called my father. When Sebastian discovered I'd returned and invited me to his party, and I saw my opportunity to right both his and my father's wrongs."

We all leaned forward at this point. Mary was about to explain to her version of that night.

"Sebastian said he was unveiling a new machine. I had no doubt this was the Lightning Gun that his younger self had spent so much time imagining. I would steal it and rid the world of his presence forever. It was a hastily concocted plan. I had only a week to prepare. There were so many hiccups, and I was relying on Humberdt, poor darling Humberdt, to carry it out for me."

Katie sat up a little straighter as Mary said this. It did feel good to be right. I was also thinking about how Mary ought to learn what constituted animal cruelty.

"We were late to the party because Humberdt was having a difficult time recognizing the gun from the diagrams I showed him. He also didn't trust me to give him cheese after it was finished. Chimps and abstract thinking, you know. Bad combination," she said this as though griping about a precocious toddler. "I was getting worried, so I brought the leather case with an entire round of cheese in it just to show him. I didn't think anyone would think anything of it. If Sebastian asked, I would say I forgot he was lactose intolerant. Humberdt would nip in there, steal the gun, jump down and escape around the back of the estate and through the countryside where I would pick him up a mile away once the party was over. I did give him a very thick sweater." She added defensively.

"Then *you* showed up, Wendell, and things got a little precarious. I didn't expect Sebastian's telephone to be in the study. That was when Humberdt was supposed to go in there. He must have fumbled the gun in surprise and shot Sebastian. I was on the balcony when I heard the noise and thought something terrible must have happened to him. But when I looked into the study, he was gone. The plan was still a success."

"Why didn't you destroy it once you had it?" Katie asked. Why did you pin it on Bellamy?"

"Can you blame me for wanting revenge?" Mary didn't sound apologetic in the slightest. "It certainly wasn't in the original plan. I was about to destroy it, but I also wanted to study its secrets. Technology like that could be used for good as well! Of course, I had no idea Bellamy was hiding up in your tower until I saw the poppy fireworks that one night. I knew at once it was him. They were his signature every Christmas, mixing up his chemical flowers to impress the locals. I knew I could kill two birds with one stone, frame my father, and get rid of the gun. I stole up there during the festival while everyone was distracted and put it there while he slept. I don't know why you were hiding him, Katie." Her expression turned ugly. "He's a bad man who deserves none of your compassion."

"That's not true."

Mary crossed her arms as Katie spoke.

"I don't know all the details, but I think he was trying to do the right thing. Trying to stop Sebastian, I mean. That's why he was on the run. Why he and Sebastian fell out so publicly. Mary, he was shot once with the gun already and lost his memory. He didn't even remember you, his own daughter."

Lost his memory. Souls. Amber. My brother, laying pale as a ghost in a hospital bed. I pictured someone, waking up lost and disoriented in a different body. There was no way...

"Katie." I'd interrupted the conversation, but by the graveness of my expression, they quieted. "I think we've been missing a big piece of this puzzle. Two people were struck by lightning on the very same night. Two Autos went missing. I think my brother might be awake after all."

Just then, a noise like a staticy parrot startled us all. Katie fumbled for her radio and put it on speaker. The quavering voices sounded as though they were speaking through miles of rain, the words coming in intermingling, splintered phrases.

"Anybody out there? This storm is—" the sound of wind whistled in the background along muffled shouts of "—whole place is flooded—booths overturned—power gone out—"

Then a second voice, coming in through another channel.

"Code—Oh bother there's no code for this—hospital's been robbed—two Autos—lizard people? —The guests—the opera

374

fellow, Evangeline and The Duke—dragged off. Couldn't stop them!"

And the final transmission, dreadfully clear even through the static,

"Two bodies stolen from the ward! Sebastian Shaw and Timothy Billings!"

~34~

The Tinman Drinks Tea

He became increasingly aware he was speeding towards certain doom at upwards of a hundred miles an hour. The Lamplighter was folded like a large paper crane into an equally tiny mining cart. Tunnels wooshed past in a frightening blur. That anything so small could go so fast was astonishing. The Cellist sat behind him in a second cart, the two attached by a rattling bolt. His had a cushion and a handle that controlled the speed. He did so with practised deftness. The Cellist appeared much more at ease here, as if these lightless passageways suited him much better than the outside world.

The Lamplighter chanced to turn around. "Er, where exactly are we going?" he shouted.

The answer wasn't promising. "Silence, you recreant milksop, unless you'd like to hold your head in your hands."

The Cellist had become increasingly Shakespearean ever since he'd gotten his memory back. Regardless, The Lamplighter got the gist and didn't say anything more.

He understood this was a ploy. The Cellist intended to trap him as soon as he was inside the manor and considering his tendency to gut and maim his victims, he could only assume it was some unfathomable usefulness keeping him alive. It was only the slim hope of Wendell being held captive that had him walking headfirst into The Cellists' plans. *I must be ready to put up a fight again.* He surreptitiously flexed his many fingers. He threw a punch in the darkness which didn't feel right. *I really should have listened to that Thai boxer in Phuket,* he thought, *instead of doing what the name sounds like.*

When the harrowing ride finally ended, The Lamplighter was instructed to put on a blindfold. The Cellist procured a stretch of fabric very clearly from Laura's Lingerie. He had no choice but to put the pink thing on.

They climbed and emerged somewhere with fresh air and grass. Then it was stairs clinking under his metal feet. The Cellist led him through twists and turns. The stillness of the air indicated they were now inside of a house. Shaw manor. The feeling of dread increased with every detour. His hand was placed on a bannister, and they descended. At last, they stopped in a room that was cavernous by its echo. There was trickling water nearby. He tentatively lifted the corner of his blindfold and was slapped.

Cello music filled the air and the sounds of trickling water stopped. Two pairs of footsteps tapped sharply across the marble floors. Something stood very near.

The Cellist poked his bow between the blades of The Lamplighters back and The Lamplighter nearly impaled himself when the rumbling started. Whatever was emerging before them, the vibrations of its arrival radiated outwards in waves that had him rattling like a rock in a tin can. *It must span the entire room,* he thought. *Far bigger than me. Far bigger than anything.* The combination of fear and sightlessness sent him scrambling in the opposite direction, but a sharp jab in the ribs prevented his escape.

"If you aren't more spineless than a malingering jellyfish," came the snarl. "You will walk forward when I say. Go."

Stifling a whimper, The Lamplighter stepped forward. His toe prodded a set of descending steps. The muted grey beyond the blindfold was swallowed by black. They were underground once more. He felt the presence of The Cellist in front of him. The rumbling began again and a monstrous mechanism—it must be some sort of door—closed behind them. This place was as still as a tomb. It reminded him of the catacombs in France. They had the same sepulchrous foreboding, the air bone dry and devoid of breeze.

Finally, The Cellist removed his blindfold. It made little difference as this new tunnel was pitch black. He fancied he felt there were other things in the room. A brush here. A distant footfall there. But when he reached out, he found nothing except that the walls had narrowed. The Cellist walked ahead, humming. It was now or never. The Lamplighter made a lunge for the smaller Auto. As he did, something hit him.

Plink.

A ball of light dropped from the ceiling in front of him to land on his leg. Instead of bouncing off, it stuck on, clinging with a pair of chicken-like claws. Its insides quivered with strange glowing jelly.

Plink. Plink. Plink.

They dropped like spiders, the little glass orbs in the ceiling. In no time, hundreds of tiny luminous globes had piled onto him. He stifled a cry of horror. His metal limbs crawled with the feeling of a thousand tiny legs. One arm dropped, weighed down as if by a bowling ball. Then the next, and the next. Within seconds, The Lamplighter was brought to his knees, covered in the seething mass.

"Do you like my new pets?" asked The Cellist, turning back. He inspected his gloves for dirt. "I've been developing them for some time now. Very useful when it comes to surveillance. The Amber is suspended within a jelly-like electrical fluid mimicking the composition of the eye. An image flashes on the retina, like so…"

The Cellist plucked one from the stuck robot. He shook it, causing the Amber iris to goggle this way and that within its glass confines.

A burst of light flashed. The Cellist showed it to The Lamplighter. Displayed in a warped fisheye across the wide retina, was the scene in the corridor; the huge robot bogged down by what looked like a murder of Christmas baubles.

"You see? They are not only useful for gathering information, but for catching those who might wish to sneak upon me unawares. Very durable—if somewhat uncoordinated." He set the creature down and it trotted unsteadily on a pair of stick legs, back to its pack. "I call them The Horde."

The Lamplighter shook his head to dislodge one of the orbs that was crawling over his mouth.

"What do you want with someone like me?" he asked. "You have so many others to do your bidding. Where is my brother?" But even as he asked, he knew the answer.

"That boy was never down here. I'm sure it'll please you to know he escaped. Somehow." The light of the Horde cast the nooks and crannies of his carved face into vengeful relief. "But I will find him. He is in league with Bellamy Dumont, who stole something very precious from me."

"The Lightning Gun?" asked The Lamplighter.

The Cellist only shook his head, and with a crooked finger, he beckoned to the ocular Autos. Like the receding tide, the orbs bumped and jostled their way off The Lamplighter. He found he'd been put in chains.

They emerged into a vertical antechamber. The tall thin room was pockmarked with thousands of holes. As they walked, The Horde scurried up the walls around them. One by one, the little globes crawled and clanked against one another to disappear into a hole of their own. It took The Lamplighter a moment to see the two doors that branched off the chamber. The first was a tall archway curtained by beige gauze. Dim shapes that either moved or were given the illusion of movement by the fabric, shifted beyond. The Cellist drew past it. The second door was gunmetal grey and made of thick iron. A chill seeped into the air around it. As they drew closer, The Lamplighter could see that the door was covered in ice, growing in crystalline spikes that made the dull metal glitter as if it were enchanted. He had no doubt whatever was beyond it was far from magical.

The Cellist pulled him close. "You asked me what I need of you. Your mistake was in the question. I need *The Lamplighter*."

380

Wrenching the handle and sending a shard of ice skittering between them, The Lamplighter gasped as frigid fog that engulfed them. A sharp shove sent him sprawling forwards into the icy chamber and impact on cold tile jarred his shackled limbs.

"Wait!" He wriggled around onto his stomach. But the door shut with the soft hiss of a hermetic seal. He was alone.

The Lamplighter took a minute to get out a few ungentlemanly curses he'd learned over his travels. Then he took stock. From his inconvenient vantage point on the floor, he saw a long low room lit by caged lamps. The light from them was surreal. Each radiated a hyperborean blue which further permeated the chill. The walls themselves were pierced with hundreds of circular doors each the size of the lid of a large rubbish bin. The corridor appeared to stretch on forever. *Must be some kind of a storage facility,* he thought. Weapons, perhaps? No, The Cellist wouldn't be so stupid as to put him in there if that were the case. Amber? Perhaps that was a special condition of the mysterious stone, that it needed to be kept very, very cold.

Speaking of the cold… already the subterranean frost was beginning to affect his joints. As a human, he imagined he would have sustained frostbite in minutes. As an Auto, he was more impervious, if he had been completely dry. But the tunnels outside had been humid, and a sheen of condensation across his chest had already chilled into diamonds of ice. He knew it would not be long until the delicate mechanisms hidden inside the hard carapace of his body slowed and stopped, succumbing to the ice that adorned this place like Christmas tinsel.

With all six arms in chains, he was too top heavy to propel himself upwards, so he went with the other option. The Lamplighter kicked his feet up to inch himself across the ground. There was a grinding scrape as he made slow progress towards the door nearest him. Finally, he was within pulling distance. With one dexterous toe, The Lamplighter's feet hooked around the metal handle. He pulled, clenching his jaw. The door remained stuck and he tried harder, bracing against whatever traction the cold marble would give. With a small explosion, the ice-seal around the opening broke. The drawer slid out easily, stopping at about two metres in length.

"Hah!" With triumph, The Lamplighter levered himself up, using his mouth to bite the side of the drawer. Then he was on his feet, hunched and shackled, but on his feet. "Take that!" he jerked his chin unsteadily at the iron door. The Cellist had underestimated him once again. He *would* get out of here. Then he looked down and saw what was in the drawer. His heart sank.

She looked to be made of ice. Ice greyed the black lashes. Ice stiffened the long black hair, crackling like straw as it brushed against the sides of the drawer. Ice covered the little woollen coat, the tips of her fingernails, and the mottled purple lips, which had once been plush and young. The crystallised girl lay doll-like within the confines of the metal chamber.

"Oh god," he whispered. "Please, please don't be dead."

She could not have been more than fifteen. She could have been anyone. She might have been funny or serious or adventurous. Now, she wasn't any of those things. She was dead.

Or was she?

He thought he could see the barest rise and fall of her chest. Where was the journal? Wendell would know what to do. Before leaving the hillside, The Lamplighter had tucked it into his own chest. There was a space there, between his neck and shoulder blades and it had been an odd yet comforting feeling to have it safe there. He lowered his chin to examine the cavity. The hollow space beside the Amber was empty. It was gone. He sank to his knees. Of course, he couldn't help her. He wasn't even sure *he* was alive.

When he looked up again, the thousands of doors seemed to press in on him, warping in that terrible blue hall. Unseen bodies piled in his mind's eye, closer and closer until their dry, frozen flesh crackled against him. The Cellist had done this. How could he possibly someone capable of that? The cold was doing its insidious work. Alone and freezing underneath Port Larkeney, The Lamplighter was slowly losing function, spikes of ice jamming joints, slowing arms and legs until every movement was like wading through molasses. The Amber within his chest was the only flame that didn't die out, slowly flickering in and out like a small bird in a vast metal cage. Perhaps hope could have kept The Lamplighter awake. But he had none of that now.

He didn't know how long he'd slept, or if sleep was even possible for a creature like him. All he knew was that he'd dreamt of Melati, and her embrace had been wonderfully warm...very warm...growing warmer now. Ow! Hot! Hot!

The Lamplighters eyes opened wide, and twin beams of light shot from them. A plume of steam wafted up through the air. It was coming from him. His first thought was: *I've caught fire! In an industrial freezer!* He scrambled backwards, forgetting that his arms were chained. As he did so, two small footsteps thumped across his chest. There was a piping noise that reminded him of home, and of Wendell.

"Toot!"

Oh, glorious *toot*! Impatient and belligerent as such a sound could be. Genie! The stumpy teapot stood atop his chest, industriously pouring hot water through the cracks in his carapace. Finally, it reached his mouth, and the warmth unfroze the hinges of his face. He babbled questions at her.

"It's so good to see you! How did you get in here? What are you doing?"

But as the water fell, he could feel it melting his frozen joints and loosening the stiffened mechanics of his person. Suddenly, he was able to sit up. He tested his torso delightedly.

"You wonderful teapot, you!"

She let out a whistle that seemed to say, "Clearly."

The Lamplighter slumped. "But there's no use. We can't beat The Cellist. Do you know what's in this room?"

Genie answered with a sad *toot toot* and vigorous bobbing. But undeterred, she hopped off his chest. They didn't have much time before the water inside him froze again.

"I don't suppose you have the keys to these?" The Lamplighter shuffled the padlock around. Genie turned on a heel and trotted back down the halls. The Lamplighter followed doing a set of knee jumps to keep spikes of ice from forming.

Further down, the light was sparser, the arctic tomb giving way to the subterranean. Genie stopped. There, in between two widely spaced drawers, was an enormous twisty network of pipes. The largest of these was a forearms width and bulged in odd places like a satisfied python. Of course! A place like this needed to get its cold air from somewhere. Genie had found out where it was pumped. He imagined with some amusement the teapot rattling through the pipes like an overlarge ping pong ball. She jogged up to the largest opening and scissor-kicked a small object from the darkness.

"What's that you've got there?" His eyes widened. "You found it!"

He nudged the leather journal with a foot. He must have lost it in the tunnel with The Cellist. Had she been following him this entire time? He wasted no time in sitting cross-legged and opening the book with his other toe. Somehow, it felt like their party had grown, Wendell's helpful voice guiding the way. They might not have the keys to the lock on his arms, but this might do just as well.

"You've really thought of everything," he said to the teapot. "I distinctly remember an illustrated page of picking locks with unconventional materials. We were imprisoned eight times together, you know." That really made him think on how he'd learnt nothing from those experiences.

With a clank more satisfying than any sound he'd ever heard; the chains fell around him. He stretched his arms and flexed his fingers. There was only one problem. One arm, the bottom left to be exact, dragged uselessly behind him. It felt like a numb tooth. The journal had called for a long slim piece of something stiff, like a stick or the quill of a hedgehog. Having none of those things handy, Genie had opted to search among the frozen bodies, but The Lamplighter couldn't bring himself to do it. In the end, he'd fished around in an arm for the lucky piece. It worked for the padlock, but putting his arm back together proved impossible. The Lamplighter swung his torso experimentally and the arm swung too, like a sad rubber glove.

"Crackers," he muttered.

Toot! Genie chirruped at the door impatiently.

He raised his hands. "That thing's half as thick as I am. What do you want me to do?"

But luck was with them, because at that moment, the lock turned. Voices drifted from the other side. The Lamplighter slumped into a prone position. Genie hid behind him. Two slithery voices slid their way through the crack in the door.

"We've got them, Ssebastian. Jusst like you assked. Yoursself, very dashing, even in ssleep—"

"—and the ugly one. The besspectacled boy. All boness and limbss. Can't ssee why you'd want him."

"Nevertheless," The Cellist's voice echoed down the hallway. "I have my reasons." The door opened wider. With one eye, The Lamplighter caught sight of a coppery gold tail and a wide flat head with green eyes. Then he saw the person hanging limply in the Auto's arms. *It's me!* It was incredibly unnerving to see himself— his *human* self. It wasn't a nice feeling. *Have I always looked so peaky?*

"Would you like usss to put them in the deep frrreeze?" The lizard people were posh. They rolled their rrs and mimicked one another's unctuous tones. He got the sense they were man and woman. Were they sentient as well?

The Cellist's footsteps drew closer. "For the time being. Big things are finally happening. Accidents have turned their way into fortune. Huh. Ophidia, what happened to your tail?"

The female creature sounded abashed. "Nothing, Sebasstian. I'm sstill getting ussed to the body."

There was a sudden bang and a screech. The voice that followed was as icy as the freezer.

"*Don't* lie to me. I am the man who gave you new life. You, who ought to call me *God*."

"Y-yess. Yess Ssebasstian. I mean, Ssir. I mean, oh god, please, please don't take it. Not the Amber!" The Auto gave a low moan of pain.

"What. Happened?"

"Assailantss in the creep," answered the other quickly. "I don't know how they followed us. There wass a big one who clubbed her like a great gorilla. Then, there actually wass a gorilla. Or chimp or ssomething."

"A chimp...?" The Cellist stopped, puzzled.

"Yes, and three otherss but we couldn't quite make them out. Two women and a boy, I'd ssay."

THE HENCH-LIZARDS
(YOU HAVE GOT TO BE KIDDING ME)

"Quite a little party there is then," he paused. "On second thought, don't put the bodies in there. I will take them myself. Just retrieve the pods."

"Are you ssure?"

"Cart. Please."

A cart with several floppy gloved shand rolled by the opening.

"Get ready," The Cellist called. "Our departure will be sooner than planned."

"Yess, Ssebasstian." The two echoed in unison. Footsteps faded away. The door opened fully, and two metallic, reptilian creatures entered the freezer. The Lamplighter suppressed a shudder at their wide, sharp-toothed mouths.

"Terrifying, that man," said the smaller one.

"He *wass* a man. Now he iss ssomething elsse."

"And sso are we," said the other scornfully. "You know, when I said I wanted to be part of his revolution, I didn't quite think it would be as a *rreptile*. In fact I succinctly remember assking to be *lady*."

"You're sstill a lady my darling. Now you ssimply lick your eyeballss," the taller of the two said soothingly.

"Debassing is what it iss. He intends to humble us. Well, it's only a matter of time. Once we find the Black King, it won't be long before Ssebasstian is answering to *uss*."

There was a heavy slide as an empty drawer was removed from its cavity. The male lizard grunted, heaving it onto the floor.

"Yes," the lady lizard nodded more cheerfully, picking up the other side. "And, as they say, two headsss are always better than one."

"*Toot!*" Genie whispered as she was hoisted into the air.

"Trust me," said The Lamplighter, cradling her to his chest.

Was it possible, he wondered? He'd noticed his ability for climbing seemed to apply to any surface, but would it work against gravity? Shrouded in the dark between lamps, he touched one arm to the ceiling, then another, and another. To his surprise, The tips of his metal fingers stuck to the ceiling as if magnetised and he could move them easily from one position to the other. He swung his legs vertically, pleased to find that they too could stick to the ceiling. Oddest of all, his sense of direction shifted. Up was down.

The floor of the freezer became the ceiling. After a moment, he was off, crawling silently above the hench-lizards. Genie sloshed uneasily in his grip, sprays of hot tea melting the ice in his joints as quickly as it formed. They were moving out of the darkness now. If the two Autos happened to look up…He reached the heavy iron door without so much as a sound.

"Ouch!" The taller lizard rubbed his head. "Did you jusst sslap me?" he demanded.

"Why would I sslap you?"

"I don't know," said the other irritably. "You jusst said you didn't feel like a lady, and sslapping ssomeone is very unladylike behaviour."

"I didn't sslap you."

"Well then who did?" The first lizard didn't sound in the mood for humouring, but he turned around anyway. And got slapped again.

"There'ss a hand right there."

The smaller one peered at the hanging appendage. "A metal one. That wassn't there before." They looked up.

"Crackers," said The Lamplighter, waggling his dead arm uselessly.

"Grab it!" shrieked one lizard.

In a flash, The Lamplighter had detached himself from the wall and hit the ground running.

"By order of The Cellist—!" the taller one began.

The Lamplighter ignored him and launched himself through the opening. The brim of his hat scraped it, sending sparks pinging after him. He shoved one of the golden geckos aside. There would be no chase.

"No!" cried the twin Autos in unison, but their cries were cut short as he closed the heavy door and locked it.

The Lamplighter breathed heavily in the antechamber, the Amber in his chest pulsing rapidly. "I did it," he whispered to Genie disbelievingly. "I got out of there."

In the warmer air, he felt himself begin to thaw, arms and legs feeling less like they were swimming in frigid water. There were two paths now; the dark tunnel from which he had come, and the strange archway where nebulous shapes moved behind the gauze. He remembered what one of The Cellist's lackeys had said. There was a party coming. Could it be Wendell and Katie? *I can't let him save me again.* He gripped Genie tight, whispering half to her and half to himself.

"If The Cellist wants a Lamplighter, he'll get one." He stepped into the unknown.

~35~

Chasing The Storm

The sky roiled and revolted. Godly strikes of lightning lit the world afire. Distantly, the sea dashed and battered the shoreline, slopping thickly into the little cove of Port Larkeney like an overfull cup. Out in the countryside, in a little goat farm, rain pummeled the five figures running to the car. Katie shut the door and gunned the engine.

"Everybody in?" I asked, facing the back seat.

There were three nods of assent. Melati, her hair oil black from the rain and sodden in her puffy jacket grunted. What little remaining space was filled by Mary and Humberdt who looked grim in matching sweaters. The whole car smelled of wet wool.

"There she is!" The young detective slapped the wheel victoriously as the car came to life, for once, without a hitch.

Mary had insisted on coming with us. Did I relish the thought of having a half-deranged woman in our backseat, with very open access to my neck? No. But there was nowhere else to leave her, and with the Inspector unconscious and all officers busy at the carnival, the police station was out of the question. For now, Melati was more than enough insurance.

As we were running out, Katie had asked the goat farmer a strange question. "Do you have any goggles?" she'd asked. "And gloves—we'll probably need gloves."

Her trademark mysteriousness made me want to strangle her, but there was no time for that. Mary had shoved a box of gardening supplies into the boot, and we were off.

I was becoming increasingly worried that we were heading straight towards the enemy with no plan and no weapons. The car flew violently over a small hill, and I hit my head against the ceiling. The monkey was howling, Melati was yelling at the monkey to shut up, Mary was yelling at Melati for being insensitive, and Katie was singing both parts of "Don't Go Breaking My Heart" as some kind of calming exercise.

The wipers could hardly beat the water back fast enough as we flew down the streets. Katie squinted through the windshield as we travelled at frightening speed through the storm. The Constabulary Carre rattled as though it were about to fall to pieces, and for that period, my fear of Katie's driving completely obliterated all else. With a vicious turn that elicited a chorus of nauseated groans from the back seat, we swerved onto the rough main road that led back into the town proper.

"*Katie!*"

She was steering with one hand as she looked down at her belt, unclipping the radio. She looked up just in time to avoid a wire fence.

"What is wrong with you?" I cried. "What if you'd crashed into the hospital?"

"We're not going to the hospital."

The walkie talkie crackled to life. "Twill here. Status of hospital victims. Which way did they go?" She swerved to avoid a stray cow.

"Saunders here," came the trembling static. "The lizard people crashed out the infirmary window. It looked like they were heading away from the festival just off Main Street."

"Has it been evacuated?"

"Ghost town, copy. Hell of a storm."

"Copy."

"They'll be gone by the time we get there," I said.

"Yes," said Katie, "but I think I know where they went."

Cheeky mannequins in corsets and camisoles posed motionless in the pink frosted windows of the Shoppe. The five of us; me, the detective, Mary, Melati, and the monkey stood in front of it like the members of an extremely eclectic folk band. Humberdt was rubbing his sore bottom and Melati massaged her head where it had bumped against the tin roof of the car for the past twenty minutes. As nice as it was to be on solid ground, I turned to Katie.

"Seriously?"

She nodded. "After triangulating, or rather octagonalizing the robberies, *this* is the only place it could be. The only place nobody wanted to search."

"Not that I'm complai—ouch!" I received a swift punch to the shoulder.

The door was unlocked. There was a sinister jangle as Katie pushed it open and swept her torch light around the room. It was eerily quiet inside, the rain muffled to a dull roar. I saw glimpses of pink and white chequed wallpaper, some rather impractical things made of lace, and three changing stalls that looked as though they'd been bulldozed. What had happened here? Behind me, Mary and Humberdt crept quietly. Melati brought up the rear to prevent their escape. All was quiet.

Thump. Thump. Thump.

It came from the far side of the room.

"Hello?" Katie called.

THUMP. THUMP.

"Mmph!"

There was a rattling crash as a cabinet drawer fell to the floor.

With ginger steps, the detective crossed the room and shone her light behind the counter. "Laura?"

The owner of Laura's Lingerie was blotchy-faced from screaming through the extra-stretch Missy-Sterious stocking that was tied around her mouth. When Katie removed it, she gripped the counter and stood up shakily. She refused to talk until I'd supplied her with a half-warm cup of tea.

"T-two days. Two days I've been back here." She dried her mascara-stained cheeks with the pair of stockings and gulped the cup in one.

Katie put her arm around the woman. "It's alright. We're here now," she soothed. "What happened?"

"The night before the festival, I c-came to see if I could catch that no good panty-thief by surprise again. I'd been suspicious for a while. There were things being moved around the shop and clothes missing for the past couple of weeks. I thought he'd come back, and I didn't bother to report it because I was sure I could handle it." Laura looked away with embarrassment. "I was wrong. It wasn't him. Two huge Autos! In my sh-shop!"

Her face starkened as she relived the event. "The white one saw me at once. What a horrible face he had! It was like a *bug* with all of those moving pieces. He and his partner—huge, like a spider. T-tied me up and left. When they didn't come back, I thought, maybe I was in the clear, but I couldn't get myself out. I screamed and screamed, and no one heard me. Then, not t-two minutes ago, two more come barreling through my door."

"The Lamplighter and The Cellist?"

"No. These were gold or something. Horrible, ugly things, slithery with green eyes. Looked like lizards or geckos. And-and they were carrying b-bodies."

"Bodies?" I kneeled in front of Laura. "Where did they go?"

All she could manage was a shaky finger, pointing to the third changing room which had been left the most intact. Katie thrust the door open.

"Great galloping gingersnaps," she breathed. "It's all here."

Piled high into the corners of the tiny space was every knickknack, appliance and decorative garden gnome that had gone missing in Port Larkeney. Half were stripped to junk. Crushed parts littered the scene. The debris clustered a large, gaping hole in the floor. Here, a whole section of tile had been slid away to reveal a yawning darkness.

"All these weeks. They've been hiding out here," she said.

Abruptly, she stood up and walked out of the shop towards the car. I followed, curious. Outside, the rain had lightened to a misty drizzle. She approached to the boot of the car and shoved her shoulder against it. I went to help her and with our combined weight, we succeeded in getting it open. Inside was a large and lumpy-looking burlap sack. Katie seized this, slung it over her shoulder, and handed me the box of goggles and gloves.

"What's—" She opened the sack.

Horrified, I jumped back. "You could've killed us all!"

Katie huffed. "I'm not that stupid, Wendell. I put duct tape on all the holes. Although, now that I look at it, do they look funny to you?"

"Funny?" I cried, bordering on hysterics. "You mean the twenty Panamanian Death Peppers you could have gassed the car with, melting the very skin off our bones?"

"No," she said and picked one up with a gloved hand, holding it up to the light of a nearby streetlamp. She shook it. "They're bulging a lot more now that I've disconnected them from the vine. Sounds like a coconut in there. Sloshy."

"Katie!"

She was already striding back to the shop. I hurried after her as she donned a pair of clear goggles.

"Once upon a time, you said the acid in these things was strong enough to corrode metal. I wasn't going in there without a backup plan, Wendell."

No matter how I tried to dissuade her, the young detective remained adamant. Once inside, Katie explained to Mary, Melati, and Humberdt about the peppers and how they worked. She gestured towards the tape that bunged up the gas holes in the football-sized vegetables. Her plan of action was to rip one off in the face of an Auto, point, and shoot. I hoped it wouldn't come to that.

In tense silence, we donned our gear, and each selected a pepper. They looked deceptively cheery with their huge red and white stripes. A Christmas candy, a fairytale fruit. I searched the box and drew out the last pair of goggles. They were green and rimmed in leather like aviator's goggles. The lens was thick as bottle glass, and I could hardly see out of them.

Mary's eyes widened when she saw me wearing them. "I thought I'd lost those," she murmured.

I didn't have time to ask what she meant by that. Katie was already lowering herself into the tunnel. I would have to use what protection I could.

One by one we descended. It was a short fall, but the darkness was foul and salty. A slow, drip-drip somewhere in the cavern gave an idea as to how big the tunnel actually was. The floor was mercifully dry, even if the walls were sticky with grime. The tunnel stretched two ways.

Katie raised the torch. "Which way?" she asked me.

I stared down the tunnel, my heart thudding. What did my journal say about tracking? I couldn't think, not without it in my hand, the comfort of the leather cover, and the entries, each of which I knew by feel of the pages. I gestured soundlessly.

"Move," said Melati.

She pushed to the front and sniffed the air. After a moment, she pointed due west, heading away from the main street. "This way. I sense Timmy's musk."

Melati took the lead this time, her heavy footsteps beating a quick rhythm as we set a clip down the passage. I felt like an idiot. Was I completely useless without my book? What would happen when the danger really started, and we would have to face Sebastian Shaw for real? I tried to swallow the anxiety budding in my chest. I would be brave, for my brother.

Katie's light caught the flash of gold.

"Oi!" Her beam swung upwards, and a serpentine tail flicked out of sight. A scraping, scampering noise echoed down around us. The chase had begun.

It was a raucous darkness we tore through, blind, every other sense heightened. The sounds of footsteps, listening for the metallic scrape, bodies colliding as the tunnel grew narrower and wider at intervals, and the ever-growing smell of the sea. Katie's torch swung as she ran, catching glimpses of our quarry. In the low light of the tunnel, the coppery gold appeared to move like fluid. Their long sleek bodies undulated up the sides of the tunnel, larger than a man. The two heads were broad, flat, and ugly with wide reptilian smiles.

Then we lost them. The five of us slowed to a jog in the darkness. Here and there was an odd clang or footfall, but we'd reached an intersection and the noises were getting further away.

Katie swept the light in circles. "Do we just pick one?"

"No," said Mary. "Wendell, put on the goggles."

"What?"

"Just put them on!"

Fumbling with the straps, I lifted the lenses and snapped them firmly over my eyes. Immediately the tunnel took on a ghostly greenish hue. Reddish shapes darted around me like phantoms. The biggest one was Melati. The tall slim one, Katie, and the fuzzy indistinct shapes of Mary and Humberdt.

Then I saw them. Slung on their backs were two bodies in hospital gowns. They slithered down the middle tunnel. Pale faces lolled lifelessly barely three metres ahead, the heat of their bodies showing up as dull orange in the goggles. My heart quickened at the sight of my brother's face, bouncing disembodied in thermal relief. The bodies of the lizard creatures gave no heat except for floating pinpricks of burning light that was their Amber.

"That way!" I said. I pointed down at the centre tunnel, forgetting no one else could see. "The middle one!"

Melati thundered past with surprising quickness. Katie trained the torch on it.

Phht.

The quiet sigh of the Sibilaverunt Mortis hissed through the darkness. A stream of something steamy prickled my skin as it whizzed past me, and in the corner of my eye I saw a jet of sizzling, compressed acid hit the Auto ahead. Katie punched the pepper as if she were trying to violently fluff a pillow. It hit the metal with a sizzle and for a moment, the golden gecko seemed almost amused. Then, the liquid began its work. The hot tang of melting metal filled the tunnel. I ducked as the pepper spit and spat through its one open orifice. In the pool of torch-light, the movement of the creature became erratic as the mechanisms inside it deadened. With that, Melati was able to catch up to it. With a firm yank, she caught the end of its tail, sending it crashing down from the wall. Tim's body tumbled with it, sprawling over the writhing creature on the tunnel floor.

"Careful!" I cried. Melati moved away from him, wrestling with the robot. It was putting up a fight, biting, hissing, and swinging its tail around like a club.

"Sorry!"

I felt a gathering of skirts bump against me as Mary and Humberdt drew up against us, blindly. Preoccupied, I wasn't able to warn them when the second Auto came back around. Someone yelled and a heavy object shattered the wall beside me. In my peripheral, the pinpricks of Amber flickered out of sight. There was silence.

I took off my goggles.

"Is everyone alright?" I called.

"The second one. It bit me," came Melati's voice. "Hard."

Katie's breath was ragged. "Swiped me. Across the face. Can't find the torch."

I put the goggles back on. The torch was lying close by, the lens cracked. I flicked it experimentally. Broken. I turned back to Katie. Her hand was pressing a cut on her cheek where the tail had whipped across. Melati cradled an injured arm.

"I cannot believe that actually worked." I stared at the deflated pepper in Katie's hands. A self-satisfied smile appeared momentarily. Then she winced as it stretched the cut on her cheek. "Are you sure the two of you are alright?" I asked again. "I can patch you up."

"No," said Katie. "We can't lose them again. Right Melati?"

"*Benar*," grunted the Indonesian girl.

"I'll assume that's a yes. Right then, let's pick up the pace everybody!"

We didn't have to go on much longer. Electric lamps now buzzed at shorter intervals the farther we walked. Soon, concrete tunnel gave way to a rougher hewn passage and a whirring, grinding sound grew ahead of us. Around the bend, the first mining cart was rolling away. The gecko creatures were shoving off into the abyss just as we entered. I ran to edge in frustration. The gaping emptiness between me and my brother was growing wider by the second. Behind me, Katie, Melati, Mary, and her monkey all looked at me for direction. I noticed a second cart, left conveniently behind. I placed my hand on it and was reminded vividly of the way my father patted the car whenever he announced a road trip.

"Alright," I said. "Everybody in."

~36~

The Devil's in the Landscaping

The tunnels rushed by in blackness, speckled with a weak smattering of stars. They left trails of vermillion light behind them, flickering in our vision as if unwilling to leave. It was the first time I'd ever seen the Amber mines up close.

As we flew through them, some part of me wondered why they weren't more impressive. Here and there were little dots of the stuff followed by long expanses of nothing. The walls were deeply gouged as though stripped of all material. I didn't like this. It felt as though the deeper we travelled, the deeper into Sebastian's system we went, weaving and sneaking through the dim veins and bloodstreams until we reached the dark centre. His laboratory.

The tracks were still going when the mining cart lurched to a stop, leaving our stomachs to play catch-up. The tracks ahead of us were vertical, which explained the two heavy clamps and rollers in the front. The motor under the cart whined, bumping repeatedly against the wall of the pit. We were too heavy.

I was the first out, and it took a moment to steady myself. It had been an uncomfortable ride. Everyone's nerves were tight as bowstrings, searching for any lizard or humanlike shapes in the speeding gloom whilst trying not to jostle the sack of volatile peppers. Still, it wasn't as bad as riding in Katie's car.

"So that was how Sebastian managed to mine his Amber," Mary said shakily, lifting her skirts as she climbed out. "He was underneath us the entire time."

"I don't know about anyone else, but I'm looking forward to giving that man a good thumping." Katie cracked her knuckles matter-of-factly.

Melati seconded that in her rudimentary English. "Me too. Thump him good."

I examined the vertical tracks. We'd been so close to my brother and proceeded to lose him by seconds!

"Well nobody will be thumped if we don't get a move on," I said. "There's a door up here." The tracks were easy to climb, and I soon reached the top. The trap door opened easily on a spring latch, and I was rewarded with a cool gust of wind. It was raining.

I lifted myself up onto wet grass. I'd emerged into a small courtyard, bordered on all sides by white balconies. The sound of running water was close by and I caught sight of the fountain in the center of the grass.

"Ugly thing, that." Katie appeared from the ground as if by magic. The cover to the tunnels was camouflaged with tufts of turf. Nobody could have ever guessed a subterranean entrance to be here.

The fountain in question might have been grand. It was certainly exquisitely carved, made of the same bone-coloured marble that limned the house, but it was a far cry from the noble Grecian statues that dotted estates like these. The subject in question sat slumped on the watery plinth in a rumpled two-piece suit. His weathered, hollowed face was both expressionless and imploring. Water poured from his eyes in an endless stream. I felt a sudden shiver of déjà vu although I couldn't tell why. When we were all up, Mary echoed what I was feeling.

"I don't like this," she said. Her boots squelched on the wet lawn. "It feels like a cemetery."

"Tracks," Melati pointed immediately at the ground. She'd taken charge of the sack. It bumped lightly on her shoulder as she moved. "Long tail." She licked a finger, holding it up to the wind. "Two prisoners."

The indentation in the grass pointed into the northwesterly corridor. From there on, Melati led the way using her finely tuned hunting skills. I checked behind us again and again. The sound of our wet boots echoed loudly through the manor, not to mention my sense of direction was thoroughly confused by the endless corridors and blue parlours with the same nondescript furnishings.

At length, Melati lost the tracks. She stopped in one of the rooms to gather her bearings and we took a brief rest. Melati and Humberdt slumped onto a sofa. Melati sat meditatively in a corner.

Katie urged me to stop pacing.

"It's too quiet," I muttered. "Every room is practically the same. Who designs a house like this? It feels like a trap."

She put a hand on my shoulder. "Aye but calm down just the same. You're just on edge."

I didn't like her treating me like a nervous dog. "We're tracking a couple of dangerous Autos who are going to slice and dice my brother into tiny little bits and pieces just like that diced rat we found at the boathouse. *Of course, I'm on edge.*"

"I know. But we've got to stay calm."

Katie, who fluctuated between fainting and bouncing off the walls was telling me to stay calm. It was strange times. I shoved my hands into my pockets. I wasn't about to tell her the truth— that I was nothing without my book and I was a nervous wreck without it. It would only worry her to find out I was not at all the plucky adventurer she somehow thought me to be. One of us needed to be the brave one.

"Here."

She walked over to the bag Melati set down and rifled through with her usual lack of regard for the grenades of pepper acid inside. The detective withdrew something red and plastic about the size of my missing journal. She set down the mini transistor radio in front of me.

"Some tunes might help cheer you up. Always helps me. I think it would be alright if we played it *really* quiet. I was thinking The Jackson…"

I stared at her uncomprehendingly. "Why on earth would you bring that?"

"I just thought—"

My nerves had reached their limit. "This is why no one takes you seriously, Katie." I snapped. Mary looked up. "Listening to disco music will not change the fact that we could very well die! Maybe if you just stopped to—"

I'd seen something. I stopped and peered around the doorway but the white flash curling around the frame had gone. Could've been my reflection. Perhaps. When I turned back, Katie looked hurt.

"Thing!" Melati yelled, whose burgeoning English limited her to such descriptors. "Thing, thing, thing!"

In the hall opposite, there was a distant slam and we scrambled to our feet, following Melati. We ran across more eerily similar rooms, balconies, and courtyards. At length, I could see the two lizard Autos scampering just yards away, the bodies bouncing on their backs. Katie passed a glance at the fourth fountain of the day, a woman with her knees high and skirts in a bunch, as though she were trying to escape the streams of water that danced at her feet.

"Really, what does a guy need with all these bloody fountains?"

"Sebastian was always one for grandeur," Mary answered between breaths. "He wanted fountains and gardens and palaces all to himself. He's got it now. Though where he is…"

"Do *you* even know?" I asked. We turned right into a drawing room. "All this time you said you knew him—that if he had a secret laboratory, you'd be able to find it."

"Pshh. Of course. No one knows him better than I. Not even Bellamy himself." A shadow crossed her face at the name. She still hadn't found it in herself to forgive him.

I kept performing backwards glances. After the flash of something I'd seen outside the courtyard, I couldn't shake the feeling we were being followed. *The hunters hunted*, I thought with a prickling of the neck. We were in Shaw's domain now. All the while we kept running, banging through closed doors and occasionally catching glimpses of the reptilian pair.

Eventually Katie and Melati slowed at the edge of the stairs I found myself in familiar territory.

Melati's head whipped around. "Where go?"

We'd come all the way back to the front of the house with the great marble stairs and chequered foyer. To our left and right was the mirrored ballroom and study. On the first floor, the foyer led out into a library on the left and another hall on the right.

The detective swore. "Great galloping gingersnaps, those two are more slithery than…well I can't exactly say a pair of snakes…"

Melati's shoulders drooped. She turned confusedly and told me in her roundabout way, that it was as though they'd simply vanished from thin air. All eyes turned to Mary.

"Where do we go from here?" I asked.

She took a moment. "Blasted clogs," she grunted, taking off her shoes and rubbing her feet. "I don't see them simply leaving the house. No, the entrance must be…the library!"

With sudden abandon, she flung the shoes down the staircase where they bounced with a pinging sound. She led the way down, moving lighter on socked feet. "He always was a fan of hidden entrances. I remember us reading books about spies and castles and secret passageways, but time and time again, he was always drawn to the revolving bookcase."

We turned into the library. It was a surprisingly small, circular room with low arched ceilings and that ever-present chequered marble.

"Search every inch. Pull out all the books," she directed. "I'm sure it's here."

Four of us immediately got to work. Melati stayed in the doorway, shaking her head.

"Track stops there." She pointed to the middle of the foyer.

"Yes," said Katie impatiently as she prodded around a tome on electrical theory, "but people don't just vanish into thin air. They vanish around revolving bookcases and secret trapdoors."

An entire, expensive-looking set of encyclopaedias flew past her head as Humberdt made quick work of the shelves. I was busy examining the drawers and poking the large globe in the centre of the room. Pretty soon, the little library was stripped.

Mary's arms were full of books. Corkscrew strands of black hair stuck to her forehead. "I don't understand. It should be here."

I turned to her. "Hardly a deduction, was it? I can only imagine how far behind my brother we are while we're waiting for you to make your guesses."

"My guesses are the best thing you've got!" Mary snapped.

"The best thing for my brother would be not turning into human sashimi by a madman in a robot's body!"

"Guys," said Katie.

"And I suppose that's all my fault?" said Mary. "I'm trying to *help* you. Why can't you understand that?"

"I don't know, perhaps because you lied about practically everything." I looked to Katie. "Back me up here. Of anyone you should be angry at Mary."

The detective's voice was curiously strained. "Oh, I would. But it seems we've got bigger problems at the moment."

I followed her gaze.

Previously blocked by Melati's bulk, there was something— no—many things, moving in the foyer. The white creatures lurched from side to side as if searching for something. Us.

"The fountains!" Katie whispered. "I should have known. The devil was in the landscaping."

The foyer looked home to a strange and awkward dance party. White figures limped, strutted, clicked, and prowled across the floor. They left trails of water behind them from freshly abandoned posts. There were many familiar faces. I recognized the old man in the rumpled suit, a few "deceased" politicians, dukes, duchesses, and some with reporter's tweeds and polaroid cameras carved round their necks. At least the twin kings, white and black were still in their alcoves, but the water in their basins had stopped running.

"We need to keep looking," Mary sounded panicked. "Melati, perhaps if you close the door, they won't see us."

A brassy lisping voice suddenly echoed violently across the floor. "Library! Intruderth in the library! Let'th Gettem!"

Eleven heads turned simultaneously.

"Out we go then!" cried the detective.

Katie ducked just in time as a solid ivory fist occupied the space where her head had been. She pulled me out with her and suddenly we were skidding across the slick floor. I made the lucky mistake of losing my balance and just avoided the tip of a cane aimed between the eyes. Together we ran up the stairs.

"Alright Wendell, just like we practised," said Katie. There was a fierce calm in her eyes. Half up the grand staircase, we were surrounded. Autos to the front and back of us. People turned to cold blooded killers.

"Practised?" I gripped the banister. "Nobody in the history of planet Earth has practised for anything like this in their entire lives!"

"There's a first time for everything then."

Katie had somehow grabbed the sack of peppers. With a gloved hand, she lobbed me a pepper and grabbed one for herself. Miraculously, I caught it by the stem just in time to see the first Auto advance. Katie was ready for it. Delicately, she peeled back the tape on one of the bumpy nodules of her pepper. Elbows bent at a ninety-degree angle, she squeezed. The acid pink liquid arched high and hit the Auto square in the face. In seconds, the robot began to shiver and shake. The marble outside was less affected by the liquid, but the cracks and crevices housing delicate machinery posed vulnerable entrances for the acid to do its work. The Auto, a man in the two-piece suit, took a few more jerky steps forward before he collapsed. His Amber eyes flared briefly before going dark.

"Wendell!" The goggles were sweaty in my palms. Useless here. My feet refused to move. Why couldn't I move? "Wendell. *I need help.*"

I stared, frozen, at the oncoming Autos. My book had been my good luck charm. I'd used it to compartmentalize my fear into a handful of sentences that happened to someone else. Now it was gone.

A woman with a long, haunted face thrust an umbrella tip at me and I stumbled backward and fell painfully onto the sack. Peppers rolled every which way. One of them burst under my heel.

The foul-smelling liquid jetted out in a puddle just inches from my feet. I jerked my foot away before the acid could eat into my boot. The white head of the Auto swivelled slowly before making eye contact with me. Her hands outstretched in ghostly talons.

Boogie nights baby
Oh, shake that booty
Boogie nights

The tinny music issued from the floor. The transistor radio—I must have knocked it when I'd fallen! Oh god, I was going to die to the sounds of boogieing and booties. Katie had stopped shooting, mystified. The marble woman with the umbrella was dancing.

It wasn't a graceful dance by any means. The act looked almost unwilling, as if the mechanisms of her body jumped and jived of their own accord. Something dim resurfaced in the back of my mind. Bellamy had said—and Sebastian's Autos had now confirmed—that the properties of Amber were activated by music. Was it possible that the quality of music changed the way the stone made its host behave?

The woman's Running Man caused her to slip on the puddle of peppery gunk. Her white face sank, sparking, into the acid. I turned back to Katie. She was silent and open-mouthed. In unison, we broke into incredulous grins. She chucked the little radio into one of the enormous vases that stood on either side of the bannisters. Suddenly, the sounds of "Last Train to London" echoed across the vast space. We snapped our goggles back on. Katie palmed another pepper. There wasn't anything to lose.

The Autos around us paused, as though caught in a game of freeze dance. Slowly, spasmodically, they made their way up the stairs, battling the effects of the music. The disco slowed them, but they were still coming.

Katie was preparing for a fourth shot, mowing the statues down wherever she could spot an opening. Some fell, but others continued onwards until I was forced to grab the stone umbrella from the felled woman and throw it. With my field of vision greatly decreased and everything a greenish blur under the tinted lens, I realised why they weren't going down. In each one of them, the Amber was in a slightly different spot, perhaps to ensure not all of them could be felled in exactly the same way. Katie couldn't

408

have known, but I could see it, flaming stars in a field of green, tails of light whispering through the cracks in their armour.

"Twelve o'clock," I shouted. "Head! Go under the jaw."

Katie aimed for the head of the lurching assailant, sliding down to squeeze the pepper in the exposed crevice between neck and jaw. In my heat-rendered vision, the pinpoint of Amber above its shoulders flared momentarily before going out. The robot crashed to the ground.

"Eight o'clock. Chest. Right side!"

GLOP! Another down.

Below us, I could see the others through the crowd. Melati was a one-woman team, making a sizeable dent in the attackers as she whirled her heavy fists. She stole marble limbs, using them to smash faceplates and cave in chests without style or grace, but in devastating, sledgehammering blows.

Mary and Humberdt were getting on alright by themselves, although the goat farmer seemed to be running out of ideas. In a rare opening, I shouted at her and threw down a few peppers. She scurried to retrieve them and ripped off the tape. The creeping marble journalist behind her went down in a mist of pink.

"Oncoming. Two o'clock. Neck."

SPLAT.

I lifted the goggles. This time I didn't hear a crash. A ghostly woman in a pinafore was still advancing. Her neck was covered in goose-egg pearls.

"It's not working!"

Katie aimed the pepper at her again, but she was hesitant. The sack was running low and there were still so many. I cried out as as a glancing blow caught the detective to the head and she slumped across the steps. A man with round features and a pair of pince-nez withdrew his fist and turned to me. Water dripped in pools down his impassive face. I slipped the half empty pepper from her limp hand and stood in front of her. I cocked the stem.

SPLAT.

The man jerked and shuddered as the bright ooze clogged the systems in his stomach. But as soon as he was gone, another replaced him. This Auto was black as coal and shiny as glass. It was one of the two bearded kings that guarded the stairwell. Someone called my name.

Mary and Humberdt had been captured. They struggled against the grip of the white king. Melati was faltering, overwhelmed by the sheer number of assailants. We couldn't keep fighting like this. We needed to find a way out. The entrance to the laboratory was here, but where? I shot at another Auto and felt movement behind me. Katie stirred. I allowed myself one look at her. Her eyes were a brighter green than ever, vivid against the trickle of blood down her temple. She gazed glassily at the fighting around us.

"It's here," she mumbled. "The entrance. It's under the stairs. I just don't know how to open it."

"What?"

But her eyes were closed once more.

The Black King was drawing nearer, so close I could see the concentric circles of his cheeks, hewn from blackest obsidian. *Under the stairs.* I looked down at all the fighting, the marble figures, and my friends reduced to game pieces on the chequered floors. Then I had it.

Katie was slowly getting to her feet when I bowled into her, locking her elbow around mine.

"What are you—?"

"Hang on," I said. "We're going down."

The Black King made a sudden lunge for us, and I abandoned all reservations, swinging my legs around the banister. A razor-sharp hand grazed the side of my face, but by then, we were slicing through the air, down and down the wide bannister of the grand staircase. Katie and I stumbled off into the fray. Fortunately, most of their attention was circled on Melati. The White King pawned off Mary and her monkey to the grasping crowd. He was claiming Melati as his next target. She saw him and readied herself, wide legged as a sumo wrestler.

"Don't fight him there," I shouted. "Lead him to the white square by the door."

She looked confused.

"Please," I cried hoarsely.

410

Melati did as she was told, skipping away from him toward the square. Now all I had to do was worry about the terrifying midnight figure coming down at us. I let go of Katie's hand and searched for the second square. It was at the very base of the stairs, and it meant walking right towards him.

Katie pulled me back by the scruff of the neck. "What are you doing? He'll kill you!"

I stepped from her. "I know what I'm doing." At least I hoped I did.

"Wendell!"

I ignored her, took a deep breath, and stepped on black. The Black King met me there. His gnarled hands reached for me and circled around my neck, tugging painfully at my hair. I gulped and twisted. I was running out of air. *Please please please work.* Things were getting fuzzy and dark, my body jerking and revolting against the loss of oxygen. There was a clunk, sounding as if it came from the end of a long tunnel. The ground beneath me dropped an inch and the pressure increased on my neck. All I could was that black face with the coal black beard.

As quick as it had come, the choking pressure was gone. I stumbled backwards. The world came back into painful focus. Katie steadied my back as I drew shallow breaths.

"How did you do that?" she demanded.

I rubbed my watering eyes to take a look at the unmoving figure before me. The Black King's hands were at his sides once more. He was as immobile as a chess piece. Around the room, the same thing happened. All of the other marble men and women were frozen in their poses, reaching, kicking, and clawing. To any unfamiliar with the scene, it would have looked like an eccentric tableau of ill-placed statues. The White King was stock still on the chequered isle directly across from us. Melati looked bewildered. She edged around, still swinging her fists.

"I wouldn't worry about that," I said, and I had to repeat it because it came out in a rusty squeak. "We figured out Sebastian's secret. They'll think we're him for now."

As if on cue, the room began to rumble, and Katie and I watched in awe as the staircase itself began to lift. It wasn't the entire staircase, which would have been an impossible enterprise even for Shaw himself, but a narrow opening in the middle.

"My apologies Masther Shaw," came a grovelling voice from the door. "I had no idea it was you. I thought I had justht theen you pasth through here." The doorknocker's half-blind eyes rolled every-which way, bringing back unpleasant memories of the first night here.

"Oh, shut it," said Katie.

~37~

The Museum at the Edge of the World

In a slow, single file we descended. It must be something about the underground. It quiets you, magnifies every noise, making the walls feel closer and closer with every deafening heartbeat. Sebastian Shaw certainly seemed to have a penchant for it.

There were caged lamps at intervals like there had been in the tunnels. This place was constructed of nicer stuff though. The black and white tiles of the upper manor extended into its buried counterpart. The walls were black and polished stone. Glints of light passed liquidly over sanded bedrock. We walked, or rather limped, onwards. Katie headed the group, hand pressed to her temple and cut cheek. Mary had a twisted ankle and a welt across her forehead where she'd been cuffed by one of the marble men. Humberdt seemed relatively unharmed but shivered unhappily. Melati sported several bruises and a black eye. I couldn't help but stare at her. I'd never met someone so powerful. This Amazon who had travelled across the world for love—for *my* brother. Words really do show a different side of a person.

My throat hurt intensely. It felt like Black King's grip was still there, sending lances of pain into my brain. I focused on what shallow breaths I could manage. We were in a bad way, but not as bad as it could have been. In fact, we'd figured out Sebastian's secret entrance. We were one step closer to finding Tim. The only problem was, we were out of peppers. Mary suggested nervously that we might go back and regroup but both Katie, Melati, and I shook our heads. We'd come too far to turn back.

There wasn't long to walk. The corridor soon widened into a narrow circular room. *A hive*. That was my first impression of the space. The walls were covered in thousands of holes, each harbouring god knew what. There were two other entrances leading out. One was an iron door studded with bolts. The other was elegant archway shielded only by a thin gauze. A dusky glow filtered through the fabric.

Katie broke the indecision. She strode up to the iron door and put her hand to the lock. "It's cold!"

It *was* cold. A miasma of chill radiated from the door and frost crept around the edges. Where a few metres away was a normal temperature, close to the door our breaths plumed white in front of us.

BANG.

Something enormous rattled against the hinges. She jumped back, colliding into me.

BANG. BANG. BANG.

Bits of ice sloughed off. The sliding lock suddenly seemed awfully flimsy.

"Er, maybe we should try our luck with the other one," said Katie.

"No." I stared determinedly at the door. "What if it's my brother in there, trying to get out? This is just the sort of thing The Cellist would do."

"Or it could be Sebastian's popsicle robot of death as yet unfit for public consumption."

I ignored my misgivings and stepped up to the door again. Tim?" I called it as loudly as I dared. "Is that you? It's me, Wendell."

Silence.

"We've come to let you out. Tim?" I turned my ear to the door. "I...know you might not remember me, but I've really missed you."

A sudden, deafening volley of bangs pounded from the other side of the door. I backed away.

"I don't think that's him."

There was a scuffle behind us. Melati was holding something in her hand that was struggling to get free. The little ball emanated a crisp radiance between her fingers. Two chicken-like copper legs kicked in vain.

"Caught rat," she said.

Katie raised an eyebrow. "They have rats in Indonesia, right? Because that is definitely *not* a rat."

The thing in her hand suddenly went limp. Melati's expression changed. It was buzzing, the light in her hands growing brighter.

"Let go of it for Pete's sake!" Mary cried.

A shutter click and a blinding flash. The Indonesian girl yelped and shielded her eyes. She dropped the ball and the lens shattered on the tile. For a brief moment, I saw the blue iris and pupil, rolling upwards as if suspended in jelly. The thing limped to its feet, kicked and rolled in the opposite direction toward one of the holes in the wall.

"Grab it!" Mary shrieked.

Humberdt was the first on it. He bounded towards the Auto and crushed it with a gleeful crunch. Thick luminescent fluid oozed from the broken creature. There was a collective sigh of relief. Then we looked up. They leered at us, watching, goggling, and spying in a vivid spectrum of glass irises through the holes in the wall. Hundreds of enormous eyes. More and more emerged to peek from their burrows in the rock. Humberdt whimpered and paced. A swathe of irises followed his every move.

My gaze ricocheted between the exits. The tunnel, the door, and the archway. To go home, to face certain danger, or the utter unknown.

415

A high-pitched whine began to fill the room. It was getting as bright as daylight. Brighter even. So dazzling that white became the all-encompassing colour. Out of the corner of my eye, I saw Mary running back the way we'd come. She was abandoning us! I made to chase her when something grabbed me and pulled me under the arch.

In the ensuing seconds, I was dashed painfully against something hard, propped up, and gently patted. Dazed from the action, I waited for the world to stop spinning. There was a blur of tartan and blond to my left. Katie had been captured too. I really hoped she was just asleep.

Something large and grey with big yellow eyes crouched inches from my nose. It was giving me the vigorous and concerned dusting. My head throbbed something awful.

"Did they get you? Were you photographed?" The voice was unfamiliar and familiar at the same time, hollow and metallic as though it came from inside a bell. "Were you photographed?" it repeated.

"What?" The thing came into focus, and I nearly dashed myself against the rock again.

The Lamplighter crouched in front of us. It was larger than life up close, barrel chested and shaped like a spider. Five spindly arms arched out of its back, rotating with meticulous dexterity as they adjusted the sheets above me. I looked up to see I was in some kind of tent. It reminded me of the sort my brother and I used to make as kids with a broomstick in the middle.

The huge yellow eyes peered at me again. "Wendell? Were you?"

"I—no. At least I don't think so."

"Good."

I was enveloped in a crushing hug. "It's so good to see you," said the voice. "I have so much to tell you."

When all I could manage was a choked garble he let go.

"Sorry, sometimes I forget I'm a huge robot. Sorry," he stammered again. He pressed one of the five hands to his broad metal chest. "It's me. It's your brother, Tim. Do you recognize me? I should probably explain because you look, I mean *I* look…"

His voice trailed off as I returned the hug. The metal was cold. He smelled odd, like fish and snow, and…tea.

"I know enough," I said.

Then he was crying, as quiet as it was possible to. There were no tears, but his stiff metal jaw moved up and as he sobbed.

"These past weeks have been so terrible. I didn't know who I was, who you were, who anybody was. The Cellist—I mean Sebastian Shaw—took me in. He told me terrible things—that we had to hurt people. I didn't want to. I never meant to. I tried to stop him. I don't know what happened, but we remembered who we were in the end. Now, he means to hurt us all. I hate this, Wendell. Being an Auto. All I want is to be a person. A real flesh and blood person and see Mum and Dad again. I want to have a sandwich and a long sleep. I think…" he paused, trembling. "I think all Autos are like me. People, I mean. It's the only explanation. He's done something to us with that gun so they don't remember who they are and they'll do whatever's asked of them."

"I know," I said. "It took us a bit to figure it out as well, but we did, and we came to rescue you. Speaking of which, what are those things out there? And where are we?"

"The Horde. They keep watch over Sebastian's laboratory and report any intruders back to him. As long as you didn't get caught in the flash you should be alright. As for where we are…" He crawled to the far side of the makeshift tent, taking great care not to entangle his many limbs in the fabric. He listened for a moment, then beckoned me to a lifted corner. "Look for yourself."

I got to my knees and peered underneath. Spotlights reflected on the glossy tile. Somewhere nearby, water lapped gently.

I turned back to him. "It looks like a gallery."

It was a gallery and a studio to rival that of Michelangelo, Donatello, and Rodin. The museum stood at the very precipice of a natural bay. We were inside a vast cave, I assumed one of the many natural caves that bordered the shoreline of Port Larkeney. The mouth was a distant light across the calm pool. There the storm raged on, but in here, Sebastian had built a testament to his achievements.

417

The museum was made up of long avenues of marble plinths upon which were velvet-lined display cases. I couldn't see much from my vantage point, but I could make out one of the nearest. A cracked monocle lay beneath the glass and on the plaque was a name.

Davies. The old man Franklin witnessed. Each one was a token, I realised. Sebastian took mementos of those he captured. That was the museum part. Our side was the studio, the area built for tinkering and torturing. Most of the pieces here were covered in cloth and bolts of fabric shielded much of the gallery from view. There was a trestle table nearby with a coppery prone form that looked more skeletal than human.

I turned back to my brother. "Where is The Cellist n—"

His hand clapped over my mouth. It was bitterly cold. Before I could protest, he held up a finger. Under the sheet, a row of the little eyeballs scuttled, inspecting the floor for dust. Repeated clicks, almost like budgie chatter heralded their arrival. After a moment, they turned the corner and were gone.

Behind us, Katie stirred.

My brother wrung his hands. "Crackers. She's waking up. I can't believe I'm meeting someone looking like this."

"Don't worry. She'll be more scared of you than you are of her." I said dryly.

Katie's shifted and I had to act fast. Last time I put a hand over her mouth she'd bit me, so I used the edge of her coat. The detective's eyes opened and widened at the sight of us. The Lamplighter tried to make himself as small as possible.

"Don't be scared," he waved his hands in front of her wide eyes. "We haven't formally met. I'm Wendell's brother, Tim, and I'm usually much better looking." He leaned towards me, whispering, "She knows about the whole Auto thing, right?"

"Yes."

Katie looked from me to The Lamplighter, then back again. She slowly spat out the hem of her coat. "I've heard so much about you," she said. "Is it true you read the entire series of *My Chiropractor is Actually a Muscular Werewolf Man?*

"What? No. Maybe. Wendell!"

I pretended I didn't hear him.

418

My brother then remembered Genie and introduced me to my own teapot which had inexplicably come alive as well. It shot a bit of water at me when I tried to pick it up. I didn't remember it being so rude. With all introductions out of the way, it became abundantly clear that my brother didn't have an inkling of a plan to take down The Cellist.

"That's your thing," he said. "I thought I could just hide for a while until I figured it out, but I still have nothing."

Great. I stretched out my legs as far as I could in the tent and thought. Even if we were able to gain the element of surprise, if one thing went wrong, we would be overpowered in an instant. I thought about Mary running away and Melati, strong but completely out of her depth. My brother had no idea she was here!

"Tim," I began, "I need to tell you something."

At that moment Katie pushed me aside. "I need some air. This tent really traps everything." I glared at her. "Not pointing fingers. Just saying, it's a bit ripe, and one of us is an Auto with no real orifices."

"It wasn't me!"

Then I caught a whiff of what she was talking about. It was strong and fishy. I pinched the fabric of the tent and brought it to my nose. The smell made my eyes water and whatever was on it came off grimily in my hands.

"What is this stuff?"

The detective crawled over. "Ah. Seal oil. Fishermen here use it all the time. Keeps the salt and the rust from growing in the engines. Smells like death. Sorry I assumed your flatulence, Wendell."

I took up another clump of the fabric, rubbing circles in the oily canvas. "Don't be sorry. I think we've got our plan."

The canvas came in handy for sneaking through the empty gallery. My brother tied two bolts to his feet, effectively muffling the iron toes. Katie and I took off our shoes. We couldn't wait for The Cellist to come to us, so I'd thrown a boot at a passing member of The Horde. With a flurry of panicked clicks and flashes it set off towards its master. Not far behind, so did we.

419

The little orb took us on a haphazard route through the gallery, weaving between displays and statuettes. I caught glances of what the macabre museum housed. A child's toy, a watch, a shrivelled-up thumb under the spotlights. As we walked, I let a spool of canvas thread drop from the large ball in my hand. It was a close thing, following the Auto undetected. It was sort of like a game of stop and go as we hurriedly disguised ourselves behind benches, carvings and whatever else could be found (except losing meant…dying.) At length, the Auto stopped at a man-made river running through the center of the gallery. A circle of people stood at the water's edge, sniffling and pleading.

We found cover behind three conveniently placed statues. I watched as the little eyeball creature ran ahead to the group at the water's edge. I tugged the thread around my finger as we settled in. Good. It was still holding. On the other side, the tiny Auto advanced carefully. Billius Brum's voice shook like a quivering bass string.

"Please. Whatever you're going to do, don't do it. Sebastian! I thought we were becoming close. Friends even! I thought you invited me to make amends. Surely what I've done doesn't warrant *this*."

Three of Shaw's dinner party guests were tied to chairs at the edge of the river. Was he going to shove them in? They struggled futilely. There was nowhere to run. The Cellist walked around the side of a small Parisian coffee table. It had been set for tea with a silver platter of baguette slices and liver spread. He picked up a thin-bladed butter knife and bread, proceeding to liberally distribute liver across the slice.

"Billius," he said. "Ever the icebreaker. I was waiting for that question. It's always my favourite part when they ask me *why* because I get to tell them, and then they get scared and start crying some more, and then I say, well, maybe I won't do it, and they say, 'really?' and I say, 'No. Pop!'"

He mimed shooting with his fingers, but all eyes were trained on the Lightning Gun hanging from his shoulder. There was another round of crying that was silenced as quickly as it began.

"You want to know why, Billius Brum?" continued The Cellist. "Because you are an insufferable man with a big mouth.

420

You are an arrogant, untalented alcoholic who rubbed dirt on my good name. Frankly you're a hazard to yourself and others out of sheer flammability. I think the world would be better off without you, don't you?"

"N-no!" stammered Billius. "I can tell you on very good authority that some of the world likes me. Ask any woman over the age forty-five!"

The Cellist scratched his chin and thought. "Perhaps I am being a bit harsh. I'll tell you what. If you sing me a better version of the play you botched that night, I'll let you go."

Billius stopped sniffling and looked up. "Really?"

"No. Pop!"

A brilliant streak of light burst from the Lightning Gun, crackling in a thousand-fingered arc across the space. It struck him dead in the chest. The opera singer convulsed violently once, twice, three times, before he was completely still. The Cellist dusted off the gun and went back to his canape. He was just about to open his mouth when the smallest of the captives cut in.

"You think you're doing something," sneered Evangeline Grey (who was wearing a brown toupee.) "You think you can enslave the world with that thing? What about people like me? People with complicated split souls or whatever the hell it is that I am. Those people will remember who they are no matter what you do to them."

"I'll put you in an automated hand-mixer, then and we'll see how far you get," The Cellist answered coolly. "Bon Voyage, Franklin." The lightning shot across once more and the little woman, man, and whoever else they were, shuddered and slumped.

The Cellist popped the canape into his mouth without further interruption. His expression narrowed as he chewed. Without warning, he spat. A gob of dry, masticated liver and bread hit the floor.

"Bugger. I can't taste any of it." In a considerably worse mood, he turned to the last person.

"Non! Non! I beg of you, Sebastian," the Duke babbled a stream of desperate French, which The Cellist ignored.

"You never did anything wrong. I just wanted your land. Plus, you remind me of a toad. I hate toads. Pop!" The Duke of Dillmont collapsed.

Katie was taking tiny shuddering sips of her thermos. I couldn't look anymore. I closed my eyes, pressing myself against the sculpture. The little Auto waited until the seizure had run its course, then it bumped against The Cellist's foot, bouncing up and down.

He picked it up. "What is it? What is that image? A boot? Well, I don't wear...oh. Of course." There was a guilish delight in his voice. "Lead the way then."

A fierce hope rose in my chest. The plan was working. They were going to find the boot. The plan was simple. As soon as I felt the barest tug on the string around my finger, I would use Genie's heat to set fire to the string of oil-covered canvas I'd threaded throughout the gallery on our way here. The Cellist, amidst the tarp and the string would be hopelessly entangled in a cat's cradle of flame. I fingered the string in anticipation. *Never thought I'd be so excited about burning a man alive.*

The Cellist's footsteps rounded the corner and disappeared. I waited with bated breath for the tug. Any minute now. Any minute. I turned to my brother. My giant robot of a brother. That would take some getting used to. His big yellow eyes swivelled toward me. He needed to know Melati was here.

"Before we go out there," I said, "I should tell you—"

Katie grabbed my arm. "He's coming back around."

"What?"

"He's coming back."

The Lamplighter stiffened. "It knew," he breathed. "It knew we were following it. It was bringing *us* to him."

"Sneaky little b—" The swear died in the detective's throat as a long silver blade appeared at her throat.

A singsong voice danced in my ear.

"One little boot and what do I find? Two shoeless children in the wrong place, at the wrong time."

~38~

Whatever Happened to Good Old~ Fashioned Murder?

The bitter irony of the situation wasn't lost on me. The very statues we'd been hiding behind held us fast—and wouldn't you know it, the statues were actually of the guests! That kind of thing was getting old quick.

The Marble Billius Brum's features were grotesquely overexaggerated. His roman nose was as long as a snowman's and his thick, wide-lipped mouth gaped stupidly. He took both Katie and I by the arm in a bruising grip. The Duke crawled on hands and knees in a toadlike gait. His eyes were even more miopic, his body more rotund, his hands and face covered in a bubbling array of boils and warts. Evangeline had been fashioned into some kind of hideous god. Her head was faceted and diamond like. Six faces cried, laughed, grimaced and howled in silence. A ten-year-old girl, a twenty-something with long ringlets, a young man, a leathery old man, a round-cheeked fellow with a walrus moustache, and a middle-aged woman with a severe face and sharp bob. The two of them worked together to secure The Lamplighter, pouncing on his struggling form and pinning him face-down to the floor with a mighty crash.

"*You were a spy.*"

Death glimmered a hairsbreadth from my nose as pale as moonlight as The Cellist padded along the water's edge. "A fink. A tinkering turncoat snake in the grass." His voice hissed as the bow slid through the air. "You followed me that night, didn't you? You were watching me, figuring out my secrets. How to get past my fountains. How to get past the Kings at the stairs. Nobody would ever suspect a little lost twelve-year-old boy, asking for a telephone."

"Seventeen actual—sorry, carry on."

Clicks and chitters preceded a small cluster of The Horde as they jostled their way up to The Cellist. The little eyeball Autos came bearing sheets and long wood platforms. One by one, the slumped bodies of the real, lightning-struck guests were manoeuvred onto the slabs and covered in white sheets. They were then carried swiftly away, their purpose served. The Cellist waited for the Autos and comatose guests to disappear around the bend. He turned back to me.

"Who are you working for? The CC?"

"What?"

"Don't play dumb with me." The point of his bow drew an unwavering line down my neck, and I tried not to swallow.

"The CC aren't above hiring children. *I* was a child," he said. "Their members are dwindling. But they might seek revenge in the form of a twelve-year-old boy and a tall girl in strange pants."

"He's not working for anybody!" The Lamplighter strained his head against the grip of the Duke and Evangeline. "He figured it all out himself! We're going to stop you. We're going to stop you and take the gun and when I'm back in my body I'm going to—to punch your lights out!"

The Cellist looked taken aback at the sudden outburst. Then he started to laugh, a deep and throaty chuckle that sounded almost musical as it vibrated the bow strings at his neck.

"All of you thought this was a good plan, did you? Hah!" There was no heat in his breath, only dead air. "Perhaps

424

you're good at solving puzzles, boy, but do either of you have a degree in theoretical electromagnetism? Do you understand the unwavering rules that govern the nature of life and death? Your brother will never be human, just as I will never be human…and I'm quite looking forward to that, although I will miss my zebra steak tartare. Just like you can't "unkill" someone, you can't put a soul back once you've taken it out. Amber cuts the tags and burns the receipt. Sorry to disappoint."

"You're lying," spat Katie. "I don't trust a word of it."

The Auto shrugged. "It matters little to me. You've learnt my secrets. I hope you're prepared to die with them." He clicked his foot in perfect metronome. "Now, I've got somewhere to be, so let's make this quick. A little electrocution, I think. I'm wearing white and blood is such a bother to get out. Hop along then. Straight line."

We were shoved into a straight line at the edge of the river. Nose down the barrel, I got an unpleasant look at the machine that had caused so much harm. It was burnished brass with a nozzle-like end. Inside was a rotating chasm of metal prongs that spun around and around, gathering up electricity in a mechanical whirlwind of piranha teeth. Globes of fuschia plasma were slotted into the side. Their pink tongues flicked at me through the glass. As I watched, a ball of brilliant blue light formed in front of the gun, as if it were pulling energy from the air itself. My entire body felt like it was part of the current. My ears hummed and buzzed; every inch of my skin prickled on end.

The Cellist cocked the gun with both hands, idly testing the trigger. "What happened to the others in your little rescue party, I wonder? Had the sense to run far away I expect. Pity…I was looking forward to gutting that giant bloody chimp you hired to steal my gun. All that hairless wrinkled skin. Felt like being robbed by my great grandmother."

An electric breeze crackled in our hair. Katie's hand squeezed mine and I looked into a pair of green eyes that no longer knew what to do.

"Don't give him all the credit," said a familiar voice. "After all the hard work I put in."

The barrel lowered as The Cellist turned toward the newcomer.

"Mary."

The goat farmer stood a yard away, her hands clutching her skirts, her chin high and trembling. "Going to turn me into one of your robots, Sebastian? Was that your plan all along? You invited me to your party to seek your revenge, just as you did to all those poor people."

"No, I—" For once his glibness seemed to evaporate. He stared at her.

"Save it. I waited a long time to say this to you. It was I who tried to stop you. Yes, I wasn't even brave enough to do it myself. Yes, I used a monkey. But now, I think I can face you myself." She took another step forward. "You hurt so many people. You took advantage of my father. You corrupted him. I think I can forgive him for that, but you? Not a chance in the world."

An ugly snarl crossed The Cellist's fine features.

"Who said I wanted forgiveness? You just liked having the little crutched boy around. You liked me best when my dreams were as small and crippled as I was and all I wanted in the world was the walk the countryside with you." He spun the bow around a gloved finger. "Well sorry love, but I've moved on."

Mary threw something. Hard. Sebastian ducked, laughing scornfully. He raised the gun once more and pulled the trigger.

CRACK.

A solid body in a fuzzy sweater collided with the copper barrel. Humberdt knocked into the Lightning Gun, scrambling after the cheese Mary had thrown. Ten stone of hungry chimp were enough to send the gun tumbling from The Cellist's grip and the Auto himself sprawling. The gun hit the floor, still vibrating with a full charge. With a bang, the gun went off. Katie and I ducked as electricity hit the Marble Billius Brum full in the face.

Arctic light enveloped his head, and the Auto lost all motor control. His jaw jiggered in a skeleton grin his limbs began to flap.

Someone grabbed my collar. "Let's go!"

Billius the Auto released us, his arms flailing as power overloaded his systems. There was a screech as the spooked monkey swung away from us towards the mouth of the cave. Through the forest of stone hands and glass displays, I glimpsed Sebastian and Mary's final dance. The white metal man and the black-haired woman. For a moment, I saw the two children from the photo: a pale, scholarly boy leaning on a crutch, and a young girl with cheerful squinty eyes and wild black hair.

The Cellist pulled her close. "You should have killed me when you had the chance," he whispered. "Whatever happened to good old-fashioned murder, Mary?"

"Humberdt!" She called, looking desperately around her. "Humberdt!"

The bow flashed. Her scream echoed and died throughout the cavern like a falling bird. I ran, barely falling, tripping forwards at every turn. I became aware of the pain in my finger. There was a red ring, blistered and peeling at the knuckle. A bit of blackened thread hung from the skin. The canvas string was gone. Burnt.

"Gingersnaps," Katie swore.

The threads, hung with meticulous care throughout the gallery, had finally caught. Bright flame was zigzagging across the string, catching on everything it touched. Ahead of us, Katie stopped. In our blind escape we'd somehow circled back to the studio. Our plan had worked too well. Heat seared the edge of my vision. The salty stench of seal oil billowed black smoke from the tarpaulin. There was a crash, and a blazing robotic armature barricaded the way we'd come. She threw her hands up in the air.

"This is just great! Trapped in our own trap." She spun in a circle, searching for a way out of the mountains of flaming cloth.

"What do we do?" I asked.

Katie ran a hand through her hair. Sweaty soot and dried blood glistened on her face. "I don't know. Mary is… and we don't have anywhere to go." Suddenly, her expression changed. "Do you hear that?"

The distant music soared and moaned, a melancholy call that rose up over the smoke, resonating in my ears long after each note was gone. The detective yawned unexpectedly.

"You can't breathe in the smoke!" I cried.

Katie shook her head and yawned again. "It's not that. I'm just so tired all of a sudden." She stumbled forward and caught herself on the edge of a table. Sweat dripped down the tip of her nose.

I was feeling strangely tired too. The fire and chaos faded to background noise. Going to sleep would be a nice thing, I thought as I listened to the music. I could be burned alive and think it was nice and toasty.

Movement caught the corner of my eye. Something squirmed around under one of the flaming sheets.

"I want a glass of milk," I mumbled.

"That would be *amazing*. This stuff tastes gross." Katie waggled her thermos at me, and I snorted.

"Pfft, they're looking at us." She giggled. "Stop looking at us!" Blurry red stars were igniting in the eyes of the unfinished statues. A disembodied hand limped comically from under the sheets toward us. The fingers bent and it hopped towards us, scuttering and dodging the flames. The nails looked very sharp.

"That is pretty weird," I observed, yawning.

Katie nodded. "Don't see that every day. Alright," she drew her coat around herself and curled up on the ground. "Goodnight Wendell."

"Goodnight, Katie."

The hand sprang at my face. That was probably bad. Something brown and fist-sized knocked it out of the air. Then the brown and fist sized thing slapped me hard across the face. It *was* a fist! The world suddenly sharpened as bits of rag were stuffed in my ears. I blinked away tears and massaged my cheek.

"You hit me!"

Melati only grunted before going and slapping the detective hard across the face as well.

"Don't listen," she said.

The fire was catching faster than before. The little circle we stood in was narrowing by the second. "Brahms' Lullaby" played around us. The music that had nearly sent us into deadly slumber was awakening Sebastian's other creations. Nearby, a torso with no head propelled itself forward on two arms. Melati picked it up easily and threw it against a pair of disembodied legs. They toppled like dominos. We wasted no time running through the opening.

The outer gallery was less affected by the fire but catching quickly.

"Where were you?" I asked Melati.

428

"Freezer. I fight lizards. But no time to wrench to heads off."
A look of regret crossed her inexpressive face. "You need help
more."

At that very moment we were shoved aside by the two fleeing
creatures.

"Ssorry," said the first lizard.

"Coming through," said the second.

"Watch out," one of them warned me. "There'ss a monsster
back there." Its voice trailed away when it saw Melati. She
growled.

"To the ship!" The other hissed. "He'll leave uss behind if we
don't make it." The two slithered speedily away, but not before I
saw that both their tails had been tied in a knot.

Water, we needed water. The edge of the gallery couldn't be
far away. If my brother had escaped, that was where he would go.
The ground began to rumble as we made it to the edge of the river.
Spinning from side to side in search of The Lamplighter I nearly
slipped. The tile was wet, water slopping over the sides of the river,
spitting and bubbling as it made contact with the flame. Something
big was emerging from the river.

A ship.

The Waltz was painted in curlicued font across the side of the
machine, but I'd never seen something so unlikely to waltz in my
entire life. Engines groaned, iron creaked, and water slid off the
round body in sloughs as it rose with demonic grandeur above the
river, smoke, and fire. It belched steam of its own through a
whirling mass of pipes and blades. On bladed legs, the submarine
began to move with the eerie lurching scuttle of a crab. A metre
above the water and rising still, I spotted two figures making their
way up the gangplank. One was small in a white coat. The other
was grey with six arms and big yellow eyes. My heart sank.

Katie read my mind. "We can make it," she said.

Water plumed against the bank of the river. *The Waltz* was
moving faster now, the pincer legs gathering speed, riling up the
water and sending iridescent oil trails behind it. *I couldn't jump onto
that thing.* We stood inches away from the water as walls of metal
rose before us.

A ledge was coming up. It was some kind of viewing balcony. I tried to convince myself it was the same as traversing the century-old, suspended bridges in the jungles of Puerto Rico. I felt for my journal and my hand closed over emptiness.

"I can't!" I said to her.

She grabbed my hand. "Shut up. One, two—"

We jumped. The railing missed my hand by a centimetre and my stomach dropped. Somewhere above, Katie screamed. Iron and brass sped by as I plummeted toward the crisscrossing legs. I reached out and grabbed wildly. My hands scrabbled against bolts and vents. The water churned closer and closer.

At the last moment, I hooked something, or rather it hooked me. My injured neck jerked horribly, and I saw stars as the hood of my parka caught on an overhanging pipe. I shot a hand up to grip the pipe and relieve the blinding pressure on my neck. The pipe was unpleasantly hot, and I couldn't stay like this for long, but I was alive. After a moment's search, I found a foothold hoisted myself up. The submarine seesawed under my feet as I desperately clawed my way upwards. The sounds of fighting grew over the ridge. I needed to get to the top of the submarine.

~39~

Rock the Boat

The Lamplighter knew it was the end as soon as he stepped aboard *The Waltz*. He wasn't sure how he knew. The feeling came with the music. It was gentle, soft, and sweet. A goodnight. It weakened his limbs, making his metal head heavy and tired. There was no use fighting. He'd run and run, and The Cellist had still caught up to him. The Cellist lowered his bow. "Brahms' Lullaby" ceased, and The Lamplighter knew that it was all over. Wendell, Katie, and the lady with monkey had all tried for nothing. There was only one thing he was really scared of now. He hoped against hope that his brother had had the sense to leave him behind.

"Come on!" The Cellist snapped.

The cold barrel of the Lightning Gun jabbed into the nape of his neck. "I'm going, I'm going."

As they walked up the gangplank to the crawling submarine, he thought he saw a flicker of light. He dismissed it, trapped in his own whirling thoughts. But soon, the flicker of light became difficult to ignore. It grew around them engulfing everything it

431

touched. Fire. Wendell had set fire to the string. It was burning everything in sight. The statues of course were impervious, but the tarps, the sketches and schematics, and the uncased displays were all going up in flames.

"This is all your fault!" The Cellist was livid. His ivory face twitched, the insectile plates rearing back until he could see the black cog work underneath.

A golden blur suddenly pushed between the two of them. The Cellist stuck out a foot and the lizards let out a *hurk* as their tangled tails caught.

"What are the two of you doing?" he snapped. "Where have you been?"

The two Autos were a pitiful sight. One had a double-legged limp. The other's head twitched as its dented neck erupted in sparks.

"L-l-l-"

"Spit it out!"

"L-locked inside the freezer, Ssir." Said the one with the broken neck. "They s-sent that g-g-great big girl in after us. Barely ess-c-caped with our livess."

"A girl! A girl did this to you?"

The first shook its head vehemently. "Not jusst any. She had fissts the ssize of lamb legss, Ssir. An utter abomination."

The Cellist looked like he might just set his own head aflame. He spoke with gritted teeth. s"Get back out there and wring those children's necks!"

The two Autos looked at one another, then at the fire where Melati certainly lay in wait, then at Sebastian.

"As much assss I'd love to…" said the first.

"Ssorry. N-n-no c-can do," said the other.

Before he could protest, they'd slithered past him into the open hatch of *The Waltz*. Fuming, The Cellist shoved The Lamplighter up the gangplank and onto the small flat top of the submarine. The ship was almost at its full height, and as it rose ever higher, more of the destruction became visible. Smoke engulfed gallery in a red haze. Twitching machines writhed in a sea of pale marble bodies. The Cellist palmed his gun, his fingers twitching over the knobs with an almost feverish intensity as he watched his beloved laboratory burn to the ground

"Where are we going?" The Lamplighter asked.

The Cellist raised the weapon and stared down the sight. "We're going to a place that makes the rest of this meaningless." A flicker of something might have been remorse crossed his face. "You understand, don't you? We've done some great things together. Stolen a lot of stuff, hurt a lot of people, had some good times out on the town, but I need my mindless machine back. A Lamplighter that lights whatever lamps I ask of it. It's a long journey ahead." The ball of electricity gathered outside the barrel once more, enshrouding the two of them in a halo of light.

The Lamplighter dropped to his knees as the barrel pressed against his head. All around them, the fire blazed. The panorama of the burning museum on still water was as beautiful as it was chaos. Amidst of it all were three running figures. Wendell, Katie, and…a figure more bewitching than all the statues combined. Her blackest hair and bronzed skin emerged through the tongues of flame. She to stop at the water's edge as the other two circled round. For the briefest moment, they made eye contact.

The Waltz was already ten yards away from the marble embankment. A narrow but impossible gulf. Fight surged through him again.

"Melati!" he roared and lunged forwards. She too, made to jump. She couldn't have known it was him, yet somehow, she did. But at that very moment, The Cellist pulled the trigger.

Familiar white-blue light swallowed him whole, crackling and howling like a hurricane. He tripped and fell, landing with a clang against the iron surface of the submarine. The shock went straight through him, electric fingers shuddering through his machinery and mind.

Another voice rose through the din. "If you want to get Wendell's brother, you'll have to get through me first."

The Lamplighter rescinded his initial thoughts about Katie's weird pants. They actually looked very dashing, whipping in the wind around her ankles as the detective stood between him and The Cellist. The convulsions wracking his body felt very distant.

433

He must have fallen, he thought, because everything was sideways. To his left, the blurry figure of The Cellist balked.

"For god's sake," he exclaimed. "You just won't die, will you? Don't you understand it's futile? I've already shot your friend's brother. He won't remember a thing about himself come morning and I'll make him do things that are a lot worse than stealing a hairdryer!"

With each shudder, Tim felt a bit of himself slipping away. He couldn't remember why he was here. Where were they going? Who was this strange girl so bent on saving someone's brother?

The Cellist evidently decided to humour her. He stepped up close to the detective. "What are you going to do exactly? You don't have any more of those ridiculous peppers. Mary is gone, and her monkey too. Better think quickly now. We're almost at the mouth of the cave. Twenty seconds and it's open waters and bye bye bellbottoms."

The girl only reached into her pocket and withdrew a tiny red transistor radio. The last dregs of "Rock the Boat" spilled out. The Cellist stared. Then he started to laugh. He laughed and laughed until he doubled over. But when he tried to straighten, he couldn't.

"What's—going—on?" he stuttered as his hands moved of their own accord in an embarrassing parody of The Funky Chicken.

"Never underestimate the power of good disco."

Katie made a lunge for the gun, but The Cellist snarled and chickened away from her. He had more control over his own facilities than the mindless Autos of the manor. She sprang again and he darted back. But the effects of the music had taken their toll. He fumbled the gun in his traitorous body's attempt at The Sprinkler and dropped it.

The Lightning Gun skidded end over end on the curved surface, propelled by the pitching movement of the ship. It stopped finally at the foot of the observation dome. A brass telescope protruded from the top like the lantern of a deep-sea fish. Around them, the water was growing deeper and darker. The mouth of the cave yawned closer. The Lamplighter could see the full moon filling up the sky. The girl with the bellbottoms traded looks with The Cellist. A momentary acknowledgment. Then they ran.

In The Lamplighter's last moments of consciousness, he saw someone else—a familiar face with unruly curls and slightly too-large nose. He fought the final throes of lightning, forcing his metal fingertips to move as he reached into his chest. He pressed something into Wendell's palm. "Here's your journal," he said. "I bet you were worried sick."

~40~

The Last Stand

I stared at the book. My journal. The engine roared and salt spray mixed with tears stung my eyes as I watched my brother lose himself for the second time. The leather was cream brown in the growing full moon. In the end, it hadn't helped me all that much.

I clutched the side of the observation dome, digging my fingers into the hinges and clinging for dear life as *The Waltz* rolled like a panicked horse. On the opposite side of the submarine, two figures faced off. Katie and The Cellist. I would never reach them in time.

Something edged out from underneath the fallen body of The Lamplighter, struggling within a makeshift sack. I crawled over, bracing myself against the narrow railing on the top of the ship. Genie nosed eagerly to get out, hot with excitement or fury. I shook my head and motioned towards the water below. If we jumped, we could still make it before the rapids of the open ocean.

"It's over."

She brushed my hand insistently.

"Stop it!" I swatted the teapot away, an impenetrable lump rising in my throat. "We're done."

Genie tooted and a jet of water scalded my already burned hand. I stifled a cry, twisting away. That was when I saw it. The Lightning Gun was at the foot of the dome, right there for the taking. It was too heavy to lift or push it over the side. Lightning gathered and pulsed deep within the delicate systems of the machine, piranha prongs spinning in a clockwork dance. Katie and The Cellist were running for it. Would water be enough to stop him though?

I took the teapot in my hands. "Genie, boil."

A jet of water shot from the teapot, arcing over the slippery hull of the submarine. The two figures stumbled in their desperate race. Katie's coattails flapped like moth's wings as her feet touched lightly across the surface of the ship, but The Cellist was faster. He wasn't human after all—not anymore. He overtook her and reached for the gun—which was when the explosion rocked the chamber.

Boiling water met with ice blue electricity in a final deathly collision. No, not water. The air had turned pink, stinging my eyes with a vitriolic peppermint stench. As the teapot wriggled out of my grasp, I realised what she'd done. Genie had managed to capture the last of our Panamanian Peppers and boil it within herself.

"Genie!"

Holes appeared in the porcelain surface, as Genie, my wonderful, ungainly teapot, was eaten away by the acid. Across the ship, tendrils of energy tore the air asunder in a million branched tree. Then everything went blue.

I met the water with a smack that took my breath away. Inky silence soon engulfed me. A deep chill numbed my limbs, and the rolling wake of *The Waltz* forced me under again and again as I fought for breath. Before anything else, I shimmied out of my parka, glad of the fact I wasn't wearing boots. It floated dimly off as I kicked away from it. I did keep one thing though: my journal. I pocketed it, then surfaced to look for Katie.

She was a few yards away and sinking fast. Unconscious, the detective was tangled in the weight of her clothes. I swam over and wrangled her favourite coat off. She would thank me later.

Far away and growing further still was the submarine. Its huge shape was dipping deeper into the water now. The remnants of the explosion remained in my vision. The arctic light, Katie's dismay, The Cellist's face still bent in determination, reaching, as his beloved machine destroyed itself. Watching it go, I thought I saw a lone, white figure dragging something down into the hatch just before it disappeared beneath the waves.

The museum was burning fully. An acrid fog obscured much of the wreckage. All around us, featherlight embers twisted and spun like falling stars. I noticed a large shape swimming towards us. Melati moved through the water in powerful strokes. Wordless, she scooped up Katie and proffered an arm. Together, we made for the shore.

~41~

A Port Larkeney Christmas

Marcus Chevral rubbed his elbows more than was strictly necessary, probably checking to make sure the editorial patches of his tweed jacket were still there. The walls were a loud burnt orange. Framed papers behind the desk proclaimed headlines like "World Hunger is a Problem for the Starving," and "Five Reasons Why Itchy Forearms May be a Sign of Gangrene."

I looked over at Katie. Her knee was bouncing, and she was scanning the room, looking everywhere but Marcus. We were in a mid-sized office in a mid-sized building. The company in question was the base for *Globetrotters Monthly*, the mid-sized newspaper my father worked for. The tall window to my right had a pleasant view of Southwark. It angled towards a small rain-soaked park. In the last five minutes, I'd seen no more than two bicycle accidents, a hairy environmental protest, and a small dumpster fire.

I wasn't sure why we were here either. The story had already been published and we'd already gotten the money. There had been radio silence about how it had done—that was, until Marcus's enigmatic call two weeks after publication.

I chewed my lip. Perhaps it had been recalled. Perhaps it was MI5 speaking through the balding editor, wanting to ask *questions*. I thought I'd been meticulous in leaving out the significant details about Sebastian Shaw. Maybe we hadn't been careful in telling our story to the press? To friends and family?

Marcus leaned forward on a red pine desk masquerading as mahogany and adjusted his half-spectacles in a way that reminded me of Tim.

"I'm sure you're wondering why I rang you," he said.

Is this what being sent to the headmaster's office was like? I wouldn't know. I'd never been to a proper school. There was a pile of papers and a copy of our edition on the table in front of us. The sight of it filled me with a mixture of dread and excitement. Was this what my father always talked about when he submitted his articles? It was your voice, floating out there for anyone with pocket change.

"Just tell us already!" Katie burst out.

Marcus looked up, surprised.

The young detective coughed. "Sorry."

"Yes, well. I suppose I have kept you in suspense. Sorry for that, but it was particularly difficult to reach you in Port Larkeney. You gave me a nearly illegible number and none of my letters seemed to go through."

"That'll be the seagulls for you. They hate organised postage. Sort of the anti-homing pigeon over there."

The editor sighed. "Are you sure you aren't willing to set up base here in London?"

"Base?" I repeated.

"London?" asked Katie.

He raised an eyebrow. "You mean the two of you aren't—? I see this isn't something you've thought about in the long term. Look, what I've been trying to tell you if you ever answered my letters, is that the two of you have become somewhat of a cultural phenomenon *here*."

We looked bemused and a stack of letters was pushed exasperatedly towards us.

"*These* are for you. They've been piling up in my office for the last two weeks. You need an official address, and I am *not* your publicist. That said," his put-uponness disappeared, "they all want to speak to you. Not just reporters, but writers, news anchors, and grammar school students who seem to think the two of you are the new detective duo, if not simply heroes."

"Well, I don't know about that," said Katie, but she was already grinning, taking the paper and reading it again for the hundredth time.

The news didn't bring as much joy to me. "I don't see why we should talk to them. We already gave our statement to the police. Katie and I don't really want to draw attention to it. It was a sensitive case at the best of times."

"You've made that clear when you handed in your story and dropped off the face of the earth," Marcus said coolly. "But it's not about that. Remember, you wouldn't even have published it if not for our relationship with your father. If you'd be so gracious as to take a grain of my professional wisdom, you'd take this as far as it goes and run with it. It's not the 1860's anymore. You two are Holmes and Watson off the page. Young, fresh. We can do something with that."

"We didn't exactly plan it that way," I said.

"And that's what makes it great! It's boy and girl, brains and brawn, tall and slim, short and—"

Katie coughed loudly.

"I was going to say scholarly," said Marcus. "Look, take the letters. Respond to them if you like or hole up in that backwater Irish town of yours for another three months. I don't care. But we do have a proposition for you should you decide to make the smart career move. We've got a case for you. It's eccentric, high profile, and discreet. Perfect for the two of you. Only, you haven't much time to accept, and in return, we want an article like this one, fast, adventurous, but more glamorous. A splash of romance maybe?"

Katie leaned forward. "What is it?"

"I can't say much about it as of now—some kind of death on The Royal World Tour. It's a cruise circling the globe, eight weeks. One of our writer's cousins got a telegram from a friend on the Tour. It's very long and very expensive. They'd just left Tilbury a

443

week earlier when one of the toffs kicked the bucket. It's a suspected suicide, emphasis on the suspected. There's no police, no publicity. Best of all, people at sea don't get *Globetrotters Monthly*, so they won't know you.

"The strangest part of it all, is that they intend to go on with the tour as though nothing has happened. Here's the schedule." He slid out a map from the bottom of the pile. "They won't stop for a while yet, but it's a big ship and it shouldn't get too far. We've already come up with a backstory for the two of you. Two rich kids related to our informant, but perhaps not to each other considering the obvious. Typical, spoiled. Missed the boarding because they were out partying but got bored and requested a dinghy sent to get on between here and Italy."

"Italy!" she breathed.

Marcus winked. "No one will be any the wiser. Think of it as a paid vacation for all you've gone through. With a sprinkling of possible murder."

I frowned. "You want us, two teenagers, to infiltrate a cruise ship and dig into these people's private lives. Just for a good story?"

Another, small smile spread across his face. He'd been suppressing something, waiting for the proper question to prompt it. "Well, not just that. It seems like one of the people on board knew Shaw. I don't know who—the informant is quite close-lipped on the matter. *It's perfect.* Another installment of the story that's rocked the headlines of the world."

"I'll do it!" said Katie.

"No." I stood up. "I submitted this piece because my father couldn't and not doing so would have butchered his relationship with your company. You weren't doing us a favour—it was a demand. Because your people wouldn't give him any allowance when my brother was lying half dead in the hospital of that *backwater town*." I pushed the papers back at him. "This was a one off."

Marcus stiffened. Then, silently, he stood and went to hold up the door. "*Globetrotters* is offering you the chance of a lifetime. I see you're not as smart as you made yourself out to be in that piece."

I said nothing and walked out. The hallway was the same atrocious orange, and there were similar framed instances of prized newspapers with idiotic headlines. My father's work wasn't even up here. I shook my head. If this was what journalism was…

I realised Katie wasn't with me. The door at the end opened once more and she was speaking with him. I heard his voice, low, in a last-ditch attempt. "All I'm saying is, it never hurts to have a publisher in your pocket, Ms. Twill. It doesn't require training to become a licensed private detective agency. *Twill and Billings*. It has a nice ring to it."

* * *

The grey thronging streets of London gave way to grey countryside in the train windows. Katie stared at me. I didn't look up from the cheap novella I'd picked up in the souvenir shop. Of course, that never deterred her.

"Well, I'm relieved it did well." The detective folded her long legs awkwardly into the tiny compartment. "Did you hear what Marcus said? Cultural phenomenon. We're sort of famous now. Did you see that girl in the street who came up to me?"

"The one that asked you for change then tried to spit in my hair? Yeah, I remember."

She folded her arms. "After I poked her in the eye, she seemed to remember who I was. She said my face was on the papers she used for stuffing the holes in her box."

"Picture of fame."

"I don't know why you're so upset."

I closed my book. "I only submitted that piece out of necessity–because it's only fair we pay your mum back for all that time we stayed at the Palaces. *He* wants to drag us back out there. Capitalise on stuff we would have done anyway. Pry into people's lives for what? Just to become one of those stupid framed papers on the wall?"

"It's not for nothing. He says he has a lead on Shaw."

"Really?" I raised an eyebrow. "You trust Marcus Chevral? For all we know, it's his lead is just someone who knows the name.

445

I seem to remember Shaw was never particularly keen on getting to know any of the guests he invited over. If we accept that job, it's more than likely we'll be stranded for months in some watery mausoleum with ten versions of the Quislings breathing down our necks."

At the mention of the Quislings, I paused. The old couple had not been accounted for in the aftermath of the Carnival. In the police investigation after, a secretary told them that Ludlow Quisling left a message at The Piquant Palaces saying the couple would be going away for a while. It was highly suspect. I shook off the lingering thoughts. "There's more important stuff to do here. We still haven't covered half of that freezer."

"...I didn't think about that," said Katie.

"Exactly," I opened the book once more. "You'll see I made the right decision. People like that, they just want the drama and that's it." Over the top of my book, I saw her mouth twisting. She looked out the window and said nothing more.

It was another three hours to Holyhead, then onto a ferry. A cab was waiting by the time we disembarked. The familiar dirt roads back to Port Larkeney brought a feeling of relief. Over the past couple of months, the little town had begun to feel like home in a way nowhere else had. My eyes had just begun to close, lulled by the bounce of the uneven country, when Katie spoke.

"You just said no. Just like that. For the both of us. You didn't even ask me."

I raised my head. "I'm sure you can go back and ask him to take you on," I said sleepily. "I don't think it'll make much difference whether it's one or both of us."

"Right. Why didn't I think of that?" She said it with such chill that I sat up completely.

"Is something wrong?"

"No."

But we didn't really talk after that either, and things were still tense when we arrived at the Piquant Palaces.

Mrs. Twill and my parents were sitting at the tables closest to the door. They sprang up in unison when we entered the pub.

My father was the first to us. "How did it go?" His beard gave off the smell of hot cider. "What did Marcus say? He didn't ask you to sign any sort of non-royalty contract, did he? Snakes, the lot of them. But most of them are wonderful. Nicest people you'll ever meet. Great folks. But also, bloodthirsty gnats."

My father had taken a keen interest when I told him I was going to be submitting the story of what had happened these last few months—of how Katie and I had surreptitiously solved the case of Sebastian Shaw, and the theft of the Lightning Gun. It was far from the whole story. Mary Belsize was dead after all, lost within the destruction that was Shaw's gallery, but in our version of the events, she'd run away, and destroyed the gun, claiming it to be the downfall of humanity. (That last part was technically true.) The explosion of the Lightning gun had happened in the vicinity of all of the guests, causing the comatose bodies of Billius Brum, the Duke of Dillmont, and Evangeline Grey to fill the remaining beds of the Port Larkeney Hospital. The lack of testimony helped my revision of the case.

I told the story of how an eccentric millionaire organised a dinner party to show off his new invention, how Sebastian Shaw had been too cavalier with the gun, and left it in his study where anyone could have found it. Mary was a bereaved family member, believing Shaw to be the reason for her father's villainy. Using her familial knowledge of him, she'd decided the best way to get her revenge would be to destroy his most precious invention—the Lightning Gun. The local CID *had* found train records of her leaving Shangana, Africa at the time of the first article calling for Bellamy Dumont's arrest. She'd changed her name and other identification before boarding a plane for Ireland.

Under the pseudonym Mary Belsize, she'd simply moved into the old house and never taken visitors. Nobody knew where Bellamy Dumont had lived. Nobody asked and nobody came. She farmed goats, waited for her father to return, and when he didn't, she found Sebastian and plotted her revenge.

As for hard evidence, the hair in the study found and documented by the police was enough to pinpoint the matter on

447

Humberdt, as was the written testimony that had been collected by the guests on the day after the dinner party. Everyone had an alibi for each other. I tried making it look as though Mary thought she was saving the world from a greater evil. A misled and semi-delusional woman, not a potential murderer. She deserved that much after sacrificing herself for us.

I knew the public would read the account far differently. It ended up being a five-page story of high-profile drama and horror, splashed in with a few personal details about the newfound partnership between Katie and me. My father had recommended that. He said people wanted to hear about the human stuff. The friendships and the fights, not just the gory details. To my surprise, I ended up with a newfound appreciation for his work. I suppose I'd always thought of what we did as a kind of lying, glorifying the places we went and making long-suffering ordeals into grand adventures. But they had been grand adventures to my father, and the public was a frightening animal. In the end, I'd had to lie for the protection of those I cared about. For Port Larkeney.

Katie and I made the decision not to tell the whole story for a few reasons. Not only was it unbelievable, but I suspected that many of the people who owned papers like these were in Sebastian's pocket, perhaps even in on his secret. A few surviving pages from his laboratory had confirmed that fact. He'd bankrolled several prominent political figures, blackmailed a few others, and deals had been struck with a shadowy organisation I vaguely remembered him mentioning. The CC. Katie agreed with me, and the watered-down version of *A Lamplighter in Larkeney* went public. For now.

These days, I spent my time piecing together what Sebastian had left behind. I went down to the burnt laboratory day after day, picking through spent booby traps and trying to find anything that would indicate where The Cellist had gone. It was the relief you get from finishing a marathon, until you realise that the finish line has moved and there is still so much further to go.

Things were far from finished. The Cellist was still out there, God knew where. My brother was with him, and his memory was

448

lost for the second time. His body was here at least. I'd found him in one of the pods closest to the door in the cryo-freezer. It lay, gently defrosting in a spare bedroom at the Palaces. I comforted myself with the fact that he was alive somewhere. There was hope he would remember himself again.

Katie was helping the panic-stricken members of the town, assisting with damage control with the businesses that had been caught in the storm on the night of the Capsicum Carnival. Unbeknownst to us, a hurricane-like squall swept in through the narrow streets of Port Larkeney, the strongest in recorded history. It had damaged much, breaking windows, toppling trees and splintering signed signs. The Carnival itself had been ruined in a matter of minutes. Streets were flooded, tents toppled, and the only upright cover in the flooded plaza was Big Bertha. Half the town had flocked beneath the enormous pepper for cover, making Mrs. Twill's pride and joy even more beloved than before. The Piquant Palaces and its Pepper Picking Saturdays had never been so popular.

As for the Inspector, it had taken Wimbelow several weeks to recover from the concussion and dislocated shoulder that were the consequences of being flattened by a wooden door and walked over several times. He did try to publish his own version of the events, wherein a corrupt and narcoleptic Katie Twill was in a secret plot to harbour Bellamy Dumont and steal the gun for themselves. I had been right.

The true story sounded so ridiculous that it was rejected by even the local newspaper as libel against a town hero. Katie was reinstated as detective with a promotion on the horizon. Wimbelow, in a fit of rage, put padlocks on all of the senior police officers' wheelchairs. It wasn't long until he quit and went back to his hometown where it was said, began a prolific hobby of creating stained glass art featuring fire-consumed peppers.

As for my parents, things had been rocky for a couple of days. I told them about our adventure by handing them the unsubmitted article. Both of them had taken their time (and numerous pastry-accompanied apologies) to digest the lies I'd told him over the past couple of weeks. It frustrated me that I still couldn't tell them the entire truth. Eventually, they understood that I had gone to such lengths to help my brother, even if it hadn't been enough.

We spent long hours discussing the future. My father, in fits of grief-laden frustration, would call multiple specialists around London, comparing treatments and price plans. Whatever way you sliced it, Tim's care was expensive, and I doubted the four shamans, six electricians, and local exorcist combined could lift my brother from his coma. My father decided to take the desk job at *Globetrotters*. It pained me to see the stoic resignation settling on his face. He had looked so worn lately; his fuzzy, moon-like grin replaced by grey melancholy. It felt as though our family would never be completely whole.

Despite this, my parents told me that I ought not to feel tied to them. I knew they felt bad about the years I'd spent travelling. I was free to go to university, spend my days how I liked, and figure out what it was I actually wanted to do. I'd spent time thinking about this, guiltily spinning fantasies of university life and freedom amongst my peers. But deep down, I knew it was just that, a fantasy. I would keep searching the world for my brother's cure if I had to. The holidays were approaching with melancholy. Katie and I weren't speaking, and Bellamy had sequestered into himself in the attic after hearing of his daughter's death. It wasn't much of a change as he was still on the run, except he refused to see anyone at all. Some Christmas this was going to be.

On the morning of, I didn't want to get out of bed. We'd be heading back to our transient home in London soon. The check from my article would cover our stay at the Piquant Palaces. I was reluctant to leave. The red goose-down bed with its faintly spicy, cinnamony scent had helped me sleep better than anywhere I'd ever been. I wondered with gloom if my departure would come before Katie, and I could patch things up…whatever it was that had happened between us.

Eight in the morning looked dusky as evening. Mist swirled thickly in the windows and white flakes spiralled past like falling

450

sugar. They glowed multi-coloured as they passed the windows, flaring briefly in the Christmas lights that adorned the Piquant Palaces year-round.

"Merry Christmas!" Mrs. Twill beamed as I entered the pub. The whole place was thickly decorated in wreaths and tinsel. The fire roared merrily in the grate. The place smelled of hickory smoke and warm bread. Katie passed with a tray of drinks.

"Merry Christmas," I said to her.

She ignored me and took her plate to the far side of the room with Melati. The Indonesian girl had made a solemn pact to stay with us until Tim was rescued.

My parents joined me for breakfast as I sat down.

"Alright, son?" My father evidently noticed I was even gloomier than usual. He was staring at me over a newly acquired pair of reading glasses and a sheaf of hospital brochures that had recently replaced the travel ones. I composed my expression.

"I'm fine."

"Did you say something to her?" asked my mother.

Another side effect of the article. My parents had become extremely interested in the detective and I. Something about me never having friends.

"No," I sighed. "Maybe. She's just being dramatic."

"Does she do that often?" he asked.

My mother stirred her eggnog. "I didn't take her for the type."

Out of the corner of my eye, I watched the (perhaps overtly) cheerful conversation between Melati and Katie.

"I said something a couple of days ago and she's making a big deal of it." I continued, somewhat defensively. "I was being the logical one. Marcus offered us another job and I said no in the meeting. She got mad that I didn't ask her opinion, and I said she should go it alone if it mattered so much. Now she's giving me the silent treatment. What's that look for?"

My mother had a wan smile. "It's your father's fault for giving you such a large nose. You can't look past it."

"What?"

"Wendell, how would you feel if someone said your friendship didn't matter one way or another? What if they told you they could have done everything by themselves, and it would have turned out exactly the same?"

I snorted incredulously. "That is not what I said! I told her she could go if she wanted. It's better for us both anyways. It's not like I'm going to see her again once we leave." I sat back.

They were hinting that I apologise for some vagary. If Katie was being moody about something, that was probably just some girl thing, wasn't it? In any case, I convinced myself that being irritated with her would make leaving Port Larkeney easier.

The day went on and brightened a little, though the weather didn't get any warmer. A group of snow-bedraggled carollers buttoned up to the ears appeared at the doorstep and sang a quick, muffled *Holy Night* before dispersing down the hill.

At one o'clock, the pub was full of people, drinking, toasting, and laughing. I sat reading by the fire. Katie helped in the kitchen. Out of the corner of my eye, I watched her. She didn't seem grumpy. She was laughing and talking with the patrons. She caught my gaze, and her face went icy. I looked away quickly and spent the next few minutes heavily concentrated on my book.

Mrs. Twill tapped me on the shoulder. She was holding a small roast chicken generously stuffed with sprigs of rosemary. "Would you carry this up to Bellamy for me? He ought to have some Christmas cheer, whether he wants it or not."

"Sure."

I felt a sense of calm as I left the hubbub downstairs for the cool, open air of the roof. I balanced the chicken on the crook of an elbow and made my way up the ladder one rung at a time, before emerging onto the roof.

Up here, the whole of the town lay shrouded in a misty white and the barest hints of chimney smoke made their way through the fog. I couldn't even see the sea. My boots sank through fluffy snow as I made my way across the balcony. The lights of the dome were on, and I didn't bother knocking. Bellamy would've only told me to leave.

"Bellamy?"

I opened the door and stopped. Katie sat on one of the crates. Her face froze as I entered. A steaming tray of potato au gratin lay in her lap. The little cot on the side of the room was empty. I couldn't think of any way to break the uncomfortable silence, so I simply brandished the chicken like a train ticket before entering.

"Where is he?"

She shrugged. I set it down.

"This was probably her idea," said Katie suddenly. "Bring us up here at the same time so we're forced to make up."

I scowled. "I can't make up for something I didn't do."

"Typical," she sneered.

"If this is a girl thing—"

"Girl thing!"

"Yes! You won't tell me anything. All of sudden you're mad at me and I don't know why."

She ignored the question and went to the door. "Where is that old man anyway?"

There was something about the cot, the air, the room that struck me wrong. The room was colder than usual, the usually crackling potbelly stove was dead. The cot and makeshift worktable of crates were barren, pushed to the side.

I turned to her. "You don't think he—?"

Katie's eyes widened. She rose and pulled back the sheets, peering under the bed. "No, no, he wouldn't."

The only thing left in the room was a framed photo. It was a picture of Bellamy and Mary two decades earlier that had been found at Mary's house. A beaming father and his wild haired daughter in a sunny pasture. She held it up. Desperation wracked her voice. "Would he leave this behind?"

I walked to the door, squinting out into the thickening snowfall. Any sign of footsteps would have disappeared by now. "Maybe she was the reason he left."

She pushed past me into the snow. "Bellamy? Bellamy!" Her words rang out and died in the wall of mist surrounding the Palaces.

There was no answer.

"We'll split up," I said. "Maybe he's still here."

"No." Katie stared at the imprints of our boots. Her fingers curled. "If he wants to leave, he can have his Christmas cheer without us. I didn't expect much from him."

"Katie," I rounded on her. "He lost this daughter."

"Well, I lost my dad!"

She shouted it at me, and I stepped back in surprise. Our breath plumed in the hair, frozen in the moment. Then all the energy seemed to leave her, and she fell with into the snow.

"Katie!" I stumbled over in the knee-high snow.

Katie was face up in the pillowy fall as if making an angel. Her eyes were closed, the rims of them frosted with white flecks. It didn't take long for her to wake. I reached out a hand and she sat up, leaning against the wall of the balcony. I stood beside her, looking out over the town. The storm swirled around us, soft and quiet.

"It's all well and good for you," she murmured. "You've got both parents. Most of the time, I can deal with the way things are, but around holidays is when I miss my dad the most." She sighed. "Bellamy doesn't deserve what I said, and maybe I'm being too harsh. My mother does deserve to be happy. Perhaps I ought to move on too. It's silly to keep searching after all this time."

"Katie," I said. "I can't imagine what it must be like to lose a parent. You shouldn't feel like you have to move on."

"Yeah…" she turned to look at me. "You know, when you said you were leaving Port Larkeney and going back to your normal life I was happy for you. You deserve that much. But then we had that meeting with Marcus, and it seemed like you didn't care what happened to me either way." A rueful smile crossed her face. "There's not a lot of choice for company in Port Larkeney, unless you count vindictive twelve-year-olds and rheumatic war veterans. So, for most of my life it's just been me, and when we started solving this case, sure it was scary, but sometimes—"

"It was great." I sat down beside her.

She nodded. "I suppose I just didn't want that to end."

I reached into my pocket and took out my journal. I turned it over, not opening it. "You know, I've been to about a hundred different countries and seen more cultures, traditions, and people than I can name. The thing is, I haven't kept a single pen pal. Not

454

one. My brother had seventy-six. Do you know how many letters I had to translate?" Katie looked like she was calculating so I shook my head.

"The point I'm trying to make, is that I'll make a pretty bad partner, Katie. I do care if you went on that cruise. I'd be happy for you and sad I wasn't there to make sure you didn't fall overboard asleep and drown. I just don't know if I want another adventure. But I'm not going away. Not just yet. I want to stay here and keep looking. If your mother will have me, of course."

Katie opened her mouth in delighted response and unbidden, I sneezed explosively in her face.

"Sacre Bleu!"

The both of us jumped. Bellamy stood in front of us, gesturing madly. His thick winter coat and grey hair were dusted pure white, and he was waving a long grey cylinder.

"What on earth are you doing out here? Are you trying to freeze your *derrière*? Teenagers zese days. Idiots! Nincompoops!"

"Bellamy!" Katie ran and wrapped him in a tight hug. "I thought you made a run for it."

The Frenchman blinked in surprise. "Ran away? I was only gone an hour."

"But your things," I said. "Your tools were all gone when we went in there."

"I moved my workstation to ze spare room downstairs. Up here, I can feel my nose hairs shrivelling, amongst other things."

In the next second, he was pushing us out of the snow and down the ladder. Making sure the third-floor hallway was clear, we slunk into the spare room. The little bunk was strung up with theories, schematics, and drawings each featuring the remarkably featureless metal cylinder. An array of tools that wouldn't have looked out of place in an operating theatre or torture chamber were lain out on the bed.

I hadn't realised how cold it was until I began to thaw. Then I became aware of the wetness on my behind. Katie was shirking her defrosting coat. Reconciling whilst sitting in the snow was one method I could do without from now on.

Bellamy bustled around, clearing the bed of tools. "Jeane told me you would be up here, and I came to share ze news when I saw

455

the two of you sitting in ze snow like a pair of *chèvres sourdes*. What was that?"

"An airing of grievances," I said.

"A passing of germs," said Katie, wiping her face disgustedly.

Bellamy made a face. "I don't want to know what zat means. Anyways, I have figured it out!" He held up the long metal cylinder for the third time. "Zis! Ze thing that I stole from Sebastian so many moons ago. I discovered what it contains.

"It's only been six months," said Katie.

"Yes, well it took me a long time. I thought at first it was a knick-knack, or scrap metal. But Sebastian claimed I stole something great from him and it could only be zhis."

"That's what you were doing all this time?" I asked.

Bellamy nodded gravely. "I will make ze man who killed my daughter pay a thousand times over. But first, I must discover his secrets. Fourteen days and fourteen nights I tested it, sampling the metal, searching for hidden levers, trying to unscrew the cap. In ze end, it turned out that ze cap unscrewed anti-clockwise." He threw his hands up in the air "But what I found has made it worthwhile."

He unscrewed the head of the cylinder and withdrew a stiff roll of paper half the size of the bed.

"It's a map of the world," Katie murmured.

Bellamy smoothed it, his electric blue eyes gazing at it with triumph. It was a beautiful map, new and laminated, each of the continents minutely detailed down to the smallest tributary. On it, several places were circled, varying wildly in distance, from Eastern Europe to the South Americas.

"You think The Cellist will hit all these places?" I asked. "But there's no telling which he'll go to first."

"Hold on," said Katie, taking his position. "That's definitely familiar." Rooting in her pocket for the folded slip, she withdrew the map Marcus Chevral had given to her laid it down next to the other. The two maps were nearly identical down to the last red circle. She turned to me, and I saw that familiar look again—the one that was impossible to refuse. "Do you know what this means, Wendell?"

I rubbed my temples, preparing for a headache that would last more than a day. Eight long, watery weeks to be exact. "That Christmas has come early?"

"Exactly."

She winked and fell asleep.

About the Author

Amelie Butkus is a nineteen-year-old writer and illustrator. What little information she can divulge is that she likes to write books about doomed dinner parties, enormous peppers, and the best places in the galaxy to get a decent sandwich. She currently lives somewhere in a town between some landmarks along a stretch of road that might or might not be somewhere in a larger country. Or right behind you.

Made in the USA
Monee, IL
26 April 2023

32570173R00267